Available in from Mills & Boon Special Moments™

PLAIN JANE AND THE PLAYBOY

"I'd like to kiss you at midnight. If that's all right with you."

He was actually asking if it was all right to kiss her on New Year's Eve?

Someone in the crowd began the traditional countdown…

"Ten, nine, eight –"

"And you are?" Jorge asked.

"Seven, six, five – "

"Jane Gilliam."

"Four, three – "

Was it his imagination, or was there a new spark in her eyes? She was definitely arousing him.

"Two – "

He drew her into his arms.

"You're not really going to kiss me, are you?" Dream or not, it was still hard to believe. And yet she *so* wanted to believe.

"One!"

His lips covered hers as cries of "Happy New Year!" echoed through the crowded room.

Jane didn't hear a single sound other than the pounding of her heart.

VALENTINE'S FORTUNE

"You always seem to be rescuing me."

His arm around her seemed to tighten fractionally. "I can think of worse things."

Her heart was climbing towards her throat. Her gloved hands slid over his, but she didn't know if that was to push his away or to keep him from pulling away. "Darr – "

His head lowered. His jaw grazed her temple. "Just answer a question for me."

She turned her head, looking up at him, and felt everything inside her grind to a breathless halt. "What?"

"The night of the fire, you said there was no one for us to call for you. No husband. No boyfriend. Was that the truth?"

"Yes." That, at least, was the bald, naked truth.

"Good," he muttered and pressed his mouth to hers.

First published in Great Britain 2010
Harlequin Mills & Boon Limited,
Eton House, 18-24 Paradise Road, Richmond, Surrey TW9 1SR

Plain Jane and the Playboy © Marie Rydzynski Ferrarella 2009
Valentine's Fortune © Harlequin Books S.A. 2009

Special thanks and acknowledgement are given to Allison Leigh for her contributions to the FORTUNES OF TEXAS: RETURN TO RED ROCK mini-series.

ISBN: 978 0 263 87945 2

23-0210

Harlequin Mills & Boon policy is to use papers that are natural, renewable and recyclable products and made from wood grown in sustainable forests. The logging and manufacturing processes conform to the legal environmental regulations of the country of origin.

Printed and bound in Spain
by Litografia Rosés S.A., Barcelona

PLAIN JANE AND THE PLAYBOY

BY
MARIE FERRARELLA

VALENTINE'S FORTUNE

BY
ALLISON LEIGH

 MILLS & BOON®

PLAIN JANE AND THE PLAYBOY

BY
MARIE FERRARELLA

Marie Ferrarella has written over one hundred and fifty novels, some under the name Marie Nicole. Her romances are beloved by fans worldwide. Visit her website at www. marieferrarella.com.

To
Margaret Watson,
for reams of e-mail
and priceless
support.
Thank you.

Chapter One

Red, the extremely popular restaurant located in Red Rock, Texas, and the realization of a dream by José and Maria Mendoza, had closed its doors to the public this holiday evening.

But it was far from empty. The premises had been rented out to Emmett Jamison who, along with his wife, Linda, both former FBI agents, oversaw the Fortune Foundation, a philanthropic organization now in its fourth year. The guests at the New Year's Eve party included key personnel at the foundation, as well as every single member of the Fortune family who could walk or crawl within a fifty-mile radius.

Included, too, were a large number of friends, not the least of whom were more than several members of the Mendoza family. There were so many people packed inside the converted former hacienda—said to have once belonged to distant relatives of Santa Ana—that guests were spilling out onto the inner courtyard, despite the cold temperature. The press of bodies generated its own heat.

Good cheer abounded, mixing with the occasional strains of festive music, some of it coming from the old-fashioned jukebox, some of it from the five-piece band that Maria had hired at her son, Jorge's behest. Christmas carols meshed with both Mexican and country music. It was a veritable potpourri of everything that Texas stood for.

Almost everyone seemed to be having a good time, if noise could be considered a barometer of fun. The only true difficulty was in maneuvering through the throng, and in locating people the crowd had swallowed up.

So when Jack Fortune all but walked into his brother-in-law as Jorge finished placing a fruity, mixed drink on a comely young woman's table, he took advantage of the situation.

Hooking his arm around his brother-in-law's neck, Jack said playfully, "Hey, there's a vicious rumor making the rounds that Jorge Mendoza is actually here without a date." Hearing Jack's voice, Jorge relaxed, lowering the tray he was about to use as a weapon. "I've been defending your reputation," Jack continued, releasing his hold on Jorge, "saying that it just wasn't possible, this being New Year's Eve and all."

"I'm afraid that you've been wasting your breath, Jack," Jorge said, turning around to face the man who made his sister Gloria's world spin on its axis. Out of the corner of his eye, he saw Gloria making her way toward them. "The rumor's true. I didn't bring anyone to the party."

There was a very good reason for that, but Jorge kept it to himself. The current lady in his life, Edie, was hinting broadly about their relationship. She wanted an honest-to-gosh commitment from him, even though they'd only been seeing each other for about a month. And while it had been a very enjoyable month, with several memorable moments, none of it was earthshaking enough to prompt him to make the relationship permanent.

He felt sure that neglecting to invite her to share New Year's Eve would send her a message about his intentions. So he'd opted to go it alone tonight, thereby dodging a very real bullet with his name on it.

"Is it terminal?" Jack asked.

Confused, wondering if he'd misheard, Jorge leaned forward. "Is what terminal?"

"Your illness," Jack answered. "You're sick, right? That's got to be the reason you didn't bring anyone. I've never known you to be without female companionship for more than, what? Fifteen minutes at a time?" Jorge went through women the way his father, José, went through clean undershirts in a hot kitchen. "Legend has it you tried to pick up a candy striper in the nursery the day you were born."

Jorge laughed, shaking his dark head, his deep brown eyes crinkling. "I'm not sick, Jack. I thought I'd just help Mom and Dad out tonight. You know, wait on tables, tend bar, mix drinks—"

"Flirt with every woman under the age of a hundred," Gloria interjected, completing her older brother's sentence as she came up to join him and her husband. She hooked her arm through Jack's, but her attention was clearly on Jorge.

"Right." Jorge saw no reason to deny that charge. He believed in enjoying himself whenever he could. And flirting was his inalienable right. Flashing his thousand-watt smile, he repeated, "But I'm only here to help out. Besides," he confided, "if I brought someone with me to this little fiesta, Mom would immediately think it was serious. You know what she's like." In her time Maria Mendoza had been on each of his now-married sisters' cases. "She'd be writing out wedding invitations right after the stroke of midnight." He considered that, then amended, "Maybe even before."

"Mom just wants you to be happy, big brother," Christina chimed in, coming in at the tail end of the conversation, her fingers firmly laced through her husband Derek's. It took a little maneuvering to join the threesome.

Jorge gave Christina a lecherous wink. "Mom and I have a *very* different definition of happiness."

"I'll say," Sierra agreed sarcastically, as she and her husband, Alex, came up to join the other two couples and Jorge in the impromptu family meeting.

"Mom wants to see you married with a family and you just want to go from woman to woman, gathering honey like a drunken bee going from flower to flower."

Jorge rolled his eyes. "A *happy* drunken bee," he emphasized.

Gloria rolled her eyes. There was no changing a leopard's spots and it seemed that there was no changing Jorge. He was going to be a playboy until the day he died.

"You're hopeless," she told him with a sigh.

Again, he saw no reason to deny the truth. He was what he was—a man who loved women. And from where he stood, there were so many women out there to love.

"Exactly," Jorge responded, the same killer, boyish grin that had made many women weak in the knees gracing his lips. He leaned into Gloria, as if to impart something confidential. "I'd give up trying to change me if I were you. Now go dance with your husband, Glory," he urged, then turned to his two other sisters. "You, too, Sierra, Christina. Don't harass the help. I have drinks to make and pretty women to wait on," Jorge told them just before he turned away and faded into the crowd as he headed back to the bar.

Gloria shook her head. A sigh escaped her lips. "There goes one unhappy man."

Jack took Gloria by the hand, deciding that his brother-in-law had a good idea. He pressed his hand against the small of her back and slowly began to sway in time to the music. "Oh, I don't know. He didn't seem all that unhappy to me."

Men could be so dense, Gloria thought, seeing only what was on the surface and nothing more. "Ever hear of the expression, laughing on the outside, crying on the inside?"

This was not an argument he was about to win, Jack thought, and he was far too shrewd a business-man to continue fighting a doomed battle. Espe-cially not on New Year's Eve.

"You're absolutely right," he told Gloria solemnly. "Jorge's a very unhappy man."

Gloria knew sarcasm even when it was disguised as surrender, but she didn't want to fight. She did, however, want some kind of solution. She wanted Jorge to be as happy as she was. She'd found marriage far preferable to the single life—as long as it was to the right person.

"Can you come up with someone for him?" Gloria asked suddenly as he swung her around in the little bit of space he'd staked out for them.

"Then I'd be the unhappy man," Jack pointed out. Gloria looked at him, puzzled. "You know Jorge doesn't like us interfering in his life."

None of them liked people butting into their lives, but sometimes, it was just necessary. For their own good. "I just don't like seeing him so alone, Jack."

Jack glanced over his shoulder. Jorge was behind the bar again, mixing drinks and talking to a well-endowed young blonde who seemed to be hanging on his every word. And having a great deal of difficulty remaining in her dress.

"Trust me, Glory. Jorge is never alone for more than four minutes at a time. Five, tops."

Gloria looked at her brother. She had an entirely different take on the scene. The woman was a bimbo. Happily-ever-after didn't happen with bimbos.

"Men," Gloria huffed.

Jack smiled broadly in response. "Glad you noticed that." His eyes gleamed as he looked at his wife. She was every bit as gorgeous, as sexy, as the day he'd fallen in love with her. "What do you say, right after midnight, we—" Jack leaned in and whispered the rest of his thought into her ear.

Gloria's eyes widened and then her lips curved in deep appreciation. Thoughts and concerns about Jorge and his lifestyle were temporarily placed on the back burner. The far back burner.

"You're on," she told her husband.

Pleased by her response, Jack continued dancing with his wife.

Maria Mendoza paused and momentarily stopped worrying if there was enough food to keep this crowd well fed, and just took in the happy revelers. Moving back, she found herself, quite by accident, bumping into Patrick Fortune, the retired president of Fortune-Rockwell and father of five of the people here. More importantly, a good friend for several decades.

"Your son is making my daughter very happy,"

she said to Patrick the moment he was within earshot. Patrick had been the one she'd turned to several years ago, enlisting his help to find a suitable husband for Gloria, her once very troubled daughter.

Maternal pleasure now radiated from every pore as Maria spoke to the tall, distinguished, redheaded man at her side.

Patrick silently lifted his glass of white wine in the general direction of his son and daughter-in-law. He was as pleased by the union as Maria was. It was nice to see Jack happy for a change.

"That did turn out rather well, didn't it?" he said proudly.

"And it was all your doing," Maria reminded him, more than willing to give credit where it was due.

Ever modest, Patrick didn't quite see it that way. "All I did was call him home to help Gloria get her new jewelry business on its feet. Chemistry did the rest."

"Chemistry," Maria allowed with a slight nod of her head. "And a lot of lit candles and prayers to the Blessed Virgin," she added with more enthusiasm. And then she sighed, thinking of her two sons. "But no amount of prayers seem to be working when it comes to Jorge—or Roberto for that matter." Both represented two rather sore spots in her very large heart. "Roberto didn't even think enough of the family to come home for the holidays." He lived in Denver now, so very far away. She'd called her first-born twice, only to get an annoying answering machine both times.

And no return call.

Patrick knew how hurtful that could be. "The boy's busy, Maria," he told her gently.

"Boy," she echoed the term her friend had used. "He's my eldest. How can Roberto be a boy when he's forty years old?"

She knew better than that, Patrick thought. "Because, to us, no matter what their age, they will always be our children. Our boys and girls." Finished with his wine, he set the glass down on an empty table. "Which is why you worry, Maria," Patrick pointed out. Good humor highlighted his aristocratic features. "Stop worrying," he advised. "Things will turn out all right in the end. You did a good job raising them. They're good people. All of them. Once in a while, it takes a little extra time for them to find their way," he told her. "But they always do in the end." He smiled encouragingly at her. "You just have to have faith."

Maria sighed. He really believed that, she thought. "You truly are an amazing man."

Taking Maria's hand in his, he gave it a gentle squeeze. "Don't worry," he repeated. "And if it makes you feel any better," he added, "I'll look around and see if there's anyone suitable to put in Jorge's path."

"Thank you, old friend," Maria replied with enthusiasm.

"Maria," a deep male voice called out just then, slicing through the noise. *"Ven aca.* I need you." The blend of Spanish and English had an urgency to it. Maria turned to see her husband, José, waving to her, beckoning her toward the kitchen. "We are running out of your special tacquitos."

"Coming, my love," she called back. Saying "thank you" one more time to Patrick, the petite woman burrowed her way through the crowd of people to reach her husband.

Patrick Fortune remained where he was, watching the object of his old friend's concern a moment longer.

The last thing that Jorge Mendoza resembled was a troubled, lonely young man, he thought. Even though he claimed to be working, Jorge, ensconced behind the bar now, appeared to be having the time of his life. He was moving from one young woman to another, seemingly taking orders for drinks and lingering to flirt, most likely mentally compiling yet another list of names and accompanying phone numbers. The young man was a modern-day Casanova, clearly enjoying both his freedom and the hunt.

Eventually though, Patrick was convinced that Maria Mendoza's wayward son would realize that "freedom" and the hunt were definitely not nearly as important as the love of a good woman—the *right* good woman. And he was a romantic, Patrick thought. He believed that there was someone for everyone. There certainly had been for him.

"Looks like the family's out in full force," Jack commented, coming up beside his father, Emmett Jamison at his side. Gloria was a few feet away, talking to Emmett's wife, Linda, about a necklace Linda wanted fashioned.

"Most of them," Patrick corrected. Although his sister Cynthia's children were here, Cynthia was conspicuously absent, despite the invitation to attend. It looked as if the estrangement between them was going to go on a little longer, he thought. "Look, I wanted to run something by you, Emmett."

"Business, Dad?" Jack asked. "I thought you were the one who finally said all work and no play—"

"This is about family," he explained to Jack, then turned back to Emmett. "Nothing worse than having your own son preach at you, especially when he's throwing your own words back at you," Patrick told Emmett. "I was hoping you might find positions at the Foundation for several of my brother William's kids. It might help bring the rest of the clan closer together."

Emmett nodded, always open to anything the older man had to say. "I'll see what I can do."

Patrick patted him on the shoulder. "Can't ask for anything more than that."

Patrick Fortune and Jorge's sisters were not the only ones observing the playboy's progress from woman to willing woman. Jorge was also an object of awe for Emmett's adopted son, Ricky, who was nursing a very serious case of envy. Envy that encompassed both the charming Jorge and his best friend, Josh Fredericks. Josh was a suave seventeen and had a steady girlfriend, Lindsey, on his arm, while he, Ricky, was a very unsure-of-himself fourteen.

It seemed as if everyone here had someone but him—and that woman sitting over in the corner by herself, he noted. Jorge seemed to have not just one but a harem of women. Every single one who came up to the bar left with a smitten smile on her face.

How did he *do* that?

Working up his courage, Ricky finally made his way over to the bar, and Jorge. But when he reached the bar, all he could do was silently observe. Jorge was a master at work.

It took Jorge a few minutes to notice the teenager. Wiping the counter down in front of him, Jorge flashed a grin as he shook his head.

"Sorry, Ricky, afraid all I can offer you is a soda pop or a Virgin Mary." The boy looked at him a little uncertainly. "That's a Bloody Mary without the alcohol," Jorge explained, lowering his voice so as not to embarrass the boy.

Ricky shook his head. "Oh, no, no, I don't want anything to drink," he protested, stuttering a little. Tongue-tied, he got no further.

Jorge threw the damp towel behind the bar and leaned forward, creating an aura of privacy despite the crowd. The boy looked like he wanted to talk, but didn't know how to start. Jorge felt sorry for him. "Then what is it I can do for you?"

Ricky felt more uncertain than ever, more awkward than he had in a very long time. But it was now or never. Clearing his throat nervously, he looked around to make sure that no one in the area was listening.

"I want to know how you do it," he finally said.

But Jorge couldn't hear him. "What?"

Ricky repeated himself, this time a little more audibly. "I want to know how you do it."

Obviously hearing did not bring enlightenment with it. "Do what?"

This was going to be harder than he thought. Ricky licked his lower lip, which had suddenly grown even drier than his upper one had.

"How do you get all these ladies to flirt with you?" he blurted out. "I've been watching you work all night and there had to have been at least twenty of them." Old and young, they all seemed to bloom in Jorge's presence.

"Twenty-six," Jorge corrected with a quick conspiratorial wink, then said simply, "They're thirsty."

"They're not coming over to the bar for the drinks," Ricky protested. He might not be a smooth operator, like Jorge, but he was bright enough to see that ordering a drink was just an excuse, not a reason. "They're coming to talk to you." He paused to work up his flagging courage. "How do I do that?" he wanted to know. "How do I get them to come to me?" And then he added more realistically, "Or, at least, get them not to run off when I come to them."

Jorge laughed gently, taking care not to sound as if he was laughing at the boy. He'd never had that problem himself. Women had always come on to him, even before he discovered the fine art of flirtation. But he could feel sympathy for the boy who seemed so painfully shy. "They don't run off from you, Ricky."

Ricky knew the difference between truth and flattery. "Yes, they do. I asked a girl in my class to come with me tonight and she said she couldn't. She said—" He paused for a second, working his way past the embarrassment. "She said her mother wouldn't let her stay out that late."

It was a plausible enough excuse, Jorge thought, although the girls he'd known at Ricky's age had bent rules, ignored parental limitations and come shinning down trees growing next to their bedroom windows just to see him for a few stolen hours.

"How old are you again, Ricky?"

The boy unconsciously squared his rather thin shoulders before answering. "Fourteen."

"Fourteen," Jorge repeated thoughtfully. "Well, she was probably telling the truth, then." He did his best to appear somber. "When my sisters were each fourteen, my father would have chained them in the stable to keep them from going out with a boy, much less staying out until midnight."

That didn't seem like a good enough excuse to assuage his ego. "But it's New Year's Eve. Besides, times have changed," Ricky pointed out.

The boy had a lot to learn, Jorge thought. "Parents haven't," he assured the boy. "And, if you want some advice—"

Ricky's eyes widened and all but gleamed. "Please," he encouraged enthusiastically.

"First, you have to have confidence in yourself." He saw the disappointed, skeptical look that entered the boy's eyes. Expecting the secret of the ages, he was receiving an advice column platitude. "You can do it," Jorge continued. "No girl is going to want to go out with you if you act like you don't want to be around yourself. Understand?"

A little of Ricky's disappointment abated. "I think so."

Jorge nodded. Since no one was approaching the bar at the moment, he decided to be more generous with his advice. "And this next point is the most important thing you'll ever learn about dealing with a woman."

"What?" Ricky asked breathlessly, Ponce DeLeon about to uncover the fountain of youth.

Jorge lowered his voice. "When talking to a girl, always make her feel as if she's the prettiest girl in the room."

Ricky swallowed and glanced over at Lizzie Fortune, the girl who made the very air back up in his lungs. Lizzie was a distant Fortune cousin, just in town for the holidays. His heart had melted the moment he laid eyes on her this evening.

He didn't have a snowball's chance in hell with someone who looked like that. And he doubted that Jorge's magic formula would have any effect on Lizzie.

"What if she already *is* the prettiest girl in the room?" he wanted to know.

"Then it's even easier," Jorge told him. "You can handle any girl. Just have confidence in yourself, Ricky, and the rest will be a piece of cake."

Ricky was still more than a little uncertain. Just breathing was enough for someone who looked like

Jorge. But for someone like him, it wasn't that simple. "And this always works?"

"Always," Jorge said confidently.

But he could see that Ricky still had his doubts. The boy definitely needed a demonstration, Jorge decided. "Tell you what," he proposed. "You pick any girl in this room and I'll have her eating out of my hand in no time."

Ricky's eyes widened far enough to fall out. "Any girl?"

"Any girl," Jorge agreed. "Just make sure she's not married. We don't want to start any fights here in my parents' restaurant."

Ricky was perfectly amendable to that. "Okay," he agreed, bobbing his head up and down. He was already scanning the crowded room for a candidate.

Ricky stopped looking when his line of vision returned to the woman he'd spotted earlier, sitting by herself at a table. There was a frown on her face as she regarded her half-empty glass and she was very obviously alone. It was a table for two and there was no indication that anyone had recently vacated the other chair.

There was even a book on the table in front of her. Was she reading? Whether she was or not, there seemed to be an air of melancholy about her, visible even at this distance.

"Her," Ricky announced, pointing to the woman. "I pick her."

Chapter Two

Rising to the challenge, Jorge attempted to focus in the general direction that Ricky indicated.

The woman was clearly the stereotypical wallflower. She was sitting at the corner table all by herself, twirling a lock of long curly brown hair around her finger, the festive lights shimmering off her shiny green dress.

"Hey, man, I don't want to get arrested just to prove a point," Jorge protested. When Ricky looked at him quizzically, Jorge added, "She looks like a kid."

Ricky shook his head. "She's not. I heard her talking to someone earlier. She works for some kids' literacy foundation, tutoring them and sometimes holding fund-raisers to buy extra books. I think it's called Red Rock ReadingWorks," Ricky volunteered. He looked at Jorge expectantly. "She's gotta be at least twenty."

Jorge grinned at the boy's tone. He was thirty-eight himself, but he doubted Ricky knew that. "Then she's ancient, huh?"

"Hey, I'm fourteen. Everybody's ancient to me." Feeling as if he'd just put one foot in his mouth, Ricky quickly added, "Except you, of course."

Jorge's grin widened. "Nice save," he commented.

Ricky glanced back toward the girl at the table before looking up at his hero again. Jorge hadn't made a move yet.

"Backing down?" he wanted to know.

Nothing he liked better than a challenge, although, given his experience, the young woman at the table didn't look as if she'd put up much resistance.

"Not a chance," Jorge told him. He looked around and then saw one of the restaurant's employees at the far end of the bar. Perfect. "Hey, Angel," he called over the din. The man looked in his direction and raised a brow. "Mind taking over for me for a few minutes? I haven't had a break all night."

Jorge was the owners' son and what he wanted, he would have gotten without question even if he wasn't so affable. Angel nodded and came around to the other side of the bar.

"No problem."

Untying the half black apron secured around his slim waist, Jorge surrendered it to Angel. He felt invigorated. He was back in hunting mode.

Jane Gilliam had really hoped that coming to the party tonight would help her shake off the dark mood that had all but enshrouded her these last few days. Three days to be exact.

Three days since Eddie Gibbs had unceremoniously, and without prior warning, dumped her.

She probably wouldn't have even known she was being dumped, at least not for a few more days, if it wasn't for New Year's Eve. She'd impulsively asked the man she'd been seeing for the last six months to this New Year's Eve extravaganza that her close friend, Isabella Mendoza, had invited her to.

Eddie had listened to her impatiently and then he'd turned her down. She hadn't been prepared for that and when she'd asked him why, Eddie had bluntly told her that he would be spending New Year's Eve with someone else.

With his new girlfriend.

Jane could feel the sting of tears starting again and she passed her hand over her eyes, wiping them away. Up until that point, she'd thought that *she* was Eddie's girlfriend. But somewhere along the line in the last month, a month in which Eddie had been making himself increasingly scarce, he had decided that he "could do better"—his very words, each tipped in heart-piercing titanium—and found himself someone else.

The only trouble with that was that he'd forgotten to tell *her*.

Jane let out a long, shaky breath. She supposed she should have seen it coming. After all, it wasn't as if she was a knockout. And cute guys like Eddie Gibbs didn't stay with mousy girls like her, at least not for long.

Women, Jane silently corrected herself. *Women.* She was twenty-five years old. At twenty-five, you weren't a girl anymore; you were a woman.

A very lonely woman, Jane thought glumly, looking into the bottom of her glass. The drink had long since become watered down, the ice cubes melting into what had once been a fruity piña colada. It had turned the liquid into an exceedingly pale shade of yellow.

She needed to get out of here, she told herself. At this point, she didn't know what she could have been thinking, agreeing to come here with Isabella. Seeing all these couples, whispering into each other's ear, clearly enjoying themselves, was just making her feel more hopeless.

More alone.

Besides, it was getting pretty close to midnight, when the New Year was ushered in with heartfelt, soulful, passionate kisses. Seeing all these couples wrapped in each other's arms, kissing in the New Year was much more than she was going to be able to stand.

Up until three days ago, she thought she'd be kissing Eddie at the stroke of midnight. Now, she thought dejectedly, she'd probably be the only one here who had no one to turn to as the glittering silver ball on the wide-screen, flat-panel television reached the bottom of the pole and sent off an array of wild, blinding sparklers to greet the incoming year.

She didn't need to see that.

Didn't need to feel like a loser.

Again.

Jane glanced at her watch. Less than ten minutes left before midnight. That didn't give her much time to make her escape.

As if anyone would notice her leaving, she thought mockingly. She'd come here with Isabella, but there had to be a taxicab out there somewhere, didn't there? This was a big night for inebriated people. Cab drivers made their money on nights like New Year's Eve.

"Freshen that up for you?" asked a deep, melodic voice directly above her.

Jane realized that the voice—and the question—belonged to one of the waiters. He was obviously asking about the drink she'd been pretending to nurse for the last two hours. She'd already set the glass aside. The colorful little umbrella was drooping badly, mirroring the way she felt inside.

"No," she replied politely, "I was just…"

The rest of her thought vanished, as did, just for a moment, her entire thinking process. All because she'd made the mistake of looking up at the owner of the low, rumbling, sexy voice.

The man who had asked the question was, in a

word, beautiful. Not just handsome—although he was quite possibly the handsomest man, up close or on the movie screen, that she had ever seen in her life—but actually teeth-jarringly heart-stoppingly beautiful.

He had soulful brown eyes that she could have gotten lost in for at least the next ten years, and straight black hair that was just a little on the long side. Tall, lean, muscular, with jeans that emphasized his slender hips—and every move he made— whoever this man was, he made her think of a young lion.

On the other hand, his smile made her think of nothing at all, because just seeing it effectively turned her very intelligent and active brain to the consistency of last week's mush.

Struggling to collect herself and retrieve whatever might still be left of her composure, Jane did her best not to sound as if she was currently understudying the part of the head idiot of a very large village.

"Excuse me?"

"Your drink," Jorge prodded, nodding at the glass next to her elbow on the table. "May I freshen it up for you?" Lifting it to his nose, he took a sniff. "Piña colada, right?" he guessed. And then, when she said nothing at all, he smiled again, completing the transformation of the organ that was in her chest from a functioning heart to a puddle of red liquid. "My parents have me tending the bar," he explained, "and making sure that lovely ladies like you don't have to wait too long to have their requests granted."

Lovely ladies. How could someone so beautiful be so blind? she wondered. She wasn't lovely, she was plain and she knew it.

The ball on the TV panel on the back wall looked as if it was going to begin its descent at any moment.

Get out of here, her survival streak ordered urgently.

Coming to, Jane shook her head. "No, that's all right," she told him as he reached for her glass. "I was just about to leave anyway."

He looked at her in surprise. "Leave? Before midnight?" He made it sound as if she were doing something revolutionary.

Jane lifted her shoulders in a vague shrug. The left strap of her dress slipped off, sliding down her upper arm.

Jorge, his eyes on hers, reached out and very slowly slid the strap back into place.

Jane felt as if her skin had just caught on fire. She was rather surprised that she didn't actually spontaneously combust. The puddle in the middle of her chest became a heart again and instantly went into triple time, hammering so hard she was having trouble just catching her breath.

"Doesn't seem to be much point in staying," she heard herself saying, although she wasn't conscious of forming the words.

"And why is that?" he asked gently.

Just the sound of his voice made her feel warm all over. It took her a moment to realize that he'd asked her a question and another moment to focus on the words, making sense out of them.

"People always kiss someone at the stroke of midnight on New Year's Eve…"

Not sure how to end this sentence without sounding like a loser, Jane just let her voice trail off, hoping he'd silently fill in the rest of it himself. And have the decency to leave.

"And you have no one to kiss?" Jorge asked incredulously. His eyes swept over her. She could almost feel them. "A pretty lady like you?"

Jane could feel heat traveling up her cheeks and down her throat until all of her felt as if it were glowing pink.

"I just broke up with someone," she finally told him.

Breaking up sounded a great deal better than saying she'd just been dumped, Jane thought. But even so, the lie weighed heavily on her tongue. She didn't like lies, no matter what the reason, and here she was, hiding behind one so that she didn't come across like the ultimate loser to a man she didn't even know.

"His loss."

The man said it with such sincerity she found herself believing him, even though there was no way he could have meant that. After all, they were strangers to one another. For all he knew, she was a shrew.

Jane picked up her purse, holding it to her chest. "Well, I doubt if he thinks so. He's already found someone else."

What made her say that? a little voice in her head demanded. Why was she always so hell-bent on the truth, on making herself seem like she wasn't worthy of a committed relationship? The kids she worked with at the foundation loved her. Their parents were all grateful to her, praising her for making such a difference in the children's lives. And she got along rather well with the people she worked with at ReadingWorks, as long as the parameters remained in place—she was a colleague. A professional. Her personal life—such as it was—stayed private.

"Then he's a fool," Jorge told her quietly. "And you're better off without him."

As he spoke, Jorge studied the woman before him. It was one of his favorite pastimes. Every woman, he'd come to discover at a very early age, had something that was attractive about her. Something special, no matter how small.

This one, he thought, was actually pretty, in a plain sort of way. And by that, he meant that she was pretty without having to resort to artfully applied makeup, like so many of the other women who were here tonight. She was slender, petite—he doubted if she could have been more than about five two—and she had beautiful hair held in place with two ornamental hairclips. They allowed her golden brown curls to cascade down her back like a waterfall.

But what really captivated him was her innocence. There was a certain sweetness to her, a vulnerability that he now detected in her eyes. He sincerely doubted that she was aware of it.

But he was.

Jane stood up. It was almost midnight and she

really didn't want to feel like the odd woman out, not tonight. It would hurt too much.

But as she rose to her feet, the tall, beautiful young man with the sexy, velvet voice didn't retreat, didn't even take a step back. He remained exactly where he was, leaving less than a ribbon's worth of space between them.

So little space that she could actually feel the heat of his body radiating out to hers. Or was that just her body getting ready to burst into flame?

She swallowed. Why was he standing in her way? Was he laughing at her?

But he didn't seem as if he was laughing. His smile was too gentle, too kind.

Jane took a breath. "I really need to leave," she told him.

He slowly ran the back of his hand along her bare arm. "Would you stay if there was someone to kiss at the stroke of midnight?"

Goose bumps were forming on her arm at a fantastic rate. Her throat felt suddenly very, very dry.

Idiot, he's not saying what you think he's saying. He's just asking a question. Don't set yourself up to be a pathetic loser. Again.

But despite her stern, silent warning, Jane heard herself answering, "Yes." And then, to save face, she tried to make light of the situation. "Are you planning on dragging someone over here to kiss me?"

Eyes the color of warm chocolate on a cold winter morning held hers prisoner.

"No," he told her quietly.

Okay, now she really did feel like an idiot. Served her right for trying to flirt, or whatever she'd just done that might have passed for flirting. She wasn't any good at that—never had been.

Doing her best to salvage what was left of her badly damaged ego, Jane forced a smile to her lips. But all she could manage was barely half of one.

"Well, then," she murmured, attempting to get past him. "I'd better get going."

"No," Jorge repeated. "I'm not going to drag anyone over here—I'd like to be the one to kiss you at midnight." And then he looked at her with just the right touch of shyness. "If that's all right with you."

He was actually asking if it was all right to kiss her on New Year's Eve?

Was this some kind of a joke? Men like—what was his name, anyway? Men like him didn't ask permission to kiss a woman, they spent half their time fighting off women who were trying to kiss them.

Jane took another deep breath and held it for a moment, wondering whether she was dreaming. What other explanation could there be? How in heaven's name didn't he already have a girlfriend in tow on this occasion? She would have been willing to bet, until this man with the magnetic smile had approached her, that she was quite probably the only unattached adult here.

"What's your name?" Jane finally asked him.

"Jorge," he replied. "Jorge Mendoza."

Mendoza.

It was certainly a common enough name. Even so, Jane couldn't help wondering if Jorge was somehow related to Isabella and if her friend had sent him here on an errand of mercy.

A mercy kissing.

Out of the corner of her eye, she took note of the TV screen. The glittering Times Square ball was definitely beginning to move downward now. Someone in the crowd raised his voice and began the traditional countdown, ticking off the seconds that were still left in this year.

"Ten, nine, eight—"

When the woman made no effort to identify herself, Jorge coaxed her a little. "And you are?"

Several voices joined in, more swelling their numbers with each passing second. "Seven, six, five—"

She wasn't a bold person by nature, but if this was a dream, then there was no reason to worry about consequences. Nothing to be embarrassed about in the future.

"Jane. Jane Gilliam," she told him. "Are you related to Isabella?"

"Four, three—"

"Cousin," he told her. Was it his imagination, or was there a new spark in her eyes? He found his interest being piqued and discovered that she was definitely arousing him. "Distant," he added for good measure.

"Two—"

Without any further discussion, his eyes on hers,

Jorge drew Jane into his arms. He could feel her breathing become audible and found something very sweet about the almost hesitant anticipation he saw in her eyes.

"You're not really going to kiss me, are you?" Dream or not, it was still hard for her to believe. And yet, she *so* wanted to believe.

"One!"

His lips covered hers as cries of "Happy New Year!" echoed throughout the crowded room, shouted from the announcer on the TV program as well as by the various people scattered about whose lips were not otherwise occupied.

But Jane didn't hear a single sound, other than the pounding of her heart.

Chapter Three

She'd died.

There was no other explanation for the way she felt, Jane thought. She must have died and zoomed straight up to heaven. And not even the regular heaven, but some higher plane reserved for the incredibly saintly, incredibly fortunate. Because there was nothing remotely earthly about the feelings she was experiencing right at this moment.

To the casual observer, Jane was certain that it looked as if like nothing more than a traditional New Year's Eve kiss was being shared by two people at the stroke of midnight.

A lot the casual observer knew.

There were fireworks exploding in her veins, not

to mention that her head was spinning wildly, threatening to throw her completely off balance and utterly out of control. Granted, her experience when it came to men and kissing was rather sadly limited, but even she knew that this was something unusual, something really and deliciously different. She'd never been on the verge of a complete meltdown before.

Jorge tasted incredibly sweet and he smelled even better. Everything about him aroused her.

Bold was a word that had nothing to do with her personality, outside of those times when she attempted to secure more funding for her nonprofit organization. But she felt bold now. Bold enough to press her enflamed body against Jorge's in an attempt to absorb every nuance, every fragment of this incredible experience that had taken her completely by surprise and swept her not just off her feet but off to another dimension.

Another universe.

Like a woman trapped in a mind-boggling, sensuous trance, Jane wove her arms around Jorge's neck, praying the dream she was having would never end. Praying that the moment she was in would stretch out until eternity. She'd never felt so alive, so wonderful before. And probably never would again.

He was rattled.

Few things ever rattled Jorge Mendoza. He was thirty-eight and eons away from being a boy, even though he still possessed not only a boyish grin, but boyish charm. Even in his teens, he'd been more man than boy, with a man's take on things. And heaven knew he'd kissed and been with more than twice his share of women.

Life had been good to him that way, he'd often thought, blessing him not just with exceptional looks but, more importantly, with a magnetic charm. Charm that now aided him in his professional endeavors—currently he was gathering financial backing for a trainer who raised the finest quarter horses in Texas—as well as in the seduction of willing women.

But none of that was on his mind right now. Instead, he felt complete and total, unabashed surprise. He hadn't thought that he could *ever* feel like this. Like there were rockets going off in his veins.

That kind of feeling hadn't happened to him since the first time he'd slept with a woman.

But this pretty, intelligent but obviously inexperienced young woman had just managed to do what no other woman had in the last twenty-four years. She'd jarred him down to his very foundations and made him feel like a boy on the brink of manhood again.

It was with incredible effort that Jorge managed to finally, albeit reluctantly, draw his lips away from Jane's.

Taking in a deep, steadying breath, he looked down at the young woman the way one might look at a soul-shaking revelation, attempting to analyze it. Very slowly, surprise gave way to abject pleasure.

"Happy New Year," he whispered softly against her hair.

"Right." She was rather stunned that she could actually talk rather than simply gasp. "Happy New Year," she repeated, each syllable accompanied by the mad beating of her heart. Hands down, this certainly was the best New Year's Eve moment she'd ever experienced.

His dark eyes danced, smiling directly into her soul. "So," he asked her, "what are you doing for the rest of the year?"

"Recovering."

The honest admission had just slipped out before Jane could think to stop it. But being coy was not something she had any practice at, or, truthfully, any desire to become proficient in. There'd always been something off-putting to her about women who felt the need to play games with the men in their lives.

By the same token, though, she'd discovered that since she didn't play games, it wasn't very long before she had no one to even contemplate playing games with. The few men who had passed through her life would come on strong and when they didn't get what they were after, they would just phase her out.

She refused to believe that all men were only after one thing—but so far, she had very little proof to the contrary. None, actually.

Jorge laughed at her response, amused that she was so honest. He was used to women who liked to be mysterious, to exercise their feminine wiles on him. In reality, a great many of them were about as shallow as saucers—not that he required much depth in his partner of the moment. It made things far less complicated that way.

But this one was different.

This one didn't seem at all versed in the flirtatious give-and-take that went on between the male and female of the species. Rather than being as devious as a cat, she came across more like Bambi, with all of the famous fawn's innocence.

A trace of guilt began to nibble away at him. Jorge was beginning to regret his bet with Ricky. He hadn't counted on the fact that there might very well be feelings involved. And there were. He could see it in Jane's luminous eyes.

He also hadn't counted on the fact that he would be attracted to his target. Not just physically, but in a way that he couldn't even quite put into words.

Jorge certainly couldn't pin this feeling on alcohol consumption because he hadn't really consumed any. Just one quick toast of white wine with his parents, sisters and their spouses before the Fortune Foundation party had officially gotten under way. But since then, he hadn't had anything stronger to drink than a ginger ale.

No, Jorge couldn't blame his reaction to Jane on anything other than the petite woman herself.

He wasn't sure how he felt about that, so, for the time being, he decided not to think about it.

"You're laughing at me," Jane protested self-consciously, the aura of her out-of-body experience beginning to fade just a little.

The faint pink color he witnessed creeping up her rather seductive high cheekbones was oddly arousing, Jorge mused. With the rest of the evening stretching out before him, he decided he definitely wanted to get to know this woman better and discover what made her so different from the legions of other women he'd known—other than her obvious lack of sophistication and her innocent manner.

"I'm not laughing at you," Jorge told her gently. "I'm laughing with you."

Now even she knew that was a line. Or was he just poking fun at her? "You might not have noticed," she pointed out quietly, "but I'm not laughing."

Jorge didn't answer immediately. Instead, he slipped his hand behind her head, cupping it.

For a moment, she thought he was going to kiss her again and she could have sworn that the wattage at Red went down several notches as the very room grew dark. She struggled to hang on to her consciousness.

"Sure you are," Jorge told her. "I can see it in your eyes."

The very remark coaxed a smile to her lips, whether out of nervousness or just because being so near to this dynamic, gorgeous man made her want to smile all over, she really didn't know. For the moment, she didn't care, either. What mattered was the proximity. She wanted to remain this close to

Jorge for as long as humanly possible without having to resort to handcuffs.

God, she was babbling and her lips weren't even moving.

Things like this didn't happen to people like her, she thought again. And while it *was* happening, she was just going to go with it and enjoy it.

Because she knew it was never, ever going to happen again.

"If you say so," Jane answered, her voice deliberately low to keep it from cracking.

Did she have any idea how sexy she sounded, Jorge wondered.

He had a feeling that she didn't, that Jane Gilliam had probably gone through her whole life seriously underestimating herself. It didn't take a student of women to pick up on that. He could tell by her body language and by the very way she wore her clothes. She dressed nicely, but there was no sign that there had been any extra fussing, any extra care taken. The same applied to her makeup.

He caught himself wondering about her. Really wondering about her as a person, not a conquest.

Leaning his head against Jane's, he looked into her eyes, then he shifted so that his lips were near her ear. "Who are you, Jane Gilliam?" he asked her quietly.

His breath sent warm shivers up and down her spine, and she was afraid he'd see how very inexperienced she was—he'd probably already guessed that anyway.

Why had he kissed her, she wondered again. A man

like this wouldn't have been alone any night of the year, especially not one that was considered to be the most important. She curbed the urge to ask, sensing that the answer might send her plummeting to the ground.

Jane felt as if she were trapped inside some kind of bubble—and bubbles always burst. There was no getting away from that. But not just yet.

Not just now.

Jane ran the tip of her tongue along her bottom lip. What was he asking her?

"Do you mean what do I do for a living?"

"That's as good a start as any," he acknowledged, aware that any one of a number of women he knew would have taken the question and given him some sort of existential, philosophical answer. Jane, apparently, was grounded.

His mother, he realized, would love her.

Jorge quickly glanced around, hoping that Maria Mendoza wasn't standing somewhere close by, taking all this in. She'd misunderstand immediately, especially since Jane was not like any of the other women he kept company with.

"I work for Red Rock ReadingWorks," Jane told him, tripping over the alliteration for the first time since she'd joined the organization. If she wasn't careful, any second she was going to start sounding like a chatty fool. "That's a nonprofit organization that—"

Jorge held up his hand to stop her before she

launched into a lengthy description of Reading-Works and all the services that it offered.

"I'm familiar with ReadingWorks," he told her.

She clamped her jaw shut to keep it from dropping in surprise. "You are?" The next moment, Jane realized her oversight. "Of course you are. You said that Isabella was your cousin." And the pretty thirty-year-old dropped by the storefront building where Reading-Works was housed often enough. Isabella probably had mentioned the place to him once or twice.

Jane felt self-conscious. She always did when attention was focused on her. She made an attempt to deflect it back to him. Besides, she really did want to find out a few things about this man who had set her on fire.

"What do you do?"

He glanced at the glass on the table, the one he'd initially offered to fill. "Well, tonight, I'm a bartender."

She sincerely doubted that bartending was Jorge's sole occupation. He looked far too vital, far too intelligent to be satisfied with mixing drinks and wiping down a counter.

"And other nights?" she prompted. "And days?" Jane added quickly when she realized what her initially innocent question had to sound like to him.

Broad shoulders shrugged casually beneath his royal blue shirt. His easygoing grin nonetheless created a knot in the pit of her stomach.

"A little of this, a little of that." He saw the curiosity in her eyes. She really wanted to know, he thought. Most women just wanted to see the size of his billfold—among other things. "I'm an entrepreneur," he added.

"That sounds interesting. Tell me about it."

She actually sounded genuinely interested, he thought. Before he knew it, he began talking about his latest venture.

Oh man, what an operator Jorge was, Ricky Jamison thought, standing over in a corner and watching his idol's every move. Because he was so far away and there was so much noise, Ricky couldn't hear what was being said, but he could certainly see what was going on. Within the space of a few minutes—and, from the looks of it, one hell of a kiss—Jorge had brought the bookish woman to a melting point.

Ricky sighed, shaking his head. His friend Josh and Josh's girlfriend, Lindsey, had their heads together over in the corner, sharing something private. Ricky felt a pang as he wished he had that kind of ability, to make girls fall for him.

When he was older, Ricky thought wistfully, he wanted to be exactly like Jorge Mendoza. The man was a god in his eyes.

Patrick Fortune rang in this New Year's the very same way he rang in all the others since he'd met his bride: by kissing Lacey.

His arm rested comfortably around his still-beautiful wife's shoulders as he surveyed the very crowded banquet hall. He recognized almost all the faces here, and that was his own doing—his and Maria Mendoza's. It wasn't every New Year's Eve that he managed to gather together so many members of his family under one roof. Sadly, not all of his five children and their spouses could make it. But on the bright side, his brother William and William's five children were all here, as well as Cynthia's children.

Bolder than sunlight, Cynthia had always marched to a different drummer and made her own rules, usually as she went along. Still, he wished she'd taken him up on the invitation and come. He wanted *all* his siblings here, all his nieces and nephews as well as his own children. Not because he had any special announcement to make, but just because he felt the need for their presence.

Family was everything.

The older he became, the more inclined Patrick felt to forget any past grievances that might have once caused him to turn his back on one member of the family or another. Life was too short—and it was getting shorter all the time. He'd thought that his cousin Ryan would live forever and Ryan had been dead now for four years. It seemed impossible, and yet it was true.

He still missed the man a great deal.

The swish of Lacey's dress as she turned toward him caught his attention.

"A penny for your thoughts," she said, leaning in so that he could hear her. He'd looked entirely too pensive for the last few minutes and she wondered if there was anything wrong.

Patrick laughed at the way she'd asked her question. "And that," he declared, his mouth curving in amusement, "is how our fortune continues to remain intact. Your frugality."

"Very funny." She threaded her arm through his as she looked up at him. He was still an exceptionally handsome man, she caught herself thinking. "Where are you right now?"

Patrick patted her arm. "Right here beside you, my love." He sighed. "Just missing Ryan, that's all. He used to love family gatherings like this."

Ryan Fortune had been a good man who always saw the best in people. Lacey liked to think that Patrick was the same way. She tightened her hold on his arm. "He wouldn't want you to be sad, Patrick."

Lacey was right. As always. He supposed that what had triggered his thoughts was seeing Lily tonight—Ryan's widow. Seeing her made him expect to see Ryan somewhere in her immediate vicinity. If only.

"No, you're right, he wouldn't. Just give me a minute to get my party face back in place," he teased.

Just then, someone bumped into him, hard. If there had been any more space between him and Lacey, he might have actually fallen into her, bringing her down with him. Patrick turned to look at the man who had stumbled into him.

"Sorry," the other man apologized. "I think I've

had just a little too much to drink. I'm going to get some air," he said by way of an excuse.

"Good idea," Patrick agreed, addressing the words to the back of the man's head. He stared after him for a second. There was something vaguely familiar about the man, but most likely, it could have just been his imagination. He shrugged his shoulders and returned to the party.

* * *

The man kept going, weaving his way in and out of the crowd, working his way to the front door. Once he was confident he was out of Patrick's sight, his meandering gait ceased.

One down, he thought, a self-satisfied smirk playing along his thin lips.

Chapter Four

Jane still couldn't quite believe how this evening had turned out. If it wasn't such a cliché, she would have actually pinched herself to see if she was dreaming.

Jorge had not left her side since he came to ask her about refilling her drink and then remained to utterly rock her world.

She finally understood what that phrase meant. This had to be what Californians experienced when a 7.5 earthquake hit. Even though it was after one o'clock and the kiss that had all but turned her brain to mush, was an hour in the past, the ground beneath her feet still felt as if it were moving. Her insides were still in a state of flux.

But Jorge hadn't moved on.

After he'd kissed her, all but burning off her lips, he'd stayed with her. Talked with her.

And made her feel beautiful.

Even when the man behind the bar had finally managed to get his attention and signaled to him in an obvious entreaty to return to his post, rather than seizing the excuse and leaving her, Jorge had laced his fingers through hers and had taken her along with him when he went to talk to the bartender.

"Hey, man, I need you to take over now," Angel said to him, stripping off the black half apron he'd donned earlier.

Jorge made no effort to take the apron from him. Instead, he said, "Ask Carlos to take over," mentioning the name of one of the waiters working this evening. "He owes me a favor."

Angel sighed, stashing the apron beneath the bar for the time being. "If you say so."

Jane felt a little guilty, taking Jorge away from the job he was supposed to be helping out with. "I'm keeping you."

Jorge turned toward her and smiled into her eyes, creating yet another huge tidal wave inside her stomach. "If that's what you want," he murmured.

Jane forgot to breathe again.

When she remembered, after a beat, she tried to draw it in subtly and then release it slowly. She was sure he'd noticed.

God, but she was acting as sophisticated as an escapee from a fifteenth-century nunnery. She really was going to have to get a grip on herself.

But Jorge was like no other man she'd ever met.

He was still holding her hand and that, somehow, was impeding the flow of blood to her brain. She had to concentrate in order to think.

"No, I meant…" She searched for the right words. "That I'm taking you away from your work."

"Not my work," he corrected her. "I'm just helping out, remember?"

Right, she thought, he'd already said something about that, about being a businessman, an entrepreneur, not a bartender. Damn, her head felt like a sieve, with all the information she was receiving just leaking out of every pore. She wasn't like this normally. Ordinarily, she absorbed details like a sponge and retained absolutely everything.

Not this time.

"And for the most part," Jorge was saying, his low, sexy voice working its way under her skin, thrilling her, "the party's beginning to wind down."

Even as he said it, a wave of cold air wove through the room as the front doors opened and several people made their way out into the night. It was mild as far as winters around here went, but there was no denying that it was still cold.

More than anything, Jane didn't want the evening to end. But even Cinderella had to go home at midnight, and she'd already beaten Cinderella's record by an hour.

Without thinking, Jane ran the tip of her tongue along her lips. She could still taste him. If she closed her eyes, she could still feel the pressure of his lips against hers.

This was definitely one New Year's Eve she was going to remember for the rest of her life—no matter how long she lived.

As if sensing what she was thinking, Jorge asked, "Can I take you home, Jane? Or did you drive over here by yourself?"

Why did that sound as if she was such a loser, coming to a New Year's Eve party by herself? Besides, she hadn't come alone, she'd come here with Isabella.

But it had been a long time since she'd seen her friend. Scanning the immediate area now, she couldn't find Isabella.

"I came with Isabella," Jane told him, still searching through the sea of faces for a glimpse of her friend.

The answer coaxed out another smile. "Isabella won't mind if I bring you home," he assured her.

Jane stopped searching and looked at him. "But how will she know? Isabella might get worried if she can't find me."

Now that was downright refreshing, Jorge thought, impressed. He'd hooked up with any number of women at parties who'd left girlfriends—and boyfriends—wandering around looking for them without so much as a second thought. Their focus was exclusively on their own pleasure.

Jane Gilliam was certainly different from the type of woman he was accustomed to. Maybe she

deserved closer scrutiny, he mused. Her kiss had
been a definite surprise. Maybe there were other
surprises to be uncovered as well.

"Don't worry," he told her, "I'll leave word at the
hostess desk for her. She's bound to ask there if she
can't find you."

Jane hesitated—but not too much. She *really*
wanted to be with Jorge for as long as possible.

"Well, if you think it's all right."

She couldn't keep from smiling. Everything inside
her was cheering. The evening wasn't ending yet.
She'd gotten a reprieve. Who knew, once they got to
her apartment, maybe he'd stay a while for coffee and
conversation. She loved listening to the sound of his
voice.

Amused by her shy eagerness, Jorge ran the back
of his knuckles along her cheek, then watched, fascinated, as a small nerve along her cheekbone winked
in and out as if it was flirting with him.

"I think it's all right," he assured her.

From across the room, Maria Mendoza was in the
middle of instructing several of the busboys to subtly
begin gathering up dishes that had clearly been abandoned when she suddenly noticed her son talking to
a young woman. Not just talking to her, but leaning
in the way he did when he'd singled someone out.

Squinting, Maria looked closer. For once, the
woman who had caught her son's attention didn't
look as if she was modeling all the makeup offered
at a department display counter. In fact, she looked

almost sweet. There was nothing brash or flashy about her. And the dress she was wearing wasn't cut down to her navel.

She was the kind of young woman, Maria thought as she abruptly stopped addressing the busboys, that she would have personally hand-selected for Jorge.

She knew her, she realized. Jane…something. Jane Gilliam, that was it. She'd met her once through Patrick Fortune. He spoke very highly of the young woman's selflessness and her dedication to the children she worked with, as well as her passionate pledge to help every child to learn how to read.

Several times during the evening, she'd noted that the poor girl was sitting off by herself. At one point, Jane had even taken out a book from her purse and had begun to read. While everyone else had been enjoying themselves, the shy young woman clearly felt cut off by loneliness.

Well, she obviously wasn't lonely anymore, Maria thought, pleased. Not with Jorge talking to her. Jane seemed to be hanging on his every word.

Maria's mother's heart swelled with hope and joy. Could Jorge finally, *finally* be growing up? Could he finally be abandoning that wanton side that had him going from one shallow beauty to another? Had he left that life behind him to turn his attention to a woman of substance?

She fervently hoped so. Maybe all those prayers to St. Jude, patron saint of hopeless causes, were finally paying off.

"Señora Mendoza?" Luis, one of the busboys

hesitantly tried to get her attention. "You did not finish telling us what you wanted us to do."

She needed to get over there, Maria thought, to find out if what she was seeing was real. "Do what you are paid to do, Luis," Maria told the young man. He needed to show a little initiative if he ever hoped to be anything more than just a busboy. "Must I do all the thinking for you?"

Luis looked a little chagrinned as he bowed his head. "No, Señora."

Maria patted his arm. "Good, then get to it, please."

Even as she spoke, she quickly began making her way through the revelers who were still left. But her eyes never left her target: Jorge and the young woman. Though no longer in her thirties, Maria prided herself on still being very quick on her feet when she wanted to be.

She made it to her son's side before he had a chance to get away.

Placing a hand on his shoulder, she could see that she'd caught him by surprise. Good. "Are you leaving, Jorge?" she asked innocently.

"Yes, in a few minutes, Mama." And then, for form's sake—and because he loved her—he added, "If you don't mind."

"Of course I don't mind," Maria assured him magnanimously even as her eyes covertly darted toward Jane and then back again. "You've been a great help tonight. Your father is very grateful. There were more people here than were expected."

Maria paused, waiting. But Jorge was not taking

the hint. He wasn't making any introductions. Maria was not shy about taking matters into her own hands. It was how she'd gotten to where she was now.

She turned toward Jane, a bright smile on her face. "Hello, you might not remember me, but we met—"

It was only around good-looking men that Jane found herself almost hopelessly tongue-tied, feeling about as sharp as a button. When dealing with the rest of the world, she became friendly and cheery, which was more her natural state.

She smiled warmly now at the older woman. "Of course I remember you, Señora Mendoza. Mr. Fortune introduced us last year. He speaks very highly of you every time your name comes up."

She was gracious as well as sweet, Maria thought. "As he does you," Maria responded.

For a moment, Jorge almost felt as if he were on the outside looking in. It wasn't a situation he was accustomed to. Moreover, his mother's behavior was a bit of a surprise. She wasn't usually this friendly with any of the women he charmed.

Bemused, Jorge looked from Jane to his mother. He could read his mother's mind as clearly as if the words had been written on a huge billboard and hung around her neck.

Sorry, Ma, not going to happen, he thought.

Granted, Jane was special in her own unique way and he had to admit that he was attracted and somewhat captivated by her, but neither condition meant that he was about to suddenly abandon his bachelor life for this woman with the huge, soulful brown eyes. At most, he'd get further acquainted with her, spend a little time pleasuring them both, and then move on. It was his way.

"I was just about to take Jane home," he told his mother. "She came with Isabella, so if you see her, just let her know that I've taken care of Jane's transportation for the evening."

"Of course." Maria's smile was just a tad strained as she offered it to Jane. Turning, Maria began to leave but at the last moment, she buttonholed her son and whispered a warning into his ear. "Don't you hurt this one." Releasing him, she smiled broadly. This time, there was nothing forced about it. Before leaving for good, she looked over her shoulder at Jane and said, "I hope I will see you again very soon."

Me, too, Señora. Me, too, Jane couldn't help thinking, even though she knew the chances of that happening were very, very slim.

Jorge waited until his mother disappeared into the crowd. The woman really did have eyes in the back of her head, he thought. Turning to Jane, he inclined his head and asked, "Ready?"

He wouldn't believe just how ready she was, Jane thought. "I just have to get my coat," she told him. She pointed vaguely in the general direction of the coatroom.

There was a crowd around the desk, Jorge noted. No sense in their both standing around, waiting their turn. He'd have better luck getting to the front of the line if he went alone.

"Why don't you give me the claim number?" Jorge suggested. "I'll go get it for you."

She wasn't accustomed to such attentive gallantry. Usually, she was the one running the errands. Flipping open the clip on her clutch purse, she began searching through it.

"It's here someplace," Jane murmured. She was forced to go through the purse twice before she finally located the small, square card with the red claim number on it. "Here it is," she announced triumphantly.

Jorge took the claim number from her, his fingers lightly, deliberately brushing against hers. He could see by the look in her eyes that he'd succeeded in sending yet another shock wave dancing through her body. Her reaction amused him and yet, there was something almost touchingly sweet about it.

It was enough to make him feel guilty—if he wasn't enjoying himself so much.

"I'll be right back," he promised. "Don't go anywhere."

There wasn't a chance of that, she thought. Not even if they used dynamite. "I won't," she promised.

Jane watched as he walked away, utterly mesmerized by the rhythmic movement of his hips. Utterly mesmerized by everything about him.

Jorge really seemed to like her, she thought, stunned and awed and very thrilled. She had no idea why someone like him would have even stopped to give her the time of day, but right now, she didn't want to dig too deeply. Didn't want to risk the chance of all this suddenly fading away. For now, she was going to ride this wonderful wave for as long as she possibly could.

Sighing, she closed her eyes and smiled to herself. Maybe, just this once, nice girls didn't have to finish last.

"Didn't I tell you he was terrific?"

Jane picked out the young voice from amid a sea of others and opened her eyes again. For a second, she thought whoever was speaking was talking to her. But as she turned around to look, she saw that the owner of the voice, a young teenager who looked about fourteen, maybe fifteen, but just barely, was talking to another, slightly older looking youth.

She turned back around, not wanting the boys to think that she was eavesdropping on their conversation.

But it was hard not to. The younger of the two sounded so enthusiastic.

"All I had to do was point someone out and he had her eating out of his hand in less than five minutes," he marveled. "He said it was easy, that all it took was just a matter of making the girl think she was the prettiest one in the room, the center of his attention. But it's gotta be more than that," Ricky insisted.

"Well, du-uh," Josh responded condescendingly. "When you look like Jorge Mendoza, all you have to do is stand still and half a dozen drooling women come running to you. It doesn't exactly take an Einstein to figure that out, Ricky."

"I don't know," Ricky countered. "I mean, he's a

great-looking guy and all, but this woman I picked out, she looked a little standoffish. I really didn't think Jorge could melt her as fast as he did." He shook his head in quiet admiration. "But five minutes after he came up to her, he was kissing her." He paused to laugh softly. "*Really* ringing in the New Year, if you know what I mean."

The one called Ricky was grinning broadly. She could hear it in his voice, even as Jane's heart froze in her chest.

"I think he's taking her to his place," she heard the young teenager speculate to his friend. "That wasn't part of the bet, but—"

"You actually bet him, you idiot?" the other teen asked incredulously.

Ricky bristled. "Not money," he protested. "It's just that I didn't think he could do it *that* fast. I just said the word. Like 'I bet you can't.'"

She heard the other boy scoff. "I could have told you that you'd lose."

Jane felt sick. For a second, she was afraid she might throw up.

They were talking about *her*.

That was why Jorge had approached her out of the blue—because he'd made a bet with a teenager who wasn't even old enough to shave yet.

How stupid of her to think that a guy like Jorge Mendoza would be attracted to her. To think that he might have even liked her a tiny bit.

A bet.

Jane could feel angry tears forming in her eyes.

She couldn't remember ever, *ever* feeling this humiliated. This awful.

She couldn't stay here, couldn't wait for him to come back. She never wanted to see that honey-tongued bastard again. Who did he think he was, making her the object of a bet? she thought angrily.

Clutching her purse to her chest, Jane swung around and forged a path to the front door. She bumped into people as she went, murmuring half-hearted excuses as she passed them.

It was cold outside. Remnants of snow from the last storm crunched beneath her high heels, but she didn't care.

Wrapping her arms around herself, she searched for a passing taxi to flag down.

There were none out on the street this time of night. Why? Didn't they know it was New Year's Eve?

Shivering, she hurried down several blocks and then took shelter in the doorway of an office building. She placed a call to a taxi service on her cell phone and waited for her ride.

And cried angry tears.

Chapter Five

"Patrick, if you want me to take that suit to the cleaners tomorrow, please don't forget to empty out your pockets," Lacey told her husband the next morning as she popped her head into the master bedroom.

The bright morning sun was trying to push its way into the room despite the heavy drapes at the windows that barred its passage. It was one of the rare mornings that Patrick actually slept in.

Sitting up now, Patrick ran his hand through his tousled reddish hair. Despite the odd hint of white, he still looked boyish, especially with sleep still hovering around his eyes.

He reached for his glasses on the nightstand and

put them on. The world came into focus, as did the digital clock next to the lamp.

He always thought of himself as energetic—except when compared to his wife. "Lacey, it's New Year's Day. It's a holiday. What are you doing up so early and why are we talking about dry cleaning?"

She crossed to him and stood before the bed that she had vacated more than an hour before.

"I'm up, dear husband, because, in case you've forgotten, we're having some of the family over for a late lunch today, and I'm talking about dry cleaning because someone," she looked at him pointedly, "spilled coffee on his jacket last night." She ran her hand along his stubbled face affectionately. "And just because it's a technical holiday doesn't mean that the world suddenly stops spinning."

"Technical?" he echoed, just a little perplexed at her meaning.

"Technical," she repeated. "Do you have any idea how many sales are going on at this very moment as you are lounging around in your PJs?"

Getting out of bed, Patrick groaned. "I could never understand that. Why would anyone want to get up that early just to go shopping? What kind of bargains could they possibly offer to warrant that?"

Sometimes the man she loved could be adorably naive, Lacey thought. She laughed at the look on his face, then stopped to pick up the shirt he must have dropped on the floor last night—or early this morning. He'd been pretty tired as she recalled.

"Spoken like a man who has never had to search for a bargain in his life."

"My biggest bargain," Patrick freely confessed as he came up behind her and enfolded his wife in an affectionate embrace, "was finding you and making you my wife. Anything that happened after that would only be deemed anticlimatic."

"You do know how to turn a lady's head," she told him with a warm smile. "But I'm not going to be distracted." Draping his shirt over her arm, she looked around for the suit she'd mentioned. "Where are the rest of your clothes from the party?"

He released her. "The cleaners aren't having a sale, are they?" he asked, amused.

"I just want to put the suit aside while I think of it," she told him. One finely shaped eyebrow arched over a sparkling green eye. "Remember leaving your house key in your pants pocket the last time? Remember wasting all that time, looking for it?"

Patrick inclined his head. "Point well taken," he allowed with a sigh.

He moved to his side of the walk-in closet. He'd meant to hang the suit back up, but somehow, it had only made it to the floor of the closet. Picking up the pants and jacket, he quickly checked all four pants pockets.

"Empty," he announced, handing the slightly wrinkled gray slacks to Lacey.

"And the jacket?" she asked as she dropped the pants on top of the shirt she had over her arm.

He checked the right pocket. He distinctly remembered taking out his wallet and depositing his keys beside it on the bureau. But as he slipped his fingers into the left outer pocket, he frowned. His fingers had come in contact with something.

It was a folded piece of paper and he opened it up as he removed the paper from his pocket. He had no memory of putting it in his pocket, no memory of anyone handing it to him.

He scanned the small sheet quickly, his frown deepening slightly.

"Not so empty, is it?" Lacey teased, then saw his expression. Something was clearly wrong, Lacey thought. "What's the matter?"

Not waiting for him to answer, she came closer in order to read the note, which was printed in large block letters.

"ONE OF THE FORTUNES IS NOT WHO YOU THINK."

It was Lacey's turn to be puzzled. She looked up at her husband for enlightenment. "Who gave this to you?"

He turned it over in his hand. There was nothing on the back. "I have no idea."

A touch of apprehension wove through her. "A note just turns up in your pocket and you have no idea where it came from?"

Rather than crumple it and toss it into the waste-paper basket, he placed it on the bureau. This required closer scrutiny. But not when Lacey was around. He didn't want to alarm her.

"That about sums it up," he agreed.

It was Lacey's turn to frown as anticipation got the better of her. "Do you think that it's some kind of warning?"

"I think it's some kind of waste of paper." Patrick handed her the jacket. "Here you go, one suit, as per your request." And then he gave her a quick, courtly bow. "Now, if milady doesn't mind, I'd really like to take a shower."

She nodded, the note already relegated to a thing of the past unless something more about it came up. Right now, she had a lunch to oversee.

"When you're done with your shower," she told him, "I've got a few things I need you to do."

He grinned and kissed her quickly. He'd expected nothing less.

"Of course you do."

But as soon as Lacey was gone, Patrick picked up the telephone next to the bed and called his brother, William.

Younger by a year, William had an offbeat sense of humor. This might have been his idea of a joke, although, truthfully, Patrick did have his doubts that William's humor was *this* offbeat.

"Bill," he began when his brother picked up on the other end. "It's Patrick. Happy New Year," he prefaced, getting the amenities out of the way, even though he'd just seen his younger brother less than nine hours ago at the party.

"Same to you," William responded. "You know, this is rather a coincidence, you calling like this. I was just debating calling you."

There was an unsettling note in William's voice that caught his attention. "Oh?"

"Yeah."

William paused, hunting for the right words. He'd found himself later in life than Patrick had, finally making a niche for himself with Fortune Forecasting, a company that predicted stock market trends. But ever since his wife had died last year, he'd lost his focus again and had felt adrift. He'd begun to look toward Patrick for guidance again.

"Now this is going to sound a little off the wall," he finally said, "but I just found this note in my pocket this morning. It says—"

"—One of the Fortunes is not who you think," Patrick completed.

For a second there was stunned silence on the other end of the line. And then William laughed nervously. "So it was you."

He'd obviously missed something, Patrick thought. "Excuse me?"

"It was you," William repeated. "You were the one who put the note in my pocket," he elaborated when Patrick made no response. "I've got to say, this isn't your usual style, Patrick. What's the point?" he wanted to know.

"I have no idea what the point is," Patrick said, sitting down on the bed. "I didn't put the note in your pocket, William. As a matter of fact, I found an identical note in mine. Someone slipped it into my jacket." He tried to think of when that could have happened. The restaurant was fairly crowded all night. He'd been jostled any number of times during the evening.

He heard William sigh. "Well, that makes three, then."

"Three?" Patrick repeated, not sure where William was going with this.

"Three," William said again. "I just got off the phone with Lily," he said, referring to their late cousin Ryan's wife. "She just called. Someone slipped a note into her purse. She had no idea what to make of it. I told her I thought it was someone's inebriated idea of a joke."

Patrick looked at the note in his hand. "That was my first thought, too."

"And now?"

"And now I don't know," he admitted truthfully.

He was getting a very uneasy feeling about all this. Why would someone target all three of them with this note? And were they intended as warnings—or threats?

"What do you want to do about this?" William asked.

"We sit tight until something else happens."

William sounded clearly disturbed. "Who do you think the note's referring to?"

As far as that went, Patrick hadn't a clue. "It still might be a joke, albeit a poor one."

"Nobody comes to mind?" William pressed.

There had been no long-lost second cousin, twice removed on the scene, no reason to believe that members of the family weren't who they were supposed to be.

"No one," he assured his brother. "Listen, I know you're coming over for lunch this afternoon. Bring the note with you. And tell Lily to do the same."

"What do you have in mind?"

"Nothing yet," Patrick said truthfully. "But it certainly wouldn't hurt to circle the wagons, just in case."

There was silence on the other end of the line and for a moment, Patrick thought William might offer an opinion or solution of his own. But when he finally spoke, it was just tacit agreement on his part. "I'll pass the word along to Lily."

"Thanks. I'll see you all later," Patrick said just before he hung up the receiver.

He was fairly certain he'd managed not to sound as concerned as he felt. It could very well be nothing, just some fool yanking their collective chains. But he was a Fortune and, contrary to the name, he and his family had had their share of adverse dealings.

It never hurt to be prepared.

Jorge stood in the center of the still-crowded restaurant, looking around. He felt exactly like the Prince must have just after Cinderella fled from him at the stroke of midnight.

Except that he was holding a light gray coat instead of a glass slipper. When he'd returned from the coatroom, she wasn't standing where he'd left her. She wasn't anywhere at all.

He spent the next twenty minutes scanning the room and describing her to people, asking them if they'd seen her. Finally, when he talked to the bartender who'd ultimately taken over for him, Carlos said he'd thought he'd seen her pushing her way to the front door. And yes, the man added, she wasn't wearing a coat, which had made him think it was rather odd.

Why, Jorge wondered. Why had she suddenly taken off like that? What would have made her leave without saying anything to him?

And without her coat? It didn't make any sense to him.

Everything about the woman aroused his interest.

Frustration ate away at him. He had no phone number for her, and no address either. He told himself to just go home and forget about it. But he couldn't.

Draping her coat on one arm, he took out his cell phone and dialed Information. With one hand pressed against his ear to drown out the surrounding noise, he gave the operator Jane's name and waited for a response.

She was unlisted.

It figured, he thought. Biting back a curse, Jorge stared at the coat he was holding.

What had made Jane bolt out of here like that? She'd given every indication that she liked being with him. So then what—?

"Did one get away from you?"

The question, spoken so close to him, nearly made him jump. Gloria was standing right behind him. Her husband Jack was next to her.

Jorge saw her looking at the coat, an amused expression on her face. Not what he needed right now, he thought. Squaring his shoulders, Jorge shifted the coat to his other arm. He'd already made up his mind that he was going to find Jane Gilliam and give her back her coat—and ask for an explanation—no matter what it took.

"Not for long," he told Gloria, his voice cocky. And then, just for a moment, he dropped his guard. "Did you see the woman I was with earlier?"

"The one Mama liked so much?" Gloria countered innocently. Maria had brought all three of her daughters' attention to Jorge and the woman he was talking to. "Yes, I did," Gloria added quickly before he could profess any denials. "She didn't look like your usual arm candy." Gloria patted his face affectionately. "Looks like you're finally growing up a little, big brother."

If she was baiting him, he wasn't about to bite, Jorge thought. He had more important things on his mind. "You didn't happen to see where she went, did you?"

Gloria shook her head, surprised. A woman avoiding Jorge? This had to be a first. "Sorry."

"Maybe someone told her about your reputation and it scared her off," Jack speculated as he helped Gloria on with her coat.

Gloria felt a tug on her heart, empathizing with her brother. She was certain this had to be the first time he'd ever experienced rejection on any level.

"If it helps any, I think I heard Jack's father say she works for Red Rock ReadingWorks. I could ask Mama to make sure—"

The second Gloria mentioned the organization, Jorge remembered Jane mentioning the name.

"ReadingWorks," he repeated. "That's right." Grateful, he kissed his sister's cheek. "Thanks."

Something different was going on here, Gloria thought, looking at her brother more closely. She'd never seen him like this about a girl. But then, as far as she knew, no girl had *ever* pulled a disappearing act on Jorge. If anything, it was always the other way around.

"Any time," Gloria murmured. She'd teased him about finally growing up, but maybe, just maybe, there was something to it.

If so, she thought, Mama was going to be thrilled.

January 2 was a typical cold winter day.

Jane shivered as she made her way to Reading-Works' front door. She was going to have to dip into her savings and buy another coat, she thought glumly. Wearing three sweaters, one on top of another, just didn't do the trick.

Maybe her coat was still at the restaurant, she thought hopefully. She'd call over there during her first break and inquire.

And pray that she didn't run into Jorge Mendoza.

Pushing open the front door, the warm air that met her was lovingly welcomed. At the same time, goose bumps formed all over her body.

Like the ones she'd felt when Jorge had kissed her New Year's Eve.

What in heaven's name could she have been thinking? Men like that didn't give women like her the time of day—unless, of course, there was a bet involved, she thought sarcastically.

Served her right for being so naive.

With a sigh, she shook her head. Well, it was a new year and it was back to reality for her. Time to put impossibly foolish dreams behind her.

Walking into the lounge where all the teachers gathered for their breaks and lunch, she saw that a number of her coworkers were clustered around the main table. At first, she thought that someone had brought in cookies. But then she saw that what had captured their attention was a huge profusion of flowers, nestled in a large basket that was in the center of the table.

Someone had gotten flowers, she thought with a touch of envy. She had no idea what that felt like, to have someone care enough about you to send flowers and publicly acknowledge his attachment to you.

"Who's the lucky girl?" she asked, trying to sound cheerful as she joined the group.

Sally Hillman turned to look at her, a huge grin on her lips. "You are."

Jane stared at her, positive she'd heard wrong. "What?"

"Joyce couldn't help herself," Harriet Ryan, another tutor, volunteered. Embarrassed, Joyce, the general secretary, made a strange, disparaging noise. "She read the card. Why didn't you tell us you knew Jorge Mendoza?" she wanted to know.

"When did you meet him?" another woman asked.

"Where?"

"Details, girl, give us details," Sally begged. "The rest of us are dying to know."

The questions all melded together into one cacophony of voices and noises as Jane leaned over the table and plucked the card from the basket. She felt as if she were moving in slow motion.

"New Year's Eve ended much too soon," the card said. "With affection, Jorge."

"With affection," Joyce echoed, looking over her shoulder at the card she'd already read. A huge sigh followed. "You've been holding out on us," she accused Jane.

"Yeah," Harriet chimed in. "Not very nice of you, Jane. Give."

And five sets of eyes turned their eager faces toward her.

Chapter Six

Unlike her former beauty queen mother—or maybe because of her—Jane had never liked being the center of attention. It made her uncomfortable.

"There's nothing to 'give,'" Jane told Harriet.

The women exchanged exasperated looks with one another, as if they thought she was holding out on them.

"Oh, come on, Jane," Cecilia Evans, the oldest of the group, pressed. "A man doesn't send flowers and sign his name 'with affection' if something isn't going on. Especially not a hunk like Jorge Mendoza."

Cecilia drove the point home. "*How* does he know you work here?"

Jane looked back at the flowers. They would have had her floating on air—if she didn't know what she knew. She almost wished she hadn't overheard those boys gossiping.

Most likely, Jorge had sent the flowers because he'd had qualms of conscience.

But then, she backtracked, why should he if he didn't know that she knew?

This was all getting very complicated. All she wanted to do was get to work, do what she did best, and forget about everything else.

Some people were meant to have romance in their lives and some weren't. She belonged to the "weren't" group and she was just going to have to learn how to deal with that and accept it.

More than anything, Jane didn't want to talk about Jorge or the flowers or anything that had to do with why they might have been sent. But she had never learned how to be rude or cut people off. She'd certainly never learned how to tell them to butt out.

So she lifted her shoulders in a vague shrug and admitted, "I told him where I work."

"When?" Joyce demanded excitedly. "When did you tell him?" The slender blonde shook her head when information didn't immediately come spilling out of Jane's mouth. "If I'd met Jorge Mendoza, every single last detail would have been up on my blog three minutes after I got home. Maybe two."

"I don't blog," Jane said, seizing on the stray item.

"You don't talk much, either," Cecilia grumbled. Two of the other women chimed in their agreement.

Jane pressed her lips together, suppressing a sigh. It wasn't her intention to seem secretive about the matter. It was just that she knew that these flowers, didn't really mean anything and honest though she was, she certainly wasn't about to tell her friends that Jorge had kissed her on a bet.

Some things you just didn't talk about. To *anyone*.

Looking at the circle of eager faces surrounding her, she decided to give them just the bare bones and hope they'd be satisfied with that.

"I met him at the New Year's Eve party I went to at Red, the one Emmett Jamison and his wife threw for the Fortune Foundation. I went representing ReadingWorks," she added quickly, in case any of them thought she had a special in with the elite circle of people the Fortunes usually associated with. As the one who had worked at ReadingWorks the longest, she'd been the logical one to invite. "I was afraid if I didn't go, it might insult Mr. Jamison."

They all knew that the Foundation had given ReadingWorks sizable grants in the last couple of years, and it was largely because of the Foundation that ReadingWorks' doors were opened to the children whose parents could not afford to pay for private tutoring.

"Right," Harriet said, waving her hand at Jane's explanation. "Get to the good part," she urged. "How did you meet Jorge?"

"Is he as good looking as his pictures?" Sally asked.

Jane had to be honest. She always was. There

were times when she considered it almost a con-
genital defect. "Better."

"So? Get on with it," Sally begged. "There had to
be a lot of people there."

"There were." It had been so crowded and so
noisy that she had trouble concentrating on her book
when she'd taken it out.

"So how did you two meet?" Cecilia wanted to
know. "Don't skip anything," she ordered before
Jane could say answer.

"He asked me if I wanted to freshen up my
drink—he was tending bar for his parents," Jane explained.

She knew she was being disjointed, that the facts
were tumbling out like grains of rice from a hole
in the bottom of the box, but it was hard for her to
collect her thoughts under all this scrutiny. Especially since she was still having trouble reconcil-
ing herself to the fact that the single greatest
experience of her young life was tied to a bet,
making her—in her mind, at least—the butt of a
cruel joke.

The fact that Jorge had sent a note like that with
flowers just served to confuse and complicate everything that much more.

"And then?" Sally urged when Jane didn't elaborate. "This is like pulling teeth," she complained.
"What did you do to get him to send you flowers?"

"I didn't do anything," Jane protested. *Except run
away.*

Maybe that was it, she thought. Maybe he *was*

feeling guilty because she'd bolted and he suspected that she knew about the bet.

Joyce frowned. This obviously wasn't making any sense to her, or the others. "So that was it? He asked you if you wanted your drink freshened and then he just disappeared?"

"Well, no." Jane thought about the way he'd looked at her and a smile curved her mouth involuntarily. "We talked a little. And then it was midnight and—"

The mere memory made her body tingle.

Joyce's eyes widened. "He kissed you?"

Jane nodded her head. For a split second, a wave of heat washed over her as, despite her best efforts to block it, the memory replayed itself in her head.

"Yes."

"And? What was it like?" Sally demanded.

Jane had never mastered the art of nonchalance. Besides, there had been nothing nonchalant about the way Jorge kissed. He had literally made the earth move beneath her feet. No matter what his motives were, she had to give him his due in that department.

"Pretty terrific."

"And you're seeing him again," Sally assumed eagerly, skimming her fingertip down along a plump, pink rose petal.

Despite everything, a sliver of sadness skewered through Jane as she answered. "No."

The other women looked at each other.

"But he sent flowers," Harriet insisted. "How can you not see someone who sent you flowers?"

Because he doesn't want to see me. He just doesn't want to feel bad.

Jane kept the words to herself, searching for some kind of plausible answer that would make the others back off and leave her alone. This was hard enough to deal with without pretending that she was starry-eyed and walking on air.

Just then, April, the administrative assistant, came into the lounge. Excitement pulsated from every pore as she announced, "Jane, there's someone here to see you."

Thank God, Jane thought. She didn't care who it was as long as it gave her an excuse to get away from this impromptu Spanish Inquisition before the thumbscrews came out.

Jane glanced at her watch, trying to remember her schedule for the day. It was a little early for her first student, Melinda Perez, to be coming in. She wasn't due for at least another hour. But that was all right.

"Bring Mrs. Perez and her daughter to the class-room," she told April.

April shook her head, her straight dark hair bobbing from side to side like black windshield wipers. "It's not Mrs. Perez."

That caught her off guard. Mothers usually brought their children, not fathers. Maybe Mrs. Perez wasn't feeling well.

"Okay, show Mr. Perez and his daughter to the classroom. Better yet," she decided, moving toward the doorway, "I'll do it."

April stayed where she was, a ninety-eight-pound

roadblock. She looked unsettled, Jane thought, and rather dazed, wearing what could only be termed a silly grin on her face.

"April, is something the matter?" Jane asked.

"It's not Mr. Perez either," the young girl said breathlessly.

Confused, Jane walked out into the hallway and saw why April was acting so flustered.

Jorge Mendoza stood just inside the doorway, with her winter coat draped over one arm and what looked like a picnic basket suspended from the other.

The grin on his lips was guaranteed to raise body temperatures by at least five degrees as far away as the next county.

"Hi, Jane. You forgot something at the restaurant the other night," he told her, his voice low and melodic as he held her coat slightly aloft.

By now, all of Jane's coworkers had poured out into the hallway. She could feel them standing behind her, a hyperventilating Greek chorus.

Just what she needed, an audience.

How much worse was this going to get? And why, knowing what she did, did her kneecaps feel as if they were dissolving right out from under her?

"Thank you," she murmured, accepting the coat he held out to her.

God, but he was even better looking in the light of day than he had been at the restaurant. But what was he doing here?

Maybe he'd made another bet, she said to herself.

Jorge drew a little closer to her, aware that they

were both under intense scrutiny. "Could I see you in private?"

Her uneasiness heightened. What was he up to? "I've got students coming in."

"Not for another hour," Jorge countered. He saw the surprise in her eyes and smiled. Nodding toward April, he said, "I checked."

"I can cover for you," Harriet volunteered. "I don't have anyone coming in until this afternoon."

"I can cover for you, too," Sally chimed in eagerly, her eyes never leaving Jorge.

His smile widening, Jorge gave a slight bow of his head. "Thank you, ladies. I promise I won't keep her too long."

Jane wanted to say something about the bet. Right here, right now, she wanted to give this too-handsome-for-his-own-good-or-anyone-else's a dressing down. Wanted to tell him that if he'd discovered a conscience and was here to make amends, she didn't want any part of that. She just wanted to be left alone.

She wanted to say all that. But the desire to get all of that off her chest was outweighed by the fact that she'd always hated making a scene. Jane absolutely despised displays of temper, maybe because she'd been the target of her mother's so often when she was growing up.

Whatever the reason, she swallowed her retort and kept it to herself, refusing to vent in front of her coworkers.

"All right, we can go to my classroom," she told him, resigned.

He laughed softly under his breath as he threaded his arm through hers. "First time I've ever looked forward to going to a classroom."

Several members of her Greek chorus giggled. Doing her best to ignore them—and the heat traveling up her body where Jorge was holding her—Jane led the way to the room where she did her tutoring. Jorge dropped his hand, allowing her to cross the threshold first.

Shutting the door behind her, Jane turned to look at him.

Charade over, she thought. *Time to dig up that backbone of yours, Janie.*

"Why did you come here?" she asked him.

He nodded toward the coat she was still holding. "I thought you might need your coat." He also wanted to know what had caused her to run off the other night, but for the moment, that could wait.

Jane had to admit that she was grateful to be reunited with her coat, but that still didn't explain the other thing he'd brought with him. "And you decided to pack it in a picnic basket?"

He set the basket down on the desk. "No, I packed some of my father's famous enchiladas and nachos in the basket, along with—" He rattled off several Mexican delicacies that he'd brought, ending with chocolate chip sweet bread.

The latter had always been her weakness and guilty pleasure. Had he known that?

No, of course not. How could he? Not even the people she worked with knew that about her. For the most part, she was a very private person. It had been a lucky guess on his part, nothing more.

"Why would you do that?" she wanted to know. She wasn't ordinarily suspicious, but after the other night, she'd decided that being cautious was a much wiser path for her to take.

Jorge opened the basket and took out a checkered tablecloth, which he proceeded to spread on the floor right behind her desk and chair. She watched him in surprised silence. Was he actually planning on pretending they were having a picnic?

"Because it might help make you forgive me," Jorge told her and then added an extremely soulful, "I'm sorry."

I'm sorry.

Her heart twisted in her chest. What was it about those words that could always make her forgive a myriad of transgressions and make her want everything to be right again? Was she just terminally kind-hearted—or a pushover?

Jane was tempted to say something about overhearing the two teens talking about the bet he'd made, but she hesitated too long and Jorge was talking again. Talking and burrowing his way into a heart that should have, by all rights, been hardened against him.

But wasn't.

"I don't know what would have made you run off like that, especially without your coat, but if it had to do with me," Jorge continued as he placed two plates and two sets of cutlery down on the tablecloth, "I really am sorry."

His wording made her realize that he had no idea that she'd overheard the two teens talking. And he probably had no remorse for making that kind of bet. This was a matter of ego. He was voicing a blanket apology because he just didn't like having a woman walk out on him.

She had to keep reminding herself of that, but being so close to him was having a definite effect on her thought process. As well as on her whole body.

What was the point of telling him that she'd overheard? That she knew she was nothing more than a bet to him? Saying it wouldn't change anything. So she looked away and said, "I had an emergency."

Two glasses joined the plates, cutlery and napkins. "What kind of an emergency?" he asked mildly.

She hadn't expected him to probe. Resorting to fabrications wasn't something that came easily to her, not even to save face. "The kind that made me hurry away," Jane responded vaguely.

Jorge looked at her for a long moment, then nodded. "Okay, you don't want to talk about it. I can respect that."

Too bad you can't respect me, Jane thought. But out loud, she said, "So, you see, you didn't have to go to all this trouble—"

"Well, since I did 'go to all this trouble,'" he said, echoing her words with a smile, "we might as well sit down and eat." Taking off his jacket, he folded it up into a square and then placed it on the floor in front of the place setting. He gestured for her to sit down on it. "Might be more comfortable that way," he explained.

She looked down at the food Jorge had placed on the tablecloth. It did look awfully good, she thought, especially since all she'd had today was half a Pop-Tart and yesterday, her appetite had deserted her completely and she'd hardly eaten at all.

"Okay," she agreed, sitting down on the jacket. She felt the material give beneath her. "I guess it wouldn't do any harm to eat."

"Nope, no harm at all." He got down on the floor, crossing his legs lotus-fashion. "You know, I like to think that I'm pretty good at reading people—"

About to start eating, she raised her eyes to his face. "Then maybe you're in the wrong place. We just read books here."

For as long as he could remember, women had come on to him. He'd never had a woman back away. But Jane Gilliam was definitely backing away, blocking all his best moves and his efforts at breaching her walls. Why? It wasn't ego, but curiosity and a certain fascination that spurred him on.

"Did I do something to upset you, Jane?" When she didn't answer, he took a guess. "Was it the flowers? Was sending them here embarrassing?"

She supposed that was as good an excuse to use as any. "It did put me on the hot seat."

Jorge laughed. Whenever he sent flowers to a woman, he always made sure there was maximum exposure involved, not because he was sending them but because he knew that women liked other women to see that they were the center of someone's attention. Jane was definitely different. And that really piqued his interest.

"You don't like all that attention, do you?" he guessed.

"No," she answered truthfully. "I don't."

"I have to admit, you are nothing like a lot of other women I've known." And right now, he thought, he had to admit that he was drawn to her because of that.

Jane had no doubt that he had known enough women to populate a small city. "I've always been a private person," she told him.

"A little mystery makes things interesting."

She hadn't meant it like that. Femme fatales were mysterious, not her. What you saw was what you got, she thought. But before she could say anything, Jorge was leaning forward.

Invading her space.

Making her pulse jump.

"Do you mind?" he asked.

The words left her lips in slow motion. "Mind what?" she asked in a hushed voice as he took her chin in his hand.

"You've got a little sauce right there." Moving his thumb slowly across the corner of her mouth, Jorge wiped the sauce away. "Got it."

He smiled at her just before he licked the side of his thumb.

Jane couldn't draw her eyes away. The sauce disappeared between his lips.

He'd done it again.

He'd made the air stand still in her lungs. If this kept up, her brain was going to malfunction because of a lack of oxygen.

If it hadn't already.

Chapter Seven

It took Jane a second to pull herself together and she had a feeling that he knew it. But there was no self-satisfied smirk on his face, no hint of a superior smile on his lips. If he did know what he was doing to her, he wasn't showing it.

She still had no idea why Jorge was here, sharing a picnic with her. Was this all part of his initial bet, or had it evolved into some elaborate plan to prove that he could get any woman he wanted with minimal effort? Was there some prize waiting for him at the goal line, depending on her reaction to him?

But even if it was that, why should she be his target? It wasn't as if she had some sort of reputation for being a removed, yet desirable ice princess. There was no one beating a path to her door. She was just an old-fashioned girl, someone her grandmother would have called a sweet bookworm—and her mother would have ridiculed.

If she held on to that thought, on to the knowledge that at best this was just some kind of a fleeting whim on Jorge's part—for whatever reason—then maybe she could keep a tighter rein on herself and not get carried away.

Or grow hopeful.

Just enjoy the moment, as you would if you were getting lost in a book, she ordered herself as she continued eating what, in all likelihood, was the best chicken enchilada she'd ever had. Books always ended and so would this. She had to remember that whatever was going on, however wonderful it might feel for the moment, it was all just fiction. Just like the books she loved to read.

Before she realized it, she'd finished eating. Picking up the napkin he'd put out, Jane wiped her fingers. "That was excellent," she told him.

"I'll pass that along to my father," he told her. "He'll be pleased." Jorge reached for the covered serving dish that he'd placed back in the basket. "There's more if you like."

"No, one was fine," she said quickly before he could place another enchilada on her plate. "I'll explode if I eat another one. Besides—" she smiled, nodding at the plate of stacked chocolate chip desserts "—I need to leave room for the sweet bread."

He liked the way her eyes seemed to light up when she smiled. "So you have a sweet tooth."

"Guilty as charged."

Jorge placed a sweet bread on a napkin and put it in front of her. "I'll remember that for next time."

"Next time?" she echoed.

Two small words, neither of which, by themselves, were unclear. But in this situation, combined and emerging from his mouth, she found herself unable to absorb them or figure out precisely what they meant—because Jorge couldn't possibly be saying what she thought he was saying. Wasn't this idyllic indoor picnic just a one-time thing?

"The next time we get together," Jorge elaborated and then suddenly stopped as a thought occurred to him. She'd been alone at the party, but that didn't necessarily mean that she was unattached. "Unless—are you seeing anyone?"

Not anymore, she thought. "No. I already told you I wasn't."

Her answer produced another smile on his lips. She stared at it, mesmerized. "Then it's all right if I see you again?"

If she didn't know better—and she did—she would have thought that Jorge was acting almost shy. But that was impossible. Jorge Mendoza had never had a shy day in his life. In a relatively small town like Red Rock, everyone knew everyone else, or at least *about* everyone else. And she knew about Jorge, knew that the impossibly handsome man went through women like tissues.

At thirty-eight, was it possible that Jorge had gone through every desirable woman in Red Rock and was now trolling for female companionship down at her level? Not that she thought of herself as beneath him, but the women he tended to pursue came from a more sophisticated social circle than she did. Their idea of charity meant writing a check while hers meant getting down in the trenches and becoming personally involved.

"If that's what you want," she heard herself answer. She watched his expression intently, waiting for him to shout, "April Fool's" even though they were four months shy of the date.

"Yes," Jorge told her, "that's what I want."

Even as he said the words, it intrigued him that he really, *really* meant them. Sure, he had always liked women—loved them—but he had to admit, even though it unnerved him a little, that he had never quite felt this way before.

In general, he was captivated by vivacious women who liked life in the fast lane. Women who knew that having any long-term designs on him would only be futile.

Until New Year's Eve.

This one was different, he thought, not for the first time. This one was not the kind of woman you enjoyed for an unspecified amount of time and then moved on from. Jane Gilliam was the kind of woman his mother would have called the marrying kind.

Jorge knew himself, knew that he had no desire to get married, to be tied down to one woman. But be that as it may, he couldn't seem to get himself to just walk away.

The coat he'd been left holding in his parents' restaurant could have easily been delivered to Jane in a number of ways, none of which involved his putting in an appearance. But he hadn't wanted to just ship the coat off to her. He'd wanted to bring it to her in person. And find out why she'd left the restaurant so abruptly.

More than that, he realized, he'd wanted to see her again.

He told himself that it was to prove that there'd just been something about that particular night that had attracted him to her—and now it was gone.

But seeing her, seeing that strange combination of vulnerability mixed with an endearing innocence and sense of wonder, was stirring something in him. Something that he couldn't quite identify.

Something, he thought, that made him a little uneasy. Maybe he should leave well enough alone and leave it nameless. Because, at bottom, it was something that had the potential to scare the hell out of him because he couldn't seem to exercise control over it. And he didn't like not being in control.

"Why?" Jane heard herself finally asking.

She was being stupid, she silently upbraided herself. Any other woman would have just eagerly absorbed the attention, however fleeting, of easily the best-looking man in Red Rock. By questioning she was almost guaranteed to chase him away.

And yet, she had to know his motives.

She liked things to make sense and this just didn't.

She was familiar with some of the women Jorge had been seen with and there was just no way she fit into that category. She was neither drop-dead gorgeous, nor the owner of a body whose curves could make a grown man weep.

She did have, Jane knew, a good heart, but that wasn't something that was visible to the naked eye and she was fairly certain that Jorge wasn't out to add a girl scout to his extensive collection of conquests.

"Why?" he repeated her question incredulously, not sure what she was asking.

"Yes." Summoning her courage, she decided to be direct. "Why do you want to see me again?"

No one had ever asked him that before. Every woman had just jumped at the chance. Jane was a challenge all right. "Because I'm attracted to you, Jane," he told her. "Isn't that why most men and women date one another?"

Date? He was asking to date her? As in seeing her more than once?

For one wild, wonderful moment, Jane felt as if she'd suddenly slipped into the Twilight Zone. Lost for words, she bit into the sweet cake she'd been holding in her hand. Her mouth full, she stalled for time, desperately trying to understand what was going on here.

She couldn't make herself believe that she'd hit the jackpot.

Maybe it was karma, something Isabella had

mentioned to her on several occasions. The young woman felt that life was a series of checks and balances. Isabella had told her more than once that someone as good as she was was definitely on track to be on the receiving end of something wonderful.

She figured that the New Year's Eve kiss had wiped that slate clean—until she'd overheard those two boys talking.

Jorge glanced at his watch. He was due at a meeting with a client soon. Besides, the receptionist had told him that Jane had someone to tutor in less than an hour. Even so, he felt a reluctance to get up and leave.

Standing up, Jorge extended his hand to her. She accepted it almost hesitantly. Somewhere in the back of his mind, it struck him that the feel of her hand in his seemed very right somehow. He tamped down the thought.

Still holding her hand, he pulled Jane up to her feet and wound up pulling her closely against him.

Sparks began to go off up and down her body, sending out alarms, quickening her pulse. He made no effort to put space between them. Instead, he just stood there, holding her. Making her warm.

And then her heart all but stopped as she watched him lower his head. Their lips met.

And Jane felt herself slipping into a dark, velvet-lined abyss.

Hardly aware of what she was doing, Jane laced her arms around Jorge's neck. Her body leaning into his, she kissed him back as if her very life depended on it.

And maybe it did.

Because if she hadn't kissed him back with such verve, she would have surely gone under for a third time and drowned in ecstasy.

All in all, she thought in her heart of hearts, that wouldn't be such a bad a way to go, dying with a smile on her lips.

"I guess I'd better be going," Jorge murmured, drawing back his head.

But even as he said it, he continued holding her, his hands resting on the swell of her hips. He could feel desire coursing through his body. She was arousing a hunger in him that couldn't be addressed at the moment.

But soon, he promised himself. And as soon as that happened, he knew that this attraction would fade.

It always did.

"You said you had students to tutor soon and I don't want you getting in trouble on my account."

Too late, she thought.

Jane searched her empty brain cavity for something to say. She'd never been a brilliant conversationalist, but until now, she'd been able to hold her own. That wasn't the case anymore.

"They should be here soon," she finally managed to get out.

Finally letting her go, Jorge bent down and quickly scooped up the plates and utensils, wrapping them inside the checkered tablecloth. Securing it, he dumped the whole thing into the picnic basket.

Jane heard the dishes clink against each other. Thinking that he might wind up breaking them, she cautioned, "Be careful."

He looked into her eyes, soft brown eyes that he'd discovered he could easily get lost in.

"I'm trying to be," Jorge told her honestly. But he wasn't all that sure how that was working out for him. Because if he were really being careful, he wouldn't have allowed his curiosity to bring him here. "Why don't you give me your home number and I'll give you a call?" he suggested.

Even she had heard that line before, Jane thought. She'd give him her number, but she wasn't going to hold her breath, waiting. He'd forget about calling her the minute he got into his car. Sooner, maybe.

But that was all right. This had been very, very nice while it had lasted.

Tearing a piece of paper from the spiral notebook on her desk, Jane wrote down her name and number, then added in parenthesis: the girl you kissed at midnight on New Year's Eve. Finished, she folded the sheet and handed it to him.

Taking the paper, Jorge unfolded it and read what she'd written. The smile that played on his lips was ever so slightly lopsided. He refolded the paper and slipped it into his pocket.

"You didn't have to write that down. I know who you are, Jane."

She lifted her shoulders in a quick shrug. "Just in case you come across that note sometime later and can't place the name," she explained casually.

He found her lack of ego refreshing and appealing. Some of the women he'd been with couldn't walk by a mirror without glancing at their reflection, checking to see that every hair was in place, that their makeup was picture-perfect, and that they were still as alluring as they had been an hour ago. In comparison, Jane seemed far more genuine.

"Even then I'll be able to place the name," he assured her.

She sincerely doubted it. She wasn't the kind of woman who left a lasting impression and she'd made her peace with that. "Thank you for the early lunch," she said.

Jorge gave her a slightly courtly bow and said, "My pleasure," just before he kissed her hand.

And then, as her heart launched into double time, he was gone.

But she had no time to savor the last hour or to even review a single sweet moment because suddenly the door opened again and the room was filled with every woman who worked at or volunteered at ReadingWorks. And every one of them was eager for information.

Harriet moved close to Jane, a wide grin on her face. "I guess you must have had a *really* nice lunch."

"Yes," Jane admitted, "I did." Her thoughts lingered on the feel of his lips moving over hers, stirring things inside her that had never even been touched before. No wonder he had such a following. The man was a fantastic kisser. "It was very nice."

Jane discovered that it was impossible to keep the smile both out of her voice and from her lips.

She still didn't have a clue what was going on but one kiss from Jorge and nothing else seemed to matter. At least, not for now.

This was not the time nor the place to daydream, she upbraided herself. They had work to do. The first of the students would be arriving any second.

"Workstations, ladies," Jane announced abruptly, calling a halt to any other personal questions that might be forthcoming.

She could hear cars pulling up in the parking lot. The first wave of students were being dropped off by their parents. It was time to stop obsessing about a man who was nothing more than a wonderful fantasy and turn her attention to something that actually had substance. Teaching children to read.

"Fine," Cecilia acknowledged with no small reluctance. "But don't even think about leaving without telling us everything that happened." Her eyes narrowed as she looked at Jane. "If you know what's good for you."

Nodding, Jane played along. She did know what was good for her. And it had nothing to do with Jorge Mendoza. But just for now, she could pretend that it actually did.

After all, what could it hurt?

"You, it could hurt you," Isabella insisted later that evening over the phone. It seemed that rumors were already making the rounds and, concerned,

Isabella had called her friend the moment she'd heard. Jane, Isabella was convinced, was far too innocent for the likes of her cousin. "Don't get me wrong, I love Jorge. Every woman over the age of eighteen months loves Jorge, but that doesn't mean that he's the kind of guy you should fall for. That would be a huge mistake, Jane," she cautioned. "He'll break your heart. He won't mean it but he can't help himself. He's just one of those guys who can't stay put."

"Don't worry," Jane tried to sound nonchalant. "I'm aware of his reputation."

"Good. Keep that in mind."

Sitting down in the easy chair she'd splurged on when she'd moved into this apartment, Jane kicked off her shoes and then raised her feet. It had been a long day. "What I don't know is why he wants to go out with me."

There was silence on the other end of the line, as if Isabella were searching for an explanation. "Because maybe, just maybe, he's growing up and he realizes that all the other women he's been with are just bimbos. Trust me, none of them are good enough to walk on the same side of the street as you."

She laughed softly. Isabella was very sweet. "I don't think that walking is what Jorge had in mind with them."

She heard Isabella sigh. "That's just it. He's a lover of women." Because they were cousins, albeit distant, she tried to give him the benefit of the doubt.

"I don't want you getting charmed by him until he can prove that he's finally matured."

Too late, Jane thought. She'd already been charmed. Right down to her toes. And dazzled as well. The only thing she had going for her was that she knew that it was only going to last until the next beautiful woman caught his eye. She was just a filler, a way for him to kill time.

But that didn't mean she couldn't enjoy herself. And she'd decided right after he'd kissed her today that she fully intended to.

Chapter Eight

In a hurry because traffic had made her late getting home, Jane had just slipped one arm into her coat sleeve when her cell phone rang. Taking a second to inhale deeply—she could swear she still detected a hint of Jorge's cologne on the wool—Jane dug into her purse to retrieve the phone.

Slipping the other sleeve on, she answered the call, interrupting the second chorus of a popular Elvis classic that was her ringtone of choice.

"Hello?"

A deep voice chuckled. "You sound breathless. Did I interrupt something?"

Jorge.

The sound of his voice brought everything to a

screeching halt—except for her stomach, which was in the middle of flipping over. It took her a couple of seconds to pull herself together. He was actually calling her. When she'd given Jorge her phone number, she'd never expected him to use it.

"No, you didn't interrupt anything." She didn't sound very convincing, Jane thought, not even to her own ear.

"Good. Listen, I was just in the neighborhood and wondered if you'd mind if I dropped by."

Her pulse scrambled, even as disappointment washed over her. She would have liked nothing more than to say yes and have him come over, but there were people—children—waiting for her. And children remembered promises that were broken.

She had.

"I would really love to see you," she said without any attempt at guile. And then regret filled her voice as she took hold of the doorknob and turned it. "But I was just on my way—"

The last word stuck in her throat. There, leaning against her doorjamb, phone pressed to his ear and a spectacular smile gracing his sensual lips, was Jorge.

"Out," Jane said, finally managing to get the last word out.

Closing his phone, Jorge straightened as he slipped it back into the hip pocket of his jeans. It was close to six o'clock in the evening and he'd been pretty certain he'd find her home.

Just not looking like this.

His eyes swept over her, taking in her outfit and the fact that her hair was confined in two playful pigtails. Amusement played on his lips.

"And just where is it that you're going?" he asked. "Clog-dancing?"

Her coat was hanging open. Beneath it was a wide, colorful skirt and a black vest laced up the front worn over a gleaming white peasant blouse. She had on knee-high white socks and a pair of Mary Janes.

Was she role-playing, he wondered, his interest definitely aroused. Was there a kinky side to this otherwise shy, bookish woman that he hadn't even suspected?

Just went to show that no one was as uncomplicated as they seemed.

"No." She looked down at her feet. "These are shoes, not clogs." Realizing that her answer didn't begin to address the question in his eyes and wary of where his imagination might be taking him, she hurried to explain. "I'm reading *Heidi* to the kids in Red Rock Memorial Hospital." He was still looking at the outfit she had on. The interest in his eyes intensified. "Dressing up like one of the main characters makes the story more vivid for them."

His grin went directly under her skin, raising her body temperature. "Tell me when you get around to reading them the story of Lady Godiva."

To his further amusement and delight, he saw a blush begin to rise up her throat, coloring her cheeks. He didn't think women blushed anymore. Certainly not the ones he typically dated.

Jane cleared her throat, looking away. "That's not on the list."

"Too bad." His eyes pinned her in place. "Maybe you could give me a private reading sometime."

C'mon, Jane, the kids are waiting. Get a grip. You can go to fantasyland some other time.

"I don't think you really need to be stimulated or motivated," she told him, those being just some of the reasons she volunteered her time at the children's ward in the hospital.

Right now, Jorge thought, he was plenty stimulated. He had no idea that "cute" could be such a turn-on. "You look very Heidi-ish," he finally said.

She'd never thought of Heidi as being sensual before. She did now. "Thank you," Jane murmured.

Twirling one of her pigtails around his finger, he kept his eyes on her face. "Sure I can't get you to postpone this?"

She sincerely doubted that she'd ever been so tempted to go back on her word in her life. But she *had* given her word and all she had to think about were all the times that her parents broke promises they had made to her, or worse, forgot that they had made them at all, and that made up her mind for her.

It killed her to do it, but Jane flashed an apologetic smile and shook her head. "I can't. I gave my word. They're waiting for me."

"This is new for me," he had to admit, "losing out to a bunch of kids."

"Hospitalized kids," she emphasized.

"Hospitalized kids," he repeated dutifully. And then he really surprised her. "Mind if I tag along?"

The air was cold and she quickly secured a button, pushing it through its hole before locking the door behind her. He was kidding, right?

"You want to come to the hospital with me?" she asked incredulously.

"Yes."

She tried to picture him in the ward, surrounded by small children. It wasn't easy. "Why?"

He wasn't used to being questioned as to his motives. She was definitely keeping him on his toes. "I never read *Heidi* as a kid."

Now *that* she believed. "I'm in the middle of the book," she warned.

If that was meant to make him change his mind about coming along, it failed. "Don't worry, I'll catch up," he assured her. "I've been told I'm bright for my age," he teased.

She was out of excuses and if she was being honest with herself, she liked the idea that he wanted to come with her. It made him seem more human to her.

"All right," she agreed, "if you're sure you want to do this. My car's parked over here." She nodded in the general direction of the carport and then led the way to her space.

Jorge kept pace with her and then watched the way the wind played with the ends of her hair as she unlocked her side of the car. Opening the door, she hit the lock release. His door was opened.

"Is this part of your job, too?" he asked as he got into the small, economical foreign vehicle. "Reading to kids in hospitals?"

"No." Leaving her purse on the floor between her and the door, she put on her seat belt. "I wanted to do something meaningful and this was the only thing I could think of—entertaining the kids at the hospital by reading to them."

His seat belt was giving him trouble. He had to extend it twice before he could get it to fit into the slot.

"Wouldn't it be easier just to donate a couple of video games and maybe a secondhand game console?" he suggested.

"Easier, maybe," she agreed looking over her shoulder as she pulled out of her spot, "but not nearly as rewarding." Books had always been her saving grace, her safe place to go when things became difficult to deal with. "Books spark the imagination."

He thought of some of his friends' kids. They spent hours glued to a television set, their fingers flying across a keypad. "So do video games."

She supposed video games had their place, but she had never cared for them. "Most video games are about blowing things up. Books build minds."

There was a note of passion in her voice, as if she were defending old friends. "Bet you read a lot as a kid," he said.

She'd taken a lot of teasing for that, but that had helped her develop a tougher outer shell. "Anything I could get my hands on," she confirmed. "I loved to escape into stories." It wasn't until the word was out that she realized her mistake.

"What were you escaping from?" Jorge asked, his curiosity aroused.

If she'd had more time, she would have come up with some vague, acceptable story. But the question was here and now. She had no choice but to fall back on the truth. "Parents who yelled at each other and ignored me."

He hadn't anticipated that kind of an answer. His parents had always been there for him, even when he hadn't deserved it. Sometimes he forgot that he was one of the lucky ones and that not everyone grew up with a support system to fall back on.

Not that he ever did, he thought, but it was still nice to know it was there if he needed it.

"Must have been rough," he sympathized.

She shrugged, glad that she had an excuse to avoid his eyes. The last thing she wanted to see there was pity.

"Other people had it worse." She suppressed a sigh. There was no changing the past. "They were just two people who should have never gotten married. To anyone," she added. Her father had been completely into his work and her mother had been completely into herself. They didn't need outsiders in their lives and they certainly didn't need to be responsible for a child. "I used to wonder why they got married in the first place."

Jorge thought of all the times he'd seen his father sneak up behind his mother and steal a kiss or nuzzle her. He'd grown up thinking that all parents loved each other and demonstrated their affection.

"Did you ever ask them?"

"I asked my mother once," she recalled. "She said it seemed like a good idea at the time." A rueful smile curved her lips. "One of the longest conversations I ever had with her."

"Do you have any brothers or sisters?" Having someone sympathetic to turn to could help take the edge off rejection.

Jane kept her eyes on the road, even as her mind revisited the past. Even with the distance of time, it was painful to recall. She shook her head. "One mistake was enough for them."

"Is that what they told you?" Jorge could feel his temper suddenly materializing out of nowhere, flaring and aimed at people he wouldn't have recognized if he tripped over them on the street. How could people say something that hurtful to any kid, let alone their own?

"In a way," she recalled. "When I was six, one of the girls at school bragged about getting a new baby sister over the summer. I came home and asked my mother if we could get one and she looked at me for a long time and then said that when people made mistakes, they were supposed to learn from them, not make another one." She could feel his eyes on her and she flushed, glancing at him. "I didn't understand what she meant at the time, but I figured it out later."

The sadness in her voice was hard to miss. But there was no condemnation.

"And you're not bitter?" he asked in amazement. A background like that was perfect for producing loners and serial killers, yet here she was, sweet and generous to a fault, working at a job that he knew for a fact paid very little, just because she wanted to help children.

"Wouldn't change anything if I was," she theorized. "Besides, they did the best they could."

Jane's reasoning eluded him. "How do you figure that?"

"I never went hungry." *At least, not for food,* she thought. "I had shelter, clothes and a library card." Mentioning the last item made her smile fondly. It was one of her best childhood memories. "My father took me to get it when I was seven. The only outing I remember with him, actually," she confessed.

There were no picnics, no trips to amusement parks, no family vacations in her past. She grew up in a house with two self-involved adults, very much alone.

Maybe the man was a workaholic, Jorge thought. "What did your father do for a living?"

"He was an engineer. Aerospace," she added. A sigh accompanied her next statement. "He was away a lot. NASA had him on speed dial," she said with a small laugh. "I think he just used work to get away from my mother." And inadvertently, her, she added silently.

"And your mother?"

Her mother.

There were no fond memories when she thought of the woman, no nostalgia, no sense of any connection at all. Her mother was just a beautiful woman who happened to have the same address as she did.

"My mother peaked at nineteen. She was Miss Texas in the Miss USA Pageant that year. She came in third and said that she was cheated." Jane shrugged, as if she wasn't sure whether or not to give that claim any credence. She did know that, as far as looks went, she had always been a huge disappointment to her mother. "After that, she became a professional shopper."

"She shopped for other people?" He'd heard of those, but thought they were generally employed by celebrities who had trouble going out in public. There was no one like that around here.

"Not other people. She shopped strictly for herself." She remembered feeling hopeful the first few times she recalled her mother coming home with shopping bags full of things. But there was never anything in them for her. And after a while, she stopped hoping. "She was only happy when she was buying things. That was why my parents argued rather than talked to each other," she explained. "My father claimed that she spent money faster than he earned it."

"And did she?"

The short laugh had a sad sound to it. "Absolutely."

Making a left turn, Jane pulled onto the hospital compound. She hadn't realized that she'd talked all the way here. It certainly hadn't been her intention to go on and on like that.

"Well, there you have it." She tried to make a joke of the fact that she'd revealed so much, "My whole life story. Not exactly a page-turner, was it?" There was a parking structure straight ahead. She drove into it and parked her vehicle in the first space she could find. Turning off the engine, she turned to look at him. She was surprised that Jorge hadn't tried to jump out of the car. "I didn't mean to bore you."

"I wasn't bored," he protested. If anything, he'd gained new respect for her.

"Now you're just being polite." She released her seat belt. "Shoelaces have more exciting backstories than I do."

Jorge grinned. The novelty of a modest woman hadn't grown old yet. "I don't usually talk to shoelaces," he told her.

She laughed shortly. "You know what I mean."

"Yes, I do," he acknowledged, "and you're wrong." He saw her raise her eyebrows in a silent question. "I don't find you dull or boring."

This bet that Jorge had going—the one that involved her—it had to be for quite a lot of money, she thought. She couldn't conceive of any other reason for him to be so accommodating, so nice to her.

Picking up her purse, she then leaned over the seat, reaching into the back for a large book whose edges were gilded in gold. On the front cover was a young woman who, at first glance, Jorge thought, bore a remarkable resemblance to Jane. A second look made him realize that it was the hairstyle and the clothes that were responsible for the likeness.

However they both had a fresh-faced appeal, he noted, although Jane was obviously older. But definitely not by much. She could have easily passed for a schoolgirl.

Jane got out of the car. Waiting until he followed suit, she hit the security lock. They walked toward the hospital's main entrance.

She tried to give him one last out. "You know, the hospital has a really good cafeteria. The food's not as good as what your father prepares, but the coffee's decent. You could wait there if you wanted to."

Reaching the entrance, he waited for her to go through the electronic doors first. "Why would I want to do that? I came along to see you in action, not to drink watered-down cafeteria coffee."

"It's not watered down," she assured him. "As a matter of fact, it's pretty strong. Designed to keep sleepy interns on their feet."

In action.

He said he wanted to see her in action. Somehow, she'd never thought of those words being associated with her. *Action* referred to the dynamic people in the world. She wasn't dynamic, she was just a person who did whatever needed doing.

Yet Jane had to admit that a part of her was glad she wasn't able to talk him out of coming to listen to her read.

Another part was nervous for the same reason.

"Okay," she said. "Just remember, this was your idea."

"I'll remember," he assured her, striding to keep up with her as she wove her way through the ground floor to the elevators on the far side of the building.

Jane hurried out the moment the silver doors parted on the fourth floor children's ward. And narrowly avoided crashing into an older woman dressed in immaculate hospital whites.

Rather than be upset at the near collision, the woman offered up half a prayer of thanksgiving. "Oh, thank God you're here," she cried. "I thought you weren't coming. I would have had a rebellion on my hands." She sounded completely serious.

"We had a little traffic," Jane explained. By now, the nurse had stopped looking relieved and had focused the sum of her attention on the man directly beside her. "Adrienne, this Jorge Mendoza. He told me he's never read *Heidi* and wanted to hear the story."

The nurse's eyes were all but shining as they skimmed over Jorge. Had there been more time, there might have been questions, or at least inane conversation. But Adrienne's first order of business was to maintain peace and that was giving every indication of disappearing if she didn't get Jane into the room—fast.

"You'd better hurry and get out there, Heidi.

Some of those kids have been waiting for over twenty-five minutes," Adrienne told her.

"Twenty-five minutes?" Jane echoed. She shrugged out of her coat, draping it on her arm. "I thought we agreed that they weren't supposed to gather together in the lounge until I got here."

"We agreed but they didn't," the nurse corrected. "They all started coming into the lounge on their own right after dinner. I don't think you realize how much they look forward to you reading to them or what a big hit you are."

Silent up until now, Jorge put in his two cents. "Jane has this tendency to underestimate herself," he confided to the nurse.

Jane caught the look in the head nurse's eyes as they shifted from Jorge to her. She could swear she could almost hear the woman applauding her.

As if she had anything to do with Jorge's being here, Jane thought.

But there was no time to protest or ponder over whatever accolades the woman was silently awarding her. She had a pint-sized audience eagerly waiting to hear the further adventures of a plucky little girl who lived in the Alps with her grandfather.

Leaving her purse on a chair, along with her coat, Jane picked up her book and walked into the next room.

The walls were decorated with paintings done by patients and the room was littered with toys, some worn, some fairly new, all scattered about on small tables.

The children broke into a cheer when she walked in. Some were sitting on the floor, others took their places at the miniature tables. A couple of the children were in wheelchairs.

"Hi, kids," she greeted them cheerily. "Sorry I'm late."

She sounded, Jorge thought as he took his place by the doorway, like a completely different person than the woman he'd met on New Year's Eve. Confident, poised and full of fun.

Definitely a woman he wanted to get closer to.

Chapter Nine

For the most part, children were not among the vast number of people with whom Jorge had daily contact. He didn't know how to talk to them or what to expect when he was around them.

So it was with a degree of interest and no small amount of fascination that he watched the group within the lounge become captivated almost from the moment that Jane began to read.

And they remained that way, spellbound by something he would have bet money should have bored them to tears. After all, the story of *Heidi* was a gentle, peaceful one, relying on emotions more than drama. As far as he knew, nothing exploded, nothing even made a loud noise.

But for more than an hour, all there was was the sound of Jane's voice as she provided both the book's narrative and the voices of all the different characters in the timeworn classic. As he watched and listened, Jane became Heidi, then Peter, the goat herder, and, most delightfully, she became Grandfather, in all the blustery glory that eventually gave way to a loving man.

There was no other sound in the room, no whispers to distract the others from story. Every pair of eyes, and that included those of the nurses, were unwaveringly on Jane as she breathed life into every word, every nuance, vividly creating scene after scene for her small audience.

The woman was definitely gifted, he thought. He would never have guessed that she had this talent. And when she finished for the evening, he was almost as disappointed as the children.

"Can't you do a little more?" one of the girls begged. Her eyes were bright blue and she had a head full of golden curls.

Jane smiled, but she shook her head. The book remained closed, a bookmark marking where she would start reading the next time. "It's late and someone has to get to bed."

"But I'm not tired," the little girl protested, ending her sentence with a pronounced pout.

"I meant me, Faith," Jane told the girl with a laugh. She went through the motions of an exaggerated yawn. "I've had a very long day and I'm pretty tired." Enthusiasm entered her voice as she continued. The woman was a born storyteller, Jorge thought. "But just think, that gives us another day to get together and see what happens to Heidi now that she's in the big city."

"Will you come tomorrow?" another little girl begged. She looked frailer than the first girl and had a red and yellow bandanna tied around her head.

Jane smiled at her as she gently ran her hand along the girl's bandanna. Ordinarily she came by twice, sometimes even three times a week. She'd already put in her three days. But how could she find it in her heart to say no to someone who was obviously so much braver than she was?

"I'll come tomorrow, Betty," she promised.

Several of the younger children, including, to Jorge's surprise, the boys, cheered.

Herding the children together, the nurses began to empty the lounge. Jane waved and said a few words to each and every child who left the room. Only once they were gone she picked up her book and, holding it to her chest, glance in the direction where she'd last seen Jorge.

She half expected him to be gone.

But he wasn't.

He was right where he had been for the last seventy-three minutes, leaning against the doorjamb on the other side of the room. Now that the children were gone, he crossed to her. Jane attempted to read the expression on his face. While open and friendly, it still gave nothing away.

There was another layer to the man, she thought,

one that he kept private and under wraps. She couldn't help wondering what he was like, deep down inside, when he wasn't being the extremely seductive Jorge Mendoza.

"You are a very interesting person, Jane Gilliam." He was close enough to whisper the words. Why did everything that came out of his mouth make her heart beat faster? She had a feeling that he could make her pulse spike simply by describing the weather.

She couldn't guess what was going through his mind. Was he being sarcastic? She'd never thought of herself as particularly interesting. "Because I dress up to read books to kids?"

That was part of it, but it wasn't what he really meant. "Because you give so much of yourself. Tell me, after you give all that away, is there anything left over for you?"

She didn't feel herself particularly depleted. "Oh, there's lots left over for me," she assured him.

This volunteer work was only a small part of her life, although she was thinking about expanding it. Red Rock Memorial Hospital wasn't the only place where children were forced to remain while they underwent treatment for conditions they didn't understand. The fact that these treatments made them better—most of the time—compensated for the discomfort and loneliness they experienced. The nurses could only do so much and she wanted to help.

Jane firmly believed that as her diminutive listeners became involved in the worlds she verbally created for them, these small patients were transported to lands they'd never been to before, and that helped alleviate their loneliness. And, for a little while, their fears.

"Have you had dinner yet?" Jorge asked. As if on cue, her stomach rumbled and he grinned. "I'll take that as a no."

The sounds coming from her stomach embarrassed her. There hadn't been time to eat. "You don't have to keep feeding me," she told him.

He studied her for a moment. She fidgeted ever so slightly. "You're an independent woman, aren't you?"

She hadn't thought of herself that way, but she realized that he was right. Independent women probably weren't his type, but it wasn't in her to lie. "I've had to be."

To her surprise, he nodded as he took in the information.

"Fine. I have nothing against independent women." The grin made her weak—hunger had nothing to do with it. "And to prove it, I'll even let you pay."

A laugh escaped her lips as she reached for her coat. "I'm not *that* independent." She had to watch every penny if she wanted to continue the work she was doing.

"No problem," Jorge assured her as he moved behind her and helped her slip the coat on. "I like playing the man."

He didn't have to play at it, she thought, enjoying

the way his hands felt on her shoulders even through the coat. Jorge *was* the man. *All* man.

"Do you mind if I go home and change first?" she asked as they walked out of the building.

There were far fewer people around now as they crossed to the parking structure where she'd left the car. Evening had descended, weaving shadows in and out of the landscape.

"If you want to," he answered. "Although I think you kind of look cute in knee socks." She felt his eyes sweep over her as they reached her car. "Actually, if you stay in that outfit, someone might call the police to have me arrested for endangering the morals of a minor."

Getting behind the wheel, Jane glanced at her reflection in the rearview mirror before buckling up. "I don't look that young," she protested. Although maybe the pigtails did cut a few years off her age, she decided.

She looked like a teenager in his opinion. "Let's put it this way," he said, his seat belt clicking into place, "in that outfit you don't run the risk of having Boy Scouts fight over which one gets to help you across the street—they'd be fighting over which one gets to kiss you at the movies."

He had a silver tongue all right, she thought, turning her key in the ignition. But she was a realist and while his words sounded pretty, she knew it was all just empty flattery. She wasn't the kind anyone would ever fight over.

"You must know some pretty desperate Boy Scouts," she commented as the engine came to life.

"You know, you shouldn't do that," Jorge told her seriously.

She thought he was referring to the car stalling out. "Do what?"

"Sell yourself short like that."

"I don't sell myself short," she told him. Looking both ways, she slowly inched out of the space. "I know exactly what I am and what I'm not."

"And what are you?" he asked, curious to hear what she had placed in the plus column.

She made a right at the end of the winding road, leaving the hospital compound. "I'm hardworking, generous, fairly intelligent and very loyal to my friends."

"You forgot kind to small animals and children."

She heard the smile in his voice, and it coaxed one from her in kind. "That goes without saying."

"And what aren't you?" he pressed.

"Pretty," she answered simply, mentally putting a barrier between herself and the word, the way she always did.

That smacked of an insult—and a deep wound. "Who told you that?"

She shrugged as she merged the vehicle into the main thoroughfare that led away from the hospital and eventually brought her to her apartment complex. "No one had to tell me that. I have mirrors in my apartment."

It wasn't a mirror that had made her feel this way, he thought. It was someone who mattered. "They need to be replaced, because you're not seeing what I see."

She wished he'd stop that, stopped saying all those nice things that weren't true. Because she was liable to start believing him and then she'd really be setting herself up for a fall.

"My mother told me I was plain," she finally said. "It really seemed to bother her that I wasn't pretty." She spared him a quick glance before focusing back on the road. The full moon looked as if it were traveling with her. "Mothers aren't supposed to lie to their children."

"They're not supposed to, no, but not every mother should have been a mother," he reminded her. Hers certainly didn't win any prizes, he added silently. "Maybe yours was jealous."

"Of me?" Jane asked incredulously just before she laughed. Really laughed.

It had a nice sound, he thought, even if it was at her own expense.

"Of you," he repeated. "A lot of 'beauty queens' are very shallow and very jealous of anyone who might steal the spotlight from them. Especially as they get older. Trust me, I've known more than my share of those." Women who saw lines in the mirror that weren't there, who were afraid of getting a day older, a day beyond their prime.

He didn't sound as if he liked those women very much. "If that's what you think of them, why did you hang around them so much?"

When he'd been younger, there'd been more than his share of older women, women who were drawn to his sensuality as well as his youth. "Maybe that's why I'm not hanging around them anymore."

But you will be. Once you win your bet or get tired of your charade, you'll be back with those beautiful, vapid women, she thought.

And the thought filled her with a sadness that took more than a moment to shake.

"You know," Jane said twenty minutes later as she unlocked her apartment door, "If you've changed your mind about going out to eat, that's okay."

He'd never known a woman who constantly presented him with avenues of escape. Didn't she want to go out with him?

"I haven't changed my mind," he told her. "If anything, I'm hungrier." His eyes met hers. "How about you?"

She wasn't hungry as much as she was walking on air. Every time he looked at her like that, she became airborne. It was a struggle to remain grounded. Anchored. She kept reminding herself that none of this was what it seemed and that as long as she just enjoyed herself and didn't get carried away, it was going to be all right.

But it wasn't easy.

"I'll just be a minute," she promised, shedding her coat as she hurried toward her bedroom. She tossed her coat onto the sofa as she passed by it.

He saw her bedroom door close and for a moment, he felt a strong urge to open it and follow her inside. But he was fairly certain that if he did, it would spook her and he didn't want to do that. Didn't want to drive her away or traumatize her.

The winning over of Ms. Jane Gilliam was going to take time. The very thought intrigued him because he'd never had to coax a woman before. That he did, he supposed, was part of the attraction he felt. He had to admit that he'd never taken time to really get to know the woman behind the face and body before. Ordinarily his goal had always been gratification—both his and that of the woman he was with.

The latter had always been part and parcel of the deal. That way it worked out to everyone's mutual benefit. But this time around it was different. Different in a way that he didn't quite understand. But he meant to. And right now, there was nowhere else he wanted to be.

Less than five minutes later, the bedroom door opened.

Had she changed her mind?

Or was that a silent invitation for him to enter?

Jorge took exactly one step toward the bedroom before Jane came out, wearing a simple black pencil skirt and a powder blue pullover. Taking a complete inventory in less time than it took to say the phrase, he found his gaze lingering on her legs. Did she realize that she had killer legs? Probably not, he decided.

"That was fast. Most women I know—including my sisters," he added purposely so she wouldn't think he was just comparing her to the women he'd gone out with, "take that long just to reapply their lipstick."

She'd always been able to get ready at a moment's

notice. It evolved from a sense of knowing she'd be left behind if she kept either of her parents waiting the few times that they actually took her someplace with them.

"Not much to fuss with," she told him. "Besides, I was afraid you'd change your mind if I took too long." She'd almost said, "come to your senses," but she'd managed to stop herself just in time. "Are we going to your parents' restaurant again?"

He heard the barely suppressed note of eagerness in her voice. "I'd rather not." She slipped on her coat before he could help her with it. So he opened the door instead. "Unless you like eating with an audience."

Crossing the threshold, she looked at him, puzzled. "I don't understand."

He waited as she locked the door.

"Most evenings, my mother's there to help out. She has a wonderful memory." Whether Jane knew it or not, she was exactly what his mother would have chosen for him. "She sees you with me and I guarantee she'll take it as a sign that her prayers have been answered."

She'd never thought of herself as the answer to anyone's prayer. The last guy who'd unceremoniously dumped her just before New Year's had made that abundantly clear.

At the risk of sounding dumb, she said, "I still don't understand."

He led the way to guest parking, where he'd left his sports car.

"My mother is a wonderful woman who has what she feels are very simple wishes. She wants to see all of her children married—and she's willing to move heaven and earth—and everything in between—for that to happen. My sisters now are all taken care of, so my mother concentrates all her efforts on getting my older brother, Roberto, and me, married off."

As long as she was on her own and not a drain, her mother didn't care how she lived her life. "You should appreciate that your mother cares so much about your happiness."

Hitting the security lock, he opened the passenger door for her.

"I love my mother." His eyes lowered as she slid her legs in. "But her definition of happiness is not necessarily mine."

She waited until he got in on his side. "Meaning you never intend to get married?"

That sounded as if it was carved in stone. He shook his head.

"Meaning I don't intend to get married now. There's always tomorrow," he added, letting her in on his private philosophy.

Glancing at her before he pulled out of the parking spot, he noted that the smile on her lips had more than a hint of sadness to it.

"Not always," she told him. "My father always thought he'd have all the time in the world to do what he wanted to do 'tomorrow.' But for him, tomorrow didn't come."

Jorge read between the lines. "How old was he when he died?"

"Forty-two."

And although she had never managed to make her father proud of her the way she so desperately wanted him to be, she still missed him a great deal. Struggling for a moment, she managed to tamp down the melancholy feelings that were rushing through her.

He'd done it again. This was the second time she'd done this in the space of one evening.

Jane looked at Jorge ruefully. "How is it that I keep pouring out my soul to you?"

"Maybe I'm just in the right place at the right time," he suggested. "Besides, I like that you let me in like that." And he did.

Jorge decided not to tell Jane that most of his conversations with women revolved around vapid, empty subjects. That he hadn't dated them for their minds or for the desire to have a stimulating, challenging exchange of ideas.

Certainly none of those women had ever donated her time to do something meaningful. Money, yes, time, definitely not.

He made a right turn at the end of the complex. "So, Heidi," he teased. "What are you in the mood for tonight?"

She knew he was asking her about food, but from out of nowhere a single word shot through her brain. *You.*

She was only grateful that she managed to keep

her mouth shut. Otherwise she would have been so mortified she doubted if she would have ever recovered.

"I'll leave that up to you," she told him, having no real preference as long as she was with him. "I'm easy," she added.

The moment the phrase came out, she turned a bright shade of pink.

"I mean—"

He laughed as he eased onto the brake as the light turned red. "Don't get so flustered, Heidi. I know what you meant."

But even so, the phrase she'd used couldn't help but fuel some pretty wicked fantasies in his brain....

Chapter Ten

Several hours later, they were back at Jane's door.

Jorge waited as she looked through her purse, searching for her house key.

It had been an interesting evening for him. He'd gotten to watch her perform for the pint-size patients at the hospital, and then he'd spent an enjoyable hour and a half at the restaurant, talking to her.

Just talking.

Not planning a seduction, nor being confident that this was merely the second act, to be followed by an evening of lovemaking. He was simply sharing a meal and conversation, enjoying Jane's company more than he'd anticipated.

It was a little, he thought, like watching a flower

unfold during one of those nature programs that his mother liked to watch.

Jane was becoming less shy and more animated. He really liked the way her eyes lit up when she talked about something that captured her passion.

And he was surprised that her conversation touched on such a diversity of subjects. For such an initially soft-spoken person, it occurred to him that Jane had a huge frame of reference. She was able to intelligently discuss classical literature and popular music, as well as advances in medicine and technology, among other things.

He began to think that somewhere along the line, the petite woman had somehow committed an encyclopedia to memory.

"I just remember what I read," she'd told him, looking pleased that he'd noticed her intelligence.

"Everything?" he asked in amazement.

Sure, he'd heard about people who could retain things to such a degree, but he'd never encountered anyone like that. For him, studying in school had always been a chore. But then, he had been a rebel. He had never liked being forced to stay in an enclosed area. As far as he was concerned, life was a huge schoolhouse and he learned far more by experience than he ever had by reading.

Jane, he'd come to realize, was his exact opposite. And even though there was that old saying about opposites attracting, he'd never given it any credence until now.

"Everything," she'd answered. He could see that

she was watching him to gauge his reaction. She'd probably been teased about how smart she was, he thought. Some men were intimidated by intelligent women. He'd never had that problem. "I just have to read it once and I remember it."

"Must be pretty crowded in there," he'd speculated, lightly tapping her forehead with his finger.

She'd smiled at him then, that blushing smile he found endearing because it was so honest, so devoid of any guile.

He'd taken his time with dinner because he'd known instinctively that once he brought her to her door, that would be the end of the evening. He wasn't the kind to force himself on a woman—he'd never had to, but even so, that would never have been his style. And, as he had already come to realize, Jane was in a class by herself. She wasn't the kind who topped off a night out by a night in.

But now that he was standing here, about to say good-night and take his leave, Jorge really didn't want to. As much as he didn't want to push, to have her do anything that was out of character for her, he didn't want to just walk away.

Jane could feel her heart doing a little dance in her chest. Feelings were madly scrambling through her, at war with her own code of ethics.

Common sense kept telling her there was no future with this man. Today, tomorrow, next week, whenever he tired of the chase—or won the bet— Jorge would vanish, move on to the next woman who caught his fancy or became a challenge to him.

And she would be left behind with a huge hole in her heart.

She knew herself, knew that if she let these mounting feelings within her lead her astray, she'd only be hurt that much more when the inevitable breakup came.

And yet…she wanted him. Wanted him to want *her*.

Was she crazy?

Or simply just that attracted to him?

Jane opened the door and then turned around to face him. It took her a second to find her voice.

"Thank you for a lovely surprise," she told him. Jorge cocked his head, as if he didn't quite follow her line of thinking. "I didn't expect you to drop by," she explained. "And I certainly didn't think you'd be willing to actually come along and put up with story time at the hospital."

The corners of his generous mouth curved. "And miss seeing you in that outfit?" he asked. "Not a chance."

He ran his hands along her arms, struggling to keep himself in check. He knew damn well that all he had to do was kiss her, *really* kiss her and he could seduce her. It wasn't that he thought of himself as irresistible. There was no ego or self-flattery at work here—he just knew what he was capable of.

He also knew that while the seduction would most likely be excruciatingly sweet, the guilt that would follow—and the pain he would cause—would be difficult to deal with. Nothing was worth that.

"I'd like to see you again, Jane," he told her and saw surprise blossom in her eyes.

She almost asked why. Was there more to the bet than she knew about? Had it escalated? Did it come in parts? Was the end goal to take her to bed?

No, she couldn't make herself believe that Jorge would actually be party to something like that. Kissing her on a dare or a bet was one thing, but the other—no, not him. She didn't care what his reputation was. If he *were* like that kind of man, he would have already made his move, would have attempted to get her into bed.

But he hadn't pushed.

Maybe, she mused, that was his strategy. She wasn't sure. All she knew was that she didn't want to give up seeing Jorge as long as possible—on her terms. He made her feel special, even if he confused everything inside her.

Maybe she was supposed to sound blasé, Jane thought, like the women she knew he was accustomed to. But that wouldn't be her and ultimately, if she tried to sound like one of those women, that would be lying. Because she wasn't feeling blasé.

Excited was a far better word for what she was experiencing.

"I'd like that," she told him.

"Me, too."

Framing her face in his hands, he brought his mouth down to hers and ignited a skyful of fireworks inside her head. She threaded her arms around his neck as much for support as for contact. The kiss deepened and she did her best to return it in kind. She didn't want to just be on the receiving end of this lightning in a bottle. More than anything, she was desperately trying to give him a reason to return.

To want to kiss her again not because it was part of a bet, but because he enjoyed it.

She had no idea how sweet she tasted, how inflamed she made him, Jorge thought. Or how much he wanted to push open that door that she'd unlocked. How much he wanted to scoop her up into his arms and carry her to her bedroom to make love with her.

And how hard it was not to.

So instead, he savored the kiss, letting it go on as long it was safe to. Just before his control cracked, Jorge broke contact.

There was pure mischief in his eyes as they looked into hers.

"Sleep well, *querida*," he murmured just before he turned on his heel and walked away.

Querida.

Beloved?

He'd called her "beloved"? Her hammering heart went into double time as she sighed and slipped inside her apartment, locking the door and then leaning against it, her eyes fluttering shut as she relived every fiber-shaking moment of his lips on hers.

She hugged herself. Life had never felt so wonderful and even if it was fleeting, right here, right now, this moment was hers to savor.

* * *

Jorge's footsteps on the asphalt seemed to echo into the silence of the night as he walked back to his sports car. A part of him couldn't believe that he was actually walking away from Jane. She was so very ripe for the taking—and he'd wanted her.

But he had to admit that this route—if it turned out to be a route—was far more intriguing and enticing. He'd never held out before, never not availed himself of what was right there before him.

Never wanted the chase, the pursuit, to continue before.

Never met a woman like Jane before, he thought, walking toward guest parking. She was a woman of substance, of integrity. She was a woman he wanted to get to know from head to toe.

Slowly.

Maybe he was just bored with his life, Jorge reasoned. Bored and looking for something different, some way to divert himself.

Or maybe, he thought as he unlocked the driver's side of his vehicle and got into it, he was in over his head. Maybe he should get out now, before something happened that he couldn't foresee. Or even worse, not be able to control.

The thought haunted him all the way home.

Walking into the house, Jorge headed straight for the small bar he kept in the living room. He reached into the cabinet without looking and took out a bottle of his favorite whiskey.

Jorge poured two fingers' worth into the chunky glass that stood on the counter. Downing the drink quickly, he briefly entertained the idea of another shot, then decided against it.

He didn't need to numb himself—he needed advice. He needed to talk to someone he respected. That didn't leave a large pool to choose from.

Although he dearly loved each of his sisters, he knew without being told that they would all be taking Jane's side of it. They might love him, but they were women first.

Damn, he wasn't sure *what* it was that he wanted to hear.

For a moment he thought about calling his father, then quickly abandoned that idea. Talking to him wouldn't help, not about something like this. It had been more than forty years since José Mendoza had been out there, making his way through the minefield of dating. For that matter, his father didn't even have any experiences to fall back on.

As far as Jorge knew, his mother had been his father's first girlfriend. His *only* girlfriend. And José Mendoza had found that the best way to get along with his wife was to always back her up and agree with her.

What he needed, Jorge thought, was to talk to someone who had walked in his shoes. Was still walking in his shoes.

There was only one person he knew like that.

Taking a breath, Jorge glanced at his watch. Roberto lived in Denver these days. He tried to remember if there was a time difference between Red Rock and Denver and couldn't. But at most, it was only an hour, he reasoned. That still didn't make it too late to call his older brother.

Roberto, as he recalled, never went to bed before midnight. At least, he hadn't when he lived in Red Rock. Pausing to remember all the numbers in their proper order, Jorge pressed the keypad accordingly.

The phone rang several times and then the answering machine picked up.

Jorge swore under his breath.

Tempted to hang up, he decided to wait out the machine on the off chance that Roberto was either screening his calls or unable to get to the phone before it launched the answering machine.

When the "beep" finally went off, Jorge began to talk.

"Roberto, are you there? It's me, Jorge, and I'd really like to talk to you." He paused for a second, waiting, but nothing happened. No one picked up. Tamping down his irritation, he said, "Okay, well, when you get this, you know where to reach me. I—"

There was a noise on the other end and, for a moment, Jorge thought that the machine was cutting him off. But then he heard his brother's deep voice come on the line. "Jorge? What's wrong? Did something happen to Mom? To Pop?"

"Nothing happened to anyone," Jorge was quick to assure him.

He heard his brother mutter something unintelligible under his breath. Clearing his throat, Roberto asked, "Then why the hell are you calling so late? Date go sour on you?"

Jorge heard a small, amused sound follow the question. At least Roberto hadn't lost his sense of humor, he thought.

"No, it didn't turn 'sour' on me. But that *is* why I'm calling."

There was a prolonged pause on the other end of the line. "It's been a while since I've seen you, Jorge. Maybe that's why I'm not following this. What the hell are you talking about?"

Jorge sighed. "Okay, let me start over again."

"Go for it," his brother encouraged magnanimously.

Jorge took a breath before beginning. "There's this woman—"

He heard Roberto chuckle to himself. "There's always a woman."

Irritation got the better of Jorge. "You want to hear this or not?"

"Sure, I'm not going anywhere—except maybe back to bed," he said the last word pointedly. "Go ahead."

His brother was going to bed early these days? Jorge refrained from asking. Instead, he leaped to the center of his problem.

"She's different."

The word covered a broad spectrum of things and Jorge wasn't being very specific or informative. "Different how?" Roberto wanted to know.

"I don't know." That was part of the problem. He

couldn't quite put his finger on what exactly made Jane stand out for him, but he gave it a shot. "For one thing, she's not a knockout. But she is pretty," Jorge added quickly.

"Okay." Roberto had never known his brother to go out with a woman who wasn't. "I take it that you've slept with her."

Now that he thought about it, Jorge realized that any woman he'd taken an interest in, he'd slept with. Until Jane.

"No."

"No," Roberto repeated incredulously, certain he hadn't heard right.

"No," Jorge echoed, a touch of annoyance entering his voice.

There was another long pause on the other end of the line before Roberto finally said, "I see."

"See what?" Jorge demanded. Since when did Roberto talk in code? "Because I don't."

Rather than answer, Roberto had his younger brother backtrack in his narrative. "Why haven't you slept with her?"

"Because she's not the type for a one-night stand," Jorge told him. He didn't know if that irritated him or made him proud—and the ambivalence was driving him crazy. "She teaches kids how to read, Roberto. She dresses up like one of the characters in the books she reads and goes to the hospital to entertain sick kids."

"Uh-huh." He made it sound like a doctor analyzing symptoms.

Jorge caught himself bristling at the sound. "What's that supposed to mean?"

Rather than explain any further, or even deal with his brother's newfound dilemma, Roberto sighed. There was almost a hopelessness about the sound.

"Look, Jorge, I'd like to help you out here, I really would. I'd like to be able to say something insightful to you to make everything fall into place, but the truth of it is, I'm probably the *last* person you should come to asking for any kind of romantic advice."

He hadn't expected to hear anything like that from Roberto. As far back as he could remember, his brother, who'd once worked in construction and was now heavily into real estate, still managing to maintain a fantastic physique, had always charmed the ladies. There'd never been a problem when it came to Roberto's love life, unless, maybe, that it had involved too many ladies at the same time.

"Since when?" Jorge wanted to know.

"Since I had a reality check."

It was obvious to Jorge that whatever the problem had been—or was—Roberto was not about to disclose it. Jorge switched subjects for a moment. "Why don't you move back home, Roberto? Mom and Pop miss you. So do the rest of us."

"Yeah, well maybe someday," Roberto said evasively, giving him no more of an answer than he had the last time he'd asked his brother to move back to Red Rock. "Look, I really have to go, Jorge. Good luck with this woman—" he paused for a second "what did you say her name was?"

"I didn't. It's Jane," Jorge told him. "Jane Gilliam."

"Well, good luck with this Jane." Roberto sounded as if he was about to hang up, then apparently had a change of heart because he stopped to add, "And welcome to the club."

There was a "click" on the other end of the line. Roberto had hung up before he could ask him exactly what he'd meant by *that*.

Chapter Eleven

"More flowers?"

It was half a question, half an announcement as Sally walked into the lounge several afternoons later. Her hands were wrapped around an ice-blue vase that was stuffed to overflowing with a dozen and a half plump pink roses that had just been delivered to ReadingWorks' door.

Setting down the vase on the table, she gave Jane a long, envious look.

"Just what is it that's going on between the two of you?" she asked. The slight smirk on her lips testified that she thought she already knew the answer to that question.

"And does he have any brothers?" Cecilia wanted

to know, wistfully skimming her fingertips over one of the roses.

As she did so, the card that had been tucked in between the long-stemmed roses came loose. It fell to the table like an open invitation.

Seeing it there, Jane fairly sprinted across the room. She managed to get to the small envelope before either Sally or Cecilia had a chance to pick it up and read what was written inside.

"Yes, he does, I think," Jane told Cecilia. "An older brother living in Denver."

"That's right—Roberto," Cecilia remembered now that Jane mentioned it. "I always wondered why he flew the coop."

Sally paused, trying to remember. "It had something to do with Francine Fortune, didn't it?"

Jane shook her head. She was uncomfortable discussing things she felt that Jorge would rather keep private. "I have no idea. I don't pump Jorge for information."

Harriet walked into the lounge, carrying a new shipment of books meant for school libraries in the poorer sections of Red Rock, a wicked grin gracing her full mouth. She put the box of books down on the floor. "What do you pump Jorge for?"

Jane turned a bright shade of scarlet almost instantly. She could feel the color, rising up her throat, traveling along her cheeks.

"Nothing," she answered tersely as she ripped the envelope open. Focused on reading the note inside, she didn't realize that Sally was right behind her. The older woman rose up on her toes in order to be able to read over her shoulder.

These blushing pink roses reminded me of you, Jane read. *Looking forward to this Friday. Love, Jorge.*

She had less than a second to savor the words.

"So, what does he do to make you blush?" Sally wanted to know, a huge grin accompanying the question.

Startled, Jane swung around, pressing the note to her breast to keep anyone else from reading it.

"He probably just grins at her," Harriet speculated. "That seems to be enough to get her going."

Cecilia draped her arm around Jane's shoulder and gave her a quick squeeze. "Don't mind them, honey. Right now, you're probably the only one in the group who's getting any and they're all just trying to live vicariously."

Jane pulled away, offended at the implication and at the cavalier way the other woman regarded lovemaking. In her eyes lovemaking was supposed to be something special, not a way to just while away the time.

"I'm not 'getting any,'" Jane insisted. "It's not like that."

Harriet looked at her as if she'd just announced to the world at large that she had landed on Mars. "Let me get this straight. You and Jorge aren't sleeping together?"

Jane shook her head adamantly. "No." The single word practically shot out of her mouth.

Harriet's dark eyebrows drew together. "And he's sending you flowers."

"Obviously," Sally answered before Jane could say anything.

Her eyebrows returned to their rightful positions as the smile on Harriet's face widened. "And he's 'looking forward' to Friday night." She repeated the phrase as if there were a conclusion to be drawn from the simple wording.

Jane definitely didn't care for the barely veiled implication.

"We're going to see a play," she told the other women defensively. "And then we're going out to dinner."

"Followed soon after by 'dessert,'" Harriet interjected.

Cecilia was the oldest and, consequently, the most like a den mother. "Leave her alone," she told the other two women. "Whatever she's doing she's doing it right." She turned to Jane. "You just enjoy yourself, kid. And don't do anything you don't want to do," she underscored deliberately.

Harriet looked stunned. "How could she not want to go to bed with Jorge Mendoza?" she wanted to know. "How could *any* woman not want to go to bed with Jorge Mendoza?"

"Your three o'clock student is here, Jane," Sally announced suddenly, seeing the gangly, dark-haired preteen and his mother walking up to the door through the side window.

Jane offered up silent thanks as she hurried off to

the classroom without another word. It was a relief to get back to what she felt she did best. Teaching children how to read.

She didn't have to look at the calendar to know down to the second how long she and Jorge had been seeing each other. She and Jorge had been seeing one another now for almost three weeks. Three weeks of expecting the phone not to ring even as she prayed it would. Three weeks of trying to brace herself for the inevitable onslaught of loneliness while simultaneously making bargains with God for just one more date. Just one more hour with him.

So far, God was saying yes and the phone was ringing at regular intervals.

As Jorge pulled his car into the last available space in guest parking, Jane thought of the comments the women at ReadingWorks had made the other day when the roses had arrived. She knew they were a little envious of her, although she didn't think they were actually jealous. They were too nice for that.

She also doubted that they believed her when she said she wasn't sleeping with Jorge.

But she wasn't.

He had been nothing but a perfect gentleman each and every time they went out. Not once had he even tried to push the issue of sex, silently or otherwise.

Maybe, she thought as they walked up to her door, he didn't really want to. Maybe he thought of her as a respite. A rest period in between his trysts.

For all she knew, he could be seeing someone else even now. He hadn't said anything about only seeing her and no one else. Hadn't even asked her if she wanted to date him exclusively or be free to go out with someone else.

Right, she thought, as if there were actually any danger of that happening. She wasn't exactly beating men away from her doorstep with a stick—or even a toothpick. She never had.

When they came to her door, Jorge leaned one hand just above her head, creating a very intimate alcove for just the two of them.

"You look pretty tonight," he told her. The smile on his lips was golden. It worked its way straight to her insides, turning everything upside down. As usual. "I don't think I told you that earlier."

Every word he'd said to her was forever pressed between the pages of her mind. "No," she whispered. "You didn't."

"Well, you do," he affirmed.

Crooking his finger, Jorge placed it beneath her chin, raising it up just a fraction. His lips touched hers almost in slow motion, as if he were a high school freshman seeking his first kiss instead of the experienced lover everyone knew he was.

Jane instantly felt herself melting, her heart hammering so hard, she was certain he had to feel it pounding against his chest. No doubt about it, whether he kissed her quickly or slowly, deeply or lightly, the man's lips evoked the same kind of reaction from her. Within moments of contact, Jane could feel her inner core heating up, could feel desire and passion galloping through her.

The kiss deepened, taking her to places she'd longed to explore—with Jorge. Each time, he took her a little further. This time was no exception.

And then, just as abruptly, just when she thought that this time, Jorge was going to go further than he had before, perhaps sweep her into his arms, carry her into her apartment and finally make love with her, it all stopped.

Drawing his head back, Jorge fought to regain his grasp on control.

It wasn't easy.

This time, despite all his silent promises to himself, despite his pride in always being able to pull away whenever he decided to, he'd almost gone over the edge. And he knew it.

And it scared the hell out of him.

Scared him because she'd tempted him more than any other woman he'd ever been with. Made him want her with a fierceness that he was completely unaccustomed to. A fierceness that almost wrenched control out of his hands. He didn't like that. A man who lost control could do things he wasn't proud of.

"I'd better go," he told her in a whisper, his breath feathered along her face.

Disappointment sprang up instantly, riding roughshod over her. The words came out before she could stop them. "Why don't you want me?"

He stared at her, not sure he'd heard correctly. "What?"

"Why don't you want me?" she repeated. "The women I work with, your cousin, Isabella, *everyone*," she emphasized, "says that you're a fiery Latin lover." She didn't know where she was getting the courage to continue, but she pushed on. "That no woman is safe with you—that no woman *wants* to be safe with you…"

And then, for a second, her courage flagged along with her self-esteem and her voice trailed off. It took her more than a moment to grab on to a second surge of courage. "But you don't want me."

He laughed softly to himself, shaking his head. Oh God, was she ever wrong.

Ever so tenderly, he lightly skimmed his fingertips through her hair, pushing back the curls that had fallen into her face. He looked into it for a long moment.

"Is that what you think?"

Fidgeting inside, Jane wanted to look away. She forced herself to maintain eye contact. She was tired of being so mousy, so low-key.

"It's hard not to," she told him. "I mean, you kiss me and make my knees weak and just when I think that you're going to press your advantage, you don't. You back off instead."

"Advantage," he repeated the word she'd used. She'd made his point for him—even though it was hard to stand by it when she looked so damn wide-eyed and tempting. "That's the key word. I don't want to take advantage of you, Jane."

Jane heard only what she thought she heard. Proof. "Then I was right." It was hard to keep the hurt tears back, but she managed. "You *don't* want to make love with me."

She couldn't believe she was actually saying that to him, but just this once, she had to make her feelings known. He'd worked her up to the point that she thought she was going to explode—and then he'd just backed away, leaving her to deal with this bubbling cauldron of frustration and desire.

"No, I don't want to take advantage of you," he repeated. "There's a difference."

Unspoken words weighed heavily on his conscience. Each time he saw her, they grew a little heavier. He'd never intended to tell her this, had never wanted her to find out. Especially once he'd gotten to know her. He was ashamed to admit that he'd been a party to something so juvenile. But Jane deserved the truth, he thought, even if it was going to make her hate him.

Heaven knew he couldn't blame her if she did, but he fervently hoped that somehow, she could find it in her heart to forgive him.

She deserved the truth, he thought again, but she didn't deserve to be hurt.

It was a hell of a dilemma he found himself in. Damned if he did and damned if he didn't. And what was worse, he would be hurting someone sweet and innocent who shouldn't be made to feel as if she were nothing more than a pawn.

God, he wished he'd never started this. But then, if he hadn't, he might never have even noticed her. And that would have been a terrible shame.

He paused for a moment, then decided that this confession was best made in private, away from any passing strangers.

"Can we go inside?" he asked.

"All right." Turned away from him, she took out her house keys. Jane tried not to notice that her hand was shaking as she unlocked the front door.

She turned on the light switch by the door. For some reason, the light seemed to accent the darkness. Nerves tap-danced through her.

She shouldn't have pressed the issue, she upbraided herself.

Jorge slowly closed the door behind them. The sound of the lock slipping into its groove seemed louder than it usually did as it ricocheted around the quiet apartment.

Damn, this was hard, he thought. But it had to be done, had to be said. Had to be gotten out into the open and out of the way.

He took a breath, then said, "I haven't been completely honest with you."

Here it came. "You're seeing someone else," she guessed.

Unexpected, the question took him aback. "No."

Was he lying? Was that why he'd hesitated? No, he wasn't like that. She couldn't make herself believe that he could look her in the eyes and lie.

She took another guess. "You're seeing me because you're resting up in between women. Taking a break from being a lover."

It was hard for him not to laugh out loud at that

one. The corners of his mouth curved, though, betraying his amusement. "No."

Then she had no clue where he was going with this. "Okay, I'm out of guesses."

That was because her mind didn't stoop to this level, he thought. She didn't think in terms this low.

Damn, he wished he'd never talked to Ricky Jamison that night. This had all started out innocently enough, as an object lesson. All he'd initially wanted to do was give the boy some confidence. It had never been his intention to hurt anyone.

Nor had it *ever* been his intention to fall for the woman Ricky had selected.

He needed to couch this in the best possible terms he knew how. "I want you to know that I wouldn't hurt you for the world."

Jane felt herself bracing for a blow. She didn't like the way that sounded, but she was the one who had asked, who had pressed him to tell her why he didn't want to make love with her. Whatever came now was on her head, not his. "But?"

The word shimmered between them, a gunshot waiting to go off.

He ordinarily didn't have any trouble framing his thoughts. But right now, it felt as if his mouth were filled with shards of glass. "Do you remember New Year's Eve?"

That was an odd question, she thought. "I'm twenty-five years old," she reminded him. "Senility isn't supposed to set in for at least another forty, fifty years or so." It was her turn to smile, amused. "Yes, I remember New Year's Eve."

"There were a lot of people at the party that night—" He was stalling and he knew it. Jorge forced himself to get to the point. "Including Ricky Jamison. Emmett's adopted son," he added in case the name was unfamiliar to her.

She didn't know the son, but she knew the father. And his wife. "Emmett Jamison," she repeated. "The man who threw the party, right."

Each word felt like a heavy marble in his mouth. "Anyway, Ricky was feeling pretty down on himself that night and he asked me what he could do to get a girl to pay attention to him. He said he'd been watching me and I made it seem easy," Jorge added with a careless shrug, wanting to make sure she understood that he didn't regard that as a compliment. "Ricky said he had no idea how to even talk to a girl." Jorge paused, taking a breath. "I told him that it was simple." Did that sound as pompous as he thought it did? "All he had to do was just pay attention to whoever he was talking to." He stopped. That wasn't what he'd said—he'd whitewashed it. If he was going to tell her the truth, it had to be the entire truth. "Actually, what I said to him was to make the girl feel like she was the prettiest girl in the room. Ricky wanted to know if that always worked and I said yes.

"He still looked pretty uncertain so I volunteered to prove it to him. I told him to pick someone out and I would show him how it was done." He felt like a total heel, slimier by the moment. Well, he'd come this far, he might as well finish. She could probably guess the rest, but he would confirm it. He took a deep breath. "That someone was you."

Jane said nothing. Instead, she looked at Jorge for a long moment, surprised that he would admit this.

Was it guilt that had him confessing?

Or could it be that Jorge actually had feelings for her?

More than likely, he was probably just telling her that the game was over and that he didn't want to continue with it anymore.

The silence felt as if it were dragging on and on. Each second killing him.

"Say something," he implored. Jorge knew he deserved a tongue-lashing. Why wasn't she yelling at him? Calling him a lowlife? Why was she just looking at him like that? "Say *anything*."

And then Jane said the one thing he never expected.

"I know."

Chapter Twelve

"Y ou know?"

Jorge stared at Jane, certain he had misunderstood.

"Yes," she told him quietly, her subdued tone not giving him any kind of a clue as to her emotions. "You had a bet."

Jorge continued studying her face, looking for some kind of sign he could recognize, some feeling that he could identify.

"When?" he wanted to know. "When did you find out?" And then the answer suddenly came to him. Things began to fall into place. "When I went to get your coat," Jorge realized. "That was why you disappeared, wasn't it?"

She would have thought a man as smart as Jorge would have figured that out a long time ago. But then, he'd never been on her side of the fence, never dealt with humiliation.

"Yes, that was why. I didn't want to be the butt of a joke. Even yours."

Dear God, she made it sound almost like an apology when *he* should be the one apologizing. The one trying to make things up to her. Regret and shame drenched him.

He tried to make sense of the pieces before him. "Then why did you go out with me?" he asked. Heaven knew he wouldn't have if the tables had been turned—unless he was out for revenge. But that wasn't Jane. Jane Gilliam didn't have a vengeful bone in her body—he was willing to bet his soul on that. "When I showed up at ReadingWorks with your coat and the picnic basket, why didn't you just tell me where to go?"

Her next words confirmed what he'd been thinking. She shook her head.

"That's not me," Jane told him. "I don't like causing scenes. Besides, everyone there thought that I had hit some kind of romantic lottery." She slipped off her coat and draped it on the back of the recliner near her.

"And," she went on, "if you must know, I was just kind of curious how far you'd take this bet. Besides, I have to admit that you're so very good looking, so very charming, it's hard to think of you as an evil, self-centered jerk I should have just sent on his way."

"I'm not a jerk," he protested. "I'm not evil," he insisted. "But what you said about self-centered…

maybe you're right. Maybe I don't see beyond my personal space. Or, at least, I didn't."

He slipped his arms around her, drawing her in a little closer. Relieved that she didn't pull pack. He would have deserved it if she had, but he was glad she didn't.

"It took you to make me realize that. To broaden my way of looking at things." Unlike some of the lines he'd fed other women in the past, this time he meant every word he was saying.

A smile slowly, shyly, stole over her lips. "You don't have to say all that," she told him. "You've already got me."

It surprised Jorge that her words actually excited him, stirred him in a way he hadn't been stirred in a very long time.

But before he could go forward, there were still loose ends to tie up, air to clear.

"I'm not saying it to 'get' you, Jane. I'm saying it because it's true. I honestly don't know what it is about you, whether it's your innate goodness or because you always seem to look for the best in people, but you make me want to be the best person I possibly can. For you."

He thought she'd be pleased. Instead, she shook her head. "You should be the best person you possibly can be for *you*."

Their eyes met for a long moment. "I don't deserve the best person," he told her, his meaning clear. That in his opinion, *she* was the best person. Far better than he.

She smiled. "Yes, you do." For possibly the first time in her life, she felt in control of a situation. Or at least an equal in it. But she didn't want to be in control. She just wanted to share whatever was about to happen. "Now, are you going to kiss me?" she asked, thrilled at her own boldness. "Or are we going to talk all night?"

He smiled into her eyes, liking this brand-new layer to Jane that he'd uncovered. "We could talk if you wanted to."

Her eyes on his, she slowly moved her head from side to side. "Uh-uh. Maybe later."

Actually, she was really praying for later, really hoping that once this moment blossomed and played itself out, that Jorge would still want to stay here, still want to be with her and just lay beside her. At least for a little while.

His mouth curved invitingly, exciting her. "Whatever you want."

The next moment, his lips were on hers as he tugged at her pullover, loosening it and then dragging it away from her body. For a split second, his lips left hers, only to recapture them hungrily a moment later as her pullover cascaded onto the rug at her feet.

Jane shivered against him, even though she was sure her body temperature had gone up by several degrees, erupting in flames as his hands stroked her arms, her shoulders, her bare sides.

Hungers and sensations she was entirely unfamiliar with went racing through her.

She was aware of everything, yet all seemed to be

happening inside a blazing haze. One that would consume her at any moment.

Strong, gentle, urgent fingers were unzipping her skirt, coaxing it down her hips. Goose bumps materialized on her arms from the intimate contact. Her breath was coming in smaller and smaller snatches as excitement all but constricted her lungs.

Jane struggled to concentrate, to do something beyond merely being a vessel that was swiftly being filled with all these delicious feelings as Jorge freed her from her clothing one article at a time.

She wanted to *do* something, to make him feel the kind of anticipation that she was experiencing. She didn't want to disappoint him.

Desire pulsed within her, coloring everything in hues of red.

Only vaguely was she aware of unbuttoning Jorge's shirt, of pushing the dark blue material off his shoulders. She was acutely aware of her skin seeking the warmth of his.

It was almost as if she were on automatic pilot, flying blindly into territory where she had never been before, hadn't even known of before, much less had a knowledge of its terrain.

All she knew was that she didn't want this to stop.

When she felt his lips move to the hollow of her throat, she thought she would just implode right then and there.

Instincts took over, instincts she hadn't even suspected she had. Instincts that drove her to do things she hadn't even *thought* about doing.

Jane mimicked Jorge's earlier movements, stripping off his clothing, letting her eager mouth roam over his throat, forging a passage along his bare, muscular chest. She felt him shiver. Empowered, her lips, teeth and tongue passed over his hard, taut skin.

She thought she heard him catch his breath and the very sound sent ripples of wild excitement through her. It gave her the courage to continue on her journey, the courage to *hang* on even while a part of her just wanted to fall back and absorb all that he had to offer. All that he was doing to her.

Jane wasn't certain just how it happened, but somewhere along the line, they wound up near the piles of shed clothing, on the floor.

Their mouths sealed to one another, they rolled into one another, switching positions as the momentum overtook one of them or the other, fueled by eagerness to be submerged in as many sensations, as many passions as humanly possible.

He'd been in the presence of expert lovers before, women who knew just what to do to work a man into a frenzy, bringing him to his knees. Knew how to make him want the final act, the climax, more than life itself.

But there was something more at work here. Something that he couldn't begin to reconcile or work into his vast knowledge of what made people, what made *women* tick. When it came to Jane, along with what he could testify was an expertise, a finesse that was hard won and long in formation, he could have sworn there was an innocence at its core.

How was that possible?

How could she be a consummate lover and yet an eager novice at the same time?

Who was this woman really? More important, he thought, how could he make her want to remain with him?

Jorge heard her whimper in sheer ecstasy as he skimmed his lips over her abdomen. Watched in fascination as the muscles there quivered in response, even as she raised her hips to him in an open invitation.

Slowly moving his heated body over hers, watching desire bloom like twin dark flowers in her eyes, Jorge gently kneed her legs apart.

Beginning to enter, he stopped, startled as resistance met him. Not hers, but an actual physical barrier.

That could only be for one reason.

Stopping, Jorge raised himself up on his elbows, pivoting over her body as he looked at her in confusion. "Jane?"

She made no response. He wasn't even sure if she'd heard him. Instead, she thrust her hips up against his in a hard, swift movement that he could no more resist than he could will himself to stop breathing.

Her mouth quickly sealed itself to his as a cry of pain was about to escape. The sound was muffled against his lips.

Jorge was aware of rigid tension shooting through her body for an instant before it relaxed once more.

The next moment, she began to move against him in a timeworn rhythm.

Unable to resist, to tamp down his own needs and back away, Jorge got caught up in the rhythm. He took the lead, his hips sealed to hers the same way his mouth was.

And the tempo of the dance they engaged in grew quicker and quicker until he found that they were racing toward that final moment, that final sensation that would make them both feel, just for the tiniest split second, immortal.

He felt her tense again, but this time it was in a good way. She'd tensed and held on to him with both hands digging into his shoulders. It was as if she were desperately trying to hold on to the moment, on to the godlike sensation that was completely covered with extreme happiness.

But even as she held on, it began to break apart, to fade away into the mists, leaving behind two spent, heated bodies in its wake.

He felt her breathing grow steadier, felt her relaxing in almost a dreamlike state.

Rising up on his elbows, Jorge withdrew from her. Then, in a fluid motion, rather than just get up and walk away, he laid down next to her. Pressing a kiss to her forehead, he tucked one arm around her as he held her to him.

Confusion held his conscience prisoner.

How did he even broach this?

He'd never been in this position before. Virginity had only been involved once in all his liaisons, and it had been *his* virginity that had been lost, not that of the woman he had made love with.

"Why didn't you tell me?" he finally asked.

Here it came, she thought. The moment she'd been dreading. It had been that obvious to him.

"Tell you what?" she murmured.

Her voice sounded different than usual. Was that wariness he heard? Defensiveness?

He couldn't tell.

Maybe he was mistaken. Maybe she wasn't a virgin. Maybe she was just built very, very small.

No, he knew what he knew and this time, he had to take responsibility for what he'd done from the start rather than just hope that the subject would never come up.

"Why didn't you tell me that you were a virgin?" Jorge wanted to know, enunciating each word slowly, carefully.

She fought back the embarrassment, the suddenly feeling of vulnerability. "You mean you missed it on my business card? Jane Gilliam," she recited, "BA, MA, and, oh yes, PV."

"PV?" What the hell was PV? He'd never come across that degree.

"Professional Virgin," she elaborated. "Possibly the last one over the age of twenty in this part of Texas."

He hadn't meant to embarrass her. If anything, he was the one who was embarrassed. Embarrassed by his cavalier treatment of her when she should have had a better introduction to this world.

"Jane—"

"If I told you I was a virgin, would you have made love with me?" It was almost an accusation rather than a question.

He had to be honest with her. "No."

His answer stung, shooting an arrow straight into her heart. But she hadn't expected anything else. She'd just hoped…

"Well, there you have it." She stared up at the ceiling rather than look at him. She couldn't bear to see the disappointment in his eyes—or worse. "That's why I didn't tell you. Because I knew you didn't want to waste your time and considerable talents making love with a woman who couldn't return the favor."

Because she was staring at the ceiling, he took her chin in his hand and turned her head, forcing her to look at him.

"I wouldn't have made love with you—no matter how much I wanted to—because a woman's first time is supposed to be special."

That temporarily stopped her in her tracks. Jane looked at him for a long moment, trying to decide if it was just an excuse he was hiding behind, or if he could actually mean what he was saying. He was Jorge Mendoza. That alone made it special.

"What makes you think it wasn't?" she asked incredulously. "That was why I chose you. I wanted you to be the first."

And the last, but I can't tell you that. You'll run out the door, naked, to get away from me.

"You still should have told me," he insisted.

No, she shouldn't have. "Then you wouldn't have been the first," she countered.

Yes, God help him, he would have. He wouldn't have been able to get up and walk away, not after they'd gone that far. He wasn't made of iron, only flesh. "I would have gone slower."

A sad smile crept over her lips. "Any slower and I would have caught fire," she told him. "Don't worry. I know that this doesn't mean anything to you. I'm not about to chain you to my bed—if we were in bed," she amended. "I just wanted—"

"Will you be quiet?" he told her.

But she needed to get this out. This could be the last time she'd ever see him. "I—"

"Obviously not," he said more to himself than to her. "Okay, only one way I know how to handle this," he told her.

And the next minute, moved in a way he'd never been before, wanting Jane all over again when by all rights, he should have been spent and all but asleep, he gathered her to him again and brought his mouth down on hers.

Startled, the moment their lips parted, she asked breathlessly, "What are you doing?"

She watched as an amused smile danced on his very tempting lips.

"If you have to ask, then I guess I didn't do it right the first time," he said against her lips.

And then there was no space for any further conversation. He was too busy showing her.

Chapter Thirteen

What the hell had he been thinking?

The question throbbed over and over in Jorge's head like a relentless tattoo five seconds after he had woken up the next morning.

He was lying beside Jane, who mercifully, appeared to be still asleep.

Their night of lovemaking, which had moved, in a flurry of clothing and passions, from the living room through the tiny hall until it had finally ended up here in her bedroom—in her bed, vividly came back to him. In living color.

Guilt attacked at the same time, coming at him from all sides, aided and abetted by fear. Fear of consequences, fear of what this all ultimately meant.

Jane wasn't the type of woman a man had a one-night stand with or even a brief affair. She might have protested last night that she didn't expect what was happening between them to mean anything to him, but he knew that in her heart, she was hoping that it did.

And it did, which was what scared him.

He wasn't husband material. He wasn't even boy-friend material, Jorge thought. No matter how good his intentions might be, he knew himself. Knew that before long, another woman would attract his attention, catch his fancy and he'd be off, leaving Jane behind and breaking her heart.

Or, worse, he'd remain with her and grow to resent the shackles that bound him.

Why the hell had he slept with her? He couldn't even blame this on anything he had to drink because he hadn't had anything to drink. If he'd been intoxicated last night at all, it was with the moment—and her.

She was still sleeping. He needed to go. Now, before there was a need for dialogue.

Very slowly, moving a fraction of an inch at a time, Jorge drew away from Jane until he was finally out of the bed.

His clothes, Jorge recalled, were still in the living room. That left him to make his way to the living room stark naked. He couldn't take the sheet off the bed. Half of it was on her side. He didn't want to risk waking her up for the sake of modesty.

When the hell had he started to care about that? he

wondered suddenly. It felt like everything about him, about the way he conducted his life, was going through some kind of upheaval. He couldn't deal with this.

With stealth movements, Jorge began to slowly tiptoe toward the door. He'd only made it halfway when he heard rustling behind him.

Jane.

Was she just turning in her sleep, or was she awake? Summoning courage, he forced himself to turn around to look at her.

Their eyes met.

And the look in hers told him that he didn't have to bother coming up with excuses. She knew what he was doing. Fleeing without saying goodbye.

But he had to say something, didn't he? Besides, the excuse was actually true, it just wasn't the main reason he was going.

"I have a meeting," he told her.

God, did that sound as lame to her as it did to him? He tried to remember the last time he'd actually felt this awkward and couldn't. What had this woman with the deep, soulful eyes done to him?

"Okay." Her response sounded almost cheerful.

Sitting up, she wrapped the sheet around herself like a toga before she swung her legs off the bed and onto the floor.

This was just what he *hadn't* wanted. A prolonged goodbye. "You really don't have to get up," Jorge told her.

"I was going to make you coffee," she informed

him with a smile. Then, as if reading what he was thinking, she emphasized, "Not breakfast, just coffee." As if accepting anything to eat would somehow bind him to her, but coffee was universally acceptable. "Besides," she went on, "I'd like some coffee, too."

"Oh, all right." The words came out incredibly stilted.

Jorge sounded almost nervous, she thought. Did he expect her to jump him because he possessed the most perfect male body ever created? She did her best to concentrate on his face, but just being in the presence of his nakedness was enough to raise her body temperature by several degrees. She did what she could to seem unaffected.

"Why don't you get dressed and I'll work on the coffee," she suggested nonchalantly. Oscars, she thought, were given for lesser performances.

As she walked passed him, her eyes deliberately focused on the doorway, she heard him call out her name. "Jane—"

Jane glanced over her shoulder, careful to make only eye contact. "No food," she assured him with a smile, "Just coffee to wake you up for the meeting."

"Right."

She walked to the kitchen as he quickly went to the living room.

You would have thought she was the experienced one and he was the newly deflowered virgin, Jorge thought, disgusted with his reaction, with his sudden inability to sound aloof, as he hurried into his clothes. She was handling this with a lot more grace than he was.

Dressed, he walked into the kitchen, brought there more by a sense of contrition than by the deep, enticing smell of brewing coffee. Jane was still wearing the sheet, artfully tucked around her to allow for movement.

He had to admit, as eager as he was to be on his way and put what he viewed as a big mistake behind him, the thought of reaching out and unraveling the sheet did captivate him for a second.

No. He wasn't going to get entrenched any further. He shouldn't have slept with her—he wasn't going to compound it by doing it again. He had to leave, quickly, while leaving was still an option.

But he couldn't leave without saying something, now that she was awake. That would be the coward's way and he had never been a coward. He wasn't about to become one. "About last night, Heidi," he began, trying to deflect some of the seriousness by calling her the nickname he'd previously given her.

Jane stiffened. She'd really hoped that she would have been able to cling to her fantasy a little longer. More time to pretend that life could actually arrange itself for her benefit just this once. But she didn't want to ruin the memory of what she did have by having him stumble through some kind of awkward apology or, equally bad, an excuse. That would only taint everything.

"Last night was last night," she said as she poured out two inky cups of coffee. Turning, she placed one on the counter before him and then took hold of the other with both hands. "And today is today," she added with a smile that clearly absolved him of any and all sins he thought he'd committed.

The flood of relief he felt was brief, nudged quickly aside by a sense of confusion. She was acting as if last night hadn't meant anything to her.

"That's it?" he asked, bewildered.

"That's it," she confirmed. "Why?" A small, knowing smile curved her mouth. "Isn't that the way you usually view these encounters?"

Actually, it was. It was his vague justification for moving on, for giving in to the restless wanderlust that came over him periodically, every time he saw a beautiful face or an inviting body. And there was *always* a beautiful face or an inviting body within easy reach.

But admitting it seemed almost sordid. Still, he couldn't very well deny it, could he?

"Yes."

She studied him for a moment, as if trying to formulate a response. "Then why do you look so surprised?"

"Well, I thought that you— That we—" He couldn't find the right words to finish the sentence.

Jane found them for him. "You didn't think it would be this easy?" she guessed. "Did you think I was going to wrap myself around your leg and hold on for dear life? Ask you what you wanted to name the children when they started coming along?" She paused to take a sip of her coffee while he stared at her, for once in his life completely speechless. "I might not be all that experienced, Jorge," she went on, secretly congratulating herself on how calm she sounded. "But I'm not stupid. The prince does not forsake his kingdom for a scullery maid. For Cinderella, maybe, but definitely not for the scullery maid."

That *really* took him by surprise. "Is that how you see yourself?"

"Symbolically," Jane elaborated. She was still smiling complacently at him, as if none of this left a scar or cut deep. "I have no regrets, Jorge. If I'd said no, you would have backed off. I know you would. I didn't want to say no. I knew exactly what I was doing last night—" And then she amended, "Well, most of the time. A few times I was a little out of my head." The smile on her lips filtered into her eyes as well. "But that's just because you do what you do so well."

His guilt increased a thousandfold because she was being so incredibly understanding. He would have done better if she'd ranted at him, called him names. He felt both off the hook and like a consummate heel for feeling that way.

"Jane, I don't—"

She glanced at the clock on the wall. "Didn't you say you have a meeting to go to?" she reminded him, not letting him finish again.

He did. And if it actually wasn't so important, he might have opted to remain.

But it was better this way, he told himself. Jane was giving him a way out, letting him take his leave gracefully and go out the door. He was the one who was spoiling it.

This was just the kind of exit he appreciated.

Putting his cup down on the counter, Jorge paused to brush a quick kiss against her cheek.

"You really are one of a kind, you know that?" he told her quietly.

Her response was glib. "I'll be sure to have that added to my business card, now that I have to have the PV removed." She was smiling as she said it.

That was the way he remembered her as he made his way out the door. Smiling.

That was the way she wanted him to remember her. And he'd left not a moment too soon.

Jane wasn't sure how much longer she could have kept up the charade, how much longer she could have had her lips continue to form that mindless smile that was all but glued in place.

Not easy smiling like that when your heart was shattering into a thousand pieces right there in your chest, she thought.

Her shoulders sagged as she abandoned her half-finished coffee. Wrapping the bottom of the sheet around her arm to keep from tripping on it, she went to the living room and began to pick up her discarded clothing one piece at a time.

And as she did so, last night vividly returned to her, replaying itself in her head. If she closed her eyes, she could even feel Jorge's hands on her, gently gliding along her flesh. Could smell the scent of his skin as he held her close to him.

No matter what she'd said to Jorge just now, or pretended that she believed for his sake, she knew she was in love with him. Had fallen in love from the moment he first walked up to her.

But that was for her to deal with, not him. He could never know, could never even suspect, what it was she felt for him.

And, truth be told, she'd gotten more out of their brief time together than she'd ever hoped for. Jane nursed no false image of herself. She knew all her good qualities. Being a bombshell was not among them.

And yet she, the bookish, mousy daughter of a former beauty queen had managed, just for a little while, to be with a man who invaded so many women's dreams. Be with him in every sense of the word.

That was more than most women had, she thought. Certainly more than she had ever thought she would have outside of her daydreams.

Jane stood there for a moment, clutching the clothes she'd worn last night, trying very hard not to give in to the tears that were suddenly forming inside her.

Last night was nothing to cry about. Last night was something to celebrate.

But today, this morning, well, that was something actually worthy of tears, she silently admitted. Because she knew that Jorge wouldn't be back. She had given him his freedom, his exit line, and he had seized them both with relief and gusto.

At least he wouldn't think of her as some clingy, pathetic female.

The thought was supposed to give her solace. But it didn't.

She sank down to the floor where she stood, the sheet pooling haphazardly around her as her tears fell freely.

Sally glanced at the table as she walked into the lounge. It had gotten to be a habit.

"No more flowers?" she asked Jane, who was the only other one there.

More than a week had passed since she'd watched Jorge walk out her front door. A week in which it was everything she could do not to break down while she was out in public.

She wasn't entirely sure how she had managed that. Jane had thrown herself into her job, working out elaborate reading schedules for each child she tutored. After work, she doubled up on the number of hours she volunteered in order to fill her evenings and weekends. She needed to keep busy every single moment. She didn't want to be alone with her thoughts until she could keep them from instantly gravitating toward Jorge.

She was still working on that.

True to her expectations, Jorge hadn't called, hadn't tried to get in touch with her at all.

Why should he?

She'd been his challenge. Now that he'd met it,

been victorious over it, there was no reason to return to the scene of his triumph. After all, there were so many more fish out there in the sea. Prettier, more accomplished fish.

But none of them is ever going to love you the way I do, she told him silently.

As if that mattered to him. He seemed to be doing just fine with those empty-headed beauties who gravitated to him.

"No, no more flowers," Jane replied, trying to keep her voice level and distant. Praying that Sally would be satisfied and just move on.

Obviously, God wasn't answering prayers lately, because all of hers were going by the wayside.

Rather than leave the room, Sally crossed to her and hooked her long arm through hers. The older woman gently drew her over to the sofa.

"Something wrong?" she asked, lowering her voice even though they were the only two people in the lounge.

Jane shook her head, avoiding eye contact. "Nothing's wrong."

Sally tilted her head, trying to get her to look in her direction. "But you two are still dating."

"We were never really dating," Jane told her. She shrugged, doing her best to seem as if none of this bothered her. "Jorge was just…spending time with me."

Sally frowned, trying to understand. "Isn't that what dating is?"

"Not in the real sense of the word," Jane answered sadly.

But she didn't want to get into it, didn't want anyone to know about the bet. It made her seem pathetic and Jorge shallow. She didn't want anyone to think of him that way. She actually understood what he'd been trying to do.

"I'm not his type," was all she said.

Sally looked at her, mystified. "Did he tell you that?"

"No," Jane admitted. "But look at the women he's been seen with."

Sally made a dismissive sound. "None of them hold a candle to you."

Jane laughed sadly, shaking her head. She appreciated what her friend was trying to do. But that still didn't change anything. "Sally, you're sweet, but you're my friend."

Sally sniffed. "I also have 20/20 vision and even better instincts. You are very attractive—when you let yourself be," the woman underscored. "You're also a woman of substance. Any man would be thrilled to have you in his life."

Sally made it sound as if there were men lining up three deep outside her door. "Don't seem to be many of those around," she quipped.

Sally slipped her arm around Jane's shoulders, giving her a comforting squeeze. None of the women who worked here had escaped being dumped by someone they thought was in their life for the long haul. And Jane, the youngest, had had more than her share of heartaches.

"Want to come over tonight, let your hair down? Vent?" Sally suggested.

That was the last thing she wanted to do. Because she knew she'd cry when faced with too much sympathy and she didn't want to cry. Didn't want to talk about it until she could do so calmly.

"Thanks, but I've got to be at the hospital. We're starting a new book. *Peter Pan.*"

Sally looked at her in surprise. "You're all finished with *Heidi?*" She'd only started that just before New Year's Eve.

Jane looked away. "Extra readings," she said with a shrug.

Sally sighed, accepting defeat, at least temporarily. "Well, you know where to find me if you change your mind."

Leaving Jane in the room, Sally headed for the door. Jane's students were coming soon and she needed to do a few things before they arrived. Just about to reach for the door, she stepped back quickly as it was swung opened. Harriet burst in, her face contorted with horror. "Have you heard?" she asked.

Sally exchanged glances with Jane. "Heard what?" Sally asked.

"Red is on fire," Harriet declared like a news-caster reporting a breaking story.

Sally's eyes widened with amazement. "The restaurant?"

"No, the color," Harriet retorted with obvious impatience. "Yes, the restaurant."

Jane said nothing. Grabbing her coat, she was already running to the front door.

Chapter Fourteen

Jane didn't even remember getting into her car, or turning the key in the ignition. But somehow, she got out here, on the road, driving faster than she'd ever driven in her life. Fervently praying for all she was worth.

Turning sharply, Jane sucked in her breath as she quickly righted her wheel again. She'd missed colliding with an SUV by inches. With her heart hammering wildly, she saw the driver roll down his window and heard him swear at her. All she could do was wave one hand in a helpless gesture, hoping he'd see her in his mirror and understand that it hadn't been on purpose.

Swallowing, trying to calm herself down, her

heart was still pounding louder than the song that was playing on the radio. With a frustrated twist of her hand, she shut it off. She didn't want music at a time like this, she wanted silence.

Instead, she heard the jarring peal of sirens.

Fire trucks.

Fire, she thought hopelessly. There was a fire. And from the smoke she saw rising in the air, even at this distance, she knew in her heart that it had to be coming from Red.

An icy hand passed over her and she shivered even as she found herself sweating.

Jorge was there.

Inside.

She didn't know how she knew, but she did. She knew with a certainty that went all the way down to her bones. Fear squeezed the very air out of her lungs.

Jane drove faster.

One minute, he was sitting by himself at his table for two, finishing a meal he'd barely tasted. There was nothing to even hint at what was coming. This was Red, the restaurant that was almost like another member of his family. Jorge was more familiar with every nook and cranny of the two-story establishment than he was with the spaces in his own home.

He'd come here searching for a sense of peace that had been eluding him for the last week. Ever since he'd walked away from Jane.

The next minute, just after the first whiff of smoke

seemed to come out of nowhere, suddenly he saw flames racing toward the dining area from the general direction of the kitchen.

It was just after two in the afternoon and most of the regulars who came here for lunch were gone. Only a few stragglers remained, the ones who had no boss eyeing the company clock, no lunch hour that had come to an abrupt end.

A scream pierced the air, followed by the word *Fire,* and suddenly the room was in motion. The few customers who were left jumped to their feet, knocking over chairs as they stampeded for the front door.

Jorge's eyes were riveted toward the kitchen. The noon cook, the busboys, the waitresses—and his father—they were all in there somewhere, lost behind that growing curtain of flames.

He had to get to them.

To his father.

Jorge poured his glass of water onto the napkin he'd just discarded, then fashioned a bandanna out of it, covering his nose and mouth as he hurried toward the belly of the fire.

"Pop!" he yelled, projecting his voice into the flames. "Pop, are you there?"

He thought he heard someone calling back.

Or maybe it was just the groan of the fire. But he couldn't take that chance. He knew that after the lunch crowds abated, his father liked to retreat to his small office behind the kitchen to go over tallies. The older Mendoza hadn't come out to see him yet, so that meant that he was still there. Trapped by the fire.

"Pop!" Jorge yelled again. He crouched low to avail himself of any oxygen in the room.

That was how he wound up stumbling into Juan, one of the part-time busboys who was groping around blindly and heading in the wrong direction.

The fire was growing more intense.

"That way!" Jorge yelled over the roar of the flames. Grabbing Juan's shoulders, he physically turned the thin busboy around because the latter couldn't seem to comprehend what he was saying. Wide, frightened eyes looked up at him. "My father," Jorge shouted at him. "Have you seen my father?"

The light seemed to dawn on Juan. "In his office," the boy blurted out. Juan moved his hand about wildly, not realizing that he was pointing toward the salad bar. The latter had become a casualty of a fallen overhead beam.

"Go!" Jorge ordered. "Go that way!" Again, he pointed toward the front of the restaurant. The double doors were still untouched by flames—but for how much longer?

He pushed the busboy toward the doors, then turned back into the restaurant. Feeling incredibly light-headed, Jorge wove in and out, looking for a path to the office that wasn't completely obstructed by flames. Flames were hungrily devouring everything around him.

The heat was unbearable.

What if this was it? his mind screamed. What if he was meant to die today? Here, in the place where he had practically grown up.

In the place where he had first met Jane.

Jane.

Oh, God, he was going to die and she was going to think he didn't love her. That he didn't want her.

He could have had a life with her, Jorge thought in despair, and he'd thrown it all away. The very reason he was here today was because he was desperately trying to bolster his spirits. Deep down, he'd known that turning his back on making a commitment to Jane was the wrong thing to do, yet he was still trying to talk himself into it.

Not anymore.

He'd gotten turned around, Jorge realized, fighting back a panic. Both in his life and in trying to make his way to the kitchen.

The napkin covering his nose and mouth was dry.

He had to get his father out. And he had to live. He had to survive this so that he could tell Jane he was an idiot.

"Pop!" Jorge yelled again, charging through the kitchen, flames swallowing him.

This was a bad one, Darr Fortune thought as he jumped off the fire truck before it came to a full stop. Quickly, he removed his gear from the vehicle.

Red was being destroyed. Hell of a shame. He'd eaten here himself a number of times.

Hell, he suddenly realized, he'd been here New Year's Eve with his dad and siblings. Who would have ever thought that he'd be back four weeks later, fighting to save it? If there was anything left to save.

Behind him, several of the other firefighters were attaching the hose, preparing to douse the two-story building with a flood of water. With any luck, they'd be able to save some of it. With more luck, it would matter that they did. Sometimes, structures struck by fire were so far beyond repair that knocking them down and beginning over was all that was left to do.

Damn shame, Darr thought again.

As he secured the tank, he was suddenly jostled from the side. Turning, he saw a brown-haired woman run past him. She'd obviously broken through the barricade that had been hastily put up.

The damn fool looked like she was running straight for the burning building!

"Hey, hold it!" Darr yelled after her. "You can't go in there!"

Jane didn't even slow down to look at the firefighter. "I have to. He's in there. I know it. I have to find him," she cried.

Suddenly, she felt herself being grabbed around the waist by a powerful arm and lifted off the ground in one swift, seemingly effortless movement. The firefighter swung her around 180 degrees away from the restaurant entrance.

"Lady," Darr said as patiently as he could. "I understand how you feel, I really do, but you can't go in there."

She wasn't going be talked out of it. "I have to. I can't let him die in there." She was struggling not to cry, not to let her imagination go any further than it was right at this moment.

"Him?" Darr asked. According to the person who'd called in the fire, one of the patrons, the few people in the restaurant dining area had fled.

"Jorge," she cried. She tried to move past Darr, but he merely blocked her again. "Jorge Mendoza."

The guy whose father owned the place. Darr was vaguely aware that Jorge Mendoza had some kind of a reputation for being a class-A Romeo. He clearly had to be one hell of a lover if this one was willing to risk burning to death trying to find him.

Trying to be gentle, Darr pushed the woman back to the barricade.

"Saving him is my job," he told her, trying to get her behind the sawhorse. "Let me do it."

Just then, a bedraggled, soot-blackened busboy staggered out through the front door. Coughing madly, he gasped in gulps of air. Unable to stand, he collapsed to his knees.

Darr made his way to the boy. The brown-haired woman darted past him, running to the fallen busboy.

Dropping to her knees beside the gasping Juan, Jane cried, "Is Jorge in there?"

The boy nodded vigorously, still trying to drag in enough air to answer her. "He…pointed…the…way…out…for…me," he finally managed to get out.

That was all she needed. Jane scrambled up to her feet, about to run to the double doors.

Again, Darr stopped her. "Murphy!" he yelled to one of the other firefighters.

About to run to the building, the heavyset man,

who looked as if he'd be more at home on a football field, responded to his name and turned to look at Darr.

"Yeah?"

"Keep an eye on this one before she's burned to a crisp," Darr ordered, physically taking hold of Jane by the shoulders and moving her over to Murphy.

"But you don't understand." She tried to wiggle out of the firefighter's grasp and couldn't. "He's in there. I've got to get to him."

"You won't do him any good dead," Darr told her matter-of-factly, hurrying to the restaurant. "I'll tell him you're waiting," was his parting comment to her.

Double-checking the last of his equipment, the stocky, muscular firefighter charged into the burning inferno.

And it was just that. An inferno.

It was hard to see, hard to move. The interior of the dining room looked like it was one continuous sheet of flame.

To the left of the entrance were the rest rooms. That avenue hadn't been discovered by the roaring fire yet, but it was only a matter of seconds before it was.

Darr pushed open the door closest to him. It led to the men's room. "Anyone in here?" he shouted, his voice made surreal by his mask.

The doors all appeared to be unlocked. A quick scan of the floor told him that the area was unoccupied.

Most likely, any patrons or help this close to the

entrance had bolted the second they'd heard cries of "Fire," he thought.

About to move on to the dining room, Darr decided to give the ladies' room a quick check first. Just in case. He shouldered the door opened and yelled out the same question. He received the same answer. Nothing.

But just as he began to withdraw from the room, Darr saw her. Or rather, he saw her legs, peering out from beneath the last stall.

Hurrying over, he shoved open the door and found a young woman on the floor. It looked as if the smoke had gotten to her.

"Lady, lady wake up," Darr ordered.

Her eyes remained closed. He had no time to try to get her to come around. Kneeling, Darr scooped her up into his powerful arms. His equipment felt as if it weighed a ton as he struggled to get back up to his feet. By contrast, the unconscious blonde felt as if she weighed nothing.

"C'mon," he quipped to the unconscious woman as he hurried out with her in his arms, "this is no place to take a nap."

His voice gave no indication of how grateful he was that he'd decided to check the ladies' room.

Jane was just about to dart under the arm of the distracted firefighter when she saw him.

Them.

Jorge and his father.

The older man, sooty and coughing, was leaning heavily on his son. From where she was standing, they looked like two sides of a pyramid that should, by all rights, collapse but was determined not to.

"Jorge!" she screamed. The next second, she broke into a run and was sprinting across the parking lot. She vaguely heard the firefighter who'd been keeping her away from the restaurant yelling after her, but she was not about to stop. Not until she had assured herself that what she was seeing was no mirage. Not until she'd satisfied herself that Jorge was alive and well, and unhurt.

Jane reached Jorge and his father just as Murphy caught up.

José looked as if he was barely standing.

"Oh, my God, is he all right?" Jane cried, immediately going to the older man's other side to help prop him up.

Murphy took over, moving Jane out of the way and grasping the sagging José about the waist.

"He needs oxygen," Jorge told the firefighter, struggling to talk without coughing. It felt as if his lungs were filled with stifling ash and smoke. He gingerly relinquished his own hold on his father. "Careful," he warned just before a coughing fit finally took over.

"I need a paramedic here!" Murphy called out.

Two ambulances had already arrived, butted up side by side on the extreme left of the parking lot. Two teams of emergency medical technicians came running over even before Murphy called for them. One team took charge of José Mendoza while the other two attendants turned their attention to the woman that Darr Fortune was just now carrying out.

But all Jane could see was Jorge. It was a struggle to keep fear from taking over and rendering her useless.

"Are you all right?" she demanded even as she ran her hands along his arms, his face, his torso. She needed to assure herself that he was whole, that she hadn't just conjured him up out of the flames.

Then, before Jorge could attempt to answer, she kissed him, unable to express her incredible gratitude that he was alive any other way. The next moment she pulled back as if a hot poker had speared her, afraid that she was stealing what little oxygen he'd been able to drag back into his lungs.

He was alive.

She felt like laughing and crying at the same time. "I had to come," she explained, shaking. "As soon as I heard, I knew, I knew you were inside."

Her tears began to fall freely. Jane didn't bother trying to stop them. What was the point? She wasn't trying to maintain a facade or somehow guilt Jorge into reconsidering their nonexistent relationship. She was just relieved that he wasn't a victim of the fire.

"This doesn't mean anything," she said, referring to her tears. "I'm not trying to make you feel guilty or anything, I just— Oh God, you're all right. You're alive." She flung her arms around him again, sobbing.

Which was why Jane wasn't sure she heard what she did.

There was noise all around them. The roar of the fire, the din of the firefighters as they fought the flames for possession of the restaurant. The voices of the paramedics as they were attending to the fire's survivors, not to mention the noise coming from the onlookers who had gathered behind the barricades.

Everything conspired to play a trick on her ears because she could have sworn she heard Jorge say, "I love you."

But she knew that was impossible. That went beyond wishful thinking. That came under the heading of hallucinations.

Until she heard it again.

And then a third time.

Lifting her head, Jane looked at him, stunned. Bedraggled and covered with soot, he still managed to look incredibly sexy. She saw his lips form the three words a fourth time.

Feeling as if she'd just slipped into some parallel universe of her own design, she could only stare in wonder. "Jorge?"

"I love you," he repeated again, his voice growing stronger. As if to help imprint the words into her brain, he grasped her by her arms. "I didn't realize how much until I thought I was going to die in there. And thought about what I was losing, what I had so stupidly thrown away." His eyes looked deep into her soul. "A chance at real happiness."

Oh, how she wanted to believe him. To clutch the words he was saying to her heart.

But she knew better.

"That's just the adrenaline talking," she told him gently.

For some reason, she felt herself growing calm, as if she was the one in control of the situation. It was up to her to make it right. She wasn't going to hold him to promises made at a time like this. It wouldn't be fair of her.

"No," Jorge insisted with fervor, "it's me talking. For the first time, it's me. And for the first time, I'm not afraid to say it. Because I understand what it means." God, he must sound like a loon to her. "I love you," he repeated for the umpteenth time.

"All I could think of in there was that I was going to die and you wouldn't know how I felt."

"You made it clear how you felt," she reminded him quietly. "The last time we were together." She was going to say that she understood, that men like him couldn't be captured, contained, held to promises that the rest of the world made routinely. But she didn't get the chance.

"That was the coward talking," he told her with feeling. A coughing fit interrupted him for a moment. When he got his breath back, he continued. "I'm not a coward anymore."

"I'll say," Murphy, the firefighter who'd handed his father over to the paramedics said as he came up to Jorge. "If you hadn't saved him, your dad would have died in this fire."

"I guess that makes you a hero," Jane told him with pride, threading her arms around his waist and leaning against him. For now, she was content just to hold on to Jorge and not his words. She knew he'd take them back within a few minutes.

But that was all right. It was enough for her that he was alive.

Chapter Fifteen

"No, no, it is not possible."

The vehement protest was coming from José Mendoza. Bundled in a warm blanket that was draped across his shoulders and sitting on the rear step that led into the back of the ambulance, the senior Mendoza had just pulled off the oxygen mask that the paramedic had placed on him to facilitate his breathing.

The gray-haired fire chief did his best to remain patient in the face of all this emotion coming his way. "Mr. Mendoza," he began again in an even voice, "it only stands to reason—"

The sound of his father's voice momentarily diverted Jorge's attention away from Jane.

But as he headed over to his father to see what was going on, Jorge took hold of Jane's hand, silently indicating that she should come along with him to investigate. What concerned him concerned her, and vice versa.

Now and always, he thought, hoping she would give him the second chance he longed for.

Crossing to his father, he put his hand on the older man's shoulder. He felt his father tense. "What's the matter, Pop?"

José frowned and jerked a thumb at the chief. "The chief thinks that the fire was started by one of the kitchen crew."

"Not on purpose," the chief was quick to point out, although his expression indicated that he wasn't entirely sure about that, either. "But you have to admit that grease fires happen in restaurants, Mr. Mendoza. Especially when there's such a high volume of food being prepared."

"No, no, no," José insisted with even more feeling. "My people are careful. They treat this place like their own kitchen—"

The chief looked as if his point had just been made for him. "Mishaps happen in people's kitchens every day, Mr. Mendoza."

"Not my home," José informed him with dour finality. "There must be another cause for the fire. A faulty connection, something that was not caused by human error."

José was clearly issuing a challenge to the fire chief.

His father was working himself up, Jorge thought, concerned. The old man's heart had been through enough today. This couldn't be good for him.

"Pop, take it easy," Jorge counseled. "Nobody got hurt—"

"Except for Red," the man said mournfully, looking over Jorge's shoulder at what was left of the smoldering building. The fire, miraculously, was almost out. Rather than the beautiful, proud building that had stood there just this morning, there was now a half burnt-out shell, some of which was on the verge of collapse.

All those years, just burned away in an instant.

"We've got insurance for that, Pop," Jorge reminded his father gently. "It'll be rebuilt in time for the wedding reception."

"What wedding reception?" Both José and Jane asked at the same time, their voices blending and echoing one another.

Jorge grinned, his eyes going from his father to his love. "Mine—and Jane's."

The horror in José's face brought on by Red's destruction vanished instantly. Wriggling off the ambulance step, oblivious to the blanket that fell from his shoulders, he hugged first his son and then Jane with effervescent feeling.

"Welcome!" he cried as he held on to her. "Welcome to the family."

Stunned by Jorge's cavalier words, it took Jane a moment to return the older man's embrace. She stared at Jorge over his father's shoulder. What was going on here?

"Did I miss something?" she asked Jorge in complete disbelief the moment she was released from his father's embrace. "When did you ask me to marry you?"

"I didn't," Jorge confessed almost sheepishly. The next second, he was back to his normal upbeat temperament. "I just thought that, well, when two people love each other, that's what they do. They get married."

And as the words came out of his mouth, Jorge suddenly realized that he'd just leapfrogged right over the most important issue, taking it for granted.

What if he was wrong about Jane's feelings?

He peered at her face, a hint of uncertainty in his dark eyes even as he kept his smile in place. It was a matter of projecting confidence, of willing something into existence.

"You do love me, don't you?"

"Yes," Jane allowed, saying the single word slowly as if she were tasting it as it crossed her tongue.

Was she dreaming?

Was she the one who'd inhaled too much smoke, had fallen unconscious and was now floating somewhere between the real and the imagined?

Why else was this most perfect of scenarios happening?

"*Hijo*," José said sharply, a disapproving frown on his face. It was clear he felt that he had failed in the education of his second born. "A woman likes to be asked such things. You cannot take them or their answers for granted."

The fact that he was obviously on her side made Jane smile. She'd never had this kind of support when she was growing up.

Very lightly, she touched his arm with affection. "Mr. Mendoza, I think I'm going to like having you for a father-in-law."

Despite his losses and his near-death experience, barely a quarter of an hour old, José beamed at her. "'Pop,' please," he told Jane. "You must call me 'Pop.'" He turned his dark eyes on his son. "And you must ask her properly." Out of the corner of his eye, Jorge saw the fire chief quietly withdrawing. Thank God the man realized that they had time to discuss the cause of the fire later. Right now, this was a family matter and anyone outside the circle of his family didn't belong.

"Jane." Pausing for a moment, Jorge took her hand in his. His eyes never left hers. "Will you make me the happiest man in the world and do me the honor of becoming my wife?"

"Is this part of the bet, too?" she asked, tongue in cheek.

"This is not a bet," he told her. "It stopped being a bet the second I started talking to you and realized what a rare woman you were. Now, please, will you marry me?"

"Yes, oh yes," she cried, rising on her toes and throwing her arms around his neck.

Jorge sealed the proposal with a prolonged, deep kiss.

"Mr. Mendoza, we have to take you to the

hospital," the tall, wiry paramedic who had attended him was saying. He was attempting to steer the older man into the back of the ambulance.

José shrugged the paramedic's hands from his shoulders. "What hospital?" the older man demanded. "I am fine." Looking at his son and future daughter-in-law with unabashed pride, he beamed. "More than fine. Especially when my Maria hears about this."

As if on cue, his petite, dark-haired wife came elbowing her way through the crowd and rushed up to him. The expression on her face was a mix of fear and anger. Fear at what might have happened and anger at what he'd put her through, through no fault of his own.

There were tears shining in her dark eyes.

"*Dios mio,* you are alive, old man. I knew you were too tough to die."

Some of the tears spilled out as she made her declaration. No mention was made of the fact that she had prayed all the way to the restaurant, terrified of what she might find once she got there.

Maria threw her arms around her husband, holding on to his thin frame for all she was worth. "Don't you ever scare me like that again, do you understand?" she demanded. *"Never."*

"It was not something that I had planned, Maria," José told his wife. He shivered when he thought how close he had come to never seeing his wife's face again. "And I wouldn't be here if it wasn't for Jorge."

"Jorge?" she exclaimed. "Jorge was here?" she asked abruptly, looking around wildly for her son. It hadn't occurred to her that he'd been in danger as well. "Where is he?"

Smiling, José tapped his wife on the shoulder then pointed, turning her attention to the kissing couple on the side of the ambulance.

"He's fine," José assured the woman who made his life worth living each day. "And you, Maria, are going to be gaining that daughter-in-law you have been wanting for so long."

Amazed, Maria gave out a whoop of joy, throwing her arms around her husband's neck and squeezing him with wild abandon.

"Finally!" It was then that she saw what was left of Red. Saw the smoldering remains of the restaurant that had been built up by the sweat of her husband's brow. "Oh, José." That was all she said, but it throbbed with an overwhelming sadness. And then she rallied, as she always did, and her natural resilience took hold. "We will rebuild," Maria announced, "and we'll make it even better than before."

"Of course we will," José agreed, draping his arm across his wife's shoulders, already envisioning what the new, improved Red would look like, a phoenix rising out of the ashes of the old. "We need to have some place for the reception."

Marie beamed, patting her husband's chest with her hand in a comfortable, familiar gesture, the way she'd been doing for the last forty-one-plus years. "Yes, we do."

* * *

The crowds that had gathered around the barricades, composed equally of the concerned and the curious, began to slowly disperse. The fire was contained. It had done all the damage it was going to and was no longer a threat to the surrounding area. There was nothing left to witness except for the tedious details of cleanup.

Two of the people who had been milling around the perimeter of the barricade were Ricky Jamison and Josh Fredericks. Like so many others who had been drawn by the sound of the sirens, they had hung around, spectators at the scene of the fire. Fascinated by the power of the flames even as they cheered on the firefighters in their swift, mighty battle to vanquish them.

But now it looked like it was all over. Nothing remained of the blaze but the acrid smell of smoke and ashes that stubbornly and oppressively hung in the air.

Even as the boys had looked on earlier, it was hard for both of them to imagine that a few short weeks ago, they had been inside, partying.

So much could change in a few minutes, Ricky thought. He was tired of hanging back, of waiting to gather his courage in order to leap into life's pool. He'd already made a first effort.

Something he hadn't told Josh yet. He grinned to himself. Wouldn't Josh be surprised? And Jorge— Jorge would be proud of him, he thought.

Bored, Josh turned away from the barricade. He jerked a thumb to the scene behind him, dismissing it. "C'mon, there's nothing left to see here anymore."

Ricky took one last glance at Jorge, a bit of hero worship in his eyes. Even though he'd taken his first steps in the right direction, he was still envious of the man's prowess.

Ricky turned to Josh. The wind ruffled his blond hair and ran up and down his thin torso. He hunched his shoulders against it. As he spoke, he did his best to sound nonchalant. Yet he could feel his heart speeding up and lodging itself in his throat.

"You know." His voice almost cracked and he lowered it. "I asked Lizzie for a date."

Josh glanced at him. "Lizzie?" He repeated the name as if she hadn't been the topic of more than one conversation between them.

"Yeah, Lizzie Fortune," Ricky said her full name, as if his friend didn't know that the girl was part of his every daytime and nighttime dream. "I've had a thing for her for a while now," he added, avoiding eye contact.

A smirk from Josh would have destroyed him no matter how much of a pep talk he'd given himself. He looked up to Josh and valued the older teen's opinion as only a fourteen-year-old could.

"Jorge told me some moves to use and I used them," he said proudly and then grinned. "They worked. She's going out with me next week."

Josh shoved his hands deep into his pockets and slowly began to walk away from the barricade. "You look very satisfied with yourself," he commented.

Shorter than his friend, Ricky lengthened his stride to keep up, trying to maintain that air of nonchalance that Josh always had. "I am. Who knows, this could be the start of something really big. Lizzie might even fall for me."

In response, Josh said nothing. Instead, he just snorted.

Ricky looked at him, confused. He thought his friend would have been happy for him. He'd cheered Josh on when he'd started going out with Lindsey.

"What's that supposed to mean?" he wanted to know, taking offense.

Josh shook his head. His expression seemed enigmatic and far away.

"Nothing," he said dismissively. "Just be careful what you wish for, that's all," Josh advised. There was a distant look in his young eyes as he added, in a voice that was far older than he was, "Love isn't all it's cracked up to be."

Ricky's brow furrowed as he struggled to make sense of what Josh was saying. Why was he acting like that? Only one answer, he realized. "You and Lindsey having problems?"

Josh looked at him sharply. "I didn't say that."

"Well, what did you say?" Ricky wanted to know. He was confused and disappointed. He thought for sure that his friend would have been happy for him. Instead, Josh looked almost moody. Did he want Lizzie for himself? No, Josh liked Lindsey. They were a couple. Everyone knew that. That was part of what made him feel like an outsider. He wanted to be part of a couple too, like Josh.

"Nothing," Josh said with a careless shrug of his

shoulders. "I hope you and Lizzie have a great time together." He dropped the topic. "C'mon. If you want a ride, I've got to get going."

Ricky looked back over his shoulder at the cluster of people near the ambulance. "I feel I should say something to Jorge."

Josh looked at his friend, puzzled. "You mean about Lizzie?"

"No." What was wrong with Josh? Why wasn't he focusing? "About the fire."

This time it was Josh who looked over his shoulder. And saw Jorge kissing that woman he'd picked up at the New Year's Eve party. The one that Ricky had bet him he couldn't get so fast.

"He's busy, Ricky," Josh pointed out. "You can talk to him some other time." Impatience filtered through his voice as he lengthened his stride. "You coming?"

Ricky picked up his pace to keep up with Josh. "Yeah."

Two of the ambulances had already left. One had the woman Darr had rescued inside. The other had taken the busboy, Juan, to the hospital.

Like the rock he'd always been, José had remained where he was, with his wife and growing circle of friends gathering around him to offer their support and encouragement.

Jorge took the opportunity to draw Jane aside, away from the others. He held her hands in his and looked into her eyes, realizing that he would probably be content to go on doing that for quite some time to come.

But life went on and she had one that she'd left when the fire had broken out. He knew it was selfish of him, but he wanted her to remain right where she was, here with him.

"You have to get back to the school?" Jorge finally asked Jane.

The question nudged reality back into focus. Her eyes widened. ReadingWorks! She'd run out of there without so much as a word of explanation. They were all probably wondering where she was. Even so, she shook her head. Her place right now was here—even if he hadn't asked her to marry her. "No, I think they can get along without me for an afternoon."

"Good," he said, "because I can't." His hands tightened on hers, reflecting his feelings. "I want to spend the rest of my life with you." He'd never really explored what those words meant—and never meant them as much as he did right at this moment.

She laughed softly, shaking her head again. He might mean that now, but she was willing to bet he wouldn't later.

"You'll get bored," she predicted.

There she was wrong, he thought. "No, that's one thing I don't think I'll ever be."

She really wished she could believe that. But there was a small part of her that was a realist. Life with parents who'd offered no encouragement had seen to that. "How can you be so sure?"

He told her the truth and bared his heart to her. He realized he'd never allowed himself to be this vulnerable before. But then, he'd never trusted another woman before the way he did her.

"Because I never loved any of the other women. I love you," he declared simply. And then he grinned wickedly. "You still have that Heidi outfit you wore to the hospital?"

What was he getting at? Was he asking if she intended to continue reading to the children at the hospital? "Yes."

His grin grew broader. "Well, that settles it. I will definitely not get bored." His eyes were shining as he told her, "I've always wanted to see what it feels like to be a goat herder."

And then she caught on. And laughed. "Right. You look just like a Swiss goat herder." She ruffled his hair with affection as she said it. Who would have ever thought she'd get this lucky? To have this gorgeous, sexy man want her in his life?

Jorge leaned into her and whispered in her ear. "Use your imagination."

His warm breath created warm ripples of desire all through her.

"I already am," she answered just before she brought her lips up to his.

Jorge didn't need any more of a hint than that. He'd always considered himself pretty quick on the uptake.

This time was no exception. His lips met hers as his soul gratefully slipped back into the paradise that only she created for him.

* * * * *

VALENTINE'S FORTUNE

BY
ALLISON LEIGH

Allison Leigh started early by writing a Halloween play that her grade-school class performed. Since then, though her tastes have changed, her love for reading has not. And her writing appetite simply grows more voracious by the day.

She has been a finalist in the RITA® Award and the Holt Medallion contests. But the true highlights of her day as a writer are when she receives word from a reader that they laughed, cried or lost a night of sleep while reading one of her books.

Born in Southern California, Allison has lived in several different cities in four different states. She has been, at one time or another, a cosmetologist, a computer programmer and a secretary. She has recently begun writing full-time after spending nearly a decade as an administrative assistant for a busy neighbourhood church, and currently makes her home in Arizona with her family. She loves to hear from her readers, who can write to her at PO Box 40772, Mesa, AZ 85274-0772, USA.

For my own Valentine.

Prologue

"Miss?" The deep voice seemed to come at Bethany from a long, hollow distance. "I'm with the Red Rock Fire Department. You're safe now. Just open your eyes."

Her throat hurt. Breathing in made her nose burn. She wanted to sleep. How long had it been since she'd had a decent night's sleep? Since before…before what?

Her brain searched, but all it found was fog. Thick, choking fog.

"Come on now, darlin'. Open your eyes for me."

She was floating in the fog. Was she flying? Someone had told her if she flew in her dreams that meant something good.

A dream. That was it. She was dreaming.

"Dammit, make a hole," the deep voice barked. "She needs air."

She winced. She wanted to shrink away from the harsh command in his voice. Didn't he know she was sleeping?

"Breathe through my mask." The voice was low again. Intimate. "It'll help."

Something covered her face. She pushed at it. Tried to protest. Sucked in oddly sweet air. She turned her head away. "No." The word scraped her raw throat.

"That's it, Miss. Come on back to us. You're doing fine now."

She could follow that voice anywhere. Even up and out of her dreaming fog.

"You're safe now," he coaxed softly. A lover's whisper.

No. That wasn't right. Her lover was…where?

She frowned at the pain inside her head. "No."

"Yes, you are safe. I promise. Just open your eyes. You'll see. Can you tell me your name?"

Bethany. The name sighed through her. *My name is Bethany.*

She jerked, her eyes flying open to stare into the face of the man speaking to her.

Voices. Shouting. Sirens. Smoke. Flashing lights.

It all accosted her in that instant and fear shot through her, making her stiffen. She tried to work her hand to her abdomen, but couldn't seem to manage it. "What?"

"Can you tell me your name?"

Relief was swift, but fleeting. She hadn't said her name. Or if she had, he hadn't heard it. Not over the incredible clamoring confusion surrounding them.

She started to clear her throat. Coughed. What was the name she was using? "Barbara," she finally supplied. Her voice wasn't much more than a croak. Her brain just didn't feel like cooperating. "Burr—" *Not Burdett. Not Burdett.* "Burton." That was her borrowed name. "What happened?"

"Don't worry about a thing now, Barbara. You're safe," was all he said. "I've got you now."

He was carrying her, she realized, and just as quickly she

felt consumed with dizziness. She closed her eyes, but that didn't help. "I feel sick."

The floating, rocking motion ceased. "I'll bet. I'm going to put you on the stretcher now. Just relax."

She opened her eyes again as he settled her on a firm, blessedly steady surface. "What happened?" she asked again. He had streaks on his face. Like war paint. And shoulders wider than a linebacker. He looked armed for battle.

She realized vaguely that a large white van was next to them.

"I almost didn't find you when we were clearing the restaurant." He'd leaned down closer to her and his voice was softer. Impossibly gentle.

Comforting.

She blinked. Rubbed her eyes. Realized that they were watering.

"The smoke was thick in there. You were unconscious," he said. "They're going to take you to the hospital. Just as a precaution. Make sure you're all right."

She didn't want to go to the hospital. She wanted, she wanted…she didn't know what she wanted. "A fire," she said, stupidly. Thickly. Even now, she could see the lick of hungry red lighting the sky beyond the van—an ambulance. And beyond that, a rise of thick, cloying smoke.

Oh, God.

She slid her hand over her abdomen. Please, *please* be all right. "I came for an enchilada."

His teeth flashed. "Afraid you'll have to wait a while for that. Inhaling smoke the way you did can make you pretty woozy," he said.

It wasn't war paint on his face. It was soot. And the armor he wore was a fireman's uniform.

"*You* rescued me?"

"Yes, ma'am." She realized his grin was slightly crooked. "And you're gonna be just fine, Barbara. D'ya have someone you want us to call? Husband? Boyfriend? Who were you with at Red?"

Red. The restaurant. She'd been treating herself to the first meal out she'd had since she'd landed in Red Rock. A woman only turned twenty-five once in her life, right?

"Barbara?"

Her mind was wandering. She knew it. She just couldn't seem to make herself stop. "I'm not married." It seemed to be the only clear thought in her head. "There's no one to call."

"We've got her now, Darr." A woman and another man appeared beside the stretcher and before Bethany could marshal another coherent sentence, they pushed the stretcher and she felt herself slide smoothly into the rear of the white ambulance. The woman followed her.

But Bethany wasn't looking at her.

She was watching the fireman, still standing there.

And then the ambulance doors closed and she wanted to protest, but it was already too late, because she could feel the vehicle begin to move.

The ambulance attendant closed her cool fingers around Bethany's wrist. "What's your name, ma'am?"

Bethany closed her eyes again. In her mind, though, was the firefighter's crooked grin. His deep, gentle voice.

"Barbara." Again, the lie scraped along her raw throat. "Barbara Burton."

Chapter One

Two Weeks Later

"Y ou know you're nuts, right? Might even say you're obsessed. Face it. The woman's gone. Like a lot of folks, she was probably just passing through Red Rock, anyway."

Darr Fortune eyed his brother, Nick, over the lunch counter at SusieMae's. "Thanks for the support."

Nick grinned. "That's why you wanted me to move back here, isn't it? Give my baby bro some ego boosting?"

"Yeah. That was it," Darr agreed drily. He was the youngest of five, it was true, with an entire decade between him and JR, the oldest. But one thing he'd never particularly lacked was ego. A trait shared by his four brothers. "Didn't have a thing to do with the Foundation."

"You just wanted me to put in my time there so *your* conscience would be clear to play around with matches and rescue damsels in distress." Nick flicked the pink message slip that sat on the counter between their empty lunch plates. Around them, SusieMae's buzzed with customers. Most likely because SusieMae's pretty waitresses wore short, sassy little checkered dresses that looked as though they'd been designed by Daisy Mae, herself. "Like the blond babe you've been hunting for since Red went up in smoke."

"I haven't been hunting for her." The denial was weak, and he knew it. So did his brother, considering the way Nick snorted. "I'm only trying to follow up. Make sure she's all right. I *did* pull her out of a burnin' building." He kept his voice light. Not even Nick would know how hard that was.

"Two weeks ago, Darr. And nobody says you're not a hero. Though why you want to go into something that's on fire when everyone else with a lick of sense is trying to get out still escapes me." He pushed a pair of glasses onto his nose and picked up the message slip. "Whoever wrote this ought to be sent back to school. I can't tell the sevens from ones, and is that last number an eight or what?"

"Devaney took the message." Darr slid the message out of his brother's fingers and peered at it himself. He'd been puzzling over the writing ever since he'd found the message tacked to the board outside his quarters at the firehouse. "Except for the street—I think it's Windrose—I can't read the rest of the address he wrote down, either. And Devaney can't remember." The other man was a hell of an engineer, but he was miserable when it came to remembering the details of anything that didn't pertain to a burn. "He couldn't even tell me who called with the address."

It probably hadn't been the hospital, relenting on its confidentiality stance. More likely, it was one of the cabbies Darr had bribed. Hitting it lucky by finding the one who'd actually driven Barbara Burton away from the hospital when she had checked herself out almost as quickly as the ambulance had gotten her there.

"I'm telling you. Obsessed. You ought to put that attention into taking the next promotion exam for captain."

Darr let that pass and Nick picked up his coffee mug, which had gone empty for too long, and gestured toward the waitress behind the counter. "Hey there, sugar. Have some hot stuff any time soon?"

Sugar, more commonly known as Lorena, strolled over and leaned against the lunch counter, giving them both a healthy view of her award-winning cleavage above pink and white checks while she refilled Nick's cup. "This soon enough for you, cutie pie?"

"It is now," Nick toasted her with his cup.

"You want a top-off, Darr?" Lorena barely looked his way. Why would she? Darr was a regular in SusieMae's. Had been since he'd moved to Red Rock from California alone himself, a few years back. She'd learned quickly enough that he wasn't the kind of man she wanted—namely, someone other than a firefighter.

Nick, however, was fresh pickings.

"I'm good, Lorena. Thanks."

"Heard you're working at the Fortune Foundation," Lorena said to Nick. "A financial analyst. Guess little ol' Red Rock must seem pretty tame after Los Angeles."

"Darr got used to it well enough." Nick eyed her, his amusement plain. "And I've always been better at everything than my baby brother."

Lorena glanced at Darr. "Really." Her speculative gaze slid back to Nick's. "I might just have to test that out someday."

"Lorena, order's up," SusieMae barked from the kitchen. *She* did not wear a dress short on length and low on material. A true blessing to the thriving community of Red Rock, Texas.

Lorena straightened up in a leisurely way. "See you later, cutie." She went over to the window and collected her order.

"Maybe Red Rock'll be more entertaining than I thought it would be," Nick mused.

"Oh, Lorena's entertaining all right." Darr pulled out his wallet. "But she doesn't want just a good time. She wants a ring and a baby carriage, too."

"Now, what makes a perfectly attractive woman want to go ruining things that way?" Nick shuddered as he pulled a clip of folded bills from his pocket. "I got it."

Darr tossed enough bills onto the counter to pay for his own meal with a decent tip for Lorena included. The Fortunes might be a wealthy bunch, but he'd always made his own way on his own terms. "I'm not broke." Not that he was earning here what he'd pulled down back in California. But his reasons for coming to Red Rock had much less to do with money than to do with his sanity.

Which Nick figured he'd now lost, anyway, given his futile hunt for the blonde from the fire at Red.

Maybe he's right.

Making certain that Barbara Burton was all right wouldn't erase what had happened with Celia in California.

"Geez." Nick's voice brought Darr back from thoughts of the woman he hadn't been able to save despite his best efforts. "Nobody said you *were* broke. Maybe you'd better go find the blonde, after all. A roll with a pretty woman might make you less touchy. Most folks are happy to get a free meal."

"I'm not looking for a roll." Just a way to sleep at night.

He shoved the message slip into his pocket and grabbed his leather jacket off the empty stool beside them, heading for the door. "Or a free meal."

Nick caught up to him, pulling on his own coat. "Christ, it's cold. This time of year the weather shouldn't be much different from Los Angeles. If I'd wanted to freeze, I could've taken that job in Chicago I was offered last year. Did you see the weather report this morning? They say if the storm veers, it could actually snow here."

"Don't bet on it. I don't care what the weather reports say. It hasn't snowed here in more than twenty years." But they could see their breath, which wasn't at all usual, and the sky looked heavy and gray. "So how *are* things going at the Foundation?"

Nick shrugged, shoving his bare hands into his pockets. "They're fine. Working for a philanthropic outfit is definitely different. Red Rock is different than it used to be, too. Helluva lot bigger." They reached their vehicles—Nick's racy Porsche and Darr's not-so-new black pickup, parked slantwise into the curb in front of the busy diner. "How long are you going to keep hunting for this woman?"

Until I find her. Darr pulled open his truck door. "I'm not hunting."

"Yeah, right. You know there'd be easier chicks to have the hots for than some woman who basically disappeared in the night."

"I don't—"

"Save it." Nick shook his head and pulled open his own door. "Why d'ya think Uncle Patrick wants to meet us out at the Double Crown later? His and Lacey's place in town would be more convenient than Lily's." Lily had been married to their father's and uncle's cousin, Ryan Fortune, and after his death had thrown herself even more into the kind of good works that Ryan had always favored.

"At first I thought it must be something to do with the charity event Lily's hosting at the ranch later this month, but now I don't think so. Patrick wouldn't call in the entire family for a children's picnic. I hope to hell it's not 'cause he's sick or something."

Nick grimaced. It was all too easy remembering when their mother, Molly, had died just two years earlier. Typically though, neither one of them commented on that. "You got the shift off?" was all Nick asked.

"Switched with another guy to get it."

"Dad and the others are taking a car in from the airport, so I could pick you up on my way out there."

Darr shook his head. "I've got some stuff to do first. I'll just see you there."

"Stuff. Like your blonde." Nick shook his head again, as if he wanted to say more, but he refrained, and slid down into his car. "Later."

Darr returned the brief wave and got behind the wheel of his truck. He didn't watch Nick pull out into the moderately busy traffic on the main drag behind him. He was too busy trying to decipher the address Devaney had jotted on the phone message.

Nick was right: Darr was nuts. What else could explain the lengths he'd gone to trying to track *her* down?

Barbara Burton.

His thumb beat against his steering wheel as he waited for a rusted-out station wagon to pass.

It wasn't just her name that stuck in Darr's thoughts.

It was those cornflower-blue eyes of hers.

No, not just blue. Despite the light that night, mutated and muddled by the flashing beacons, by spotlights, by smoke and flames, he'd been able to see that bruising color. The panic in them, followed by relief. Trust. The intimate, soul-wrenching kind of trust that had absolutely nothing to do with sex and everything to do with a basic human need for connection.

That, and the discernible swell of her abdomen that he'd felt when he'd lifted her unconscious and otherwise very slender form, off that smoke-filled restroom floor.

A horn tooted.

He blinked, and shoved the truck into Reverse, backing out into the road, clearing the parking spot for the SUV waiting behind him.

For two weeks, he'd tried to coax and cajole information about Barbara from anyone and everyone who'd had contact with her the night of the fire. The best he'd gotten out of the emergency room had been that she'd left AMA—against medical advice—in a cab. That had led to some greasing of palms at all the cab companies that could conceivably service the community of Red Rock, which was located about twenty miles outside of San Antonio.

His attempts had involved a fair number of cab companies. It had meant a lot of "grease."

Darr probably would have been wiser to let Nick pay for his lunch.

He turned off Main and wound his way through a quieter, modest residential area until he reached Windrose. There, he turned left and began hunting for the first possible combination of house numbers from the message.

Four houses later, he'd netted himself two slammed doors in his face and a third, more kindly shake of a head before the door closed. In his face. The fourth house, he hadn't gotten an answer to his knock at all, but the sight of two motocross bicycles and an abandoned hockey stick in the front yard made him pause.

Barbara Burton had told him that night that she had no husband. And while he strongly suspected that she was pregnant now, she nevertheless looked too young to have children old enough to ride those bikes. Still, he scrawled a note on the back of his business card that he was looking for Barbara Burton and tucked it into the doorframe.

He returned to his truck, and headed back in the other direction. The street narrowed. Well-tended yards grew smaller and then disappeared altogether.

He grimaced when the pavement ended, leaving nothing but scattered gravel and ruts.

In the few years since he'd moved to Red Rock, he'd thought he'd learned every bend in every corner in every street. But he knew for a fact that he'd never been out this way.

He passed a turnoff just before the road started to climb. A lone house sat facing the other street and he followed it, but the address on the mailbox stuck in the weedy yard wasn't remotely close to Devaney's scrawl and he veered around back to the original road. For all he knew when he reached the top of the hill, it would end at exactly nothing, and this would be just one more wasted afternoon looking for a woman who might as well be a ghost.

He crested the hill and a small house came into view.

His boot lifted off the gas and the truck slowed, nearly coming to a stop. In his chest, though, his heart had started pounding. His hands tightened around the steering wheel.

The house—hell, it was more of a cottage, considering its size—sat about fifty yards off the miserable excuse of a road. There was no neatly trimmed, nicely bordered lawn in front of it. Instead, there was cold, bare dirt. Scrubby bushes. The cottage had probably been painted a cheery yellow once, but now it just looked faded and sad, and the open-sided carport next to it seemed to have a tilt. But there was a curl of smoke coming from the chimney, and the rear corner of a car was visible in the listing carport.

So his foot hit the gas again.

Gravel spit from beneath his tires. "Get a grip, Fortune," he muttered, and turned toward the house, heading up a virtually nonexistent driveway.

He parked in front of the cottage and when he got out, the slam of his truck door sounded loud and ungodly intrusive. He looked around. There didn't seem to be a breathing soul anywhere.

It was almost hard to believe he was still in Red Rock.

He exhaled, causing another cloud to ring around his head, and brushed his sweating hands down the front of shirt before pulling up the zipper on his jacket. If this *wasn't* Barbara's house, he was going to tear up that damn message and that would be the end of it.

No more hunting. No more obsessing.

She was a woman with her own life who didn't need complete strangers tracking her down, and finding her wouldn't change the things for him that couldn't be changed.

He rounded his truck and went up the three cracked concrete steps leading to the door and knocked.

No answer.

He knocked again, craning his head back to look at the smoke rising from the chimney. Definitely an active little blaze in the fireplace. But there was still no answer.

He knocked harder. "Hello! Anybody there? I'm with the Red Rock Fire Department," he called out. "I'm looking for Barbara Burton."

* * *

Bethany jumped when the deep voice—oh, it sounded much too familiar—passed easily through the thin door.

She pressed her hand to her heart, willing it to calm. At least it wasn't Lyle. Or worse—her parents.

She hid behind the faded curtain at the front window, and lifted the corner of the thin fabric. Just an inch. Just enough to see the front stoop.

The man standing there was definitely not her father. He wasn't as tall as Lyle, but his shoulders were about a mile wider. She'd never seen her ex-fiancé wear blue jeans—not once in the four years she'd known him—but if she had, she knew the rear view of him in them wouldn't have been as stellar as the one on her porch.

Like a hunting dog scenting its prey, the shaggy dark blond head turned at just that moment, catching her peeking through the curtain.

She jumped back, dropping the curtain back into place.

This time when her heart thudded unsteadily, it wasn't fear that her parents and Lyle had managed to track her down to press her into the marriage that was only designed to benefit them.

The thin door rattled again under the firefighter's firm knock. "Ms. Burton. Answer the door, would you? I'm not here to bother you. Not for long, anyway. I'm just, uh, just doing some follow-up."

She ran her hands down the long sleeves of her oversize fisherman's sweater. Pushed the hem farther down the thighs of her jeans. Cautiously moved around to the door and undid the lock. She pulled the door open as far as the safety latch allowed. She'd installed it herself, miraculously enough. Armed with an instruction booklet from the hardware store and using tools that the kindly manager there had let her borrow.

She eyed the fireman through the two-inch space. "Follow-up?"

He turned his light-blue eyes her way and smiled, causing faint crows' feet to crinkle appealingly into existence. "Yes, ma'am."

Her heart did a squiggly little dance inside her chest. She tightened her grip on the doorknob. "Is that common? I mean, I've never been rescued from a burning building before. I don't know the protocol, I guess."

His head tilted to one side. "It's not unheard of."

Unfortunately, she didn't know what to make of that. But the gust of cold wind blowing in through the crack was enough to jog her into action. "Just a minute." She pushed the door closed again, slid off the safety bolt, and opened it again. "It's freezing out there. Maybe you should come in." He'd saved her life, after all. Leaving him standing out on the porch just seemed impolite.

She felt a vague sense of hysteria. Such a thought could have come out of her mother's all-about-propriety lips.

His head dipped a little as he entered, and a quick vision of him tipping the brim of a cowboy hat in some old-fashioned, courtly gesture flitted through her head.

Her hormones weren't just wreaking havoc with her body. They were doing a number on her imagination, too.

She hurriedly pushed the door shut, feeling the resistance against the gusting wind. But then that left her facing *him*.

He wasn't exactly staring at her, though. No, he was too busy glancing around the modest confines of her simple house.

Home, she corrected mentally. This was her home now. And it was far preferable to the palatial estate she'd grown up in.

"You should turn that screen around in front of your fire," he said after a moment. "It's backwards."

She looked toward the fireplace, feeling foolish. In the six weeks since she'd lived in the cottage, her ability to lay a fire there had improved considerably. For one thing, she'd learned how not to fill the small space with smoke. "I bought the screen second-hand," she admitted, going over to turn it around. The cottage hadn't come with one.

What it had come equipped with was a hopelessly outdated couch upholstered in a hideous orange. A kidney-shaped cocktail table. Spindly-legged dinette set.

Anything else would just have to wait. At this point, and for some time to come, her money was too precious to waste.

She moistened her lips. The silence between them was painfully acute, broken only by the sharp whistle of wind outside and the soft crackling of the burning wood in the fireplace. "I never had a chance to thank you for what you did." She flushed a little. "I'm sorry. Do I call you *officer* or what?"

He shook his head, smiling faintly. "You can just call me Darr." His lashes were ridiculously thick.

And she felt ridiculous for noticing such a detail. He wasn't there as a prospective date, after all—even if she were in the market for such a thing. Which she wasn't.

Besides, he'd already said he was merely following up.

"Would you like something hot to drink…Darr?"

His smile widened. Enough to reveal a faint dimple alongside his sculpted lips. "That would be great."

She quickly looked away and moved over to her small, efficiency kitchen. "C-coffee?"

"Perfect."

It was perfect. And it kept her busy for a few minutes. Minutes that she should have been able to use forming something to say. Instead, she stood there at the minuscule counter, as tongue-tied as she could ever recall being, and focused on the coffee. The smell of it. The blessed act of adding grounds to the small coffeemaker. The spit and sigh of liquid when it streamed hot and fragrant into the glass pot.

Unfortunately, she could only inhale the aroma, since coffee was verboten these days. She finally looked back at him, only to find him standing at the window. He'd pulled aside the faded, floral curtain to look outside. "Do you take sugar? Cream?" Not that she had any cream. But she did have plenty of milk since it had now replaced her beloved coffee.

"Black's fine."

She turned back to her task and pulled a mug from the open shelf that ran the length of the wall above the stove and the sink. Aside from the cupboard next to the refrigerator, the shelf was about the only storage the kitchen afforded. She stood at the counter, watching the coffeepot slowly fill, feeling the tick of every second.

There'd been a time when she could at least carry on a conversation with anyone. Even a handsome stranger.

What had happened to her?

Foolish question, when she knew exactly what had happened. More particularly, *who* had happened.

She yanked the pot out a few moments too early and coffee drips sizzled against the hot plate. She filled his mug and turned to give it to him, only to start at the sight of him standing behind her. Coffee sloshed over the edge of the mug and she sucked in a breath, hastily setting it back down.

He tsked. "I didn't mean to startle you. Better run that under water."

She evidently didn't move quickly enough to suit him,

because he took her wrist, nudging her back the two steps it took to reach her sink, and turned on the ancient faucet.

Air seemed to stop up in her chest as he guided her hand beneath the cool water. She prayed that he couldn't feel the way her pulse had started racing.

"Better?" His voice was soft, brushing against her temple.

She swallowed. Nodded jerkily. "Yes. Thank you."

"Don't thank me. I'm the one who made you jump." He switched off the faucet and gently wrapped the inexpensive tea towel she'd had looped over the oven door handle around her wrist. He blotted away the water and looked at the pinkish mark that still remained on the back of her hand and wrist. His lips compressed. "I don't know what's worse than a burn."

"It hardly stings," she assured. At least she was hardly aware of it when every other nerve in her body was attuned much more acutely to something else.

Him.

She picked up the mug again, refilled it, and handed it to him. "Have a seat."

He walked to the couch. "You're not having any?"

She wiped up the spill with the tea towel and sat on one of the kitchen table chairs. "Keeps me awake at night." Her hands were brushing nervously over her thighs and she tucked her fingers beneath her legs to hide them. "Do you need to fill out a report or something?"

His eyes narrowed over the brim of the mug as he sipped the hot brew. "Report?"

"You know. Follow-up and all that."

"Not exactly."

She felt a fluttering in her abdomen. "Did the hospital give you my address?"

He leaned forward and set the mug on the table in front of him. He'd unzipped his leather jacket and it parted enough for her to see a dark blue T-shirt beneath, with a Maltese cross and "RRFD" printed in white letters on the front. "Something like that."

She tried not to let panic run rampant through her. He'd found Barbara Burton. Not Bethany Burdett. There was no reason to think that Lyle or her parents were any closer to finding her.

"If I'd gotten a phone number for you, I'd have called first. The hospital told me you'd left AMA."

She smiled weakly. Her phone number—"Barbara Burton's" phone number—was unlisted and she certainly hadn't left it with the hospital. She'd only hooked up the phone line because common sense told her that she should, given her situation. "The hospital wanted me to stay for observation. Just…in case. But the doctor told me I was fine, so I came home. It's a lot more affordable sleeping in my own bed than in a hospital one." She didn't know why she was explaining herself to him, but she couldn't seem to stop herself.

Maybe it was those kind eyes of his.

"Insurance?"

She shook her head. "Not yet." But soon.

"I don't mean to pry, but you know there *are* programs."

He meant charitable ones, she knew. Like those administered and funded by the Fortune Foundation where she'd managed to get a job as a receptionist. "I know. But I've just started a new job. I couldn't afford to miss work."

He didn't look entirely convinced. She supposed firefighters with the Red Rock Fire Department were covered with more than adequate health insurance. And truthfully, before she'd escaped from Dallas, she'd never thought about her own need for it because her parents had handled such matters. And after her parents, it would have been Lyle to see to that sort of detail.

Naive. She'd been so painfully naive. Keeping busy with attending the charity balls that *her* family had supported. Picking out the gowns for her ten bridesmaids. Selecting the most suitable china pattern to grace her and Lyle's dining table. And all the while she'd never known the real reason behind Lyle's proposal.

"Where *do* you work?"

She rose and went to the fireplace, and took a split log from the untidy stack of them on the hearth. "The Fortune Foundation." She moved the screen aside long enough to carefully stick the log on the dwindling fire.

"No kidding."

She looked over her shoulder, catching a somewhat bemused look on his face.

"Is that so surprising?" She couldn't think why it would be. *He* didn't know who she really was. What kind of frivolous, useless life she'd led before she'd escaped.

"No. The Foundation employs plenty of folks around here. It just seems kind of ironic."

She brushed her hands together and straightened. "Why?" Lordy, but the man had such a face. She'd been able to tell that even when he'd been streaked with soot and she'd been incapable of coherent thought.

"I've been hunting for you for two weeks," he admitted, still with that faint smile toying around his lips. "And there you were, under our nose all that time."

Hunting? A sliver of unease slid through her. "*Our* nose?"

"The Fortunes," he said easily. "I'm Darr Fortune."

She swallowed. "I see." Which meant he was probably rich as sin and raised in privilege.

Just like Lyle.

"Well." She brushed her hands together again. "As you can see, I haven't suffered any ill effects from the fire. Thanks to you."

She was fine.

More important, the baby she was carrying was fine.

And it was time for this wealthy, privileged, handsome man to go.

Happily, Darr took her hint. "Right." He pushed to his feet and she had the fanciful impression of a deceptively lazy cat rising out of the grass. "Like I promised, I wouldn't take up much of your time." He headed to the door, only to stop and pull something from the inside pocket of his jacket. "If you ever need anything, you just call." He handed her a small white business card.

She took it, excruciatingly aware of how carefully she avoided touching him. The Fire Department insignia embossed on the corner winked up at her. "Lt. Darwin Fortune" was printed in the center. "I'm sure I won't, but thank you."

He nodded and after a hesitation that she wasn't sure if she'd imagined, he reached for the doorknob. "Or you can call even if you don't need anything," he added with a quirk of a smile.

Her mouth ran dry. She didn't know what to say to that and all that came out was an embarrassingly inadequate "Oh."

The quirk twisted a little. "Be sure and keep that fire banked now." He opened the door.

And they both gaped at the wholly unexpected sight of snow.

Chapter Two

"Damn," Darr breathed, disbelieving. He'd never hear the end of this from Nick. "Would you look at that?"

Barbara slid between him and the doorway, peering out. "I didn't think it snowed here!"

He dragged his abruptly diverted attention away from the soft scent of her hair and looked over her head at the strange sight. "It hasn't ever since I've lived here."

She tilted her head, looking up at him, and the impact of those purple-blue eyes of hers was like a blow to his midsection. "How long is that?"

"Close to three years. The forecast earlier said the storm might veer this way, but—" He shook his head, still bemused. Hell, he was a Southern California kid despite the cowboy boots on his feet. Snow wasn't in his vocabulary unless he'd been heading out for a ski trip.

Already a thin layer of white was lacing across the hood

of his truck, only to get snatched away in a swirling gust of wind that seemed to head right through the doorway where they stood.

She shivered and quickly shut the door again, leaning back against it. "So much for forecasts." She brushed her hand through her hair, drawing it away from her smooth forehead. "Maybe you'd better wait until it lets up."

He didn't have to glance at his watch to know he was already cutting things close with the family meeting his uncle Patrick had called. It would take some time to drive out to the Double Crown as it was. And it didn't take a genius to recognize that though Barbara had made the offer for him to stay, she wasn't holding her breath in anticipation that he'd accept.

If anything, she looked nervous at his presence.

Another blast of wind whistled past her window and the bare lightbulb in her kitchen flickered. "Do you have more wood?"

She nodded. "The owners have a stack under the carport that they said I could use if I wanted." She smiled weakly. "I never thought I would be in a situation to *need* it, though. I just liked the scent of a fire in the fireplace. You, um, you don't think the electricity will go out, do you? Everything in here runs on electricity, including the heat."

She plainly hoped he would reassure her that it wouldn't. "Probably better to be safe," he said. "I'll bring in more wood for you just in case. If you've got candles or a lantern—" she pulled a face at that one "—candles, then, or a flashlight, you might put them out somewhere handy."

She moved by him, and he quickly headed out the door. But again the soft, feminine scent of her as she'd brushed past him stuck in his head.

He found the firewood stacked against the side of the house, but few of the logs had been split. He wasted some time looking around for an axe to rectify that, but didn't find one. Not even in the storage bin squatting in front of her twenty-year-old sedan. So he gathered up the pieces that *had* been split and carried them inside, bowing his head against the stinging wind.

One more armload, and he'd made a stack of wood that climbed a reasonable piece up the wall next to the fireplace. "That ought to be enough to keep you warm through the night even if the electricity does fail." She'd need wood in the morning if it did, though, which meant he'd be coming back— with an axe—one way or the other.

Her heart-shaped face seemed to pale a little more. "It's just a little snow. I'm sure it'll stop any minute."

"You're probably right," he agreed, keeping his tone easy. He moved aside the curtain again and looked out. If anything, the sky looked even heavier. Darker. He dropped the curtain again. If he was going to get to the Double Crown, he needed to get moving.

Knowing that didn't alleviate his reluctance over leaving her, though.

She had a small television sitting on one corner of a dresser across from the couch. "You might want to keep that on," he suggested. "Watch for the weather report." The snow was one thing, the plummeting temperature another. She might need to burn the wood even if the electricity held. By the looks of the cottage, he doubted it came equipped with anything other than the most rudimentary heating system.

She'd folded her arms across her chest. "I will." But she made no move toward the television and he couldn't help but wonder if the ancient-looking thing even worked. He also knew that asking if it did would probably just embarrass her. And she'd been embarrassed enough about the fireplace screen.

She had wood, he reasoned inwardly. She'd put out a few thick candles and a box of matches on the table. She had a phone. It was an old rotary-style model; a landline that didn't depend on electricity.

"Would you like more coffee?"

He shook his head. "I really do need to go," he said truthfully.

Her lashes fell. "Thanks for bringing in the wood." Her voice was almost shy.

"No problem. You've got my number."

"Yes."

That reluctance remained heavy inside him, but he went to the door, anyway. His last glance at her before he let himself out into the blowing snow showed that she hadn't moved. Her arms still crossed, her feet still planted.

And he could see the edge of the business card she was still clutching against the sleeve of her thick, oversize sweater.

He let out a breath and made himself move toward the truck. The lacy white layer over it had woven into a full blanket. He got inside the cab, cranked the engine—and the heat. His wipers cut arching swaths through the layer of snow on his windshield as he steered away from the small house. The truck rocked and jolted over the deep ruts. It took no great imagination to know that her old car would have a helluva lot more difficulty maneuvering the near-trenches even if they weren't filling up with snow.

He made it all the way down the hill, past the lone turnoff and her nearest neighbor before he stood on his brakes and pulled out his cell phone.

Nick answered on the third ring. "Should've taken that bet on the snow after all," his brother greeted. "Where are you?"

"Still in town. Tell Patrick I'm not gonna make it."

"No kidding. Well, whatever is going down here can't be

good. Even Aunt Cindy is here, acting like the Queen herself. Lily is looking pained, and that takes some work."

Darr rubbed his forehead. He was hard-pressed to think of a more gracious woman than Lily Fortune. On the other hand, Darr barely knew their father's only sister, Cindy. Aside from the fact that she'd had nothing much to do with the rest of the Fortunes during Darr's lifetime, she was supposedly pretty flamboyant. She'd spent a good amount of time collecting and discarding husbands, and had little contact with the kids she'd produced along the way.

His father and brothers fly in from California, and now his elusive aunt has come to town? Whatever Patrick wanted to meet about *had* to be critical.

More critical than a perfectly capable woman he barely knew.

"Okay. I'm leaving now," he said decisively.

"Wait up. I thought you knew. The roads have been closed. Only way you're going to get out here to the ranch is if you're on a fire truck with the sirens going and the lights flashing."

Darr muttered an oath and flipped on his scanner. It was filled with chatter about the storm. He always kept the scanner on when he was driving, but for once, his preoccupation with Barbara had taken precedence. "I need to check in at the firehouse." For emergency situations, all members of the department were expected to be on call. "Keep your phone on, will you? I want to know what's so all-fire important to Patrick."

"Will do. Any luck deciphering that address?"

Darr didn't want to talk about Barbara. If the department called him in, he wasn't going to be any more good to her than he was to the family out at the ranch. "Yeah."

"And?"

"And nothing. I've gotta run." He didn't wait for Nick's response as he disconnected the call. With his engine idling and his wipers rhythmically doing their best to conquer the snow, he called in to the department, only to be told emphatically by Devaney that the chief wanted everyone to stay put, right where they were. If the department needed him, they'd send out a vehicle to collect him. As it was, the mayor wanted to declare a state of emergency, based on the freak storm.

The problem was that if the department did send a vehicle for him, Darr knew they'd be going to the apartment he rented across town. So he reluctantly gave Devaney Barbara's address instead, and made the man repeat it back, just to be certain he could read his own miserable writing. "It's a friend's place."

"All your friends are firemen," Devaney drawled. "And they don't live way the hell and gone outside of town."

"She's not a firefighter," he said evenly, knowing that tidbit would earn him an immeasurable amount of ribbing, but it couldn't be helped. "Hopefully the charge in my cell will last until the storm passes."

"At least you'll have fun staying warm," Devaney pointed out. "That is, if you remember how all that works since you've barely had a date with a woman since you moved here."

"At least she's a woman." Darr pulled his truck around in a slow turn. "Unlike the sheep you stupidly prefer over Lorena."

Devaney laughed and told Darr what he could do with himself before hanging up on him. Darr dropped his phone on the console and worked his way back up the hill. Even kicking in the four-wheel drive, the truck struggled with the snowy climb. Once he made it, he looked back down the hill. Or what he could see of it, considering the wall of white behind him that seemed to have no beginning or end.

Realizing that if he dawdled much longer he could well lose sight of Barbara's cottage, he gunned across her yard, not even making a pretense of trying to find that rutted driveway.

He aimed toward the porch, but only made it partway before his tires hit a rut that not even his powerful engine could breach. Swearing under his breath at the owners of the cottage for neglecting to grade the drive, he grabbed his phone and the first-aid kit and a heavy-duty flashlight from beneath his seat. He zipped his jacket to the neck and ducked his head into the storm.

By the time he made it up the porch steps, snow was sliding down his collar, and his hands felt numb when he knocked hard on the door. "Ms. Burton?" The wind carried away his voice, but he yelled through the door, anyway. "It's Darr Fortune again."

The wind nearly pushed him through the doorway when it suddenly opened. Barbara scrambled out of the way before he ran into her. "Sorry." He hastily shut the door again, but it still wasn't fast enough to keep snow from blowing in over the threshold.

"That's okay." She looked startled. "Your hair looks icy! What's wrong?"

He dumped his belongings on the end of the couch and shrugged out of his jacket. Compared to the outdoors, the warmth of her cottage felt almost sweltering. "Do you have a towel? I think I'm dripping on your rug."

"I don't think a little water can do more damage to it." But she quickly left the room and returned with an oversize terry cloth towel. "Here."

He swiped it over his head and his wet neck, then tossed it on the threadbare brown rug. Standing on the towel, he managed to pull off his wet boots, and he stepped off the towel to leave them there instead.

When he looked up at her again, her eyes were even wider, running from his stocking feet up to his face and back down again. "It's worse out there than I expected," he prefaced.

Her hand waved toward the TV. She'd turned it on while he'd been gone. It showed a snowy, but decipherable picture. "The newscaster was talking about a state of emergency."

"I heard. The roads have been closed, too."

She swallowed. "For how long? No. Don't answer that. They wouldn't know that yet, would they." It wasn't a question. "You…you'll just have to stay here then."

"I'm sorry."

She shook her head. "There's no reason for you to be. It's not your fault." She looked back at the television. Then toward her nearly nonexistent kitchen. Anywhere, he noticed, but at him. "I don't have a lot of space. Obviously. But I guess we'll manage. Do you want more of that coffee now?"

"That'd be nice. Thanks."

Her smile was small, but looked genuine. She went to the counter and pulled down the same mug he'd used before. While he'd been gone, she'd obviously washed and dried it. The coffee, however, was still in the pot and still hot. Even when he sat down on the couch, he could see the small green power light on the coffeemaker.

In seconds, she returned, handing him the mug.

"Thanks."

"Are you hungry?"

"Had a late lunch."

She looked only slightly relieved as she perched on the seat of the chair. He'd starve before he'd empty her refrigerator of the contents that he suspected might be meager. "Nick and I— my brother, Nick, he works at the Foundation now."

She slanted a shy gaze toward him. "I haven't met him, but I saw the memo announcing when he started there."

"Right. Anyway, we had lunch today at SusieMae's. They make a great steak sandwich."

"I've seen the restaurant but haven't been inside."

"*Restaurant* seems like a fancy name for the place." He kept his tone calm and light. It was plain that it wouldn't take much for Barbara to jump right out of her skin. "But the food *is* good. SusieMae even has enchiladas on the menu," he added. "Never bothered having one there, though, since Red's always been the place to go for good Mexican food."

Her eyebrows crinkled toward each other over the bridge of her straight little nose. "That's nice," she said slowly.

He set his coffee mug on the spindly coffee table. "The night of the fire, you told me you'd just gone there for an enchilada."

"Oh." Her forehead smoothed out again. "I don't remember telling you that."

"Yeah. People say all sorts of things when there's a fire around their ears."

She suddenly looked painfully casual. "What else did I tell you?"

"Nothing much." There were secrets in those blue eyes. He wondered how many of them had to do with the baby he was fairly certain she was carrying. "You were pretty out of it, which is normal. You told me you didn't want us to call anyone for you." No boyfriend. No husband, she'd said.

So where was the baby's father?

"Right. I do remember that." Her hands were twisted together in her lap, and when she realized his gaze had dropped to them, she flattened them. Brushed her palms down the drawn-up sleeves of her thick sweater, as if she were merely pulling them down over her delicately formed wrists because of the cooling room and looked away from him again.

He hid a sigh. If he couldn't get her to relax that skittishness of hers, they were in for a long evening.

He didn't want to think just yet about what they'd do if he was stuck there all night.

Unfortunately, as the gray afternoon light dwindled into darkness and the snow kept falling, Darr figured he'd be finding out soon enough.

Eventually, Barbara turned on a second lamp. There were only two, and mismatched as hell, but they worked, and that's what counted. "I'd better check the heater." She disappeared for a moment down the hall.

He hoped that hall led to a bedroom, but he wasn't confident that it did. From the outside, the cottage had looked no larger than the space that he could see from right where he sat. If there was no separate bedroom, then she slept right here in this room. He had no idea when sofa beds came into production, but the couch looked as old as he was.

He heard her footsteps and he shoved the cushion that he'd started to check beneath back down into place and picked up his coffee mug again. He'd been drawing out the mug's contents, and the brew wasn't even close to lukewarm anymore. "So tell me about your work with the Foundation," he said when she reappeared. "What do you do there?"

"I'm just a receptionist." She tucked her hair behind her ear and for about the millionth time, he noticed the lack of rings on her fingers. "Nothing as important as what your brother—or any of the other Fortunes do."

"Don't kid yourself. People walking in the office over there get to see *you* right off the bat. They're going to want to open their wallets that second."

Her eyes widened, and he realized just how poorly he'd phrased that; as if her mere presence served as an example of the need for charitable donations. "That didn't come out right. I meant that you're just so pretty, people are going to naturally want to hand over cash…hell." He could feel himself flushing and grimaced. "That's not sounding right, either. You can see why I stick to firefighting."

Her lips twitched. "I think there was a compliment in there somewhere, so I'll say thank you, and leave it at that."

"I appreciate that."

Her smile grew a little wider. "How long have you been a firefighter?"

He was a paramedic, too, but wasn't going to belabor the point. "About ten years now." He plucked the RRFD on the front of his T-shirt. "Been with the Red Rock department for nearly three."

"And before that?"

"Southern California. Born and raised there." He tilted the mug her direction. "You?"

She shrugged. "Texas." She didn't elaborate. "I don't know about you, but I'm getting hungry. I'd planned on spaghetti, but I could fix something else if you prefer."

"Spaghetti's pretty much our staff of life in the firehouse," he assured. "Can I help with anything?"

Her eyebrows rose and she gave a wry glance toward the kitchen area. "Yes, you can stay where you are, so I can reach the stove. As you can plainly see, space is in short supply here."

"If it meets your needs, who cares?"

Her gaze flickered for a moment. Another small smile played about her lips as if the comment pleased her. "True enough." She went over to the kitchen area and began pulling items out of the short, old-fashioned refrigerator. "Will you eat a salad?" She held up a head of lettuce.

"I'll eat anything."

"That's good." Her smile turned impish. "Because my

skills in the kitchen aren't likely to ever net me a job in the kitchen at Red."

"Until the restaurant opens up again, nobody's doing much of anything in the kitchen over there."

"I read in the newspaper that the cause was still under investigation?"

"Yes." The initial presumption of it being a grease fire had been loudly contested by the owner. The duration of the subsequent investigation suggested that José had been right. "They'll probably issue a public statement when the investigation is complete. Should be any day now."

"You can't talk about the details," she surmised.

"Even if I knew them."

"When do you think they'll be able to open again?"

"Not soon enough for José Mendoza. He's the owner. Don't worry, though. You'll be having enchiladas there again before you know it."

She actually laughed softly, and her smile widened enough to show the perfect fine edge of her white teeth. "I'll sleep better tonight, knowing that." She turned away to face the counter and fortunately missed the hard swallow that Darr had to make.

He'd never met a woman before who could make him stop breathing with a simple smile.

He ran his hand down his face. "Your bathroom?"

"Oh. Down the hall." Without taking her attention from what she was doing, she pointed the tip of her knife over her shoulder.

There'd been no other location it could be—other than an outhouse. It also gave him an excuse to see if there was a minuscule bedroom hidden beyond the short hall, too.

There wasn't.

He looked at his reflection in the mirrored medicine cabinet hanging on the wall over a chipped, but shiny clean pedestal sink.

Nick was right. He was nuts.

The bathroom was as small and spare as the rest of the place, particularly with a stacked washer and dryer taking up one corner, but she'd hung a cheerful striped shower curtain on the circular rod above the miniscule bathtub, and stacked matching towels on the iron shelf hanging on the wall. He left the bathroom behind and passed the bare hallway walls again.

There were no personal items around the house at all. No photographs. No dust collectors, as his mother used to call the knickknacks that she'd liked having around their house when he'd been growing up.

His apartment was mostly just a place for him to sleep when he wasn't on duty, but even *he* had some stuff on his walls. His shelves. Maybe they were only ball caps from his favorite teams and a mishmash of photographs—mostly ones his mom had framed and given him—but they were still his.

Barbara seemed to have nothing.

The picture on the television was even snowier than it had been earlier, and he fiddled with the rabbit ears protruding from the back with no results.

"It's hooked up to that converter thing for the new digital signals, but I still only get a few channels," she told him, sounding apologetic.

He just wanted to see any weather report but, at the moment, the only thing he found was a decade-old sitcom, a public television telethon and a reality show. "I hardly ever turn on the TV at my place." He gave up on the limited selection and pulled out one of the chairs at the dinette table. "There's a huge flat screen over at the firehouse that gets plenty of use, though."

She leaned over and pulled a big pot out of the lower cupboard and straightened. He saw her face pale and she braced her palm against the counter, shoving the pot with a clatter onto the stove.

He made it to her in little more than a step, catching her shoulders. "Are you all right?"

"Fine." Her fingers fluttered against her forehead for a minute. "I just straightened too quickly."

"Here." He nudged her toward the chair he'd just vacated. "Sit."

"I'm really fine," she protested, but she sat, anyway.

"Head rush." He filled the pot in the sink and set it on the burner, cranking it to high. "Is there a cover for this thing?"

She pointed to the low cabinet and he pulled out the lid, dropping it on top of the pot. She'd already set out a package of dried spaghetti and a jar of sauce, and the salad was sitting in a large wooden bowl, topped with mangled tomatoes and jagged shards of carrots. He took the salad to the table. "Start on that while the water boils."

"I'm *fine.*"

He grimaced. "And stubborn, too."

She gave a disbelieving snort. "If you knew me, you'd know how far off the mark you are."

"Then eat some salad. You've already said you were hungry." He went to the pot, peeked under the lid. The water was just starting to ripple. He dropped the lid back in place. "What about salad dressing?"

"In the refrigerator door."

He pulled on the V-shaped handle. "I haven't seen a fridge like this since I was a kid. I think my grandparents had one like it."

"It's a little old," she allowed mildly.

"It's probably an antique," he murmured. Ancient or not,

the inside was considerably better stocked than he'd expected. She had a liking for fresh vegetables and fruit, and mostly lean meats. "Which dressing?"

"The vinaigrette."

He pulled the bottle out and took it to the table. She still hadn't served herself any salad, and he unceremoniously dumped a good helping on one side of her plate. "Here." He handed her the dressing.

"Are you sure I can manage?" She took the bottle and shook it, looking oddly peeved. "I *can* decide a few things for myself. Like whether I want salad this very minute."

"I'm sure you can decide. And if you want to pass out the next time you stand up, feel free."

She flipped off the bottle top and sprinkled the vinaigrette over the lettuce leaves. "You're just panicked by the idea of having to pick me up off the floor again."

"It takes a lot more than that to panic me," he assured her drily. The water was finally boiling, and he dumped a big handful of spaghetti into the pot. "Do you want me to add salt to the water?"

"I don't add it. Trying to cut down on sodium, too."

No caffeine. No salt. Combined with the items in her fridge and the distinctive bottle of vitamins on her shelf, she was probably an obstetrician's dream.

She had a clear glass mason jar that held cooking utensils sitting on the counter next to the two-burner stove, and he pulled out the largest wooden spoon and gave the spaghetti a stir. He glanced at her, only to find her watching him.

"You seem pretty comfortable in a kitchen." The idea seemed to surprise her. "Even one as dinky as mine."

"We all switch off with kitchen duty at the department." He grinned. "Some days the results are better 'n others."

"Which type of day would you fall into?"

"Better, of course." He slid a piece of spaghetti off the spoon, bit it in half and deemed it done.

She smiled and turned her attention back to her salad. "Why would I have thought anything else?"

He was glad to see that now she'd begun on the salad, it was steadily disappearing from her plate. He drained the spaghetti, tossed the sauce over it right in the pot and carried it to the table. He pulled out the chair opposite Barbara, sat, and reached for the salad. "My mom was a great cook. She did her best to teach me and my brothers how to find our way around a kitchen. It probably wasn't as effective as she'd have liked. But I can boil water and make a mean turkey sandwich."

She still looked amused. "How many brothers do you have?"

"Four. No sisters. How my mom put up with all of us is anyone's guess. You?"

She reached for the spaghetti and scooped some onto her plate. "One brother. One sister." She made a face. "I'm the baby by ten years."

"I'm the youngest, too, but there's only ten years between the entire lot of us."

She twirled her fork through the spaghetti. "Are you the only firefighter?"

"Yeah. The middle one, Jeremy, is a doctor in northern California, but the rest keep more to the number-side of business."

"Bailey—my brother—is a doctor," she surprised him by offering. "Julia's a lawyer. They're the brilliant ones." She swallowed a mouthful of spaghetti, delicately sucking in the tail of a noodle and unknowingly sending a blast of heat right down to his gut. Fortunately, her attention was on her plate.

"They're both married, but they are *all* about their careers.

And then there's me," she added after a moment. "Receptionist extraordinaire."

The world needed receptionists, too, he figured. Just like it needed guys like him. "Is there something else you'd rather be doing?"

Her gaze lifted and collided with his. "Until lately, I've never really thought about it," she admitted, then just as quickly flushed and looked down again, seeming to focus hard on her plate. "Sorry. You don't want to hear about that. It's hardly interesting dinner conversation."

"Barbara." His voice was quiet. It was all he could do to keep from reaching out and touching her hand. "Look at me." He waited until she finally lifted her lashes again and he could see those striking pools of blue. "Don't you get it? Everything about you is interesting to me."

She stared back at him. Finally set down her fork and moistened her lips. "E-even the fact that I'm pregnant?"

Chapter Three

Bethany couldn't believe that the words came out of her mouth.

"I wondered," he said, and shoved a hefty bite of spaghetti into his mouth.

He didn't seem in the least bit shocked. Instead, he was watching her with that steady, utterly calm and capable expression that she'd already come to identify with him.

"You...did? How? Why?" She narrowed her eyes and poked her fork in the air. "Did the hospital tell you?"

"The hospital wouldn't tell me diddly-squat about you, other than that you'd left AMA in a cab."

"Then how did you find me?"

"Cab drivers are a little freer with information about where they deliver their fares than hospitals are with the identity of their patients."

"I should hope so," she muttered and tried to remember how many cabs she'd used since she'd hightailed it out of

Dallas in a semi driven by a portly old man who'd reminded her of her grandfather. Most of the cabs, though, had been in San Antonio, before she'd found herself a car to buy and backtracked twenty miles to settle in Red Rock.

What was the likelihood of her parents or Lyle tracking her down through them? She'd always used cash and had avoided using the same company more than once.

If they had, she'd know it by now. At least that's what she told herself.

There was no reason to panic. *They* weren't here. Darr was.

"How far along are you?"

"Five months." She dropped her fork on her plate and propped her elbows inelegantly on the tabletop. "What *is* it about you that makes people tell you things they have no intention of talking about?"

"I'm a firefighter. People trust us."

She wished it were only that simple. But she feared it wasn't.

"I was a bartender for a while, too," he went on easily, as if there were nothing at all out of the ordinary in their conversation. "Back in my college days. Heard things then that would curl your hair tighter than a corkscrew. Saw things." He shook his head. "Nothing like when I joined the department in Los Angeles, but still. People are crazy." His lips twisted and he looked ironic for a moment. "That's a fact."

She toyed with her fork, watching him. He wasn't exactly handsome. Not in the classical sense, as Lyle was. But there was something far more appealing in Darr's masculine good looks. Something strong. Steady.

Comforting.

And she ought to know better than to let herself get sucked into the lure.

For the first time in her life, she was standing on her own two feet. It felt strange. And scary.

But infinitely better than the life she'd left behind when the only decisions she'd ever made for herself were which shoes best matched which outfit.

Darr was making a serious dent in his helping of spaghetti while she'd had barely more than a few bites.

She twirled her fork through the noodles more intentionally. If he wondered where the father of her baby was, he hid it very well.

She reasoned that asking about Darr might be a way to stem her runaway tongue before she started blabbing about that, too. "What made you want to be a firefighter?"

"Studying finance and economics in college," he said wryly. "It was pretty evident to everyone that I was *not* going to be joining my old man's firm. Fortune Forecasting."

She'd heard of the West Coast firm. Rather, she'd heard her father *talk* about the firm. Probably at one of the endless cocktail parties she'd attended at his behest. "Seems a big jump from balance sheets and marketplace trends to fire hoses."

"Not so big. I wanted to join the academy as soon as I was old enough. He didn't agree. Thanks to my mom's efforts, we compromised. I ended up with the degree he wanted, but got the career that mattered to me. Everyone was happy."

She wished she could say the same about the difference of opinion she'd had with her own parents. But the only way *they'd* be happy was if she shackled herself to Lyle.

And that, she simply would not, *could* not do.

Before she'd come to her senses, she'd wasted far too much time thinking otherwise.

"Do your parents live in California?"

"My mother passed away a few years ago. But my dad still

lives there. He's in Red Rock right now, though." He nudged his empty plate away. "Half the Fortune family is here right now. Just one big happy family reunion."

She noted his faint grimace. To her, he didn't look all that happy about it.

So she switched topics entirely.

"I have cookies if you'd like some dessert. Just store-bought, I'm afraid, but—" She broke off when he lifted his hand, shaking his head.

"Don't knock store-bought cookies." His grimace had been replaced again by that faintly wry grin of his. "Another staple at the firehouse. But I'll pass. Thanks."

Even though she felt keenly on display still eating when he'd already finished, she made herself take several more bites of spaghetti before allowing herself the luxury of pushing back from the table. But before she could reach for his plate, he rose, too, and neatly slipped her plate out of her hands. "Go on and relax. I'll take care of this."

"You've already done too much," she protested. "You practically made the entire meal."

He rolled his eyes. "Boiled some noodles. That's serious effort. Go on. Put your feet up. Isn't that what pregnant women are supposed to do?"

She pressed her lips together for a long moment. But really, what was the point in fighting? There wasn't room for them both to maneuver around the kitchen area. And he looked firmly planted where he stood, as if he would bodily block her from trying to take care of the simple housekeeping tasks if she'd tried. "Do you always get your way?" she finally asked.

His lips tilted crookedly. "On occasion."

That odd squiggle slid through her again. The man was way

too attractive for her peace of mind. "I'll see if there's some news about the storm on the television."

He smiled faintly and she had the embarrassing sense that he knew exactly what kind of effect he had on her. The same kind of effect he probably had on every woman younger than ninety.

She tugged her hair away from her too-warm face and turned her back on him as she flipped the ancient dial-style switch on the television, running through her three channels. In all the time that she'd spent alone in this excruciatingly modest little house, she'd never before wished so strongly that she'd used some of her precious nest egg to invest in a decent television.

She'd have had plenty of cash if she dared to access the trust fund left to her by her grandparents. But she knew her parents would be watching for withdrawals and would find her the moment she transferred any money.

So she'd had to make do with what she had.

As it was, she didn't know what she and Darr were going to do to pass the rest of the evening. It might have fallen into utter darkness outside the windows of the house, but that didn't mean they were anywhere near bedtime yet.

At the mere thought of *that,* her gaze slid guiltily to the sofa bed.

It would be wide enough to accommodate the both of them. If there was very little space between them.

Heat streaked through her and she pulled her focus right back to the safety of the television and its grainy picture. "Darr." She called him and turned up the volume. "The news is on."

He walked over to stand beside her in front of the television. "Sit," he told her again as the local newscaster talked about the balmy weather on the West Coast.

"Bossy," she murmured, but sat on the edge of the side chair.

"That's what gets my job done."

"You weren't bossy the night of the fire," she countered. That night was a jumble of memories, but at least one thing was clear—just how cajoling his voice had been, calling her back to consciousness.

The weather report turned local then, and they both fell silent to watch. Two minutes later, if Bethany had harbored any hopes that Darr would be heading out any time soon, they were firmly dashed with the news that there was another storm front on the heels of the one that had already hit Red Rock.

She didn't know whether to be relieved or disturbed that they would be facing the weather together.

She could not read Darr's expression, as he turned the volume back down when the news slid from weather into sports. He looked as calm and composed as ever.

"That's that," was all he said before returning to the kitchen. Without looking at her, he flipped on the faucet and squirted liquid dishwashing soap into the sink. "Don't look so worried, Barbara. I'll bed down on the floor."

"I—I wasn't worried," she protested automatically, even though it was an outright lie. What worried her, though, was not fearing that he'd expect to find some space on her only bed, but the fact that she wasn't simply appalled by the very idea of it.

She'd been a virgin when she'd become involved with Lyle. Even then, it had been over a year before she'd shared his bed. She'd known Darr, what? Two weeks, if she counted the night of the fire.

All she could seem to think about was the combustible combination of Darr and a bed.

Pregnancy hormones?

Or him?

"I'm, um, I'm going to take a shower," she announced abruptly. "While I can be certain there is electricity to keep the water hot." She didn't wait to see what, if any, reaction he gave, and hurried down the hall, closing herself safely behind the bathroom door.

She flipped on the water, running only the cold so as not to waste the hot while she sat on the closed lid of the commode, her face buried in her hands.

Hormones or whatever, she needed to get hold of herself, and fast. Darr Fortune—moneyed or not—showed all the makings of a perfectly decent man.

He could say everything about her was interesting, but she felt certain that the last thing he needed was a pregnant, runaway bride throwing herself at him.

The second Darr heard the bathroom door close, he braced his hands on the edge of the sink, bowed his head and let out a long, deep breath. He heard the water turn on in there, and ordered himself to stop imagining her shedding her jeans and that all-enveloping sweater; and clothing herself, instead, in hot, streaming water.

There were a lot more pressing matters that should be concerning him.

Like what the hell was going on over at the Double Crown.

Like whether the electricity here in Barbara's dinky house would hold.

Like how deep the snow was, and what the second storm front would bring, and if they were going to have to actually shovel out, as the news had warned people to be prepared to do.

He heard the faint, metallic jangle of the shower curtain being pulled across the shower rod, and his damnable brain went right back into that small bathroom with Barbara.

Annoyed with himself, he yanked the plug from the drain, letting out the water, and rinsed the last of the soapsuds from the dishes.

Was she a washcloth and bar-of-soap kind of girl, or did she like those puffy wadded-up net things that turned a squirt of soap into a mountain of lather?

God. He was a head case.

If he had been half as infatuated with Celia, things would have turned out a whole lot differently. But then, he'd have stayed in L.A., likely married to a woman he didn't love who was carrying another man's child, and it would have been someone else who'd have carried Barbara out of that burning restaurant.

He snatched up the dish towel and dried the big pot and the dishes, sticking them back in their spots on the open shelves. Then, with the kitchen restored to order, he went to the television and turned up the volume again, as if it could drown out the steady hiss of the shower running.

It didn't.

He threw himself down on the couch, only to get right back up again and move, instead, to the chair. He pulled out his cell phone and dialed Nick, but only reached his brother's voice mail. He disconnected, not bothering to leave a message.

He knew that Nick would call when there was something to report.

The shower was still running.

Swearing under his breath at himself, he yanked on his boots and jacket. Then, with the flashlight from his truck in hand, he went outside, where the wind had died down to an occasional gust. The air was still cold, though, and did a reasonable job of freezing through his jacket *and* the heat pooling in his guts.

She had a utilitarian porch bug light that cast just enough of a yellow tint to see the snow piled on the steps. He scraped his boot along the risers to clear the worst of it away as he stepped down them, and played the strong flashlight beam over the area beyond.

The snow was still falling, but instead of the deluge of white that it had been earlier, now it was just a smattering of flakes, catching like firefly glints in the light of the flashlight. He headed around the house to the carport and stepped back far enough to shine his light over the roof. Visibility wasn't the best, but he didn't think the weight of the snow had worsened its uneven cant.

Once things got back to normal, he'd see about getting someone out there to shore up the supporting posts.

He trudged back in front of the house again, where the snow easily reached the top of his boots. Several yards off, his truck was nothing more than a hulking mound of white. He didn't bother wading his way closer.

He could only imagine the chaos all this snow was causing the rest of Red Rock.

He looked up at the sky. No stars to speak of and a snowflake that landed in his eye. He wiped it away and went back inside, only to catch Barbara standing in the center of the living area.

At his entrance, the uneasiness cleared from her face. "I just went outside to check around," he told her. Had she really thought he'd leave her alone now, despite the conditions?

Her fingers flexed around the wide white collar of the velvety-looking robe that covered her right to her toes. "Is it still very bad out?"

"Snow seems to be letting up, but there's a good foot of it on the ground out front." Except for the occasional one he'd given his mother as a gift, he was no particular judge of women's robes. But the one Barbara was wearing looked expensive. Luxurious and so perfectly fitted it might have been made just for her.

It also seemed highly incongruous, considering her exceedingly modest surroundings.

He reminded himself that it was none of his business how she'd come to own a robe like that. Wasn't it bad enough that he'd stuck his nose into her business as much as he had?

He pulled off his jacket and his boots again, leaving them once more by the door. "It's going to take some shoveling to clear the way to the road," he said. "And that road's either going to need plowing, or a whole lot of sunshine and warmth to make it drivable."

She nibbled her lip. "I don't even have a regular shovel, much less a snow shovel."

"We'll figure out something." The town might be short of snow equipment, but that didn't mean there was none at all. And while he knew the emergency protocols would be in place by now, he also knew those measures would first be focused on ensuring that basic services were available for those experiencing true emergencies.

Aside from being cut off from the rest of the town, they had water and were warm, dry and well sheltered.

"Do you think we'll be back to normal by Monday?"

Reassuring people was second nature to him, and it was more than plain that reassurance was what she wanted. But the circumstances were extremely unusual. "Hopefully," he said. "Depends on what that second storm front decides to do. Don't worry about the Foundation office, though. If you can't get there, there're a lot of other people who won't be able to get there, either."

She didn't look particularly comforted by that, though she

did let up on the death grip she had on her robe. "I put out clean towels for you," she said. "For when—whenever you want to use them. I don't have a spare toothbrush, I'm afraid."

"Nobody expects you to turn your home into a hotel," he assured. "I'll be fine. And if you're tired, you can say so. Like I said earlier, I'll pitch camp on the floor."

"You're being very accommodating."

"I think that should be my line. You ended up with a guest you never invited."

She lifted her hands to either side, like scales. "Let's see. I give you a floor to sleep on." One hand dipped slightly. "You save my life." She leaned over with the other hand nearly to the floor. "I think I should be telling *you* to take the bed."

"Don't even try," he warned drily.

"Well." She straightened and brushed her hands together. Toyed with the silky white sash tied around her waist—which was still narrow despite her pregnancy. "As it happens, I am a little tired." She shrugged her shoulders. "It seems like I'm tired most of the time these days."

Celia had been tired 24/7. "You're growing a baby in there," he said, reminding himself to focus on the present. "Gotta take some energy to do that."

She pressed her hand flat against her abdomen. Only then was it obvious that there was indeed a distinct baby bump beneath that rich-looking fabric. "You're the only person in Red Rock I've told. And it turns out you already knew." She suddenly fixed her gaze on him. "If the hospital didn't tell you, how *did* you know?"

"I carried you out of the restaurant."

Great, Bethany thought with a wince. "If I'm that much of a whale already, goodness only knows how huge I'll be when the baby is actually due."

"Honey, you're a far cry from a whale. But you're small. And slender. And I'm a paramedic. I'm trained to notice details. Even if it hadn't been for the way you were holding your hands just like you are now." He nodded toward her, and she realized that her hands were still pressed protectively around the swell of her baby. "Don't worry," he added. "I wasn't feeling you up or anything on the floor in Red."

Her cheeks went hot. "I didn't think anything of the sort!"

"Then stop fretting," he said. "Please. Does this couch pull out, or what?"

"It pulls out."

"Okay. Here." He handed her the first-aid kit that was still sitting on the couch. "Put that down somewhere."

"I'll bet you were a Boy Scout, too," she murmured, setting the large plastic case aside while he lifted the two narrow cushions off the couch to reveal the mechanism beneath. "Be careful. It wants to stick a little. I've smashed a finger or two trying to pull it out."

He grabbed the metal bar and yanked on it, unfolding the bed with absolutely none of the difficulty that she struggled with every night. The thin mattress unfolded, too, and landed on the frame with a soft plop that made the sheets that she left on the bed flutter wildly.

She pulled the thick, tie-dyed comforter that she'd found on the clearance rack at a discount store in San Antonio out of the hall closet. "Here." She handed it to him. "You can use this. Hopefully it'll be enough to keep you warm."

"What about you?"

She reached into the closet again and pulled out another blanket as well as her two pillows, one of which she handed to him. "I don't have a spare pillowcase for you, I'm afraid. But I did laundry just a few days ago."

"I think I'll live," he said gently, with only a hint of amusement. "Barbara, I'm used to sleeping in quarters that most closely resemble a coat closet with a cot inside. I'll be fine."

She smiled weakly. Every time he called her Barbara, she felt a pang of guilt. That's what she got for lying. "The couch cushions would probably be a little softer to sleep on than just the carpet."

With the couch unfolded into a bed that ran sideways, barely two feet away from the fireplace, it was readily apparent that there were few options over which stretch of carpet would hold him for the night. Sleeping at the foot of the bed would leave either his head or his feet running down the short hallway. The other option put him directly in front of the refrigerator and stove.

She wasn't particularly surprised when he tossed the couch cushions in front of the fridge and dropped the comforter on top of them.

Feeling painfully self-conscious, she straightened the rumpled sheets on the thin mattress, and spread out the blanket on top like someone who really was just as tired as she'd claimed to be. Without looking at him, she pulled off her robe and quickly slid beneath the bedding.

When she'd escaped Dallas, she'd left with not much more than a wad of cash from her ATM, which she was still carefully hoarding, and the clothes on her back.

That, of course, had happened to be a designer wedding gown and her grandmother's pearls. The gown, though, had at least proved to be useful in the end. It had netted her enough cash to buy the old car sitting under the carport.

The only other thing that Bethany had taken with her from Dallas had been the suitcase that had already been packed for the honeymoon. She'd been able to snatch it before the chauffeur loaded it into the trunk of the limousine that was to have brought her to the church. She'd traded a good portion of *its* contents in a secondhand store in San Antonio for pots and pans, dishes, the linens they were using right this minute, and nearly everything inside the bathroom except the fixtures that had come with the place.

Now, rather than the filmy white peignoirs that her mother had deemed suitable for a new bride, which were presently stuffed in the bottom drawer of the bureau below the television along with the pearls she couldn't bear to sell, Bethany had chosen instead to wear the thick, serviceable flannel pajamas she'd bought at the same place as the comforter. She was more thoroughly covered than she was even during the day, but there still seemed something painfully intimate about wearing them while climbing into bed with Darr just a few feet away.

Then she made the mistake of sneaking a look toward him as she reached over to turn off the lamp on the little table between the couch and the chair.

He'd pulled off his dark blue T-shirt to reveal a white one that clung a whole lot more to his shoulders.

His very broad, well-muscled shoulders.

She swallowed hard and quickly snapped off the light. "Do you want me to leave on the other lamp?"

"I'll get it." He crossed to the dresser where the TV and the lamp were. "What about the television?"

She often left it on at night. Silly, she knew, but it was some small bit of noise against the utter quiet that, at night, underscored just how alone she was. "It doesn't matter."

He switched off the lamp, but left the television on, the volume turned low so that it gave off only a low murmur of noise. "I'll shut it off after the news. Are you warm enough?"

Beneath the blanket, she curled her toes inside her thick socks. If anything, she was too warm. But that condition had little to do with the temperature inside the house. "Plenty."

"G'night then, Barbara."

My name is Bethany.

She closed her eyes and pulled the blanket nearly to her nose. It made her feel slightly more invisible, but not in the least bit less guilty. "Good night, Darr."

She could hear him moving around as he settled. Heard a faint jingle that she belatedly realized was probably his belt buckle and had to brace against the torrent of images her imagination conjured up over *that*.

And then, all was silent except for the low drone of the television and the occasional gust of wind that rattled the thin windowpane and door.

She lay there, counting off the beats of her heart, then finally pushed herself up on her elbow. With the bluish light from the small television and the warm flicker from the fireplace, she could easily make out the shape of him on the floor, buried under the comforter. "Darr?"

He didn't move. "Yeah?"

"I'm glad you're here," she admitted softly.

He was silent a long moment. "Me, too."

Chapter Four

The next time Bethany opened her eyes, daylight was shining through the curtains and she could hear the distinctive sound of water running in the bathroom.

Darr was taking a shower.

She unwound herself from the blankets, only to pause when she realized he'd spread the comforter on top of her while she'd slept.

The couch cushions that had been his bed were stacked next to the door, with the pillow he'd used sitting on top.

She climbed off the bed and nearly winced at the chilly air that accosted her. Pulling on her robe helped only a little, and she quickly checked the thermostat situated on the wall by the bathroom door. The furnace was running, but the temperature was well below what it should have been.

The running water stopped, and she nearly skipped her way over to the kitchen where Darr had already put on a pot of coffee.

He'd also found her store of herbal tea bags. One was un-wrapped and waiting inside a mug, and on the stove a saucepan was filled with water. He'd obviously heated it for her tea.

Something inside her chest squeezed and she carefully poured the steaming water into the mug and took it to the table. She'd had all manner of beverages and meals prepared for her during her life. Always by a paid staff person.

This was distinctly different.

By the time Darr emerged from the bathroom, she thought she had her silly emotions back in hand as she leisurely sipped the piping-hot tea.

That was until he padded out of the bathroom wearing nothing but his jeans and one of her blue-and-yellow-striped towels looped around his neck.

She dragged her eyes from the most perfectly masculine chest she'd ever seen in her life and took too hasty a sip, nearly choking as it burned down her throat.

"You're awake." He stopped at the coffeepot and took down the mug from the shelf. "I tried to be quiet."

"You were," she managed. She coughed a little, hoping her face wasn't as red as it felt, and lifted her cup again. "I didn't hear you at all. Thanks for the tea."

"Just boiling more water." Leaning one hip against the counter, he turned to face her. His gaze narrowed slightly over the brim of his coffee mug as he drank. "The electricity went off in the night. It came on a few hours ago, but it's been cutting in and out ever since. I decided I'd better make quick use of it while it was on. Shower wasn't entirely cold."

"I didn't even notice the power had been off." She couldn't believe she'd slept so soundly with him there.

Or, maybe she *could* believe it, which was all the more impossible.

"That's why it's so cold in here." He lifted one end of the towel to run it over his wet head. The muscles in his sinewy arms flexed from the cords in his wrist and right on up to his shoulder.

She barely kept herself from chugging another gulp of too-hot tea.

"I turned the furnace up as high as it would go," he continued, blessedly oblivious to her embarrassingly juvenile reaction to his ungodly beautiful torso. "Well…damn." His gaze went to the ceiling as the furnace clicked off with an ominous pop. "There it goes again."

She looked at the coffeemaker. The power light had gone out. "At least you made the coffee in the nick of time." Her mouth fairly watered just from the aroma of it.

Or maybe her mouth was watering because of him.

Either way, the source was something she needed to stay away from.

He rubbed the towel over his chest. "D'you know if there's an axe around here?"

"I have no idea." Focusing her brain on something other than him took an embarrassingly monumental effort. "If, uh, if there is, I think it would be in the storage chest outside."

"I looked yesterday. There wasn't one."

She barely heard him.

Lyle had been an avid swimmer. He played tennis and golf and a host of sports he considered advantageous in the business world. He'd been tall, wealthy and meticulously groomed. Right down to a waxed-smooth chest that didn't hold a candle to what was on display three feet from her nose.

She exhaled carefully and nonchalantly moved away from the table and the overwhelming appeal of the dark hair swirling across Darr's hard chest.

What had they been discussing?

Wood. Axe. Right.

"I don't know where else one would be then," she told him. "The only things the owners left inside were the furniture and a few board games in the hall closet." She lifted the curtain away from the window and looked out, squinting against the reflection of light from an ocean of glistening snow. "Have you *looked* out there?"

He joined her at the window and looked out. "Yeah. This'll be one for the record books all right." His arm barely grazed hers as he turned from the sight. "I know this will probably sound kind of strange, but do you have a pair of socks that I can use?"

"Oh. Sure." She blinked. His bare feet were considerably larger than hers. "Well, we can try." She went to the dresser and pulled open the top drawer, rummaging through the meager contents before pulling out a pair identical to the ones she was wearing. "They're polka-dotted," she stated the obvious.

"And pink," he observed, grinning crookedly. "But they'll do." He sat down on the arm of the couch and pulled them on. On her, the stockings reached nearly to her knee. On him, the fuzzy cotton barely covered his muscular calves. He followed up with his own white socks, then pushed his feet down into his somewhat battered-looking cowboy boots and yanked the hem of his jeans back in place.

"I have a few extra T-shirts," she offered. She felt hot inside. "I bought them with the baby in mind." She held her hands out beyond her expanding middle. "Men's size large." So far she'd only slept in them. She went back to the drawer and pulled one out. "It'll still probably be too tight, but it's clean." It was also plain and white.

"The more layers, the better." He took it from her and worked it over his head, then pulled it down over his chest. As she'd expected, the cotton knit strained at the seams. It also lovingly outlined every rippling line of his torso, from the hard points of his nipples to where the fabric stopped short midway down his six-pack abdomen. "Got another one?"

She blindly grabbed and mercifully came out with another T-shirt and not one of her lacy bras that in the past month had become increasingly snug. "Here."

"Thanks." He pulled it on over the first, followed up with his own undershirt, and then the blue fire department shirt.

When he picked up his jacket, her stupefied brain kicked into gear. He needed more layers, because he intended to go outside. "Wait a minute. What're you going to do out there?"

"We need more firewood, whether I can find something to split it with or not. I put the last log I'd brought in on the fire about an hour ago."

"But your hair is still wet."

"Not for long." He scrubbed the towel roughly over his hair.

She went to the hall closet and unzipped the front pocket of the suitcase that sat inside on the floor and pulled out a cashmere scarf. The coordinating leather gloves would never fit him in a million years, nor would the secondhand coat she'd bought, but she took them out, anyway. If she went outside, she'd need them.

"I know," she said when he finally unearthed his head from the towel and saw the scarf she was holding. "*More* pink. But it'll help keep your head warm. I don't have a hat to my name, unfortunately."

"Beggars can't be choosers." He took the scarf and wrapped it awkwardly over his head.

She tsked. "Here. Let me." She reworked the cashmere smoothly over his tousled hair, twisted it, and wrapped it twice around his neck before tucking in the ends.

She accidentally caught his gaze with hers. His thick brown

eyelashes had dark gold tips, she realized. Basically the same burnished color as the faint beard blurring his sharp jaw. He also had a tiny scar that bisected the end of his left eyebrow.

She quickly stepped back, deliberately halting her visual feast. "Fashionable *and* functional."

"Thank God Devaney can't see me now," he muttered, and pulled on his bomber jacket, zipping it all the way to his throat.

"Who's Devaney?"

"A guy I work with."

"I wish I had gloves that would fit you. Would it help to wear socks over your hands?"

"Like mittens? Sure."

She found another pair. Her last, and this time they were purple with blue polka dots. She'd deliberately purchased the most colorful multipack she could find at the discount store because her mother would have detested them.

Childish, maybe. But infinitely satisfying.

She held them out. "Here you go."

He pushed his hands inside them. "I've even been accused a time or two of not having opposable thumbs, so socks are just about perfect. Wish me luck." He pulled open the door, stepped out and quickly shut it behind him.

She pulled aside the curtain again, to watch him head down the steps. When he reached the ground, he sank into the snow nearly to his knees. It didn't stop him, though, and she watched until he turned the corner of the house and moved out of sight.

She hurriedly gathered together a clean pair of jeans and a long-sleeved T-shirt and went into the bathroom, dragging them on. There was still enough warm water left to wash her face and clean her teeth, and she pulled a brush through her hair, taming it enough to toss it up in a clip. Then she pulled on the same thick sweater she'd worn the day before.

Her appearance-conscious mother would have been appalled.

She didn't care. Aside from her coat, the sweater was the warmest thing she owned. She laced her stocking feet into tennis shoes and immediately her chilly toes felt warmer.

She folded up the blankets, then manhandled the recalcitrant bed back into the couch, and replaced the cushions.

There was still hot water in the saucepan Darr had used, but not enough for much more than another cup of tea, which she didn't want anyway. To her, it just seemed that herbal tea was a poor substitute for fresh-ground coffee. So she added more water to the pot, dumped in a measure of quick-cooking oats and, feeling quite pioneerlike, carried the pan over to the fireplace, moved the screen and nudged the pot in next to the grate. The pan was entirely metal, so she doubted it would suffer any harm.

With a wooden spoon and a folded towel to use as a pot holder, she sat on the hearth and watched the pot, pulling it out occasionally to stir it.

Before long, the contents looked as if she'd cooked them right on the stove.

Feeling ridiculously pleased, she moved the pot to the hearth and plopped a cover on it. When Darr came in from the cold, at least she'd be able to offer him something warm for his stomach.

She replaced the fireplace screen and went to the window and peeked out again. He'd obviously made the trek to his truck because she could see the deep trench of footprints he'd left. Of him, however, there was still no sign. She went to the refrigerator. She didn't want to let out any more cold air than necessary, but she opened it quickly just to extract the plastic bowl of fruit she kept on the top shelf next to the milk.

Humming under her breath, she stood at the sink and

started peeling a large orange. The people on the cooking shows she occasionally caught on PBS made the task look much easier than it was. By the time Bethany was finished, the sections were more than a little mangled, and she was sticky with juice up to her wrists, just like usual. She dumped the pieces in a bowl and rinsed her hands, then started on a gigantic green apple. She made a better job of that, at least, courtesy of the sharp knife she'd bought at the grocery store.

She heard the rattle of the doorknob, and turned to see Darr enter with a few logs in his arms. He'd obviously made some attempt at brushing the caked snow from the legs of his jeans, but patches of it still clung to the denim and when he nudged the door behind him shut with the heel of his boot, a clump fell onto the carpet.

"No luck on the axe or a hatchet. Or anything else useful, for that matter." He carried the wood to the fireplace and started stacking it on the edge of the brick hearth. "The logs seemed to stay dry from the shelter of the carport, but they'll be slower to burn than if they were split."

"Won't that make the wood last longer?"

"Yup. Harder to get burning and slower to heat, too." He pulled the socks off his hands, then shrugged out of his jacket, eyeing the covered pot sitting on the hearth. "What's that?"

"Oatmeal." She hurried forward and using the folded towel, moved it out of his way. "Breakfast is the most important meal and all that."

"I'd have been happy with cold leftover spaghetti. Oatmeal is great." He unwound the pink scarf from his head. His thick hair stuck out in spikes and her fingers itched to smooth through it. "Anything warm sounds great. It's colder than a witch's tongue out there."

She couldn't seem to get the smile off her face and turned

back to the kitchen. "I cut up some fruit, too." She quickly set everything on the table. "Cook—" She realized what she was saying and bit off the rest of the thoughtless sentence. That Cook had always served oatmeal with raisins and brown sugar.

"What about cooking?" He pulled out one of the chairs at the table, obviously for her, and she slipped onto the seat.

"Oh." She shook her head. "Cooking isn't my forte, that's all. Not with a proper stove, much less over a wood fire. I, um, I hope the oatmeal isn't too lumpy."

He reached for the bowl of fruit and spooned some right on top of his cereal then tucked in. "It's fine." He let out a quick breath. "And hot."

She quickly hopped up again to fill a water glass. "Here."

"Thanks." He gulped down a third of the glass, then stuck his spoon right back into the hot cereal, giving every indication that he was perfectly satisfied with the ordinary fare. "So what do you want to do today, Barbara?"

"Do?" She eyed that scar on his eyebrow and wondered if he'd earned it on the job. "I don't know." She nibbled at an apple wedge.

"What would you ordinarily do on a Sunday if you weren't snowed in with a stranger?"

"Do laundry. Clean." Her lips quirked. "It takes hours to keep this place up, you know, being as palatial as it is."

His dimple flashed. "Anything else?"

"I don't know. Read. Take a nap. We pregnant women are big on naps."

"Ain't that the truth." He added more fruit to his bowl, leaving her to wonder if he knew that fact just in a general sense, or if it was from more personal experience.

From his tone, it had sounded personal and she quickly realized just how little she really knew about Darr.

He wore no rings, but what did that really matter? For all she knew, he had a girlfriend, five ex-wives and a half-dozen kids.

Just as rapidly, she dismissed the notion.

He wasn't the secretive one. She was.

"Laundry is out, obviously," he went on. "Cleaning'll take about three minutes, I'm figuring. Maybe five. Being so palatial and all." His gaze lifted, and settled on her face. "Better all around to leave napping to you."

"I suppose you're too macho to indulge in such behavior?"

The corner of his lips kicked up. He looked amused and very, *very* wry. "Too smart," he said.

Before she could decipher that, he tapped the edge of her bowl with his spoon. "Eat up. You'll want something hot in your stomach when we go out."

Bemusement slid through her. "We're going out?"

"Might as well. Better than twiddling our thumbs indoors when we don't have to. Do you know if anyone lives in the house down the hill?"

"As far as I know." She hadn't made a point of meeting whoever did, though. For one thing, she didn't know how long she'd be able to stay in Red Rock. For another, it was hard enough keeping up her false identity with her coworkers, much less even more people, like neighbors. "There's a car that comes and goes."

"Good enough for me. We'll check on them. See if they're okay. Maybe they'll have an axe we can borrow. Unless you'd rather not go with me?"

"No. That's fine." The truth was, it didn't really matter how they passed the time.

She couldn't think of anyone she'd rather be with even if they did absolutely nothing at all.

While she finished her oatmeal and fruit, he fiddled with

the logs in the fire. Whatever he did was effective enough to get a small flame started.

She imagined that after being outside for a while, it might actually be strong enough to create a small amount of heat.

Then he pulled on his jacket and the sock-mittens, and she pulled the used wool peacoat over her thick sweater and fitted her hands into the fine leather gloves. "Here." He tossed her the scarf.

"Don't you want it?"

"Head's not wet anymore. And the color suits you better."

"I don't know about that," she countered lightly. She was rapidly coming to the conclusion that Darr Fortune looked pretty darn fine in almost anything. But she slid the scarf around her neck and tucked the ends into her collar. The only thing she couldn't do anything about was her tennis shoes. She had nothing else she could wear. The shoes that she wore to the office would have been even more unsuitable.

"After you, ma'am." He opened the door and held out his arm.

She stepped out onto the porch. The air was clear and so crisp with cold that it stung a little just breathing it in. It was also silent. Sparkling. Amazingly beautiful.

"Come on." He took her hand. "Careful on the steps. I didn't notice ice earlier, but you never know."

When they reached the bottom, her tennis shoes promptly sank several inches into the snow and she couldn't help but laugh. "I feel like I have on cement galoshes." She lifted her hands to her sides. "Now what?"

"When's the last time you were around snow?"

"Last year on a skiing trip." She'd worn knee-high designer boots and a mink coat that Lyle had insisted on giving her, despite her distaste for real fur. As expert on the slopes as he was with everything else, he hadn't wanted to slow down enough to match her more elementary level. While he'd spent hours on the slopes, she'd spent hours alone in the lodge.

She should have recognized that something was lacking when she hadn't missed his company in the least.

"You ski?"

"Not very well."

He grinned. "Me, neither. I'm better on water skis, and even that ain't too pretty of a picture."

She strongly doubted that.

"Just follow in my footsteps. And if you get too tired, say so, and we'll stop."

"You make it sound like we're climbing the Himalayas." But she fell in step behind him. Not surprisingly, he was right about following in the path he cut before her. She suspected that he was dragging his boots more than he ordinarily would have to clear the way for her; regardless; it was effective. She didn't even have snow sliding down inside the tops of her shoes.

They stopped when they reached his truck, though. He used his arm to sweep away some of the snow and he tried to open the door, but couldn't.

"Did you lock it?"

"Nope. It's frozen." He squinted up at the gray sky. "Come on. You still doing okay?"

A bubble of laughter rose in her throat. "I'm pregnant, not decrepit. We haven't even made it halfway to the road, yet. And I'm fine."

"Okay." He took her at her word and headed past the truck. "Watch that rut," he pointed behind him. "Your drive needs some serious grading."

"Tell me something I don't know. I got the owners to knock some off the rent because of it." She'd been quite proud of herself for negotiating that little matter in her favor.

"I suppose that means they don't intend to fix it anytime soon."

"I'll take the discounted rent over the grading."

He made a sound, not much more than a grunt, that she didn't bother deciphering.

Everyone had their priorities. Living as frugally as she could now meant that her savings would last just that much longer when she had to take time off for the baby.

Or if she had to bolt, again.

She was strongly hoping that wouldn't be the case, though. Everything about Red Rock and her life there was the antithesis of the life she'd led before. But she *liked* the town far more than she'd anticipated when she'd deliberately chosen to settle there. The people were friendly without being too nosy. The town itself was as picturesque as a postcard. Even her small rented house had its charms.

Her foot slipped on the snow but she caught herself before falling.

That's what she got for keeping her eyes glued to the charms of the rear view in front of her, and not where she was walking.

When they made it to the road, she was glad to find that the snow didn't seem as deep. She still followed in Darr's wake, though, and by the time they made it to the bottom of the hill where the closest house was located, her muscles were feeling loose and warm despite the cold temperature that had turned her nose into an ice cube.

Darr bounded up the three steps to the front door and knocked loudly. "Anyone home?"

After his second round of knocking, the door squeaked open and a baleful eye glared out at them. "What do you want?"

"We're from up the road," Darr said easily. "Just wanted to check and see that everyone here is all right."

"And what wouldcha do if I wasn't?" the man barked.

"See if I could help, sir. I'm Lieutenant Fortune with the Red Rock Fire Department."

The door cracked open a little farther. Enough to reveal a shock of wiry white hair and a wrinkled face that looked just as cantankerous as the voice sounded. "My tax dollars paying for the fire department to go door to door? Like a man don't have enough to pay for without that?"

"Actually, I'm not on duty. But we would go door to door if we had to. Is your electricity out?"

"Ain't it out all over town?" He looked over at Bethany where she was waiting at the foot of the steps. "We got lady firemen now, I suppose." His tone made it plain what he thought of *that*.

"Yes, we do," Darr agreed. "But—"

"But I'm not one of them," Bethany inserted. "I live up there." She pointed toward the hill behind them. Now that they were standing still, even for just a few minutes, she could feel the cold seeping through her jeans.

"Fenton's place." The man squinted at her, obviously judging. "You're the blonde who drives that blue beater with the bad brakes. Better get 'em fixed, girlie, or one day you'll drive down off this road and keep on going."

She felt herself flush.

"We'll get that taken care of," Darr told the man. "Are you able to keep warm enough? Have enough food? Water?"

The man looked irritated that Darr would even ask. "Hell, boy, I got me a generator. You young kids. Never think to be prepared. That's the problem with the world today."

Darr grinned and Bethany realized that the more ornery the old man sounded, the more cheerful Darr seemed to get. "You're probably right about that," he said. "So maybe you can bail *us* out. You wouldn't happen to have an axe or a hatchet we could borrow?"

The man heaved a grunting sigh. "Hold on." He slammed the door shut.

"Friendly," Bethany murmured under her breath.

Darr chuckled. "Reminds me of the captain I had when I was a probie. Guy was grouchy as hell but he had a heart of gold." Footsteps crunching on the snow interrupted, and they looked over to the side of the house to see the old man, now bundled in a hooded parka with his khaki-colored pants pushed untidily into the tops of fur-lined boots. "Here." He shoved a long-handled axe at Darr. "Better get your butts back up the hill," he advised, glaring at them both. "Snow's going to start falling again soon. I can smell it."

"Well, you're a lot more prepared for it than most folks around here," Darr told him. He held the axe just below the head. "I'll get this back to you as soon as I can."

"Eh." The old man waved his hand. "I got others." His faded blue eyes squinted at Bethany. "She can drop it off sometime when she's squeaking her way past my house."

"Appreciate that." Darr pulled the sock off his hand and stuck it out.

The man grimaced, but pulled off his own thick glove to shake Darr's hand. "John Decker," he provided grudgingly. Then he pulled off the other glove. "Here. You can bring them back, too, when you're done. Don't argue," he barked, when Darr paused. "Can't abide arguing fools."

"Yes, sir." Darr took the gloves. "Thank you, again."

"Yes. Thank you, Mr. Decker," Bethany added.

The man gave that same annoyed grunt. He stomped up his steps and pushed through his front door. It closed unceremoniously behind him.

Darr exchanged the socks for the gloves, then balled up the socks and pushed them into his pockets. "Back up the hill we go. You still doing okay?"

"I'm fine." She strode past him, reversing the way along the path they'd already made. "Just because I'm pregnant doesn't mean I'm out of shape," she said over her shoulder. "I used to run marathons, for heaven's sake."

"Yeah? Which ones?"

"Los Angeles. Chicago. New York. I was drawn in the lottery for that one two years ago."

"Houston?"

"Oh, yeah. Every year." She snapped her mouth shut.

"I run to train, but never got involved in the marathon thing. When'd you start?"

"In high school." It was the only thing at which she'd managed to excel. Her mother had hated it, deeming it unladylike. Her father had pretty much patted her on the head, calling it just one more of her silly phases. "You?" The road started to climb.

"About then. Do you run now?"

"Not since I moved here—oh!" The sole of her tennis shoe slid on the gravel and she started to pitch forward, but Darr's arm slid around her from behind, scooping her back against him.

"Steady there." His breath was warm against her ear.

Even through all the layers she wore, she was excruciatingly aware of the press of his thickly gloved hand under her breasts; of the solid wall of him behind her. "Thanks." Her voice shook and there didn't seem to be one thing she could do to change it. Not when both her pulse and her hormones seemed to be skittering around as if in a hot pan. "You, um, you always seem to be rescuing me."

His arm around her seemed to tighten fractionally. "I can think of worse things."

Her heart was climbing toward her throat. Her gloved hands slid over his, but she didn't know if that was to push his hold away or to keep him from pulling away. "Darr—"

His head lowered. His jaw grazed her temple. "Just answer a question for me."

She turned her head, looking up at him, and felt everything inside her grind to a breathless halt. "What?"

"The night of the fire, you said there was no one for us to call for you. No husband. No boyfriend. Was that the truth?"

"Yes." That at least was the bald, naked truth.

"Good," he muttered, and pressed his mouth to hers.

Chapter Five

Darr felt her quick intake of breath; the momentary shock that stiffened her. And almost as quickly, everything about her softened. Most particularly her lips.

He'd kissed plenty of women in his life. But nothing, *no one,* was like kissing Barbara.

She murmured something against his mouth, but he didn't hear. All he knew was that her gloved hand was sliding around his neck, that she was turning toward him, that her mouth was the warmest, sweetest thing he'd ever tasted.

When she finally pulled away, gasping, pressing her forehead against his shoulder, it took all of his willpower not to lift her face to his and kiss her again. He closed his eyes, tilting his head back, and pictured Devaney's ugly mug. Anything to cool the fire raging inside him.

His leather jacket creaked when she lifted her head again, trailed her gloved hands down his chest. "It's snowing again." Her voice was faint. Her indigo eyes looked dazed.

The blood that should have kept his brain functioning had all headed south and he stared stupidly up at the fat white flakes dancing down from the solidly gray sky. She shifted, pulling away from him and he reluctantly released her. Realized he'd dropped the axe in the snow beside them.

She stepped beyond the path he'd made down the hill and lifted her arms out from her sides, looking upward. A soft laugh bubbled out of her. "Again. It's snowing *again*. Can you believe it?" She looked back at him. "What are the odds?"

What were the odds of falling in love with a woman practically at first sight?

"Astronomical," he murmured.

"I'll say." The smile playing around her lips suddenly turned impish. It was the only warning he had before she leaned over, packed up a handful of snow, and tossed it at him.

The snowball exploded softly when it hit him square in the shoulder.

"Oh. Honey." He clucked his tongue. "What was that for?"

She grinned. "Isn't that what we're supposed to do in the snow?"

He slowly, deliberately leaned over and scooped John Decker's sturdy, lined glove through the snow. Straightened and just as slowly, just as deliberately, packed the other glove around it.

Her eyes were laughing. "You're not going to throw that at me. You're the heroic type, remember? An all-around nice guy?"

"Nah." He tossed the solid ball from one hand to the other. "When it comes to water fights and snowballs—" he caught the ball in his right hand and narrowed his eyes "—I fight back."

Her hair flew out over her shoulders when she turned on

her heel, doing her best to jog through the snow, though it kept swallowing her legs nearly to her knees. She forged on, though, high-stepping diagonally away from the road toward her house. He pitched the snowball and it splattered square and harmless between her shoulder blades.

She turned, laughing, and grabbed up another mound of snow, gained several feet up the hill, then turned again and launched it at him, this time catching him right in the chest.

She pumped her arm triumphantly and darted away again, only to stop short, laughing even harder. "Wait, wait," she called as he closed the distance between them, another snowball already forming in his hands. "Time out!"

"Tired of the game already?"

She giggled and raised her foot, wriggling her stocking toes. "I lost my shoe in the snow."

"Excuses, excuses." He lobbed the snowball at her and it hit her dead center in the chest. She screeched, and started to fall, arms cartwheeling for balance.

But it was no good.

Cursing at himself, he plowed across the distance, but there was no way to reach her before she fell backward. "Barbara!" He slid the last foot on his knees and tore off his gloves, tossing them aside.

He slid his bare hand along her neck. She was trembling, her gloved hand pressed to her mouth. "Don't move. I'm sorry. I don't know what the hell I was thinking. Where do you hurt?"

"I'm not hurt!" She dropped her hand, and he realized she was laughing. "I have a foot of snow underneath me, remember?"

His relief was swift and all-encompassing. "I still shouldn't have thrown that snowball at you."

"There are worse things." Her voice was a little too blithe; a little too deliberate. "Nice aim, by the way." She grinned up at him, and that at least seemed completely genuine. "I have snow down my coat."

"We should get you inside."

"Wait." She tilted her head back in the mattress of snow. "Snow angels first." Suiting words to action, she slowly worked her arms up and down, her legs in and out. Her long hair was splayed around her head and a few snowflakes settled among the curls. "Come on," she chided. "Don't you like snow angels?"

The snow angel he was looking at was pretty damn appealing. "I'll leave that to you," he said gruffly, "and look for your shoe."

Her swishing limbs stopped. She pushed up on her elbows and dashed a snowflake off her eyelash. Her humor had just as effectively been dashed judging by the suddenly stubborn set of her chin. "I'm not that incompetent. I can find my own shoe. Where's the axe?"

"Nobody said anything about incompetence." He pulled on the borrowed gloves again, pushed to his feet and headed back to where he'd dropped the axe. The heavy head was buried in the snow; the long handle sticking up like a periscope. He pulled it out of the snow and turned back toward Barbara.

Over the snowy hillside, their footprints were like a criss-crossing map. She was hop-stepping her way around, obviously trying to keep her shoeless foot out of the snow as she searched for her tennis shoe. He could tell the instant she found it, for she immediately sat down on her rear and pulled it on.

Around them, the snow was falling a little faster. A little harder. He reached her and held out his hand to her.

She put her hand in his and he pulled her to her feet. "I'm sorry I snapped at you," she murmured.

He shrugged. "You said what you thought."

She dashed the snow from the seat of her pants with a swish of her hands. "I...well, I guess I'm used to people thinking I'm incompetent."

He couldn't help wondering *what* people. But she didn't offer more of an explanation, and he didn't ask. "Come on. We'd better get back to the house. I want to get some wood split while I can."

She sucked in her lip for half a second, then turned and dug her shoes into the snow, heading upward. By the time they made it to the porch, their original footprints were starting to fill in with fresh snowfall and the fog of their breath was even more visible. "I'll heat up something over the fire for us to drink," she said before going inside.

He continued around to the stack of wood tucked under the carport.

He'd worked his way through a decent stack of logs and into a sweat when he felt the buzzing of his cell phone against his chest. He notched the blade into the upstanding log he was using as a base and pulled out the phone. Nick. "Yeah. Who's sick?"

"Nobody. It's not like with Mom," his brother said speedily.

Darr leaned his weight against the end of axe handle and let out a long breath. "Thank God," he murmured. "Then what'd Patrick want to talk about so badly?"

"It's complicated." Nick's voice was muffled, as if he didn't particularly want to be overheard. "You still stuck out there with Blondie?"

"Barbara. And yeah."

"Hmm. Cozy."

Darr pinched his eyes shut. He didn't want to think about how cozy. And judging by the continuing snowfall, they had another night under the same roof ahead of them.

For one night, she'd been glad of his presence. What would happen after another night?

More to the point, what would happen *now,* when he'd put the monumentally ill-advised moves on her? She hadn't exactly beat him off with a stick.

But she was pregnant, and wariness screamed off her like a neon light.

"Earth to Darwin," Nick's voice slowly penetrated. "Yo, bro. You still there or not?"

He focused. "I'm here. The power out at the ranch, too?"

"Yeah, but Lily's well equipped with generators. Nobody is suffering too badly. You?"

The only suffering Darr was undergoing was owed entirely to jonesing for a woman he should know well enough to stay away from. "She's got at least half a cord of wood and I borrowed an axe from a neighbor. We're doing all right. You going to tell me what's *complicated,* or do I have to guess?"

"You could try, but believe me. You wouldn't guess. Hold on. I'm going outside for a sec." Darr could hear muffled murmuring, then Nick came back on the line. "Too many freaking people here," his brother muttered in a clearer voice. "God, I cannot believe it is snowing again. Sometime, remind me why I let you convince me that moving here was a good thing."

Darr let that one pass. The truth was, if Nick hadn't been ready to leave California, he wouldn't have left, no matter what anyone said.

He worked the axe loose and dropped the blade again into the base log. "So, what's the deal?"

Nick heaved a sigh. "Evidently, someone slipped a note into Patrick's pocket at the New Year's Eve party Emmett and Linda threw." Emmett Jamison and his wife ran the

Fortune Foundation, and they'd rented out Red for the private party. "At least Patrick figures it was during the party. He didn't even notice it until a few days later. Basically says something to the effect that one of the Fortunes is not who we think."

"What the hell is that supposed to mean?" Darr recalled the lively party and those present. The Fortune family was admittedly extensive, and they'd been well-represented at the party. So, too, had been a lot of the Mendozas. Not only did José and Maria Mendoza own the restaurant, but the Fortune and Mendoza families had long been friends.

"Good question. Patrick might have shrugged it off as a joke, except that Dad received a similar one."

"What?"

"And get this. Aunt Cindy got one, too."

"Hell." There was no pretending that was coincidence. Cindy's life had been too far removed from the rest of the Fortunes. "Was there a demand for money or something?"

"No. Not yet. That's where they think this might be heading, of course. Cindy wants to call in Ross to get to the bottom of it."

Darr squinted. Overhead, the carport creaked. Ross, a private detective, was Cindy's eldest. "I thought he and Cindy didn't speak these days."

"As far as I know, they don't. But he's just over in San Antonio and she figures he's not likely to turn down a good-paying job. He can nose around without being entirely noticeable. Everyone seemed to agree that it was a good idea."

"If he agrees." There was no love lost between Ross and his mother.

"There's that."

Standing inactive was accomplishing nothing but making

him cold, and Darr leaned over, grabbing up another log. "I'm surprised Dad didn't say something to us earlier."

"Until Patrick and he both realized they'd gotten similar notes, I don't think either one paid much attention. It's not like the Fortunes haven't been targets of all sorts of nonsense over the years. Anyway, that's the deal here."

"Yeah, well, at least nobody's dying." That's the only thing he cared about. As for anonymous notes and the motives behind them, he couldn't begin to venture a guess. Darr yanked the axe loose again and balanced the log on its rough-hewn end. "Call me if anything else comes up."

"Will do."

He shut off the phone and stuck it back inside his jacket, then swung the axe down onto the end of the log. It split clean in two. He quartered the halves, left the axe buried in the base, and began carrying the rest inside.

Barbara was sitting on the narrow brick hearth, a folded dish towel in her hand. When he entered, she turned toward the door, a smile on her face. "I made hot chocolate. Over the fire."

He pushed his heart back down out of his throat. You'd think he'd never seen a beautiful woman before. "Sounds good." He nudged the door shut behind him and carried the wood to the fireplace, crouching down to stack it against the wall.

"If you'd rather have coffee, I could make that instead. Fortunately, my coffee grinder runs on batteries."

He'd seen the grinder on the shelf. A fancy little device. And her coffee beans were top of the line, too, he knew.

Then he reminded himself that how she spent her money was no business of his.

"Hot chocolate is fine." In fact, the aroma was filling the cottage, right along with the warmth from the fireplace. Warmth that she must be feeling, too, since she'd peeled off her socks as well as that oversize sweater, leaving a pink long-sleeved shirt behind that clung to the high, full thrust of her breasts. "Let me get the rest of the wood I split, though, first."

She nodded, leaning forward to move the handle of the pot she was using for the hot chocolate. The V of her neckline gaped, giving him a gut-tightening glimpse of creamy flesh cupped by snug white lace.

He dragged his gaze away and bolted for the door, then nearly fell on his butt when his boot slid on one of the steps outside. He caught the iron rail, and shoved his glove through his hair, letting the cold air flow over him.

Maybe if he rolled around in the snow for a while, his jets would cool, too.

He stomped around the side of the house again and pushed several handfuls of kindling into his pockets before grabbing up the rest of the wood he'd cut. The wind was steadily picking up. He couldn't tell how much was fresh snow coming down and how much was just being blown around. Snow had even drifted up beneath the outer corners of the carport, banking against the tires of Barbara's car.

They'd have to shovel some out before she'd be able to move her car. Clearly, there was no point in making a start on that task just yet.

Arms loaded, he retraced his steps back to the front door. Barbara must have been watching for him because she opened the door before he could maneuver a hand free for the knob.

"Let me help you," she said, grabbing several pieces off the top before he could protest. She added them to the stack beside the fireplace then quickly moved out of the way for him to do the same. "It looks like we could heat this place for the next week with all this wood."

"You're fortunate there was a healthy supply here." He

emptied his pockets of the wood chips and long slivers, leaving the kindling more or less neatly in a pile to the other side of the hearth, and then peeled out of his jacket. The multiple layers of T-shirts followed. When he'd pulled them all off, he yanked his department blues back over his head and leaned down to start on his boots and the socks.

Barbara set a mug on the coffee table, complete with a folded napkin and a heart-shaped red-and-white lollipop, before settling in the side chair.

"Someone was giving those out at the Foundation office," she said when he picked it up and twirled the stick between his fingers. "For Valentine's Day. It's peppermint."

"That's right. I'd forgotten today was the 14th." He lifted the lollipop in a toast. "Happy Valentine's Day."

"You, too." She held an identical candy in her hand and swirled the heart through her own mug, then popped it between her soft lips. After a moment, she slid it back out and dunked it in her mug again. "Not bad."

He realized he was staring at the slick gleam left behind on her pink lips and yanked the wrapper off his own candy, shoving it in his mouth. "Isn't there caffeine in hot chocolate?" he asked around it.

"A little. Not anything like coffee. My doctor suggested it. She also said I could stand the extra calories." She made a face and pulled her shirt taut against her belly. "Like I'm not getting big enough as it is."

He exhaled carefully and moved away, carrying his various shirts over to one of the table chairs. To buy himself time to get some control over the need raging through him, he made a production of draping them over the back of it for the next time he needed to wear them.

The wind whistled around the cottage, hitting the windowpane in soft beats. The fire crackled. He flipped on the light switch next to the refrigerator, but there was still no power.

The candy was spicy against his tongue, but it still wasn't strong enough to remove the taste of the kiss they'd shared.

He crunched it into pieces and tossed the stick into the small trash can tucked beneath her sink, then looked back at her. She was staring into the fire, sliding the lollipop around inside her mouth.

God. He was dying.

"What games?" he asked abruptly.

She jumped a little and her blue gaze slanted his way. She drew out the candy and pressed her lips together for a moment. "Excuse me?"

"Earlier, you said the owners left some board games."

Her forehead smoothed. "Right." She pushed off the chair, dropped the lollipop in the trash and went to the closet that opened off the short hallway. She rummaged around for a minute. Pulled out a very expensive piece of rolling luggage. "Sorry. It's a little cramped in here." She rummaged around a little more. Out came a few flat, colorful boxes, and the suitcase was rolled back inside out of sight. She picked up the game boxes and moved them to the coffee table. "Take your pick."

Chutes and Ladders. Twister. Monopoly.

"Monopoly," he said wryly.

"I figured." She smiled faintly and ran her hand over her abdomen as she sat on the side chair again. "With this one, the only thing in my future is going to be Chutes and Ladders. And I think Twister is definitely a thing of the past for me."

He couldn't recall the last time he'd played the human-pretzel game, but his imagination had no trouble conjuring up images of the two of them playing. Whether she was five months' pregnant or not.

He grimly pulled the top off the Monopoly box. He needed to get those sorts of thoughts out of his brain or he'd be a raving lunatic before too long. "You want to be banker or should I?" She didn't answer and he looked at her. She was nibbling the inside of her lip, her hands folded neatly in her lap. "Something wrong?"

Her fingers lifted slightly. "You tell me. You're the one who seems…upset."

"Just cabin fever," he dismissed. A convenient excuse and much better than admitting that he was aching for her right to his back teeth. He unfolded the game board on the coffee table. It was such a well-used game that the cardboard nearly split apart at the seams. "Pick your piece." He dumped the playing pieces on the corner of the board closest to her.

She didn't look exactly convinced but she reached out and selected the car.

"I'd have pegged you for the Scotty dog piece," he drawled. He'd keep it light, or die trying.

"You just wanted the car for yourself," she returned and set her piece on *Go*. "Like all typical men."

He took the dog for himself and dumped the rest of the unused pieces back into the box. "Played plenty of Monopoly then, have you?"

"A time or two. When we were younger." She slid out of the chair to sit on the floor beside the table.

"Your brother liked the car," he deduced.

She picked up the stack of property cards. "And my father liked the money," she murmured. "You can do the banking. I'll do the title deeds. Unless you're one of those stick-to-the-rules kind of guys where the banker handles it all." She squared the cards with a tap on the table, waiting.

"There are a few rules I live by—" namely not taking advantage of vulnerable women "—but that's not one of them."

She began organizing the cards on the floor beside her. "What are they? The rules."

"We each get $1,500.00 to start."

She looked at him from beneath her lashes. "*Your* rules. Not the game."

He rifled through the play money. "Don't lie."

She glanced back at the cards she was laying out. He strongly wished that it was just coincidence, but the prickling at the back of his neck warned him otherwise. "Don't cheat," he added as if he hadn't noticed a single thing. "And don't steal."

"That's all?"

"They tend to cover most everything, literally or otherwise."

She laid out the last deed card and leaned her elbow on the coffee table. "I suppose they do, at that." She toyed with the dice that were lying on the board. "So are we playing for a set time or until you go bankrupt?"

Despite the prickling at his nape and her obvious change of subject, he grinned. "You didn't learn much by that snowball exchange, did you?"

"Just pass me my money and roll the dice. And then we'll see."

What they would see, he decided sometime later, was that whoever had taught her to play the game had taught her well. Fortunately for him, though economics hadn't been his career path, whiling away hours between emergency calls usually entailed some sort of pastime and he was no slouch at the game, either.

They were pretty much dead even as they broke to have some lunch—cold tuna sandwiches and canned tomato soup that she heated over the fire—and had begun playing second pieces just to spice it up when the gray light angled from afternoon toward evening and snow still spit from the sky. They'd pushed the coffee table out of the way, moved the game to the floor, and had even resorted to creating more money to supplement the bank's depleted supply.

"You're a cutthroat," he announced, not for the first time, when he landed on one of her building-laden properties to the tune of wiping out a substantial portion of his personal bank account.

"Maybe with the game," she demurred, taking the hefty rent he forfeited to her and adding it to her neat, orderly piles. By contrast, his cash was spread haphazardly next to him. His dwindling cash, that was.

"In real life?"

She shook her head. "Not so much or I wouldn't be here." She rolled the dice, and made a face when she landed on one of his particularly well-endowed properties. She handed back some of the money she'd just taken from him. "That's the fourth time I've landed on Park Place!"

She may have snatched up more properties, but he'd snagged his share, including the two biggies—Park Place and Boardwalk. With hotels, the resulting "rent" was nothing to sneeze at. "And my wallet appreciates it." He dropped the money on his pile. He knew if they called it quits, she'd be the winner with more assets, but he didn't really care. Continuing the game was as good a way to pass the time as any other.

Well. It was a safer way, at least.

"If you weren't here, where else would you be?" he asked.

Only the width of the tattered playing board separated them. "Nowhere interesting," she said, and leaned back against the pillow that she'd propped under her side. She stretched her arms over her head and pointed her toes—back inside socks once more—toward the fire. "Oh." Her hand went back to her abdomen.

"Are you all right?"

"Yes. The baby's moving." She shot him a bemused look. "I'm still not used to it."

"Do you know if it's a boy or a girl?"

"Not yet." Her lashes were lowered in concentration as her hand slowly drifted along her abdomen. "I have an ultrasound scheduled next week. If I want to find out then, they'll probably be able to tell me."

The motion of her hand was doing a good job of pulling the soft fabric of her shirt snug against her breasts.

He tried not to notice.

But he was a guy.

He noticed.

He absently rolled the dice and didn't even complain when he landed on the Go to Jail square. "Do you want to know?"

"I haven't decided yet," she mused thoughtfully. "On one hand, I'd like to wait and learn when the baby is born. On the other hand, knowing now would make it easier when I hit the secondhand store to find baby clothes." Her smile turned wry. "Not that an infant cares *what* color he or she is wearing. I just prefer blue or pink over that ever-neutral yellow. Green isn't my particular favorite, either. Fortunately, at the shop I found in San Antonio there doesn't seem to be a shortage of baby gear in any color. I'll sell you my Get Out of Jail card for a hundred dollars."

"Shark." The usual fee was only fifty. "I'll pass. What about a crib? Where will you put that?"

"I haven't figured that out yet. I wasn't even sure I'd be here when the baby came." She rolled onto her side, propped up on her elbow and reached for the dice.

"Got a bigger place in mind?"

"I meant *here* as in Red Rock."

"Town is a good place for kids." He kept his voice reasonable, though his neck was prickling like crazy. "The Foundation offers child care for its employees. Why would you want to leave that?"

"I wouldn't." She rolled the dice. "Not unless I had to."

"Why would you have to?"

She exhaled softly. "Darr—"

"Look, Barbara." He abruptly took the direct route. "Why don't you just tell me what kind of trouble you're in? Maybe I can help."

An expressionless mask that didn't fool him for a second slid over her face. "There's no trouble."

"Okay, then whatever you're running from," he said evenly. "Is it the baby's father?" It was an obvious guess.

She pushed to her knees and then to her feet, scattering her stacks of Monopoly money. "I realize it goes against your very nature, but you don't have to rescue me from anything else, Darr." She stepped over the game board and around his feet and went to the kitchen area. "I imagine you're hungry. I, um, I'm not sure what to fix for supper. Unless it's more canned soup and sandwiches." She picked up the loaf of bread they'd left on the counter after lunch. "Not imaginative, I know, but at least I can manage to boil something over the fire without ruining it."

He pushed to his feet, too, and followed her. Tension screamed from her slender shoulders and he settled his fingers on one pink-clad shoulder. "Barbara—"

She winced. Her fingers squeezed the plastic-wrapped bread. "I don't cheat," she said abruptly. "And I don't steal. And I never used to lie."

He pulled the bread out of her hand before she finished squashing it to death. "I want to help," he said softly, "but I need to know what we're dealing with."

"Why?" Her lashes lifted. Confusion clouded her eyes. "Why does it even matter to you? I'm nobody!"

"No one is nobody," he countered. "Certainly not you. Not to me. And if I haven't managed to convey that after all these hours you've been stuck with me, then I guess I'm not as good at communicating as I thought."

"I don't want you feeling sorry for me."

"Believe me, that isn't one of the feelings that is plaguing me." If anything, he was feeling pretty sorry for himself, and pretty annoyed by that very fact. "Just tell me whatever it is and we'll go from there."

"Maybe I'm a bank robber on the run."

He snorted. "Right. Living low on the hog so as not to draw attention to yourself."

"Well," she made a face, "what if I told you it was some legal problem. What would you do? Help me hide out? Turn me in?"

"I'd do what I could to help you. But I don't believe it's something like that. The Foundation runs background checks on all of its employees. You obviously passed that."

"Barbara Burton passed that," she said wearily.

He tipped up her chin. "And who is she?" he asked quietly.

Her lips pressed together. A swallow worked down her throat. She looked braced for a blow. "A friend from school."

He let out a long breath and slid his arms around her, tucking her head beneath his chin.

Amazingly, she didn't try to pull away.

Finally, they were getting somewhere.

He listened to the snap of the wind outside the cottage. "And that would mean you are... who?"

Chapter Six

"Bethany," she whispered so easily she cringed. Where was the backbone she was supposed to have grown in the past two months? Gone in a blink simply because it felt so good, so safe, surrounded by Darr's arms? It didn't even seem to matter that she knew she couldn't trust her own judgment when it came to men. The truth just pushed at her lips until the words were out. "My name is Bethany. Bethany Burdett."

"Bethany," he repeated softly. "That feels like a much better fit than Barbara." He tucked his finger beneath her chin and nudged upward. "Bethany," he said again. "Why the pretense?"

"I didn't do anything illegal," she said swiftly. Except lie about who she was to everyone she'd encountered since escaping Dallas. "And using Barb's name wasn't to defraud anyone or anything." Her old friend was living in Paris, studying art and blissfully unaware of the mess in which Bethany had found herself.

"Good to know."

She frowned warily. "You believe me?"

"I think I can tell when you're lying."

"Great." She pulled out of his arms and reached for the loaf of bread again. There was only half a loaf left as it was, and she'd managed to squash half of *that*. "So you know I've been a liar all along." She could only imagine what he must think of her.

He caught her elbows and turned her inexorably to face him again. "What I *knew* is that there were a few things that didn't add up for me. What I suspected was that you're scared of something. Or someone. And now, knowing that you're not even using your own name, I'm more convinced of it than ever."

"All right. I'm a poor liar. And you've got hero-juice flowing in your veins instead of blood. But this isn't a fire. You don't have to pull me to safety. I...I have to do this myself."

"And when does the lie stop, Bethany? You're halfway to term. Do you want to bring your baby into a world where you're still running? Still pretending to be someone that you're not?"

"The only thing that is a pretense is my name," she countered swiftly. "Everything else about my life here is real. The most *real* it's ever been!"

"Why? Because you're shopping at secondhand stores instead of designer shops?"

She could feel the blood draining out of her head and swallowed back a wave of dizzying nausea. "I don't know what you mean."

He snorted. "You buy one of the most expensive brands of coffee beans that you won't let yourself drink. The cost of that suitcase in the closet alone would probably pay the rent on this place for half a year. You might be living frugally now,

Bethany, but I'd bet my salary that it's not something you're accustomed to."

"Spoiled rich girl just doesn't wash off the way you'd think."

His lips tightened, but his eyes never lost that calm, gentle quality.

Maybe that's why it was so dangerously easy to let herself trust him.

Darr never got that look in his eyes that Lyle had when he was irritated.

"I don't think you're spoiled. I think you're—" He broke off. Tilted his head back and closed his eyes for a moment. "God," he murmured. He looked back at her, evidently shaking off whatever he'd been about to say. "It's the baby's father. That's who you're hiding from, right?"

Her throat tightened. She nodded. It was the truth. Just not all of the truth. Her parents were as thorny a problem as the man she'd nearly married.

He pulled the bread out of her grasp yet again. Folded her cold hands inside his. "What happened?"

"It doesn't matter. It's over."

"It does matter, when you feel you have to hide who you are. Honey, that's your basic damn right as a human being!"

Her eyes stung. Why couldn't she have met a man like Darr instead of a man like Lyle?

She stared at Darr's hands wrapped around hers. Strength was in the wide, square palms, the long, blunt-tipped fingers.

Strength.

Not violence.

"The first time he hit me, he blamed it on too many cocktails at a charity benefit we'd just attended." Her voice was thin with the humiliation that still burned.

Darr's fingers twitched around her hands, but he said

nothing. Just waited. As if they had all the time in the world in that snowbound cottage for her to run down the countless mistakes she'd made.

"We'd been engaged for three months by then," she added. "Marrying him satisfied everyone. His family. My family." Particularly her family, but she hadn't realized just *how* much until the day of the wedding and in a fit of temper over her wanting to wear her pearls instead of the diamond choker he'd given her as a wedding gift, Lyle had coldly informed her about the financial arrangement between him and her father.

Darr slowly ran his thumb over the back of her knuckles. "And you? Did the idea of marrying him satisfy you?"

She frowned slightly. "It...I couldn't think of a reason to refuse. The only thing I was raised to do was land a husband like him. Successful. Wealthy."

"Did you love him?" His voice was even lower. Deeper.

"I'd known him since I was twenty-one. I thought I did." Even that admission burned. "Or maybe I just convinced myself that I did because everyone expected me to." She made a face. "It's a poor excuse, but if you knew me, you'd see...well. Anyway, I found out I was pregnant and suddenly there was something more important to focus on than finding exactly the right shade of dye for my bridesmaids' shoes, and deciding between Bavarian cream or lemon-curd filling for the wedding cake." Her throat tightened. "My...fiancé didn't embrace the idea when I told him about the baby." In fact, he'd been livid. He wanted a beautiful Texas debutante on his arm. Not a pregnant heifer.

"He's an ass," Darr said. "A real piece of sh—scum."

Since Bethany had come to that conclusion herself, she didn't see any reason to argue.

"You said the *first* time. He hit you again?"

The first time, she'd retreated to her parents, expecting them to be as fully horrified as she'd been. Her father had snapped at her to stop exaggerating a lover's tiff. Her mother had wailed that Bethany needed to beg, if she had to, to get back into Lyle's good graces before he called off the wedding. The second time, she'd showed them the bruises on her shoulders caused by Lyle's punishing hands, and they *still* accused her of some imagined hysteria caused by the elaborate wedding plans and rapidly approaching nuptials. The third time, she hadn't gone to her parents. Instead, she'd run out on all of them on the very day of her wedding.

Run out on her life.

And now, it was just her and her baby. And though she worried about the future, about being a good mother, about how she would make ends meet when the only thing she'd ever been trained to do was decorate the arm of a wealthy man, she didn't regret her actions for a second.

Except that she hadn't left for good after the first time.

"Sometimes I'm a slow learner," she said. About Lyle. About her parents.

Definitely about herself.

She drew in a shaking breath and let it out in a heady stream. "He's out of our life and I want to keep it that way."

"But you think he's looking for you. That's the reason for the assumed name."

She was certain of it. Lyle wouldn't stand for the public humiliation of his bride running out on him. The fact that he'd managed to keep it out of the news was simply a testament to the power he wielded as an up-and-coming power broker. The fact that his intended was the youngest daughter of one of the oldest, supposedly most oil-moneyed families in the entire state would only make the scandal that much more juicy.

"I don't want to take the chance, just in case he is," Bethany said carefully.

"You should have pressed charges against him."

Her father was drinking buddies with the sheriff and both of them were firmly in the good-ol'-boy mold. "Maybe. But leaving was my top priority."

He was watching her with hooded eyes. "That was a good move, too."

She knew it, but having Darr commend her for it was still unexpected. And unaccountably touching.

Inside her, the baby fluttered.

Awareness accosted her over just how closely the two of them were standing.

Of the way his thumb continued to stroke, warm and distracting, over her knuckles. The back of her hand. Again and again.

And just how alone they were there in her small, rented house. She and this man whose kiss had been intoxicatingly tempting.

She swallowed against her oddly parched throat. Moistened her dry lips. She knew the wisest course would be to move away from him. To make her trembling legs put some well-needed physical distance between the overwhelming appeal of him and her more-than-apparent vulnerability to it.

But next to *him* is right where she stayed. "Darr—"

"Is it going to freak you out if I kiss you again?"

She sucked in a quick breath.

His gaze burned over her face, dropped to her lips, then returned to her eyes. She felt warm from the inside out. "You didn't freak me out the first time," she reminded. The admission felt husky. Raw. "That probably says more about me than anything." She was a runaway bride, with an attraction to her snowed-in roommate that was escalating exponentially.

But there was no judgment in his blue eyes. Nothing but

warmth. And an odd glint of humor when his lips suddenly kicked up at the corner. "I don't know that it says anything at all. So I'll be the one to admit being a little freaked."

She felt a hot flush rise up her throat and start to crawl up her face. "If you didn't want to kiss me, then why did you?"

"I didn't say I didn't want to." He caught her face in his hands. "What's unsettling is how damn badly I didn't want to stop."

Then why did you? By some small grace, she managed to contain the question and all that emerged was a faint, innocuous "Oh."

Why should she be surprised that she didn't understand this man anymore than she understood anyone else? Her faulty judgment was well established, after all. He kissed her, claimed he didn't want to stop kissing her, but was he kissing her *now?*

No. He was staring at her with those heavy-lidded, wrenchingly sexy blue eyes of his, as if he couldn't quite figure out what to do with her.

There was no mystery to solve, as far as she could tell. She was five months' pregnant and had admitted that the baby's father was a slug of a human being.

Why would he want to get involved with that, even if the kiss they'd shared *had* been explosive?

She squelched the pang and the sigh that rose with it, and finally managed to back up a step. Why would she want to get involved, for that matter?

Almost immediately, his hands on hers fell away and she was more convinced than ever that, at last, she was on the right track.

"It's getting dark in here," she said. "I'll light a few candles." And then she'd figure out what to feed them.

The last of the loaf of bread was out. She'd managed to

squash it beyond recognition. It was either eat a meal of raw vegetables—there were plenty still in the fridge—or cook something again over the fire.

She took the matchbook that was sitting on the counter and moved over to the dinette where the trio of candles waited, and struck the match. The flame trembled unsteadily as she set it to the wicks.

Behind her, Darr moved away from the kitchen area. "I'll clean up the game."

She didn't protest but when she heard the wooden clatter of Monopoly houses and hotels sliding into the cardboard box, she closed her eyes against the pang she felt.

After that, the rest of the evening passed in an oddly surreal calm. They shared the hot soup that she heated over the fire, ate peanut butter and saltine crackers, and drank the last of the milk from the refrigerator that was just now beginning to show signs of warming. They heated water in her largest pot to use for washing up—dishes *and* themselves—and he brought in yet more wood from outside while she hid in the candlelit bathroom and prepared for bed, all the while shivering in the cold, tiled room.

They didn't talk about Lyle again.

Or about kissing.

When she came out of the bathroom, he'd unfolded the sofa bed for her, and was tossing the comforter he'd used the night before on top of the cushions he'd situated once again in front of the kitchenette. He'd obviously made himself at home enough to find the blankets and pillows where she kept them in the hall closet.

Strangely enough, she felt no sense of being intruded upon. In fact, there really didn't seem to be anything odd or unusual about his presence at all.

As if he belonged right where he was in the flickering fire-light and candlelight.

She chewed the inside of her lip and pulled off the robe that had been a gift from her mother's favored fashion designer, dropped it on the end of the bed and lay down.

And stared blindly up at the ceiling.

"What's wrong?" His voice floated to her, reminding her of the night he'd carried her out of the burning restaurant.

"Nothing." Nothing more than was ever wrong at any rate, and at the moment, even those problems seemed long ago and very far away. She heard the jingle of his belt again. Same as the previous night. The sound of it, too, seemed normal.

Like they were quite the cozy little twosome, together for so long they were as comfortable as old shoes.

Only she'd never felt as if the nerves beneath her skin were ready to burst into song when it came to footwear, a pointed little voice inside her head reminded her.

Beneath the blanket, her stocking-clad toes curled and she reached down and pulled off her socks, folded them up and leaned over to leave them on the side table.

Darr, stripped only down to his jeans and that white T-shirt that hugged his shoulders, was blowing out the candles on the table.

She wondered what he usually wore when he slept.

Pajamas—even just the pants, silk or otherwise—seemed highly unlikely. She lay back down and stared at the ceiling some more, watching the shadows thrown by the fire dance around.

Everything was silent except for the low crackle of the fire-place.

That, and the busyness swirling around inside her head that would not settle down.

She finally turned on her side, scrunched the soft pillow

beneath her neck and looked at the covered mound of him stretched out on the floor. She could clearly make out his tousled hair and the gleam of the white cotton knit clinging to his shoulders.

"Was it still snowing when you went out for the wood?"

"No."

She gnawed at her lip some more. "Do you have a girlfriend?"

He didn't budge. "I jumped your bones in the snow this morning, Bethany. What do you think?"

On one hand, she recognized that he hadn't given a direct answer. On the other hand, she recognized that she believed him anyway. "Were you ever married?"

"No."

"How old are you?"

"Thirty."

"Have you ever come close?"

The comforter finally rustled as he turned on his side to face her. It was too dark to make out the expression in his eyes. She sensed, more than heard, his sigh. "Briefly."

She'd asked the question so she had absolutely no right to feel the pinch inside her at his answer. She moistened her lips. She couldn't seem to make herself drop the matter there, though. "What…what happened?"

"She preferred someone else."

Ouch. She bunched her pillow a little more. "How long ago?"

"Three years."

Which was about how long ago he'd moved to Red Rock, she remembered.

Had he left his heart in California with the woman who'd married someone else? "What was her name?"

He sighed again. "If I tell you, will you go to sleep?"

"Yes."

He made a soft sound. "That didn't really sound convincing, Bethany." There was a faint hint of amusement in his deep voice. "Celia," he added, and the amusement was gone, just like that. "Her name was Celia."

Was she beautiful? This time, Bethany wisely refrained from asking. She didn't know if it was better or worse to have a beautiful name for the faceless woman in his past.

"D'you realize that we've spent more than twenty-four hours together?" Straight. If they'd been seeing one another socially, how many dates would that equal?

"Yeah." Now he just sounded pained. "Do you need something warm to drink? Would that make you sleepier?"

"There's no milk left to warm. There's instant cocoa and water. Do *you* want some?"

In answer, he shoved back the comforter and rummaged around the counter above him. He filled the fire-blackened metal pan with water and took it to the fireplace, then sat on the edge of the brick hearth, watching it heat.

While she watched him.

Around them, the house gave an odd creak and she sat up. "What was that?"

"The house settling, probably." He barely glanced around.

"I wonder how long it'll be before we can get out."

"Tomorrow, one way or another." He retrieved mugs and the envelopes of cocoa mix that he dumped into them and returned to the hearth. Beneath the snug T-shirt, his muscles moved fluidly as he filled the mugs with the quickly heated water and stirred the contents before handing one to her.

She sat up on her elbow to take the mug. Her fingers accidentally brushed his. "Had enough of being cooped up here, then?" She kept her voice light and ducked her head over the hot drink.

"My shift starts tomorrow. Seven in the morning." He'd

made himself a mug of cocoa, too, but she noticed that he didn't drink much of it before he set it on the counter and lowered himself back to his improvised bed.

She sipped, eyeing him over the rim. She supposed if the snow had really stopped that it would quickly start to melt off. But not by seven in the morning. "How will we get your truck out of the snow?"

"I called Nick again when I was bringing in the wood. He'll borrow one of the Double Crown trucks to get here. He'll help get it out."

She fell silent. Of course he wouldn't have just waited around for conditions to improve. He was a take-charge sort of man. She had no reason to feel as if he were abandoning her.

No reason at all.

"I'll get a generator out to you, too, if the electricity isn't restored."

"You don't have to go to all that trouble for me."

"It's no trouble. Probably spend most of my next shift helping people dig out."

She sucked the edge of her lip between her teeth and set aside the mug. "Well…thank you."

"No prob." His comforter rustled and the white gleam of his T-shirt disappeared as he pulled the covers nearly to his ears.

She drew her own blanket to her chin and closed her eyes. She was even *less* sleepy now, but she would pretend to sleep if she had to.

And she would keep her mouth shut.

Darr let out a long, quiet breath when Bethany finally went silent and stayed that way long enough for him to believe she'd mercifully fallen asleep.

She was a pregnant woman. She *needed* her sleep.

He was a man burning up from the inside out and needed something a helluva lot stronger than a powdered hot-chocolate drink to make him forget it.

He threw his arm over his eyes, but nothing could block out her presence just a few feet from him.

And then he heard her voice as she said his name—little more than a whisper above the crackling of the fire—and it put his belief that she'd fallen safely asleep to a grisly death.

If he were a smart man, *he'd* pretend to be asleep. Pretend that he didn't hear that soft, tentative whisper.

Nobody'd ever figured him for genius. "Yeah?"

She was silent for a moment. A log snapped, sending a shower of glowing sparks up the flue. "You'd be warmer on the bed," she finally said.

He exhaled. There was truth in that. A finely honed, double-edged truth. "I'm fine where I am."

He heard her blankets rustle, and in the dim light he saw her push up on her elbow again. Glints of gold and red seemed to reflect off her pale hair. "I don't mind. There's room for us…for us both."

No amount of swallowing was going to combat his arid throat. He finally pushed up on his hands and eyed her. "It's not a good idea."

"Why not?"

He exhaled. "You know why." God in heaven, how could she not?

He couldn't see the expression in her eyes, but he could see the way her lashes fell for a long, silent moment. When they lifted again it felt as if even the fire was holding its breath.

She moved her hand.

And pulled back the covers.

"Bethany—"

"Don't." Her voice was husky. "Don't tell me all the sensible reasons why you think this is not smart."

"If I lay there beside you, I'm going to want to make love to you," he said bluntly. "You realize that?"

She was silent for a heart-thudding minute. "I...I'm not an idiot."

"No. You're a vulnerable, *pregnant,* young woman."

She sat up. Despite the flower-sprigged flannel she wore, he could still see the curve of her shoulder, the taut, full thrust of her breasts, silhouetted against the firelight.

"Does it turn you off? My being pregnant?"

"What'd I just say?" He shoved his fingers through his hair. "God, Bethany. I've been looking for you for weeks. I've wanted you for the last thirty-one freaking hours!"

He could see her lips part. Could hear the indrawn breath she took. Imagined that he could feel the weight of her heartbeat, throbbing in every pulse point.

"I want you, too," she finally said. Quietly. Distinctly. "Don't worry, Darr. I'm not asking for anything more. I just want to be with you. Now. Tonight."

As if he needed any more contributing forces to the erosion of his self-control. The problem was, he was absolutely certain that "now, tonight," wasn't going to be remotely enough for him when it came to Bethany Burdett.

If he were a stronger man, a better man, he'd find some way to talk her off this particular cliff. But he wasn't stronger. He wasn't better.

He wasn't anything but a man who was in a knot over a beautiful woman.

A woman in need.

Dammit. He ought to know better.

He shoved back the blankets that—if he weren't basically

conflagrating from the inside out over her—would be doing a poor job of keeping the encroaching cold at bay, and pushed off the thin couch cushions.

He could feel her gaze on him like a physical thing as he stood beside the sofa bed. "Are you sure?" His voice seemed to come from somewhere deep inside him where there still lingered a kernel of hesitation, of control.

She sat up more fully and with a little shimmy that knotted him right down to his toes, she drew her flannel nightgown up and over her head.

She couldn't have looked more erotic if she'd been doing the Dance of the Seven Veils.

The nightgown seemed to drop, almost in slow motion from her extended fingers, drifting to a soft mound right over his bare toes.

And if that wasn't message enough for his addled soul, which was drinking in the sight of her pink-crested breasts and the curve of her creamy hip as if he'd never seen such a marvel, she held out that hand to him, her fingers trembling ever so slightly. "I'm sure." Her whisper was soft. Throaty.

He closed his hand over her fingers. They felt cool against his palm. He knelt on the mattress and in some graceful dance that he couldn't recall ever learning, he turned her toward him and followed her down, his mouth covering hers.

She tasted of hot chocolate.

And sweet, mindless pleasure.

His pulse raced in his ears, as loud and furious as a firestorm. When he felt her fingertips tug at his rumpled T-shirt, pulling it free of his jeans, and sliding beneath to drift across his abdomen, he nearly came out of his skin.

"Wait." He caught her fingers in his. God help him, but he

was a basket case if just the taste of her lips, the graze of her fingertips, was enough to send him careening out of control.

She stared up at him, her hair an untidy and gut-wrenchingly sexy fan over the pillows around her head. Her breasts rose and fell with her deep, choppy breaths. "You've changed your mind."

He exhaled roughly. "Hell, no." He finished the job of yanking off his shirt himself, and pitched it off the bed to land who knew where. As long as it wasn't in the fire, he didn't care. Then he slid down beside her. "Come here." He pulled her into his arms and she moved smoothly, easily, against him, only to breathe an audible sigh when he rolled back, taking her with him until she was draped over him like the sweetest of blankets.

"Cold?"

"I should be," she whispered. "Considering I'm the naked one here."

Ripe. Naked. Glorious.

But mindful of the undeniable chill in the air, he worked the nubby blanket from beneath his hip and dragged it over the both of them. Beneath, his hands slowly slid up and down her spine, gaining only a few precious inches with each pass.

"You're making me crazy." Her words were little more than a whisper that burned along his jaw. Her knees slid to either side of his hips and she sat up, bracing her hand flat against his abdomen.

He lifted his head and caught one of those taunting, tempting nipples between his lips.

She made a soft sound. A needy purr of a sound that drove him mad. But when she reached for the waist of his jeans, he sucked in a hard breath, his head falling back. She popped open the button. And then another. Slowly. Tormenting.

He muttered an oath and yanked apart the rest of his fly, shoving the jeans away. "Come here." He pulled her back to him, and nearly cried like a baby when her hand snuck between them, circling him. Her thigh slid over his hips and in one smooth arch, she suddenly took him in. Fully. Completely.

He very nearly forgot how to breathe.

He damn sure forgot everything he'd ever known about self-control.

"I can't wait," she whispered thickly. "I'm sorry. I've never wanted anyone so badly."

He caught her hips in his hands, holding her tight. Still. But deep inside her, where she held him so intimately gloved, he could feel the very pulse of her. "You think that requires an apology?"

She lowered her mouth toward his. "Kiss me." Her whisper teased his lips. "Kiss me like you never want to stop."

The problem was he *didn't* ever want to stop.

The problem was, in the cold light of day, he figured *she* would.

His hands swept up her spine, slid over her tumbled hair and cradled her face while his mouth caught hers. And then there was just too damn much sensation to think about problems or what the next morning would bring, or even what the next hour would bring.

All he cared about was the moment.

The slide of her tongue against his.

The press of her fingertips against his ribs.

The soft cries that rose in her throat as they rocked together, as perfectly attuned as two lovers had ever been, and the fluttering, grasping spasms deep inside her that clutched him, drugged him, maddened him. And when she gasped his name and threw her head back, every line of her taut body shining in the firelight, he practically felt the top of his head blow off as he spun along with her, emptying everything he was inside her.

And then all was still.

Except for those sweet, nearly painful aftershocks working through her as her head dropped forward and she slowly collapsed against him.

His heart felt like a freight train inside his head. Her breathing was more like a marathoner's gasps. Despite the pervasive chill in the room, they were both slick with sweat. His hands were actually shaking when he closed them over her spine. "I didn't hurt you, did I?"

She pressed her forehead more tightly into the curve of his neck. Shook her head. "It…you…were perfect."

She'd drained everything out of him. He felt about as macho as a weak kitten who'd been run down by a hurricane. "Honey, there ain't a man alive who wouldn't want to take the credit when a woman tells him that, but you were the perfect one."

"It wasn't me." She lifted her tousled head. In the firelight, her eyes were dark, gleaming pools. She slid her hand over his still-racing heart. "I've never felt anything like that before. Not ever."

"Well, gee. Thanks, ma'am," he drawled after the too-long pause his addled brain took to absorb that. "Glad to be of service."

She gave a half laugh, and pressed her forehead to his shoulder again. "The aw-shucks tone isn't quite believable coming from you."

He grinned into the dark and smoothly turned her onto her back. The slight thrust of her belly was visible in the flickering glow. As were the pink nipples that tightened even more as he looked at her. "Good. But when I finish making you crazy again, you'll see that I'm not exaggerating about the service part." He ran his hand over her waist. Splayed his fingers over the burgeoning swell of her baby.

She caught her breath, and pressed her hands against his, stilling his motion. "Feel that?"

He felt plenty. The satiny warmth of her skin. The indentation of her navel beneath his thumb. The downy mound beneath his little finger. The desire rising inside him again, as if he were fifteen instead of thirty.

"That's the baby moving," she prompted.

His attention abruptly pinpointed to the firm swell under his palm. "Seriously?"

"Wait," she whispered. "There." In a flash, she pressed their hands about an inch to the right.

And he did feel it.

The faintest of small flutters. Like the wings of a butterfly scraping against his palm. "Jesus," he breathed. He slid around until his face was right next to her belly. "Hey there, peanut," he said against her. "How's it going?"

She laughed softly and lifted one hand, sliding it slowly through his hair. "You're the nut."

"So I've been told." He probably was. Just then, he didn't give a flip.

He pressed his lips to her abdomen and she caught her breath. Her fingers tightened. "Darr."

Not a protest. Just a sigh of his name.

He closed his eyes. Wondered if he was imagining the flutter of the baby that he felt against his lips and decided that it didn't matter. The baby was there and he couldn't ignore it anymore than he could ignore the idea that had started swimming inside of him hours earlier.

Long before she'd seduced him into sharing the bed.

"Marry me," he said.

Chapter Seven

Bethany stiffened. "What?"

He sat up and despite the cold douse of shock coursing through her, she couldn't help but appreciate the thoroughly masculine beauty of him. "I know it sounds crazy," he admitted, "but it makes perfect sense."

"Why? Just because we slept together?" She didn't believe for a minute that any man in this present day and age would think one should necessitate the other.

"If you need a reason, yeah. Because we slept together."

"No. No. You don't want to marry me," she countered swiftly, denying the very idea of it. For pity's sake, she'd practically had to beg him to make love to her. "It's not like you need to rescue my virtue." Her parents had essentially auctioned that off to Lyle, though Darr had no way of knowing that.

He exhaled briefly, impatiently. "This isn't a rescue."

"Of course it is. And I need to take care of myself. All my

life I've let other people do that, and look what happened!" She spread her fingers across the swell of her baby.

His gaze followed her hands and she couldn't help but swallow hard when she saw the way his gaze drifted upward, lingering on her breasts. Nor could she help the way her flesh tightened, the way her nipples pebbled and rose like they were begging for his attention.

They *were* begging, darn it all.

Every nerve in her body wanted more of his touch.

More of him.

"As my wife, you would be immediately covered under my insurance." His voice was a hair ragged and she felt a perversely feminine thrill over it. "So would the baby. I'm hardly rolling in dough, but I can still provide. We could find a house here in Red Rock. Or even build. You wouldn't have to work unless you chose to. And you damn sure wouldn't have to worry about that spineless bastard finding you. You...and the baby...would have my name." His angled jaw looked carved from stone. "Nobody messes with a Fortune and gets away with it."

What he offered sounded so easy. So plausible. So reasonable.

"We hardly know each other!"

"We know enough."

That was the problem. He didn't know enough. And she couldn't bring herself to tell him.

What would he think when he learned how little she'd truly mattered to her own family? That they'd rather marry her off to an abuser than give up the millions that Lyle had been prepared to invest in the family business upon their marriage?

Maybe Darr would end up agreeing.

Her small gains of independence were too fresh, too tender

to put to the test. If she backslid now, what would happen later when it wasn't just her pregnant self she had to take care of, but a tiny, defenseless baby, as well?

"I can't marry you."

"You mean you won't."

She slid off the bed and stood. "I mean I can't! You're a nice man, Darr. A decent man." Her gaze caught. An aroused man. "A…a really…decent man," she repeated doggedly. Goose bumps that had nothing to do with the chill in the air were dancing down her spine, and she snatched up her robe, dragging it over her shoulders.

The velvet felt excruciatingly soft against her hypersensitive skin.

His calloused fingertips had felt even better.

She dragged the belt around her waist and yanked it into a knot. If only she could tie up and put away her reaction to him just as decisively.

"And it's not that I don't appreciate your noble intentions, but truly, they're not necessary. I have to take care of myself." If she didn't do it now, she feared that she never would.

"And I'm telling you that you don't have to do it alone."

Maybe later, when she had reason to have more faith in herself, she could afford to let herself think that way. But not now. Not yet.

Not even if the offer of help came gift-wrapped in the altogether addictive appeal of Darr Fortune.

"I just—" She broke off when the house seemed to groan again. More loudly than before.

Even Darr stood. His eyes narrowed in concentration. Then he suddenly swore and snatched up his jeans.

She'd never seen anyone dress so fast. From two T-shirts to boots. "What's—"

But he'd already grabbed his coat and was heading out the door. "Stay inside." The order was terse.

The groaning turned into a high-pitched screech as he closed the door behind him and she nearly jumped out of her skin.

She hopped around tugging on her socks and pushing her feet into her tennis shoes, showing absolutely none of the finesse or efficiency that Darr had exhibited. Getting her coat was too much effort so she just grabbed the blanket off the tumbled bed, threw it around her shoulders and dashed out after him.

The cold air hit her like a fist, and the soles of her shoes slid on the steps.

She grabbed the handrail to keep from flying head over heels and paused, willing her heart back into place. She had the baby to consider! She needed to be more careful.

Another screech squealed eerily and she quickly moved off the steps. Her tennis shoes broke the crisp surface of snow and she sank down to her ankles.

"Dammit, Bethany, I told you to stay inside." Darr's voice came from several yards away and she focused on the darker shadow of his form barely visible in the thin moonlight and headed toward him. He was some distance from the side of the house, facing it.

"I don't like being told what to do."

"Then use your common sense. You don't need to be out here catching a cold." His arm came up, holding her back when she reached him. "Far enough."

She hitched the blanket higher around her shoulders and clutched it at her waist to keep it from dragging in the snow. "Is it the roof?" She hoped it wasn't, but assumed that if it were, the owners would have to fix it.

"Carport," Darr said, and swore when yet another screech rent the air, followed by a gunshot of a crack.

Bethany nearly screamed, she was so startled, and Darr pulled her close, turning his back toward the house even as an explosive crash vibrated right through their feet. Chunks of snow flew out at them, raining over their heads.

And then there was nothing but awful, horrible, silence.

"I should've known," he muttered finally, holding her tightly. His hand brushed over her head. Her shoulders. "Are you hurt?"

She shook her head and looked up. "What—" Her throat clamped shut with horror. "My car," finally emerged, sounding strangled.

Even in the dark she could make out the scene. Could see the tumble of debris from what had *been* the carport, along with a massive pile of snow, now smashed squarely down on the hood of her car.

Her caved-in car, that was.

"Don't try to get closer to it." Darr's hands closed around her again when she started toward it. "There's still one post holding up the backside of the roof, but the structure's too unstable."

She blinked back the sudden burning in her eyes. "I can't believe this is happening." It had taken her weeks to find a car she could afford, and a seller who didn't look too closely at her personal information.

How was she supposed to get around now? To work? To her obstetrician's appointments?

"Insurance should cover it."

She was twenty-five years old. She should know how things like insurance worked! And wasn't that one of the very points she'd been making only a few minutes ago?

She flopped her hands. The blanket fell off her shoulders but she hardly noticed. She had no idea how long a process it would be to get the vehicle fixed. If it could be fixed. And if it couldn't, what then? "What if it doesn't?"

"We'll figure something out."

"This is not your problem, Darr. *I* am not your problem!"

"Maybe I don't look at you and see a *problem*," he countered quietly. He turned her toward him again, snuggling the blanket once more up around her shoulders, and slipped his hand beneath her chin until she couldn't do anything but look at him. "I can *help* you, Bethany. I want to. This is all the more reason to marry me."

Her jaw set. "I've already told you no."

"You're not even going to consider it."

If she did, she'd probably cave in and agree, that's how weak she was. "There's nothing to consider," she insisted.

"You're a damn stubborn woman, you know that?"

Nobody had ever accused her of that, but she realized she much preferred stubborn over weak.

She shivered and hitched the blanket up to cover her chin and turned to eye the remains of her car. Once it was daylight, she feared the mess would look even worse.

Belatedly, it occurred to her that the mess could have been *far* worse. Several times, Darr had stood under that carport splitting wood. What if it had come down on *him?*

She felt sick at the thought. "Better the car than you."

"True. Come on. There's nothing we can do out here in the dark. You're freezing. Let's get inside."

"Do you think the house is safe?"

"The carport was definitely added after the house was built." He pointed. "See? It's separated completely from the exterior wall."

That was at least one positive note.

She headed back toward the porch. Each step she took had her shoes cracking through the snow and by the time they made it inside, there was snow caked inside the shoes, packed and freezing, all around her heels.

She peeled out of them, and her socks, and sat down on the side of the bed, rubbing her feet with the end of her blanket, drying and trying to warm them.

Darr left his boots by the door as usual and dropped his jacket over the back of a chair. With no hint of the self-consciousness that was presently plaguing her, he flipped his shirts off over his head and tugged off his socks, then shucked his jeans.

She lowered her gaze to her feet, but couldn't help peeking through her lashes as he moved around, naked as the day his mama had brought him into the world, and a whole lot more grown up. He spread his jeans across the hearth, close enough to absorb the heat but still a safe distance from the unscreened flame.

Then he stepped in front of her and crouched low, covering her cold feet with his hands and rubbing gently. "Take off your robe."

Heat streaked through her veins.

"It's wet from the snow," he added. "You don't want to get the bed wet, too."

Her hormones didn't come to a jolting stop, but they should have. "Right." Feeling even more self-conscious, she slid the robe off her shoulders.

It was one thing to strip down to nothing but skin when you were making love. It was another thing to do so when the guy rubbing sensation back into your feet was just being practical.

But he hardly seemed to look at her anyway as he grabbed the comforter from the cushions on the floor and dumped it in her lap before spreading the long folds of the robe over the side chair so it, too, would dry. Then he tossed the pillow that he'd been using onto the bed and gestured. "Scoot over."

She hesitated. "Um—"

"It's probably twenty degrees outside and the only wood we've got to get us through the night that's not buried under that carport is that stack there." He gestured at the small pile of split logs that still remained. "We're both cold. We'll be warmer in bed. Together."

She felt tongue-tied with desire for the man she'd insisted she wouldn't marry. And he *was* merely being practical.

Again.

She reached for the flannel nightgown that she'd pulled off so wantonly not all that much earlier and yanked it over her head, not much caring if he thought she was being silly or not.

With a snap, she flipped out the comforter so it spread across the bed and, without looking at him, slipped into bed beneath it. Facing the kitchenette kept her back to "his" side of the bed and she shoved her pillow under her head, pulling the comforter up to her ears.

Fortunately, he didn't say a word.

The bedsprings creaked as he joined her on the thin mattress and she tried not to be excruciatingly aware of the tiny points of contact he made along her spine as he settled himself.

He was still for only a few tight moments before he shifted again, with another creak of bedsprings.

Odd how she hadn't noticed that squeaking when they'd been giving the ancient bed a considerably more vigorous workout.

He made a muffled sound. "The floor's almost better than this thing. How do you manage to sleep?"

Defensiveness hunched her shoulders. "You weren't complaining earlier."

"We weren't sleeping earlier," he reminded her pointedly. Needlessly.

She closed her eyes, which only served to bring the still-vivid sensations he'd wrought from her into sharper focus. Making love with Darr was so completely different than her experience with Lyle had been. Then she'd just been anxious to get it over with.

Now with Darr, her insides felt liquefied, wanting only to relive the experience.

Again. And again.

She shoved aside the comforter.

"What's wrong?"

"Nothing." She pushed off the bed and went into the bathroom, closing the door behind her. It was dark as pitch inside with no electricity or candles or firelight, the tile even more uncomfortably cold against her bare feet, but that didn't stop her from accomplishing the necessary, and with her bladder happy once again, she hurried back to the warmth of the bed.

She was trying to keep the folds of her nightgown down around her calves, keep the comforter up around her ears, and find a comfortable position when Darr sighed. "*What* are you doing?"

"My nightgown's tangled."

"Then take it off." His tone was short. And it was certainly devoid of seductive suggestion.

"I don't think so." She yanked the fabric until it was straight again and well below her knees, and pushed the pillow more comfortably beneath her head.

"You need a decent bed."

"Well, this is the only bed I have."

"*I* have a very comfortable king-size bed."

"You have my heartiest congratulations."

"I don't know why you're sounding so ticked off. I'm the one who's had his proposal tossed back in his face."

Her jaws ached. "You only offered out of pity."

"The only thing I pity is our backs from the freaking springs poking through this joke of a mattress."

She stared at the dancing gleam of the fire reflecting against the metal legs of the dinette set.

Between Darr and her car, her thoughts were so jumbled that she wasn't sure she'd ever sleep.

"If I said yes—" which she had absolutely no intention of doing "—what would *you* get out of it?"

"Honey, you have got to be kidding me." His voice was arid.

Her lips twisted. She was getting bigger by the week. "Wait a month and see if you still feel remotely interested."

His arm suddenly scooped around her waist and he slid her smoothly, easily, across the space that separated them.

The surprised gasp that rose in her throat got strangled before it could even emerge when he gripped her hip and tucked her bottom snugly against him.

"Does that feel remote?"

There was no mistaking his meaning.

He was hard. Rock hard. And no amount of thin, cheap flannel between them could have hidden it.

Her paltry shore of resistance was no match for the torrent of want that swamped her. "Darr."

His fingertips flexed against her hip and for an infinitesimal moment, he pressed harder against her. "Don't worry. Evidence to the contrary, I do have some self-control. Go to sleep."

Maybe he had self-control, but she didn't. She wished that she hadn't been so set on wearing the nightgown. That she could feel his hair-roughened chest against her back and his long legs twining with hers. That his hand would slide up, over her aching breasts, or down, between her legs.

That he'd bring her again to that overwhelming, all-encompassing ecstasy that—until him, *with* him—she'd always believed was a wildly exaggerated myth.

She pressed her wrist against her mouth and remained painfully still despite the yearning inside her that imagined arching against him, savoring the magical differences between her body and his.

Eventually, his absolute calmness started to penetrate, though, and instead of bracing against her own thundering pulse, she began to feel the steady beat of his. Her short breaths found—and followed—the pace of his slower, easier ones.

And at last, without even being aware of when it happened, her muscles relaxed into the too-thin mattress, and she slept.

The next thing she knew, daylight was filling the room, creeping easily beyond the thin curtain at the window, and Darr was nowhere to be found.

She could, however, hear deep voices coming from outside. Maybe that was what had woken her.

Or maybe it was the baby pressing on her bladder again.

The alarm clock that sat on the side table was still dark, which meant the electricity was still out. She quickly climbed out of bed, visited the bathroom that was not quite as cold as it had been the night before, and went to the window to look out.

The sky was pale blue and clear with not a cloud in sight, and the horizon was lined with gold from the rising sun. It looked like a perfectly lovely day in the making.

Except that she was still surrounded by snow, the electricity was still out, and her car was still flat.

Still. Still. Still.

She exhaled, and her breath made a faint cloud against the cold windowpane.

A large white pickup truck was parked near Darr's, which had been wiped clean of snow. He and another man—presumably his brother, Nick—were wielding wide, flattish snow shovels as they cleared a track, from where it was mired in snow, to the road.

It was obviously warmer outside. Both men's heads were bare, and Darr's leather jacket wasn't even zipped up.

She nibbled the inside of her lip. At least one of them would be able to get to work.

She, however, would need to get in touch with the owners of the house about the collapsed carport, and figure out what to do about her car.

The fire was burned down to a red glow and there were no more pieces of wood stacked against the wall. Darr must have continued feeding the fire while she'd slept.

The baby jittered around inside her and she pressed her hand to her side. "I know," she murmured aloud. "He's something, isn't he?"

When she saw the two men jam their shovel blades into the ridge of snow they'd created alongside the clearing and turn toward the house, she quickly stepped away from the window. Snatching fresh clothes from the drawer, she darted into the bathroom.

When she came out again, dressed and as presentable as she could make herself, given the lack of warm water and electricity, the door was just opening.

Darr spotted her standing in the hallway immediately, of course. Since he'd arrived on her doorstep Friday afternoon, the dark shadow of beard had deepened across his angular jaw.

It just made him look that much more masculine. That much more dangerous to her shaky emotions.

"Good. You're awake." He gestured behind him, and pushed the door wider. "Come on in, Nick."

Bethany brushed her hands self-consciously down the front of her brown corduroys. She didn't suppose it had occurred to Darr that she might feel awkward with a stranger coming into her house while the bed they'd shared was still unfolded and noticeably tumbled.

She didn't know if it was ironic or not that she no longer categorized Darr as a stranger. No matter how briefly you'd known someone, she supposed that's what happened when you lived in each other's pockets for a couple of nights, made love like you were the last two people on earth and argued over a well-intentioned, albeit loveless, marriage proposal.

"Hello, Mr. Fortune." She stepped forward with her hand outstretched, ignoring the bed and the memory of all that had occurred there, when Darr's brother stepped inside and closed the door behind him. "I'm Barbara Burton. Nice to meet Darr's rescue crew." She didn't realize until she introduced herself that it hadn't occurred to her that Darr might have told his brother her real name.

Even with his shoulders padded with a thick, downy coat, it was obvious that Nicholas Fortune was slightly leaner than Darr. He was also a few inches taller. But there was definitely a similarity in the way the corner of his lips kicked up as he stepped forward to close her hand in a brief, businesslike grip. "Mr. Fortune's our dad," he said, sounding vaguely amused. "Make it Nick. Nice to meet you, too. Bet you'll be glad to get rid of this guy." He gave Darr a clap on the shoulder.

Would she be rid of him?

Now that the snowstorm looked like it was finally over, would he realize the folly of his proposal?

A quick glance toward his impassive face told her nothing. "I was glad not to be alone. Your brother's been very helpful," she demurred.

"He's good at that." Unlike Darr, Nick's eyes were brown. And openly curious as they went from Bethany to Darr and back again. "The Foundation office is closed today, just in case you were worrying about that."

Which meant that Darr had told Nick that she worked there, because she highly doubted that the man would be aware of it otherwise. They had never even met. "That's good to know."

The extra day would give her a little bit more time to solve the matter of transportation. She didn't want to use a taxi service and no bus line ran to her neighborhood. A bicycle would be fine if the road was clear of snow, but only temporarily because she just couldn't see herself riding down that hill when she was nine months' pregnant.

"Here." Darr held out his truck keys toward her, almost as if he'd read her mind. "We've shoveled a healthy path. Don't go forward or you might get stuck again. But you'll be able to back straight out to the street. A plow came through just after dawn."

She stared at the keys. "Excuse me?"

"Nick's gonna drop me at the firehouse," he continued. "I'll be on duty for the next twenty-four hours. Longer if I have to pull a double."

"Darr, I can't take your truck!"

"Well, you can't drive your car," he returned evenly. When she still didn't take the keys, he tossed them onto the table. "I called the power company. Electricity's supposed to be restored by midmorning to all of Red Rock. If yours isn't, call me. Use the cell number, not the main line for the firehouse. The guy who usually answers the phone there can't write a message for diddly. It's on the card I gave you. You might have to leave a voice mail but I'll get back to you as quickly as I can."

Before she could get in a word edgewise, he leaned down and planted a hard kiss on her lips.

"I did mean what I said," he told her when he lifted his head. "Think about it."

Bethany didn't say anything when he opened the door and preceded his brother—whose gaze was now even more speculative—outside.

She was too busy keeping her knees from dissolving beneath her.

Chapter Eight

"Think about what?" Nick barely waited until they were in the cab of the truck he'd borrowed from Lily's ranch before he fired the question.

"Nothing you need to worry about." Darr fastened his seat belt as the powerful truck—complete with chains on the tires—reversed over the clearing they'd made.

"Yeah, that helps," Nick drawled. "You went there and burned the sheets with her, didn't you?"

Since Darr considered that to be his business, he didn't answer that, either.

"Well." Nick turned the wheel and started heading down the gravel hill. "Can't say I blame you there. The girl's a looker."

"And too young for the likes of you."

"Got your protective instincts going, has she?" Nick laughed softly and Darr wished he'd kept his mouth shut.

"Don't sweat it," Nick said. "Frankly, I'm glad you're finally acting normal again."

"Hold up. Stop here," Darr said when they neared the side street and John Decker's house on the corner.

Nick obediently braked and Darr quickly hopped out and left the borrowed gloves tucked inside the old man's mailbox. There was nothing he could do about the axe at the moment, since it was buried beneath Bethany's pancaked carport. A trip to the hardware store would fix that quickly enough, though. "What do you mean, normal?" he asked, the second he climbed back in the truck.

"You know. Going out. Romancing the ladies," Nick continued the second Darr climbed back in the truck. "Having some fun, you know?"

"I'm going to marry her."

Nick slammed on the brakes again and the truck fishtailed to a drunken stop. Nick looped his arm over the steering wheel and stared at Darr. "Say again?"

Darr's jaw tightened. "You heard me."

"You proposed. You know the woman for two days and you propose." Nick looked out the windshield, as if he were trying to fathom the unfathomable. Then his sharp gaze shot right back to Nick. "Are you out of your mind?"

Darr stared back, unflinching.

"*Why?* That's taking Valentine's Day to the extreme, don't you think?"

The truth was, Darr hadn't given the holiday another thought after he'd climbed into bed beside Bethany. "Could we go now, or do you want to sit here until all the snow thaws?"

Nick, however, didn't put the truck in gear. "You know, you *can* sleep with a woman these days without going down on bended knee. I doubt anyone's going to come running for you with shotgun in hand."

"This has nothing to do with sleeping with her." And he was annoyed with himself for letting his brother egg him into admitting it.

Particularly when he could see Nick's brain ticking behind his glasses. "Oh, hell," his brother said, looking suddenly resigned. "You're trying to rescue her. That's it, isn't it? Just like you tried with Celia."

"Dammit, Nick. Leave it alone."

"Ahh." Nick rolled his head around on his shoulders as he swore more ripely. "Anyone ever tell you that you have an overabundance of conscience? Darwin. *Dude.* You don't have to make up for the rest of society's failures when it comes to some poor woman!" He shot Darr another look. "So what's her story? Grew up in poverty? Got knocked around by a drunk parent? A scumbag boyfriend?" His eyes sharpened. "That's it. I can see it in your eyes. You want to keep her from going back to the guy who beat her."

"Do you want me to *walk* back to the firehouse?" He flipped off his seat belt and reached for the door in one rapid motion.

Nick sighed noisily. "Don't be so touchy. You're the one going around proposing to complete strangers. You expect me to just whip out the attaboys over it?"

"She's not a stranger."

"Because you've been in her pants?"

"Dammit, Nick, shut the hell up!"

Surprisingly, his brother did. Nick watched him, his thumb slowly tapping the steering wheel. "Look, I get it that marriage isn't anathema to you like it is to…well, to me. But I just don't want to see you tearing yourself up again like you did before," Nick finally said quietly.

"This is not about Celia." Darr's voice was tight.

"Are you sure?"

Darr stared out the window but in his mind, all he saw was Bethany's small house and the collapsed carport.

Was he sure?

He'd slept with Celia. When they were high school sweethearts, bent more on a good time than ever after. But when they'd graduated, she'd gone her way and he'd gone his.

And he hadn't seen her again until they'd been called out on a domestic disturbance.

The guy in question had needed his shoulder sewn up after slamming it through a window before the cops could haul him in. The pregnant girl in question had needed sobering up and several months' worth of good meals.

Celia.

He'd made sure she was fed. Got her to the doctor for some very tardy prenatal care. Gave her a shoulder to lean on when she'd needed it, and done everything he could to help her get back on her feet. And when she'd begged him to keep the baby's father from trying to take the baby from her after he was born, Darr had agreed to help then, too. She was a friend. A girl he'd once cared about.

So they decided that marriage was the best course. But he'd never loved her.

And when she'd gone back to the jerk anyway, Darr hadn't done anything to stop her.

A week after that, both she and her baby were dead and not even the fact that the bastard who'd done it was rotting in jail mitigated Darr's sense of having failed to act when he could have.

He knew if he told Nick that Bethany was pregnant, his brother would be more convinced than ever that he was trying to relive—and rewrite—the past.

Telling Nick that he was in love with Bethany wouldn't get him anywhere, either.

It was hard enough to believe it himself.

And if he'd added that particular point to Bethany, he figured she'd disappear for good the second he turned his back.

"I suppose she agreed," Nick finally said when Darr remained silent. Then rolled his eyes. "What the hell. You're a Fortune. Of course she agreed."

"Just tell me what else happened out at the Double Crown," Darr answered instead. "And do it on the way to the firehouse."

Mercifully, Nick put the vehicle in gear and headed back down the street and toward town. "Not much. Lily plays a mean hand of poker. She even gave Dad a run for his money. Aunt Cindy got hold of Ross. She says he agreed to look into the notes."

"One of the Fortunes isn't who we think," Darr recounted.

"Pretty much."

"Sounds like a bunch of bull to me." The only person Darr knew who wasn't who people thought was Bethany. And she had good reason to disguise her identity.

"Bull or not, Ross should be able to get to the bottom of it," Nick said. "Nobody threatens a Fortune and gets away with it."

Which is exactly what Darr had told Bethany.

That hadn't convinced her to marry him anymore than anything else had.

He exhaled. He could be patient when he had to be. And persistent.

She'd change her mind.

It was the lack of milk that got Bethany out of the house later that afternoon.

She approached Darr's truck, with his keys clutched in her

hands, as if it were about to rear up its chrome grill like some menacing snout and strike.

She'd contacted the house owners in San Antonio about the carport. They'd promised to contact their insurance agent, who promised to send someone out to review the situation.

She'd contacted representatives of the insurance company about her car. They'd promised to send someone out to review the situation.

She'd even contacted the folks at the utility company about her continued lack of electricity, and they'd admitted that most of the town's service had been restored. And *they'd* promised to send someone out to review the situation.

Well, she'd reviewed the situation in her warm refrigerator, when her stomach wouldn't stop growling, and determined that it was time for her to take action.

Which meant taking Darr's truck.

The sun was well up in the sky and all around her the snow was melting at a furious pace, as if it wanted to retreat just as rapidly as it had unexpectedly struck. In fact, the temperature was so pleasant that she wore only a long-sleeved blouse beneath her unbuttoned peacoat, and when she braved climbing behind the wheel of Darr's truck and had figured out enough of the fancy controls, she turned off the heat and rolled the windows halfway down to enjoy the afternoon air.

She was almost giddy with gratitude that the truck had an automatic transmission. It was bad enough that she'd never driven such a large vehicle in her life; if it had been a stick shift, she'd have been just as stuck as if Darr hadn't left the truck for her to use at all.

The pretty little BMWs that her father had been bestowing upon her every other birthday since she'd turned sixteen had all but driven themselves.

Her lips firmed. Maybe if he'd been less extravagant with unnecessary cars for her, he wouldn't have tried selling her off to the man who was supposed to save their business.

She craned her neck around and slowly backed the truck across the wide yard toward the street. She probably could have managed to turn it around in a circle with the way the snow was melting, but she didn't want to take a chance when it was Darr's property she was borrowing.

Relief sighed through her when, still in reverse, she bumped safely over the curb and turned to head straight down the gravel hill.

John Decker was in his yard and she waved her hand at him as she passed. Not surprisingly, he did not return the greeting.

There were lots of people out in their yards as she drove toward the center of town. Adults shoveling sidewalks. Kids playing in the melting banks of snow. She knew if she turned down Main, she would pass the firehouse, and the urge to do so was strong.

No matter how vigorously she refused to entertain the notion of marrying Darr Fortune, she couldn't deny the part of her that wanted to debate the matter.

She'd been truthful when she'd told Darr's brother that she'd been glad he was there during the storm.

But that didn't mean they should go turning one weekend of unusual extremes into something it wasn't. So she would just have to get her fascination as far as Darr was concerned under control before she ruined things altogether.

Her hands tightened around the steering wheel as she turned in the opposite direction and tried focusing on the matter at hand.

There was no point in trying to entirely restock her refrigerator yet. For one thing, she didn't have that much cash, and for another, an electric refrigerator without electricity was as useless as no refrigerator at all. She'd wait until that matter was resolved, and then she'd find a way to get to San Antonio and the big-box discount stores there where the prices would be easier on her wallet.

Instead, she wandered the aisles of the hardware store until she found a small, inexpensive ice chest, then went to the grocery store and bought a half gallon of milk and a few other essentials that would keep her going for a few days. In the parking lot, she dumped a bag of ice cubes around the milk inside the cooler, fit the top in place, and lifted it to the passenger side floor of the truck.

"Darr, is that you?"

Bethany lifted her head with a start, staring across at the tall, curvaceous redhead who stood on the other side of the truck. "Nope. Sorry."

The woman's brows quirked together. "Sorry, too. I thought this was someone else's truck." She smiled brightly, though there was a questioning crinkle between her brows. "You look familiar. Have I seen you around Red Rock before?"

Bethany returned the smile noncommittally. "No. I don't think so." She tucked her other two bags beside the cooler and shut the door, rounding the front of the truck.

The other woman stood taller than her by half a foot, which put Bethany's head right about level with a truly impressive bosom when the other woman didn't move away from the driver's side door. "Oh. Excuse me." The woman quickly shifted so Bethany could reach the door. "I'm Lorena Evans," she introduced.

"Barbara Burton," Bethany returned. She pulled open Darr's door and reached her foot up for the high running board.

"Are you new or just passing through?"

Bethany couldn't bring herself to be rude. Red Rock was her home. At least for now, and the residents there were her neighbors. "New."

"Well, we sure put on the fine weather for you then, didn't we?" Lorena grinned ruefully. "I work at SusieMae's down on Main. Best meal you can find in town, at least until Red's back up and running." She leaned forward. "But don't tell SusieMae I said that," she added with hushed humor.

"Your secret's safe with me. I'd better go and get this stuff home."

Lorena backed away with an easy smile. "Nice t'meet you."

"You, too." Bethany pulled the door shut and started the engine. A moment later, still feeling strange sitting so high up in the truck, she drove carefully out of the small parking lot. She was quite satisfied with herself by the time she made it back to the house, and parked the truck in the same spot where Darr had left it.

There were more bare patches of ground visible now, but the melting snow also meant water and, in her yard, that particular combination meant mud. Better to stick to the area where the snow had been cleared.

The phone was ringing stridently when she carried her purchases inside. The sound was so unfamiliar that she was reluctant to answer it. But she'd made a lot of calls that morning, and some of them would no doubt result in returned calls.

So she picked up.

"Are you all right?" Darr's voice was unmistakable, though there was a loud, constant roar behind it.

"Fine." She pulled her purse off her shoulder and dropped it onto the couch that she'd restored to order after he and Nick had left that morning.

"I've been calling for the past hour."

"Oh." She moistened her lips. It wasn't demand that was in his voice. If it had been, she'd have felt no compunction whatsoever in telling him what he could do with it.

She'd had enough of *that* with Lyle.

But it was concern that she heard, and against that, it seemed she had few defenses. "I went to the store to buy a few things."

"Your electricity's back on then?"

"Well, no. Not yet."

"Hold on." She heard him speaking, muffled, to someone else, and then he came back. And still there was that noise in the background.

"Where are you?"

"On the engine. Heading back to the firehouse. We've been responding to calls all day. It's been pretty crazy."

"You're all decked out in your uniform then."

"Turnouts." He sounded amused, suddenly. "Yes, ma'am. If that image does it for you, maybe we should talk about that…thing…again."

That *thing* meant his marriage proposal, she knew, but she still couldn't help the flush that ran right down her body. "There's nothing to talk about," she said primly. "And I wouldn't have thought you'd be allowed to make personal calls while you're on duty."

He laughed out loud at that, and the strength seemed to leave her knees in a rush. She sat down on the couch with an inelegant plop. "My Cap is sitting next to me," he told her. "He saw me dialing so I guess I must be okay. I'd tell you that you can come stay at my place—I know for a fact the apartment building's got electricity—but I suppose you'll turn that down, too."

Of all the things they'd talked about over the weekend, the

only thing she knew about his home was that he rarely used his own television. And she couldn't pretend that she wasn't curious about where he lived.

A useless curiosity, she reminded herself firmly.

"I called the utility company," she told him. "They said they'll send someone to check it out."

"Good. I'll call you later. See how it's going."

"Darr, that's really not neces—"

"Gotta go," he said cheerfully, and disconnected.

Bethany held the phone out from her ear, staring at it when the background noise of the fire engine was replaced by the low drone of the dial tone. Thoroughly bemused, she leaned over and replaced the receiver.

True to his word, he called again later.

This time, she was outside dealing with the insurance adjuster that the owners had arranged.

The good news was the damage would be covered, and the carport would be replaced.

The bad news was only the damage to the actual carport was covered.

Her car was another matter.

She was heading into the house when she heard the phone ringing and nearly vaulted over the coffee table to reach it, but it stopped before she got there.

She knew it was Darr, though.

Who else was calling her these days?

The third time he called, it was nighttime and she was sound asleep in bed, and the strident ringing nearly sent her nerves right through the roof. Which is what she deserved for setting the phone on the mattress right beside her pillow.

"Third time's a charm," she said in greeting.

"Sorry I woke you."

She brushed her hair out of her eyes and turned to face the side of the bed that he'd occupied the night before. "How do you know I was sleeping?"

"I can hear it in your voice. You've got power going?"

"Mmm-hmm. Thanks for that, too." Even now she could hear the hum of the generator that had been delivered and hooked up by the three very capable and very good-looking off-duty firefighters sent by Darr shortly before dark. "How did you know my electricity still hadn't been restored?"

"I have my connections. They show you how it works before they left?"

"Yes. Your friends were very helpful and thorough."

"Joe and Marcus are both married," he said. "Don't pay any attention to their flirting."

She bit back a smile, but then let it loose since he couldn't see it anyway. "And Rick?"

"Big-time social problems. He's seriously afraid of women."

Laughter bubbled in her throat. "He is not." The tallest of the three, Rick had talked of nothing but his sweetheart. "His girlfriend's name is Elise and she's an elementary school teacher."

"Yeah, okay. You caught me."

She hadn't really, though. He was just putting on the unexpected charm to sway her to his way of thinking.

"I don't know how I'll repay you for the generator, but I will."

"I'm not looking for repayment. The generator's from the Double Crown. You can thank Lily when you meet her. And if you think I arranged it so you'd feel obliged to marry me, you're way off track. And no, I don't want your apology if that's what you're trying to come up with."

She had been. "All right. But I'm not planning to meet Lily Fortune."

"Sure you are. She's hosting a children's picnic Sunday

after next at the ranch. The department is going to be there with the engine we're retiring. Kids love climbing on a fire truck. Even an old one. For obvious reasons, I got roped into being the liaison for the event. You have to have heard about it. The Foundation's the main sponsor."

And she'd answered plenty of questions from people calling the office about its "Fortune February Fest," designed to give underprivileged kids from as far away as Houston a real Texas ranch experience, but that hadn't meant she'd be attending. "I heard they had all the volunteers they needed for the event."

"There's always room for another pair of hands at something like this. Besides. I can't go without a date."

She let out an exasperated sigh. "Nobody takes dates to an event like that."

"How do *you* know?"

Because she'd attended plenty of them with her family. The agreeable, dutiful daughter who'd dressed up and smiled prettily for the society page cameras whenever they'd turned their way. "I just do."

"Come on, Bethany," his voice dropped lower. "You want to make a new life for yourself? Start *living*. Red Rock's a good place."

Why did it affect her so to hear her name on his lips?

She twined the coiled phone cord around her finger. "Are you alone?"

"I'm in my quarters."

Which explained him using her real name.

"Means we're in bed together again," he added. "What are you wearing?"

"Flannel pajamas," she lied repressively and tugged the hem of the departmental blue T-shirt he'd left behind down around her thighs. Almost as quickly as generated electricity had flowed through her house, she'd whipped through her household chores, including the laundry. Tossing his shirt in with her jeans had struck her as an oddly intimate gesture, but she'd had good intentions of returning it to him, folded and ready to wear again.

Of course, that didn't explain why she was now sleeping in it.

"You forget, honey, just how much I like flannel."

She'd forgotten absolutely nothing.

She rolled over and kicked the comforter off her too-warm legs. "The, uh, the field supervisor for the power company finally called me back," she said, deliberately changing the subject. "He said they have to pull a new line from the box. Something like that, anyway. It'll be done by Wednesday, latest."

"Chicken," he murmured.

"That's right," she agreed without a qualm.

She heard him sigh faintly. "What about your car?" he finally asked. "You called your insurance company, right?"

"Yes." And she appreciated the fact that he hadn't tried to take over the matter for her. Instead, he'd merely encouraged her. "They said they'll let me know. They have to determine if the homeowner's insurance is responsible." And she already knew the homeowner's insurance wasn't. "You can get your truck anytime. I figured out a way to get to work." It involved the oldest transportation known to man. Foot.

It would be a couple of miles at least, but walking was good for a pregnant woman. Particularly a woman who'd been used to running every day before fear had sent her running in an entirely different way.

"I'm not in a hurry to get my truck. You can use it from now on as far as I'm concerned."

She pressed her cheek against the pillow. "You have to stop talking like that, Darr."

"Why?"

"Just…because! Because I said so."

He laughed softly, but it was drowned out with a loud, distinct alarm. "Toned out," he said. "That's us. Sweet dreams, Bethany." Once again, he disconnected before she was at all prepared for it and she slowly replaced the receiver.

Sweet dreams, indeed.

When she finally fell back to sleep every one of them seemed to be centered solely on him.

Chapter Nine

"Delivery for—" The teenage kid with a ring in his eyebrow consulted his clipboard. "Barbara Burton?"

Sitting behind the reception desk of the Fortune Foundation, Bethany eyed the enormous vase of brilliant pink and white flowers the boy was holding. She was painfully aware of the attention she was getting from the steady flow of employees moving through the lobby on their way in and out to lunch. "I'm Barbara Burton."

"Cool." The delivery boy set the vase on the desk and flipped the board around to face her. "Sign on line nine, ma'am."

She scrawled Barbara's signature on the line. "Thank you."

"You bet." He grinned. "You're not the only one around town somebody wants to make up with for missing Valentine's Day." He tucked the earphones of his MP3 player in his ear and nearly bounced out the doorway.

"Nice flowers." Julie, one of the teen counselors for the

Foundation, stopped at the desk to pick up the stack of mail that had yet to be sorted. "Better late than never, right?" Her blue eyes twinkled as she headed down the hall.

She hadn't missed Valentine's Day, Bethany thought, running her finger along one of the velvety petals of a spider mum that was as big as a dinner plate.

She'd spent it with Darr.

The phone rang and she automatically hit the button on her headset. "Good afternoon. Thank you for calling the Fortune Foundation. This is Barbara. How may I help you?"

"You look like a woman who needs some lunch."

She sat up straighter in her chair as Darr's deep voice sent shivers down her spine. "Oh? Says who?"

"Me." Darr walked through the doorway, and tucked his cell phone in the pocket of his khaki-colored cargo pants. He rested his wide palms on the reception desk and leaned closer. His blue RRFD shirt tightened over his shoulders. "Nice flowers. Should I be jealous?"

She made a face, though everything inside her was jumping around like water droplets scattered over hot oil. She hadn't seen him since he'd left her house the previous morning.

She'd talked to him.

Dreamt about him.

But she hadn't seen him, and no matter how sternly she'd told herself that what had happened over the weekend had been a result of their enforced proximity, all such common sense flew right out of her mind again when she was face-to-face with him. "You ought to know. You're the one who sent them."

The dimple beside his lips deepened. "So, do the slave drivers around here let you out for good behavior and grub?"

She tucked her tongue between her teeth. He was related in one way or another to a good portion of those supposed slave drivers. "Actually, I took my lunch hour already." And her regret that she'd done so was very real. Peanut-butter-and-cucumber sandwiches were simply nowhere near as appealing as the man leaning against the front of her desk. "I'm sorry."

"Them's the breaks." He pulled his phone out again. "I don't have all that much time, anyway, but I figured I'd give it a shot. Here." He handed her a phone. "I didn't see the truck in the parking lot."

She automatically took the phone, though she held it up curiously. "I…walked to work, actually."

His gaze sharpened on her face. "You walked? What the hell for? There's still snow on the ground for cripes sake and this place is miles from your house!"

And her feet had certainly felt it, particularly by the time she walked the last stretch to reach the three-story building on the highway just outside of town. "It's not too many miles," she countered. "If I were still running every day, this wouldn't even be an issue."

His lips tightened. "You're not running. I left you the keys, for a reason, Be-arbara."

"And I didn't use them for a reason, Darr." She kept her voice low. They were already drawing too much attention.

His jaw was a hard, inflexible line, his dimple nowhere in sight. "Do you get off at five?"

"Four-thirty."

"I'll pick you up then." He spun on his boot heel and headed for the door.

"Darr, wait." She hurriedly unhooked her headset and darted around the desk, chasing after him. "Your phone." She held it out toward him.

He didn't take it, though. "*Your* phone," he said, and pushed out the door before she could argue.

The phone on the desk buzzed, summoning her.

She wanted to ignore it. To chase after the infernal man and make him see reason. Her reason.

But she had a job to do.

Darr would have to wait. She blew out a breath and hurried back to the desk, grabbing up the receiver. "Good afternoon." She launched into her usual spiel. "Thank you for calling the Fortune Foundation…"

"Women," Darr muttered, slamming through the rear entrance to the firehouse. He stomped through the dayroom, which was filled with recliners all facing the enormous flat-screen television hanging on the wall, a pool table and a bookshelf jammed with a mess of books and DVDs.

"They're the opposite sex, son. Would'a hoped you'd learned that by now." Devaney was sprawled back in one of the recliners, an oversize book lying facedown on his chest. His hands were linked behind his curly blond head.

"That book for looks, Vane? We all know you can't read."

Devaney pitched the book at him, but Darr caught it in midair, glancing at the paper cover. A study guide. He flipped the book back at his coworker and turned to the coffee urn that was kept always full and always hot. "You're studying for the exam, eh?"

"Can't let you be the senior LT for long," Devaney said. "'Course you could leave the honors to me if you'd sit for the captain's exam, the way the chief wants you to, instead of being a girl about it."

Until Bethany, Darr hadn't had much interest in going for that promotion, even though the fire chief had practically begged him to. Lately, though, the idea was taking root in the back of his mind.

Lately, since he'd decided to get married.

He filled a mug with the brew, and proceeded to singe the skin off his tongue when he drank it too fast.

"What're you hanging around here for, anyway?" Devaney asked. "You're off today and tomorrow."

"So are you and you're here."

"Yeah, but I ain't got a life," Devaney drawled. He scratched his oft-broken nose. "And you're setting up house with that pretty blond thing over at the Foundation."

"I'm not setting up house."

"Man, I know about that generator you sent over there. And she's driving your precious truck all over town. Sounding pretty cozy to me."

All over town. But not to her job. "Who told you about the truck?"

"Lorena, when she was dishing up my extra-crispy bacon and hash browns. She's the one you were with over the weekend, right?"

"Lorena? Hell, no."

Devaney flipped him off. "The blonde. Lorena says she's the one you pulled outta Red the night of the burn. The one we all know you were trying to track down."

"Lorena's full of information," Darr returned. "She know if the fire investigator's report is in yet on the incident?"

"God, you're touchy," Devaney complained. "Guess you didn't get any after all. Some good lovin' would'a made you a mite friendlier."

Darr shook his head. "You're a sleaze, Vane. Anyone ever tell you that?"

"My mama, every day." Devaney rolled himself off the recliner and stretched. "Report came in this morning," he said with all seriousness. "Definitely arson. Chief went over to Red to talk to the Mendozas about it. I hear the whole clan is working on the place to get it open again. Imagine they'll have their wedding reception there."

"Who?"

"Jorge Mendoza and Jane Gilliam," Devaney said as if it were obvious.

"You know," Darr eyed the other man. "You and Lorena Evans are perfect for each other. You should marry her instead of clogging your arteries with bacon fat every morning at SusieMae's counter. The two of you are like peas in a pod. Whatever she doesn't know about the people in this town, you do."

"It's a filthy job, but somebody's got to do it." Devaney grinned, strolling out of the dayroom.

But not before making a production of setting the study guide next to Darr's elbow.

Ignoring the guide, he dumped the rest of his coffee down the drain and headed out, too.

He'd been on the promotional fast track in LA. Maybe if he'd been less interested in making the next pay grade, he'd have been more interested in keeping Celia safe.

It wasn't far from the firehouse to Red, but behind the wheel of the Double Crown truck he'd purloined from Nick, every second of the way reminded him of Bethany walking to work that morning.

In the short time it took him to get to the restaurant, his jaw ached from grinding his teeth. There was no sign of the fire chief's unit when he parked nearby, so Darr presumed he'd finished delivering the news about the investigation.

Though much of the celebrated hacienda-style restaurant had been damaged by the fire, the worst of the exterior debris had been cleared away within days of the fire investigator's go-ahead. Inside, though, Darr knew that the kitchen—where the burn had started—had been off-limits. Now, with the investigation completed, they'd be able to get started on repairs there, too.

He went in through the courtyard side where snow still clung in the shadows of the walls, looking highly at odds with the tall fan palms that towered overhead. The palms didn't look like they'd suffered too badly from the snowstorm, but the bougainvillea that proliferated around the perimeter of the courtyard was already brown and shriveled.

He knew from experience, though, that the colorful shrubs would recover. They could be cut down to stumps and a month later come back lush and vibrant. In California, every year his mother had carried on a running argument with their gardener to cut back the thorny bushes and every year, had complained when they'd always grown back. He'd always figured she must not have minded them too badly or she simply would have had them dug out at the roots.

In the courtyard of the restaurant, the tables and chairs with their vivid umbrellas overhead, which had been filled with diners the night of the fire, had all been cleared away; and the courtyard would have been bare if not for the old fountain in the center. It was dry for the moment, but Darr figured water would be trickling down its ancient lines soon enough. Assuming none of the plumbing had been damaged by the freezing temperatures they'd just suffered, that is.

Despite the chilliness of the day, the door to the inside restaurant was propped open and he followed the high-pitched whine of an electric saw. As soon as Roberto Mendoza spotted him, the other man straightened where he was leaning over a table saw, and the whine died. "Darr," he greeted, sliding his safety glasses off his face. "Suppose you've heard the news."

"It doesn't change the damage that's been done, but at least your dad has an official stamp on what he's maintained all along."

Roberto pushed a hand through his dark hair, leaving a trail of sawdust behind. "Someone set the fire deliberately." His voice was grim. "There are times when I'm not sure that doesn't feel worse."

That was understandable. The Mendozas were like the Fortunes. You didn't mess with them and expect to get away with it for long. "I figured José would be around here."

"He took my mother home." Roberto's brooding gaze drifted around the walls. Water stains had replaced the historic tapestries that had once hung there.

"How long are you staying before you have to get back to Denver?" Darr knew the other man was in construction and real estate development there.

"As long as it takes." Roberto slid on his safety glasses, clearly intent on resuming his work.

"Well. Tell your folks that if there's anything I can—"

"Do. I know." Roberto's smile was faint, but it was there. "You've done plenty already. You and the rest of the department are why there's something left for us to rebuild." He flipped on the saw and Darr took the cue, heading out with a brief wave.

He intended to take care of a few chores at his apartment before picking up Bethany and taking her home. Convincing her that he should stay with her for the night might be a little tricky, but he intended to do that, too.

But his phone buzzed before he reached the Double Crown truck, and that put paid to everything but heading straight back to the firehouse.

* * *

By the time four-thirty rolled around and her workday was over, Bethany had managed to work her nerves into a fine frenzy anticipating Darr's arrival.

Only it was Nick Fortune who strolled by the reception desk just as she was retrieving her purse from the locked drawer where she kept it. "Darr had to go out on a call," he said. "Multicar pileup halfway between here and San Antone. I'm here to play chauffeur."

"That's not necessary," Bethany said swiftly. Her nervous energy dissipated in a tidal wave of relief. She refused to entertain the idea that it was disappointment sinking through her.

"You have another ride?" Nick had a pair of glasses perched low on his nose, but his brown eyes peered at her over the frames. He was wearing a suit, yet managed to look as relaxed and laid-back as if he were strolling a beach in flip-flops.

And oddly, she couldn't seem to make herself utter the blatant lie that she did have a ride.

What was it about the Fortune men?

"No," she admitted. "But I can walk."

"Yeah. Darr warned me about that. Sugar, it's too damn cold for you to walk all that way." He jangled the car keys in his palm. "Come on. Easier for us both if we go along with the plan. Otherwise, that brother of mine'll drive us both up a tree. He acts like a good ol' boy, but you might have noticed he's pretty much a dog with a bone when he gets something into his head."

Bethany tucked her tongue between her teeth and wondered just how much Nick knew about the "something" that Darr had in his head where she was concerned. "I've noticed." She slid into her coat and accompanied Darr's brother out the door.

She'd expected to find the big white truck that he'd been

driving the previous morning in the parking lot, but instead he led her to a low-slung black Porsche.

Ordinarily, she would have appreciated the lines of the vehicle. But it was nearly identical to the one that Lyle drove.

Nick opened her door and waited until she'd slid down into the passenger seat before closing it and heading around to his side.

"Did he say how bad the accident was?" Bethany asked when they were on the road, heading back through the center of Red Rock.

"Bad enough they called out Red Rock and San Antonio." Nick smoothly navigated around a slower-moving truck and turned into the neighborhood that would lead to Bethany's street. "I don't know how he has the stomach for the stuff he's seen and can still go out every day knowing he might see worse." He pulled to a minimal stop at a stop sign and gave her a sideways glance. "Being married to a firefighter isn't easy under the best of circumstances."

She felt her face go hot. "I guess I don't have to wonder any longer if he told you he'd proposed."

"Darr's a straight shooter." Nick's voice was quiet. "He's strong and he's tough and I respect the hell out of him. And whatever your deal is with Darr, it's your business. I just don't ever want to see him tear himself up again like he did in California after Celia died."

She started. "How did she die?"

He slanted a look her way, looking as if he were debating whether to say anything more.

"How?"

He made a face. "The guy she was living with beat her to death."

Bethany felt nauseated.

"Darr thinks he should have been able to save her."

Bethany curled her fingers around the buttons on her coat. Tears stung her eyes and she stared blindly out the side window. No wonder Nick wasn't praising Darr's marriage proposal. "He's fortunate to have a family who cares." Her voice was thick.

She could feel Nick's gaze on her, but he'd evidently figured he'd said enough as he continued driving out to her house. When he turned up the hill, she could hear the spit of gravel under his tires. Lyle would have had a fit driving his precious car over such a road. "I should have had you let me off at the bottom of the hill. The gravel might damage your—" her voice trailed off at the sight of the unfamiliar black sedan parked in front of her house "—paint job," she finished faintly.

"Looks like you have company." Nick started to turn into her driveway. Snow still lay in the deep ruts, making them easy to spot and avoid, which only seemed to hasten the end of the journey as Nick pulled to a stop near the other vehicle.

"I'm not expecting any." The windows of the sedan were darkened, giving no hint to the identity of who might be sitting inside.

She racked her brain for an excuse, *any* excuse not to get out of the vehicle.

Her palms were sweating and her stomach rose in her throat.

If it were Lyle or some minions sent by her parents to drag her home, she doubted that throwing up all over their shoes would stop them.

"Hey." Nick touched her sleeve. "I really didn't intend to upset you. Are you all right?"

"Actually," she didn't have to fake the trembling in her hand when she pressed it to her abdomen. "I'm suddenly not feeling very well." She ducked her chin when a cramp made her gasp. "Oh, please, not now." But another spasm twisted through her.

"Not now *what?*" Nick was looking vaguely green. "Maybe we should get you inside."

She shook her head. "I'm sorry. Not inside. I—" She gritted her teeth against another wrenching pain. "The hospital," she finally managed. "I think something's wrong with the baby."

Utter silence filled the vehicle for the span of a heartbeat. "I knew it," he muttered under his breath.

Then he wheeled the car right around the other sedan, holding his hand over her shoulder to keep her steady as he rocketed out to the road. "Hold tight," he said.

There was little else for Bethany to do. The sharp pain was radiating up her spine. Down her legs.

She closed her eyes and tried not to panic but she was pretty much wracked with it when, a short while later, Nick was hustling her through the emergency room, barking for a nurse and nudging her down onto one of the wheelchairs that were sitting near the entrance.

She supposed it was the influence of the Fortune name that garnered such immediate attention, because hardly a minute had passed before she was being whisked through the double doors. One nurse helped her onto the examining table, another was pulling out blood pressure cuffs and a third was wielding a sheaf of forms. "Do you want Mr. Fortune to come back with you, Ms. Burton?"

Another pain clawed at her. "Darr," she managed, breathing hard. "Please can someone call Darr?"

"Where is she?" The emergency room doors were still sliding open when Darr strode inside, spotting Nick, who was leaning his hip against the reception desk, chatting up the starchy gray-haired woman who manned the station.

In Darr's experience, Beatrice was a true battle-ax. God knew that getting any information out of her about Bethany after the fire had been about as pleasant and productive as banging his head with a tire iron.

With Nick, of course, Beatrice was nothing but smiles.

"They ran some tests," Nick said. "I think the doc is with her." He slid off the desk. "I think I need to tell you something before you go back and see her."

"Later."

"But—"

Darr strode past his brother and pushed through the doorway.

If the highway accident he'd just come from had resulted in more injuries instead of deaths, the E.R. would have been busy as hell. As it was, the only survivors had been medevaced to San Antonio and, for now here, there was only one bed with a curtain around it.

When he stepped inside the curtain, his damn knees felt weak.

Bethany was lying on her side on the narrow bed, wearing a washed-out hospital gown with a thin blanket drawn up over her hips. "Hey." His voice was soft.

Her gaze ran over him, taking in the sight of him still in his turnouts. "You came straight from the accident?"

He'd done something he'd never done before. Left a scene early.

He rolled the metal stool close to the bed, straddling it. He closed his hand around hers. "What happened?" All he knew was Nick's version when he'd phoned Darr, and that had been damn abbreviated.

"The baby's fine," she said.

He pressed her fingertips to his lips. Thank God for that. "And you?"

"Why didn't you tell me about Celia?"

He went still. "What about her?"

Her eyes closed. "Your brother told me she died. How she died."

He muttered an oath.

"Don't be angry with him. He's concerned about you."

"He doesn't need to be. It was a long time ago and has nothing to do with us."

She didn't look entirely convinced.

"It doesn't." He slid his fingers through the ends of her waving hair. "I'm concerned about *you*. Here. Now. What did the doctor say?"

Her eyes looked like bruises above her pale cheeks. "Dr. Waite thinks I had an anxiety attack."

Anxiety they could deal with. "About what Nick told you, or about the car parked at your house?"

She moistened her lips. "He told you about it, I suppose."

"Yes." It was one thing Darr didn't want to throttle him over.

"He thinks you've lost your mind where I'm concerned."

"Nick can think whatever he wants," he said quietly. "As tight as we are, we live our own lives our own way. He's no different. This—" he wagged his finger between himself and her "—is between us. You and me. *That's* what I care about."

The tip of her nose got pinker. Her eyes glistened. "I don't think I've had anyone care…really care…in a long time." Her lips quivered and she pressed them together, clearly struggling. "Maybe ever," she finally added.

"You have someone now." He folded his arm on the narrow strip of bed beside the thin pillow beneath her head. He rested his chin on his arm. Mere inches separated them. "Who did you think was in the car?" He figured he already knew.

"Lyle." Her lips turned down at the corners.

Now the slug he wanted to pound into the ground had a name.

"It was your landlord," Darr told her softly.

Her eyes widened. She struggled to sit up, and the hospital gown slid off one shoulder. "How do you know that? The owners live in San Antonio."

He sat up, too. "After Nick called me, I asked a friend at the PD to check it out. The guy was still there, meeting some contractor to fix the carport."

She slid the gown back over her shoulder, but since the tie behind her neck had obviously come loose, it just slipped back down again. "Just the owner." She pressed her palm over her eyes. "I can't believe I was such a ninny."

"Panic doesn't have anything to do with being a ninny," he dismissed. But it was one more indication of the terror that had forced her to assume a false identity. "You're one of the bravest young women I've ever met."

Her hand slowly dropped. "How can you say that?"

"For one thing, you're not running back to the guy who hurt you." *Lyle.* He couldn't bring himself to voice the man's name, though. "You'd be surprised at the number of women who do. The women who believe the jerks when they claim to be sorry, or that they'll never do it again."

"Is that what Celia did?"

He nodded.

Her brow wrinkled. "I stayed with him even after he hit me."

"But you *did* leave. You haven't gone back. You're making a life the best way you know how. You're standing on your own two feet, honey. That's not ninny. That's brave."

She was looking at him as if she badly wanted to believe him. "Do you—"

"Okay, Ms. Burton." The statement came from the young doctor in a lab coat who shoved aside the curtain more fully with the metal clipboard he held to make room for the even younger-looking boy wheeling a mobile ultrasound unit. "Hello, Darr."

"What's going on?" Darr eyed the equipment.

"We're doing an ultrasound."

"Thought it was an anxiety attack."

"It's just a precaution," the doctor assured. The technician ignored them all as he rolled the unit closer to the bed.

"Heard they sent two patients over to the trauma center in San Antonio from that pileup." The doctor nodded toward him, taking in Darr's appearance. "You work it?"

"Yeah." He was more interested in getting the ultrasound going than rehashing the grisly scene.

The doctor had turned to set his medical chart on the short counter and was pumping antiseptic wash onto his hands. "Three of the vics were kids?" He rinsed away the wash.

"Good Lord," Bethany said, obviously horrified.

"How long before she can go home?" Darr deliberately changed the subject.

The doctor dried his hands and pitched the paper towel through the hole in the counter designed for waste. "Soon as we see how the baby is doing." He smiled at Bethany and took the rolling stool that Darr had vacated.

Evidently satisfied with the position of his equipment, the technician adjusted the head of Bethany's bed, and she lay back down. He adjusted her gown and squirted gel on her bare belly, then handed the doctor the transducer.

"All rightie. Let's see how things are going." Dr. Waite pressed the scanner against Bethany's abdomen, sliding it through the gel as he stared at the monitor. "You said this is your first ultrasound?"

"Mmm-hmm."

Darr moved to the other side of Bethany's bed. She, too, was staring at the monitor, her lower lip caught between her teeth.

He closed his hand over hers.

She didn't pull away.

"There's the baby." Dr. Waite circled his finger in front of the monitor. "Placenta looks good. Position looks good." He glanced at Bethany. Noted their linked hands and his gaze almost imperceptibly shifted to include Darr. "Do you want to know the sex?"

Bethany's gaze flitted up to meet Darr's.

Something squeezed hard inside him. "Time to decide." His voice was husky. He cleared his throat. "It's absolutely your choice."

The corner of Bethany's lips curved. She looked back at the doctor. "Yes."

Dr. Waite looked at the monitor; slid the scanner around a little more. "Looks like your son isn't all that shy," he said, smiling. "*Definitely* a boy." He leaned forward and grabbed the medical chart. "We'll send the results over to your OB in San Antonio, but from what I can see, all looks well." His pen scratched on the chart. "I'll send the nurse in to do another blood pressure check, and if you're still in the normal range, we'll get you out of here and back home." He glanced up. "Any questions?"

"No. Thank you, Dr. Waite." Bethany was still staring at the image on the monitor.

Darr sort of knew how she felt.

He could hardly tear his gaze away, either, and barely noticed when the doctor left.

"We'll print that for you," the technician said with an understanding look as he shut down the equipment. "You'll have it before you leave," he said and pushed the cart beyond the curtain that he drew back around the area.

Bethany's fingers were still twined with Darr's.

He had to swallow the knot that was still in his throat. "There's just one thing left for you to do now," he told her. "Start thinking of names for your son."

"Darr," she whispered quietly.

"What?"

She shook her head slightly. "No. I mean as a name."

She refused to marry him—so far—but she would consider naming her child after him?

It was a good thing the curtain was being drawn back again by a nurse, who pulled down the blood pressure cuff from where it was hanging near the bed.

"Don't torture the kid that way," Darr managed lightly, moving out of the way so the nurse could slide the cuff around Bethany's arm. "Believe me. Growing up with the name Darwin ain't easy."

She was silent as the nurse worked the blood pressure monitor. But as soon as the nurse finished and departed again after telling Bethany she could get dressed, she spoke.

"I'd like to think he would grow up to be as good and decent as you."

Darr sat on the bed beside her. "Then say you'll marry me."

Her eyes were wide. Color suffused her high cheekbones. "Darr—" She was shaking her head slightly.

He slid his hand along her cheek, stilling the motion. "Just say you'll think about it. *Really* consider it."

She moistened her lips. Blinked. "Okay," she finally said. "I'll consider it."

He exhaled and tipped her head and pressed his lips to her forehead. Pressing her for more could wait.

"Will you get me out of here?"

"I'll have you under your roof as soon as you're dressed."

"*Your* roof. I'd rather go home with you."

He pulled back, and though her purple-blue gaze was shy, it was unswerving. "If that's all right."

"Yeah," he managed. "That's definitely all right."

Chapter Ten

"It's not large or fancy," Darr said, as he conducted the brief tour of his apartment when they arrived. "But it's enough for me. For now," he added pointedly.

The place was easily twice the size of her rented house.

Primarily because he had a bedroom.

Bethany stood in the doorway of said room and eyed the bed—covered in a thoroughly bachelorlike blue plaid comforter—that consumed a healthy portion of the space.

"It's very nice," she assured him. Clean, and possessing a sort of emptiness that wasn't uncomfortable, but more an echo of the limited time he'd said he spent there.

He waved his hand over a dresser drawer he pulled open. "T-shirts. Sweats. Use whatever you need." Then he walked out of the bedroom. "Bathroom's there," he pointed at the opened doorway adjacent to the bedroom. "I'm sorry that I've got to leave you again."

She shook her head. Once they'd left the hospital, he'd warned her that he'd have to go back to the firehouse. "I understand. It's your job." The man was still wearing his turnout pants, for pity's sake. The heavy khaki-colored pants with orange fluorescent stripes around the bottom were unfastened at the waist, hanging over his dark blue T-shirt-clad shoulders by red suspenders.

He looked the part of the ultimate hero.

He could say that she wasn't a ninny, but what else explained her hiding out now at *his* place because she was too frightened to go back to her own?

She brushed down the sleeves of her sweater.

"Are you cold?" He immediately reached for the thermostat on the wall in the hallway.

"I'm fine," she insisted. "Go." She swished her hands toward the door. He'd already spent a good portion of the dwindling evening on her.

"I hate leaving you."

"I'll be fine."

"I know that," he said easily. "I just want to enjoy the sight of you here."

Warmth spread through her face.

And the rest of her.

His eyes crinkled then, almost as if he were perfectly aware of her reaction. And maybe he was.

"I'll be back before you have to go to work. I'll run you back to your place for clothes, get my truck, and you'll still be sitting at your desk on time tomorrow."

She nodded. He'd already gone through the logistics with her.

"There's plenty of food in the fridge," he added as he opened the door. "Make sure you feed that boy of yours. He's probably starving by now." With a flash of that deadly dimple beside his crooked grin, he pulled the door closed after him.

She exhaled and pressed her hand against the faint, rhythmic flutter she could feel.

Her boy.

She blew out a breath and looked out the large window over his kitchen sink. Though it was well past dark, she could see the street outside easily, courtesy of the tall lamppost casting its golden glow, not only over the street, but over the cluster of lacy-leafed bushes around its base. Snow was still piled over the curbs where the snowplows had pushed it, piled over the manicured strip of lawn that stretched between the sidewalk and the curb.

The white truck Darr was using had already driven out of sight.

She nibbled her lip and turned to the refrigerator. In comparison to her ancient one, the tall stainless steel model of Darr's was nearly space-age. And as he'd said, it had plenty inside. She was vaguely surprised that the contents were similar to what had been in hers before the snow hit.

Except he had a six-pack of some oddly named beer that she'd never heard of.

She poured herself a glass of milk, made a turkey sandwich and turned on the television.

His had a spectacularly clear picture, of course.

She found the nightly news, turned down the volume and gave up trying to curtail her curiosity. The dark wood bookcase against one wall contained an eclectic collection—from baseball caps to books on philosophy.

There was one shelf with several haphazardly arranged framed photographs. She picked up the largest frame—a beautifully matted eight-by-ten that obviously dated back many years. It was easy to pick out Darr. Not only did he look the youngest, sprawled on the floor in front of his seated parents, but she would recognize that crooked grin and dimple anywhere. She could even pick out Nick. He was the one wearing a violently hued, tie-dyed T-shirt. He, and the other three boys—blond-haired to brown—were standing around the adults.

And even though they had all posed, remaining still long enough for the person behind the camera to snap the shot, there was life and energy screaming from the photograph. Energy that was singularly lacking in any sort of formal studio shot. At least when it came to the chronicles of *her* family that her mother had insisted upon so that she could hang them in her father's office.

Testament to their quote-un-quote perfect family.

She drew the tip of her fingernail along the glass.

The Fortunes looked happy. The kind of happy that far transcended fortune.

She set the frame back on the shelf and peered at the rest of the photographs. Christmases. A birthday—someone's twenty-first, if the drunken pink elephant on the cake top and the laughing crowd of guests surrounding it with beer bottles held aloft were any indication.

For her twenty-first birthday, her father had introduced her to Lyle for the first time during a cocktail party thrown, not to celebrate her birthday, but to court another infusion of cash into the family coffers. At twenty-one, Bethany had been thoroughly uninterested in the family business. Maybe if she'd paid more attention, she would have realized sooner the part she was unwittingly playing in the arrangement between her father and Lyle. Instead, after a year of continual nagging from her mother about what a good catch Lyle made, she'd agreed to accompany him to the Governor's Ball. To her surprise, he'd been an enjoyable companion. Humorous and certainly handsome. And even though he could have had his pick of any number of females, he'd continued to pursue her. He hadn't even been swayed by her resistance to sleeping with him.

If anything, the longer she put him off, the more concerted his courtship became.

Of course, the more she saw of Lyle, the better her parents liked it. When she'd accompanied Lyle to Switzerland on a ski trip, she'd known that she'd end up sharing his bed. There hadn't been any bottle rockets going off inside her afterward, but that hadn't stopped him from proposing. Or her from accepting.

Everything about that was wrong. So wrong. Even if he had never lifted his hand against her, it had been wrong.

A trilling ring startled her out of her thoughts and it took her a moment to realize that it was the cell phone that Darr had given her that was ringing. By the time she'd fumbled it out of her purse, it had stopped.

She slid it open and scrolled through the numbers that he'd stored in the phone's memory.

Darr's home. Darr's work. Darr's cell phone.

She dialed his cell.

He picked up immediately. "You settling in all right?"

She felt a foolish smile on her lips and hugged the sudden warmth sliding through her close. "You haven't even been gone an hour."

"Feels longer. What're you doing?"

"Eating a sandwich." It was close to the truth. She'd taken a few bites before getting sidetracked by the photographs. "What're you doing?"

"Putting together giveaway bags for the kids next weekend. Gotta work on 'em when we can."

She sank farther into the corner of his very comfortable couch and nibbled off a corner of bread from her sandwich. "Red Rock's not *that* large. How many calls do you have?"

"Oh, you'd be surprised. Structure fires are actually the smallest percentage. The fire at Red was the worst we've seen in a while."

"I don't suppose it's easy to catch an arsonist." He'd told her the fire had been deliberately set.

"Not always. But Red Rock is a tight community. If the guy is still around, he'll make a slip sooner or later. You're not having nightmares or anything, are you? About the fire?"

"No." Amazingly, she wasn't. Her nightmares were of an entirely different sort. "Quite honestly, I hardly remember anything from that night." Except him.

Her gaze fell on the well-coiffed newscaster looking out from the television screen, his expression sober while above his shoulder rolled footage of several mangled vehicles. "You probably see more car accidents than fires, then."

"Yeah. Not too many like the pileup on the highway today, though."

"It's on the news right now." She reached for the remote and turned it off. "Watching *that* is bad enough. How do you stand it?"

"Focus on the ones who live. Some days that's harder than others. It's bad when there are kids involved. It was pretty grim."

She slid a little farther down into the couch. "I hope you haven't had to see anything worse."

"I wish I hadn't."

Which meant that he had.

"Tell me what's in the giveaway bags," she said suddenly.

"Don't want to think anymore about tragedies for tonight?"

"I don't want *you* to think about it," she said softly.

He was silent for a moment. "Whistles," he finally said, his voice low. "Fire safety coloring books."

"Anything else?"

"Snack bars donated by SusieMae's. Crayons donated by the Mendozas. And 'course we'll have the old engine there with a few of the guys who work my shift."

"What about Nick?"

He exhaled. "Even if I weren't pissed at him, he wouldn't be there. It's a kids' event and he doesn't do kids."

"You shouldn't be angry with him."

"He upset you. That's always going to make me angry—" A high-pitched alarm nearly drowned out his voice. "That's our tone," he said more loudly. Behind him, she could hear a female voice calling out numbers. "You can hear why we work on stuff when we can."

"Be careful," she said quickly.

"Honey, I'm always careful," he returned.

And just that quickly, the line went dead.

She exhaled, pressing her hand to her bumping heart. Whether it was adrenaline because of the alarm or because of Darr, she wasn't entirely certain. She had a strong suspicion, though, that it was the latter.

She finished her sandwich, tidied up the kitchen, and still feeling very much out of her depth, entered his bedroom.

The dresser drawer he'd left open beckoned and, trying not to be too distracted by the bed, she gingerly poked through the neat contents, pulling out a gray long-sleeved T-shirt and a pair of sweatpants. They'd be way too big, but the drawstring waist could be tightened, and the elastic cuffs could be folded up.

If Darr's apartment was twice the size of her house, his

bathroom was also more than double the size of hers. For one thing, he didn't have a stacked washer/dryer unit taking up one corner.

For another, not only did he have an enormous, oval-shaped garden tub, but he had a separate glass-walled shower enclosure, as well.

She hardly debated the matter.

She flipped on the water in the tub, adjusting it so that it was comfortably warm but not hot. No bath salts, of course, but that didn't matter. Just being able to stretch out in a luxuriously sized tub was enough to make her feel nearly giddy.

She didn't get out until the water was cold and she was in danger of falling asleep right there in his tub. She let out the water, then felt thoroughly extravagant by stepping into the shower and washing her hair there, before wrapping herself in one of the oversize blue towels folded on the shelf. With the comb from her purse, she worked out the tangles from her hair.

Despite looking for one, she couldn't find a blow-dryer, and she had to settle for towel-drying her hair as best she could. She'd just have to suffer the ringlet results of her shower greed.

The sweatpants were as oversize as she'd expected. The waist, however, didn't need tightening quite as much as she'd thought it would. A fact that led her to stand on tiptoe in front of the wide mirror atop Darr's bedroom dresser, studying the profile of her growing belly.

Then her gaze shifted, taking in the entire picture of herself.

Instead of the petite, sleek-haired, pampered-looking debutante she'd been, she saw a wide-eyed, tangle-haired woman.

The woman that Darr, amazingly, seemed to want.

She dropped the long T-shirt over her thickening waist and faced the bed.

Two choices.

Climb under the comforter covering that mile-wide bed, or snitch a pillow and sleep on his couch. It was certainly more comfortable than hers was—whether it was pulled out into a bed or not. And Darr hadn't made any suggestion, one way or another where she should sleep when she'd invited herself into his home.

When she'd been with Lyle, he'd made it plain that he was the one who called the shots. He was the initiator. The decision maker. And—as he'd proven when she'd become pregnant—he didn't have much tolerance when situations arose without his say-so.

If she'd ever stripped off her nightgown and invited him boldly into her bed, he'd have been thoroughly disapproving.

Darr had *not* disapproved.

She threw off her indecision and tossed back a corner of the comforter, climbing into the side of the bed away from the digital clock sitting on the nightstand.

Darr was not Lyle. And she was not a ninny.

Feeling better than she had in weeks, she was asleep almost as soon as her head hit the pillow and miraculously didn't waken until she felt the bed dip. "Darr?"

"Shh. Go back to sleep."

She peered into the soft dark night. "I thought you wouldn't be back until morning." It clearly wasn't morning.

His arm slid around her waist. "I got off a few hours early. I wanted to see if there was a snow angel really sleeping in my bed." His voice whispered over the back of her neck.

She melted.

There simply was no other word for it.

"I'm glad." She slid her hand along his arm. His warm, bare arm. Her fingers slid over the back of his hand, sliding between his. "I like it here."

"Told you my bed was comfortable."

She smiled into the darkness. "The bed's not the reason I like it."

"That works for me, too." He brushed her hair away from her cheek and kissed her jaw.

She twisted her head around and found his mouth with hers.

"Keep doing that," he murmured eventually, "and neither one of us is going to be sleeping any time soon."

"That works for me," she whispered in return. She drew their linked hands to her breast.

He let out a low breath. Through the soft knit of his shirt, his thumb rubbed across her tight nipple, making it rise even more achingly. "You need your sleep."

"I need you." She wriggled around, turning to face him. "I shouldn't, but I do."

"Need isn't a bad thing." Beneath the blanket, his hand snuck beneath the hem of her T-shirt. There was nothing but bare skin beneath.

Her voice went thready as she sucked in air at the wicked glide. "It can be bad," she managed breathlessly.

"Yes. But not now. Not this."

He grazed his fingertips over her hip. Down her thigh, drawing it over his and his mouth caught hers and he kissed her so tenderly, so thoroughly, that she forgot the cautions that wanted to lurk inside her head. And when he slipped, so smoothly, so completely into her, and her name was a rough exhale on his lips, something inside her cracked open wide.

Even though she wanted to savor him, hover endlessly in that sweet, sweet fullness, her body quickened.

She could feel his heartbeat as if it were her own. Shared the slow, deepening breaths he drew. Impossibly felt him even deeper, even fuller.

As if he were breaching her heart.

Her soul.

Tremors quaked. Built strength. Speed. She gasped his name, and his arms held her even closer. His breath burned against her ear. "Let it go."

It was too late, though. She was already spinning into the universe. And even dissolving into splintering pleasure, she could feel his, too, just as keenly, and it drove her even higher. Harder.

Tears collected behind her closed lids. Streamed down her temples. And always, always, his arms held her close as they tumbled into that beckoning, timeless abyss.

An eternity seemed to pass before the world found motion again.

She pulled in a long breath. Let it out again.

He thumbed away the tears sliding silently down her cheek. "Did I hurt you?"

She felt healed, in ways that she couldn't even begin to explain, not even to herself. "You didn't hurt me."

"Then why the tears?"

"Too much perfection," she whispered. "Thank you."

He let out a breath that seemed to come from deep, deep inside him. "Thank you."

"For what?"

"Being here to come home to." His head slowly fell to her shoulder.

A fresh wave of emotion burned the back of her eyes.

She brushed her fingers through his thick hair. Wordlessly pressed her lips to his brow.

Neither one of them moved as sleep claimed them.

Her car was still a pancake of metal, covered in wood debris, when Darr drove her to her house the next morning before work.

Nearly all the snow had melted away in the yard, leaving the ruts in her driveway looking even worse than they had before the storm.

"It's a pathetic sight," she said as he pulled his borrowed Double Crown truck to a stop behind his own black pickup. "Imagine you've seen worse, though."

"Yup." He climbed out of the truck and came around to open her door, then continued to hold her arm, even when she was on the ground. "Careful. The mud is slick."

They made it up the steps and she unlocked the door. "It'll only take me a few minutes to dress." She'd barely stepped out of the quick shower she'd taken that morning at his place when he'd popped a piece of thick, sourdough toast into her mouth. That had been followed up by amazingly delectable scrambled eggs.

She'd accused him of hiding his cooking prowess.

He'd drawled that food tasted better after a night like they'd just shared.

She'd blushed.

Until meeting him, she'd never *had* nights like that.

"You have plenty of time before you need to be at the office," he assured her now. "Pack that fancy suitcase of yours as full as it can get. We'll come get the rest of your stuff later."

He seemed to take it for granted that she'd be staying with him now.

She nibbled the inside of her lip and didn't challenge the assumption.

After all, isn't that what she wanted?

When she was with him she felt safe. Home.

So, after pulling on a slim pair of black slacks and a tailored pink shirt with shirttails long enough to cover the unfastened waistband of her slacks, she did as he suggested.

Most of the clothing she'd acquired in the last few months fit into the suitcase. She even added her toiletries, vitamins and herbal teas and there was still room to spare.

She opened the bottom drawer of the dresser and pulled out her grandmother's pearls.

The last time she'd worn them had been with the wedding gown.

Now she coiled them several times around her neck and they still looped down across her chest. Without a second thought, she nudged the drawer closed again, leaving the fancy peignoir sets behind.

Then she slid her secondhand peacoat onto her shoulders, pulled up the handle of her suitcase, and rolled it out to the porch, locking the door behind her.

Darr, wearing blue jeans and an unbuttoned plaid flannel shirt over a white T-shirt, looked up at her. He propped his hands on his hips and shook his head.

She pressed her hand against her chest, looking down at herself, but couldn't see anything amiss. "What?"

"Sometimes I can't get over it. How damn beautiful you are."

She felt herself flush. She'd grown up wearing designer labels. Now the only thing of value she wore were the pearls.

"It shows, you know," he added. "You look—"

"—fat?"

"Yeah, right. Pregnant. Definitely pregnant. You're ready to announce it to everyone who sees you today?"

She hadn't thought about it, really, until she'd exchanged his sweatpants and T-shirt for her own clothing. "Yes. And everyone who sees me tomorrow. And the next day, and the next."

His eyes were nearly the same color as the early morning sky and they crinkled. He bounded up the steps and took the suitcase by the handle, easily hefting its weight. "Good for you."

After he'd dumped the suitcase in the back of the white truck, he handed her the keys to his truck, which he'd retrieved from her kitchen counter. "This time you'll drive to the office?"

In hindsight, her refusal to use his truck to get to work seemed silly. She took the keys. "Yes. Thank you. What are you going to do?"

"Catch up on a few Zs," he said, chuckling when the heat rose again in her face. "Return this rig here to Lily's place. I'll get Devaney to follow me out there. We need to go over some planning for the picnic anyway."

Lily's place, she knew, meant the Double Crown. "Okay." She moistened her lips, suddenly feeling awkward.

His lips tilted. He hooked his hand gently behind her neck and drew her close for a slow, sweet kiss.

When he stepped back and pulled open the driver's door to his big truck, she feared her face was even rosier.

Amazingly, she didn't care.

"See you after work," he said, helping her up behind the wheel.

"See you after work," she echoed.

"Gotta drive to the office first, honey," he prompted softly. Amused.

She blinked. Realized the key was still in her hand. She fit it into the ignition and looked over at him warningly. "Don't let this go to your head."

His smile just widened.

And she knew she was never going to be the same.

Chapter Eleven

"I know I've said it about ten times today already, but this has been the most perfect day for a picnic." Lorena Evans stared up at the perfection of the cloudless, blue sky. "Hard to believe that two weeks ago everything in sight was covered in snow. And now—" She broke off, looking around them.

Not a speck of snow remained from the storm to dot the wide expanse of rolling hills and grazing land of the Double Crown. The day held only lengthening golden sunlight that counteracted the steady breeze. It had been neither too cool nor too hot.

The result? Perfect.

All around, the children who'd arrived by the busload earlier in the afternoon, continued racing from one activity to another. Even now, after having watched for several hours, Bethany was hard-pressed to determine what held more appeal for the youngsters.

The long, shining, red fire engine that was parked about a hundred yards away, midway between the banquet tables laden with food and games that the adults were tending and the main ranch house that was surrounded by a sandstone wall, or the weathered barn behind them with its tall, wide doors, thrown open to the treasures within.

It was even a toss-up to determine who was enjoying themselves more.

The adults—who not only included about a dozen volunteers from the Foundation, but a good portion of Red Rock business proprietors, and, of course, their hostess, Lily Fortune, who was every bit as beautiful and gracious as Darr had claimed—or the kids, ranging from wide-eyed kindergartners to middle-schoolers who'd rapidly lost their blasé mien the second Darr and his coworkers rolled up in the behemoth fire engine with all its lights flashing.

The department might be retiring the vehicle, having replaced it with a far more modern rig, but as far as she could tell, it didn't look all that outdated to her.

"It's an amazing sight," Bethany agreed, watching the engine as she absently filled a red plastic cup with apple juice and handed it to the little girl across the table from her. Darr and the guys who'd delivered the generator to her house after the storm all stood alongside the engine, monitoring the half-dozen kids clambering up and down through the opened doors.

"Thanks, Miz Burton," the gap-toothed girl lisped and ran off, carefully balancing her drink cup.

Lorena, working the refreshments beside her that had been provided by SusieMae's, laughed. "Barb, sweetie, you haven't looked at much of anything aside from Darr Fortune's very fine hiney since we started working here this afternoon."

Bethany felt her face flush.

"Can't say I blame you, though," Lorena added. "All those fireboys look pretty darn fine."

Devaney—Bethany still didn't know if that was his first or his last name, despite the evening of pizza he'd shared with her and Darr earlier that week—strolled to their table. He was almost skinny in comparison to Darr's broad shoulders, and his curly white-blond hair looked as if he'd dipped his head too long in a bucket of bleach, but there was something distinctly similar about the two men.

Firefighters, Bethany had rapidly learned in the two weeks since she'd essentially moved in with Darr, all seemed to possess a certain demeanor that set them apart from the rest.

"Hey, there, Barbie doll," Devaney greeted Bethany with a wide grin, though she noticed that his gaze didn't really veer away from the statuesque redhead working beside her. "Fill 'er up, would you please?"

"You got a leak out of those boots of yours, Devaney?" Lorena's voice was sweet. "You've drunk enough juice today to float a boat."

"And I'm smart enough to ask this sweetheart for a refill than to expect you to show some generosity."

Lorena made a face at him and turned to flip open one of the coolers behind them filled with ice and gallon-sized juice and water containers.

Bethany poured the last of her pitcher of apple juice into Devaney's cup, filling it nearly to the brim. "There you go."

"Thank you, darlin'." He winked and strolled back toward the engine.

"Insufferable jerk," Lorena muttered, turning back to the table. She flipped open a water jug and began refilling some of the empty pitchers on the table. "Be grateful for the one you got, sweetie. Wouldn't have thought it, but Darr's definitely the keeper sort."

"Devaney isn't?"

Lorena snorted. "The man doesn't know what the C-word means. Commitment? Please." She dropped the empty jug in the trash barrel beside the table and seemed to toss away the topic of Devaney at the same time. "So, when's that baby bump of yours due to pop?"

Bethany ran her hand over her abdomen. The bright red turtleneck that she wore didn't do a thing to hide her expanding size. To her obstetrician's delight, she'd even been up by four pounds at the appointment that Darr had insisted on accompanying her to last week. "Middle of June."

"You and Darr ever need a babysitter for that tot of yours, you let me know," Lorena said. Her expression was wry. "Seems that taking care of other people's babies is about as close as I'm going to get."

She, like nearly everyone else who'd learned that Bethany was pregnant, didn't seem to question the couple that Darr and Bethany had suddenly become, or the place that her baby would hold in their lives.

Bethany, however, still held onto her doubts.

Everything between her and Darr just seemed too perfect. Too quick. Too easy.

It wasn't that she doubted Darr. Far from it.

It was herself she couldn't quite trust.

Which was why she continued to put him off every morning when he'd ask, "Can I call the preacher now?"

She tore her gaze from Darr's unquestionably fine rear and looked at Lorena. "I guess you want children?"

"Have for as long as I can remember." Lorena rolled her eyes, shaking her head. "Which, at my age, is saying something since I'm not exactly getting any younger. And prospects in Red Rock aren't exactly expanding." Her gaze strayed back toward the fire engine.

Right then and there, Bethany decided that the next time Devaney came for pizza, she'd find some way to include Lorena.

The irony that she didn't doubt there would be a next time wasn't lost on her.

"How are you ladies doing?" Lily Fortune stopped next to them. A wide-brimmed hat shaded her strikingly beautiful face, which age hadn't even begun to dim. "Do you have everything you need? Did you take a break to eat some dinner?"

"Yes. We're fine, Mrs. Fortune," Bethany assured. The woman was about her mother's age—early sixties—but any similarity ended there. Angela Burdett's hair was as falsely blond as Lily Fortune's hair was still naturally dark. Her mother's face stayed smooth courtesy of cosmetic surgery and copious amounts of Botox, while the faint lines radiating from Lily's dark, thickly lashed eyes only seemed to underscore her exotic beauty. "Everyone's having a wonderful time."

"Yes, they are." Lily looked around with a satisfied expression. "My husband is probably looking down on all this with immense pleasure." She gave Bethany a sidelong glance. "You be sure to sit when you have a chance, my dear, or Darr will have both our heads. Oh, there's Emmett and Linda driving up. They've brought the ice cream. Excuse me, won't you?" Her long legs made short work of the distance between the barn and the graded road beyond the fire engine.

Since there seemed to be a lull in the run on beverages, Bethany did sit. Right on top of one of the large white ice chests lined up behind them. "Did you ever meet Mr. Fortune?"

Lorena sat, too, stretching her jean-clad legs in front of her. "Sure. He was a good guy. Handsome as the day is long."

Lorena tsked. "That's one thing you can say about all the Fortunes. They're a good-looking bunch. The whole town grieved when he died." She wrinkled her nose in thought. "Four years now, I'd say. Expect it'd be hard to move on after loving—and losing—a man like that. Oh, sit. Sit." She waved her hand at Bethany and hopped up when a group of giggling teenaged girls approached.

Since it did feel good to get off her feet, Bethany stayed where she was. She stretched out her legs and wriggled her toes inside her tennis shoes. Her gaze roamed over the crowd and she laughed softly when a half-pint of a pigtailed girl whooped and hollered as she beat her opponents in success- fully saddling a padded sawhorse with a stuffed horse head attached to one end, and a blue yarn tail attached to the other.

"Nobody's watching." Darr's soft voice suddenly came to her from behind. "We could find an empty stall, spread out some straw—"

She caught his hand as it slipped around her waist. "You're incorrigible."

He laughed and kissed the side of her neck. "It's your fault." He straightened. "Hey, Lorena. How's it going?"

The redhead rolled her eyes, but her smile was indulgent. "Get a room, why don't you?"

"I'm trying," Darr drawled, giving Bethany a devilish wink just for the sheer pleasure of seeing her cheeks go pink. "Come on." He took her hands and drew her to her feet. "I'm a honcho today and I'm calling a fifteen-minute break."

"Can't do much in fifteen minutes," Lorena inserted with a laugh.

Bethany's bright gaze collided with his and he felt that same emotion clamp around his heart that had only been getting stronger since the first time he'd looked into them and had seen forever. "That's what *she* thinks," he murmured for her ears alone.

She muffled a laugh against her fist and followed him into the cool, dim barn where the strong scent of horseflesh and the hay bales stacked high in a puzzlelike maze drew them into its heady hold.

Mercifully, he didn't have to look for a private corner. For the moment, the place was devoid of kids.

It was just him. Her.

And seven curious horses watching them with their liquid brown eyes from the two rows of stalls at the far side of the barn as Darr led her around the side of the mammoth hay maze toward them.

"You're not really looking for an empty horse stall, are you?"

He stopped and leaned back against a wooden rail, next to a spectacular dark bay who tucked his head over Darr's shoulder, looking for his usual treat. "Sorry, fella." He reached up and rubbed the horse's forehead. "No apple for you this time."

Bethany propped her foot on the bottom rail and reached her hand over the top, stroking the horse's black mane. "Hey, sweetheart," she crooned. "Aren't you a handsome one?"

"Barnabus," Darr supplied. "Barney for short." He pointed out the stalls on the facing row. "Double Jeopardy's the roan on this end. Pasqual, Senator Sam, Honeygirl and Mojito's the palomino filly on the far side. It's an apt name. If you don't watch that one close, she'll knock you on your butt." The rest of the horses were outside, turned out in the various corrals.

Bethany rested her cheek on her arm, looking at him. "Do you ride?"

"Occasionally. You?"

She looked back at Barney. Stroked his neck. "I used to ride almost as regularly as I ran. That's what refined young women did in our circle. We were members of the riding club, the yacht club, the junior women's league. The ones who did lunch."

"Do you miss it?"

She shook her head, then paused. "Well. Maybe the riding."

"We'll come back here after the baby's come and you can ride to your heart's content. Lily's always concerned about the horses getting enough attention."

"I like her."

"Most folks do." But he hadn't drawn her away from the crowd for idle chatter. Even now he could smell someone smoking a cigarette nearby, a reminder that they could be interrupted at any moment. But he'd been watching her all day long while he took care of his business and she took care of about a hundred thirsty kids.

And he knew he couldn't wait a minute longer.

"I put in for the next advancement exam," he said abruptly. "Captain. If I pass—" and he knew he would "—and if I get the slot—" also a given, since the chief had told him so "—it'll mean a nice little bump in pay."

Her eyes narrowed slightly. "You don't sound very enthusiastic. Is that what you want?"

"What I want—" he pulled out the small box that had been burning a hole in his pocket since retrieving it from his safe-deposit box days earlier "—is for you to marry me." He thumbed back the lid. "Maybe this will show you how serious I am."

Her eyes widened as her gaze fell on the ring. Her lips parted, but no sound escaped.

The fact that she wasn't already telling him no, or that she was still thinking about it, gave him hope.

"It was my grandmother's. She gave it to me before she died," he added. "She had blue eyes, like yours. My grandfather said the stones reminded him of the color of her eyes." There were five of them, decorating the narrow width of the white gold band, surrounding a center diamond. "I don't even know what the stones are. But she loved the ring and he loved her."

She swallowed. Her eyes had gone wet. "It's beautiful," she whispered. "But Darr—" She broke off. Touched the tip of her tongue to the center of her upper lip. "You, um, you should give this to someone you…you love."

His throat tightened. His nose prickled. He'd never considered giving it to anyone before. Not even Celia. "I am."

Her lashes lifted again. "What?"

He held her gaze. "I think I fell in love with you the first time you opened your eyes and looked at me outside of Red. And then the snowstorm hit when I'd finally found you. Hell, I don't know. Maybe God was taking pity on me so you wouldn't shut the door in my face."

"Oh, Darr."

He could walk into a burning building without a qualm, but he couldn't keep his hand steady when he slid the ring out of the box and held it between them. "I know everything up to now has seemed like one big rush. But we have the rest of our lives together to take our time. This isn't about me doing the rescue thing, though I'd lay down my life to keep you and that baby safe. *Wear my ring.* Be my wife."

"I—" Her brow crinkled as she looked up at him. "I—" She broke off when he jerked his head around, the tickling in his nose finally penetrating his consciousness.

His adrenaline spiked. He swore.

The smell of the cigarette was gone. In its place was an equally distinctive smell.

Fire.

"What's wrong?"

He pushed the ring into her hand. "Get everyone away from the barn," he said calmly, though everything inside him was leaping to get *her* out of the barn. "Don't panic anyone. Just get them to move. Find Emmett Jamison." His practiced eye raced over the stalls where the horses were starting to shift nervously.

There wasn't smoke. Not yet.

But he could smell it, and knew there would be a helluva lot of it, given the fuel available.

He knew the barn wasn't wired with a sprinkler system, but that didn't explain why the alarm—which it did possess—hadn't sounded.

Bethany had closed her hand around the ring. "What—"

"Fire." He was already sliding open Barnabus' stall gate, pulling the rope halter off the hook and stepping inside with the horse. "Go, Bethany. Now."

She turned on her heel and ran around the hay maze, streaking lithely toward the wide doorway.

"Come on, boy," he murmured to the horse, sliding the halter over his head. He couldn't let the horse bolt even if the yards outside the barn hadn't been full of children. Not when horses had been known to run back into a burning barn.

From outside, he heard Bethany's voice. "Come on, everyone," she said, and even inside the barn he could hear the surprising authority in her tone. "I need you all to walk away from the barn as quickly as you can. Come on. Line up. That's it. Head across the road. Go beyond the fire engine. Toward the wall. Quickly now."

Holding Barnabus's lead rope, Darr threw Jeopardy's halter over her neck, and ran the two horses out of the barn. He handed off their halters to a stunned-looking Lorena, saw that Bethany and the other adults were rapidly rounding up the children, moving foot by foot away.

"Vane," he shouted, but he saw that the other man was already swinging up into the engine while the probie, Rick, was waving everyone away from the area.

A high scream split the air. "Look! The barn's on fire!"

Darr swore under his breath as the more-or-less orderly retreat splintered into shock. Panic was the last thing they needed. "Emmett," he yelled, spotting him. "Get those kids under control."

But the former FBI special agent who now ran the Foundation was already trotting into the melee swirling around Bethany, his voice brooking no debate as he sharply ordered everyone to keep quiet and to keep moving.

"Get these horses to the riding arena," Darr told Lorena. It was a safe distance away from the barn. "Don't let 'em run back this way." He turned back to the door.

The smoke had arrived. With a vengeance. It slunk out of the wide doorway, sneaking up toward the sky with menacing tentacles.

He ran back inside, yanking the collar of his shirt up over his nose.

Inside it was worse.

Already, fire was licking up from the corners of the hay bale maze. Even hunched low against the smoke, he could see Mojito in the last stall, prancing; could hear her groaning in agitation. "A couple minutes," he muttered, grabbing the fire extinguisher from its holster on the wall and running along the side of the smoking maze, blasting it with fire retardant as he went. "Give me a couple more minutes."

But the rear wall of the barn suddenly burst into flame. It raced hungrily upward. Outward.

Mojito threw herself against her stall door. It shuddered violently, but the gate held.

He knew Devaney would attack from the rear, but they were only half a company with an apparatus that was three decades past its prime, and the weathered barn wall was fully engulfed.

He emptied the extinguisher over the hay maze, hoping to keep the pathway clear, then ran to the stalls and the nickering horses. Climbing on the rails, he managed to lasso halters over Pasqual and Sam. Honeygirl was nearly frothing; she was almost as panicked as Mojito in the next stall. Talking all the while, he had to slip into Honeygirl's stall to reach her. He ran his hand up her quivering shoulder. She exhaled noisily, butting her head. "That's a girl," he soothed.

Three feet way, Mojito was beyond calming. Her hooves crashed against the rails again, this time slamming against those between her stall and Honeygirl's, and the wood splintered in half, catching Darr across the chest.

Honeygirl lurched, pinning him between her half ton of terrified horseflesh and the remaining rails of the stall. He grunted, gasping for breath and pushed against her hind quarters but her feet were planted. Swearing a blue streak, he smashed his fist against the rail behind his butt, and fell backwards into Mojito's when the wood gave way.

Mojito's hooves slammed down close enough to pull hair out of his head and he rolled over, shinnying back into Honeygirl's stall as Mojito reared again, barely missing him with her flying hooves. He grabbed the halter and threw it over Honeygirl's neck, bearing his weight against the lead rope to pull her unwilling soul out of the stall.

His ribs aching, he slid up on her back, laying low. "Come on, baby," he coaxed. Her ears twitched and he could feel her muscles bunching beneath him. He leaned forward and caught the edge of the latch to Sam's stall. Honeygirl nervously side-stepped. He leaned farther. Shot the latch and barely managed to grab Sam's rope before the horse could bolt.

Honeygirl whinnied. He clucked, eked another prancing side step out of her. He nearly had Pasqual's rope.

"I got him." Emmett appeared almost like an apparition out of the thick smoke, a bandanna tied around his nose. He flipped the latch open, pulled the horse out and ran ahead of Darr toward the barn doors.

Honeygirl's legs reached out, and it was all Darr could do to keep her from mowing down Emmett and Pasqual in front of them. The heat from the burning hay scorched as they streaked past the maze, but the suppressant he'd sprayed over that side was still managing to keep the fire in check.

And then they were in the clear.

He took in the sight of the children, all evaced safely away from the outbuildings. He could see Bethany, Lily and the others moving among them. Keeping them calm.

Just the sight of Bethany's blond hair and red sweater safely in the distance was enough to keep him going.

He slid off Honeygirl. Shoved the two lead ropes toward Emmett. "Mojito's still inside."

Emmett swore. "Darr, you can't go back in there."

But he would—he *had* to. The sound of the horse's cries were audible even above the roar of the fire. He grabbed a pitcher of water off the table and threw it over his shirt, yanked the shirt up over his nose and raced back through the waves of smoke billowing greedily out the door.

The visibility was nearly nil, the wet shirt clinging to his face a poor airpack. The entire top row of the maze was an open flame, reaching all the way to the roof.

He ran low. And hard. The straw on the stall floors had ignited. Jumped from there to the wood posts. The rails.

He nipped a halter off the empty stall next to Barney's before the flame could reach it, and stumbled toward Mojito.

She whinnied piteously, the sounds of her clawing hooves wrenching through him. "I'm coming, girl." He reached the last stall. The gate was smoldering; the flames behind her singeing the ends of her creamy-colored tail.

He shot his boot through the gate and the wood shattered, sparks flying. Mojito reared up and Darr grabbed her mane, yanking her down hard. Her eyes were a blind panic. He slid the halter over her fighting head, and dragged her from the stall, away from one burning wall toward another burning maze.

She reared, nearly dislocating his shoulders, but he grimly held on to the lead, pulling, dragging.

And then, just when he could see the glimmer of afternoon sun through the roiling smoke, the ground seemed to shudder around them. The horse screamed and maybe Darr did, too, as she succeeded in yanking the lead at last free from his fists, and the rear walls of the barn caved in behind them.

He lurched, fell on his knee, scrabbled forward and nearly crawled the last few feet to the barn doors.

"You're a goddamn lucky sumbitch," Devaney hollered in his ear, dragging him beneath his shoulders out into the sunshine and halfway across the field before dumping him flat on his back and leaning down into his face. "Lucky or freaking dumb." He straightened up to stomp around in a furious circle. "You got a death wish? That was a freaking *horse!*"

Darr sat up, coughing violently and doing his own cursing over the sharp pain in his ribs. There was no sign of Mojito. The horse would stop running eventually. As long as it wasn't back into the barn, Darr didn't care.

"Your hands are burned," he croaked.

"Had to play freaking hose man for a freaking incinerator!" Devaney's voice was still loud. "Had to pull back almost as soon as we hit the attack, for all the good we did. That thing went up in fifteen minutes flat."

He finally seemed to run out of steam and propped his angry red hands on his hips. Behind them, the department's new pumper had arrived, along with a water tanker, and the smoke billowing toward the sky was turning white.

But it was obvious that the barn was beyond saving.

Now it was a matter of ensuring that the fire didn't spread on the breeze to the other outbuildings or ignite the winter-dry fields, and then dealing with the cleanup.

"Helluva picnic for them." Devaney jerked his head toward the picnic-goers. "Not exactly the kind of news you Fortunes were planning to make today."

Darr looked back toward the house. Not only did it look as though every emergency rig in the county had arrived in reinforcement, but the local news truck had rolled onto the scene, as well.

He grimaced and rolled to his knees. Hugging his arm across the gnawing ache in his side, he got his feet under himself and stood.

"Where you going?"

Talking took too much effort. He waved in the general direction of the engines.

"Hell, no, you don't." Devaney hauled him back practically by his collar. "You're sitting your butt right here until a medic can check you out." He grimaced, raking his fingers through his near-white hair. "Check us both out." He stomped around in a circle some more. "How the hell'd this happen?"

Breathing was becoming a distinct hassle. "Someone was

smoking near the barn," Darr said. Which was never wise. One thoughtless flick into some greedy fuel, and the rest was history.

Fifty feet away from them, the cameraman from the news truck was practically tripping over his feet to get footage. But it was the woman running toward him, her blond hair flying behind her, that grabbed Darr's focus.

He barely managed to brace himself before Bethany flew into his outstretched arms. "Omigod." She buried her face in his neck, only to pull back, racing her gaze, her hands over him. "You're burned." Tears streaked down her cheeks.

"I'm fine."

"You can hardly speak!"

"Just the smoke." He couldn't keep from coughing.

She slipped under his shoulder, as if she fully intended to keep him from falling off his feet. "Come on. The ambulance is here."

"You gonna drag me there?"

"If I have to," she said. But her tart voice was belied by the tears.

He closed his eyes. The air was filled with smoke, and the sweet, clean smell of her hair was heaven. He would've been happy to go with her just about anywhere. "I can't leave yet. This is the Double Crown. It's family."

"And I appreciate that," Lily came up. Her face was pale, but her spine was straight. Emmett and Linda were on her heels. "But you've done enough, Darr." She pressed her lips together for a moment, obviously struggling.

He let out a rough breath and lifted his arm off Bethany's shoulder. "Fine. I've gotta report to the chief first." Still holding his side, he headed toward the command.

Bethany pressed her hand to her mouth, watching him go. She choked back a shaking breath that was terribly close to a sob.

"He's a good man." Lily ran her hand down Bethany's shoulder.

She nodded. He was the best Bethany knew.

"You stay with him," Lily added.

She managed to scrape together some composure. "What about all the children?" The buses weren't due to arrive for another hour to transport them back home, though she knew that calls were being made to hasten the process.

"We have enough volunteers on hand. We'll take care of the children. *You* take care of him." The older woman looked around. Her hair lifted in the breeze. "If he's anything like my husband was, he won't settle for anyone else."

Bethany nodded, unable to find her voice again.

"Mrs. Fortune." A helmet-haired brunette, bearing a microphone and a cameraman in her wake, approached. "Would you mind giving a statement? I've heard that the alarm system in the barn failed. Is that correct?"

Lily sighed and with a final pat on Bethany's shoulder, turned toward the news crew.

Bethany paid them absolutely no heed. She was too busy watching Darr. The second he started to make his way back from the man wearing a white fire helmet who was barking orders at everyone, she headed toward Darr, intercepting him midway between Devaney, who was fending off a raving, teary-eyed Lorena, and the news crew, and tucked herself under his arm again.

The fact that he let her take even a minimal portion of his weight told her just how much pain he had to be in. They slowly made their way toward the rear of one of the ambulances that had arrived on the heels of the fire engines.

"This seems like a weird sort of turnaround," Darr croaked, "from our first night by a fire."

"Hush. Don't try to talk."

"You're wearing my ring."

Her fist curled. She couldn't even remember exactly when she'd pushed it onto her finger after he'd sent her running out of the barn. "Yes."

"Is that a *yes* yes?"

She pressed her lips together for a moment. "Yes." There wasn't any other answer. Not since she'd felt her heart nearly stop at the sight of him racing in and out of that barn. "Now stop talking because listening to you is making *my* throat hurt."

"You're gonna be one bossy wife," he muttered, but even through the soot and grime caked on his face, she could see the flash of his dimple.

Wife.

She swallowed hard and turned to the white-shirted EMT. "He's burned. And something's wrong with his ribs."

"Don't worry, ma'am. We've got him."

She nodded and moved back as the man helped Darr up and through the rear doors. "I'll follow in your truck to the hospital." She'd driven it to the ranch since Darr had arrived with the engine and the rest of their crew.

Darr nodded, and lifted his hand. His blue eyes looked at her above the small oxygen mask the EMT gave him.

And then the door closed, and she stood there, watching the ambulance slowly nose its way back through the throng.

Chapter Twelve

"**C**ome on, honey," Lorena said from behind her. The ambulance was long gone. "I'll ride with you over to the hospital."

Bethany brushed her hands over her wet cheeks and turned. "Thanks."

Lorena closed the last few feet between them, lifting a shoulder. "Nobody said it's easy loving a firefighter. We need all the support we can get."

Bethany looked past the other woman. She could see no sign of Devaney, however. Just a mass of confusion as the Jamisons and Lily and the rest of the adults dealt with getting the children organized. "How long have—"

"As long as I can remember," Lorena sighed. "I keep looking for someone else." She shook her head. "Problem is, nobody else is *him*." She looped her arm through Bethany's. "The cursed fool." She nearly spit. Then laughed brokenly.

This time, it was Bethany who squeezed Lorena's hand. "Darr's truck is up by the house."

It was nearly two frustrating hours before Bethany could maneuver the big vehicle around and through the blocked roads and turn through the main gate of the Double Crown to head back to town. Lorena was true to her word, not leaving Bethany's side until they reached the emergency room at the hospital where the attendant had clearly been ordered by Darr to send his fiancée immediately back to him.

"I'll wait here," Lorena told Bethany, and gestured at the molded plastic seats in the waiting room. "I want to know he's okay, too. You go on back."

Needing no further urging, Bethany went through the double doors. Darr was in the first bed, right around the corner.

His face was marginally cleaner, though a thin oxygen tube stretched from his nose to the unit affixed to the wall beside the bed.

The charred T-shirt had been removed from his wide shoulders and he was holding an ice pack against his side, but it did nothing to hide the scrapes and angry red splotches dotting his arms and shoulders.

Even his turnout pants were gone, leaving only his blue jeans in place.

"Hello, again." Dr. Waite looked over Darr's chart when Bethany stopped next to his bed. "Seems like nothing but excitement for the two of you." He scratched on the chart. "Nurse'll be by soon to dress your cuts and those burns," he told Darr. "From what I hear, you're lucky they're not worse."

"I'm lucky all right." Darr slid his hand around hers. His fingers toyed with the ring that was slightly loose around her finger. "How quick can I get out of here?"

"Still waiting on the films we took when you arrived.

Whether there are fractures are not, you've got some seriously nasty contusions. You're going to be black and blue and every other color of the rainbow before long. I want to keep you until morning for observation."

"No." Darr immediately shook his head.

Dr. Waite's lips twisted. "Of all people, you ought to know better, Darr. The FD takes a dim view of its employees—particularly a paramedic who knows better—leaving AMA after an incident."

Darr grimaced. "You're not moving me to a regular room."

"Then as long as we don't need the bed, you can stay in here," Dr. Waite countered immediately. He glanced at the clock on the wall. "And if you don't keep that oxygen in place, it might well be tomorrow night before I spring you." He tapped the side of the chart on the end of Darr's bed and strode away.

"Control freak," Darr muttered after the departing doctor.

"It's just until morning," Bethany soothed.

He made a low, impatient sound. But when he patted the bed beside him, his smoke-charred voice was anything but impatient. "Sit here." He waited until she'd stretched her hip up onto the high bed. "Are you okay?"

She exhaled. "*You're* the one laying in the E.R. this time."

"Yeah, but stress isn't good for the baby."

He rubbed his hand over her abdomen and she suspected the immediate bump inside her wasn't just a coincidence.

"Have you thought of any better names?"

She leaned down and carefully avoiding brushing against his poor, battered chest, then pressed her lips to his. "I've already told you. *Darr.* If that's too horrible for you to contemplate, then we'll call him DJ for Darr Junior."

"Ah-hem." A deep male voice interrupted them. "Sorry to

interrupt," Nick said, looking anything but. "I had to find out on the evening news that my baby brother was here!"

"I would'a called," Darr defended.

"Yeah. Once you were home and snug in your jammies." Nick crossed his arms, eyeing them with clear displeasure that didn't do a thing to mask his concern. "Look, I know I opened my mouth when I shouldn't have, but have either one of you ever heard of a *phone* call?"

Bethany slid off the bed. She'd have called the man herself if she'd known how to reach him, but judging from his expression, she doubted he wanted to hear excuses.

"You two can hash this out. Lorena's in the waiting room," she told Darr. "She wanted to know that you're all right."

Darr reluctantly let go of her hand and watched her walk away.

"I see she's wearing Grandma's ring," Nick said the second she disappeared through the swinging doors.

"I told you I was going to marry her."

"Yeah, well, I didn't know she'd agreed. You've been together what? Two weeks? This is insanity, Darr. Even you've got to see that."

"The only insanity is not marrying the woman I love," he said, coughing through his clenched teeth. "Maybe if you've ever really loved someone, you'd know that."

Nick sighed noisily. "I'm not bashing Barbara," he said. "She seems perfectly nice." His gaze was sober. "I'm just not convinced you're not trying for a Celia do-over."

Darr dropped his wrist over his eyes. God. He was tired.

But Nick wasn't finished. "How d'you know you're not just replacing her? Christ man, you couldn't have found a woman more identical if you'd tried."

"Celia's dead," Darr said wearily. "Just because Bethany's pregnant doesn't mean I'm confusing the two of them."

"Bethany?"

Dammit. "Barbara."

"Well which is it?"

"It's Bethany." Her voice startled them both.

Darr dropped his arm. Pain—inside, outside—dredged through him.

She was standing just inside the swinging doors. Her face was pale. She continued forward to set a bottle of water on the rolling table beside Darr. "The nurse asked me to bring that to you." Her voice was brittle.

"Beth—"

But she was already focusing on Nick. "My name is Bethany Burdett. If you do an Internet search, you might find a few scandalous notes about how I ran out on the day of my wedding. But unless you already knew that, I doubt that's the similarity between me and Darr's Celia that you find so objectionable."

"She wasn't *mine*," Darr said, but neither Bethany nor his brother was listening.

"You're not objectionable," Nick apologized. "I never meant to imply that you were. I just don't want to see Darr rushing into something for the wrong reasons. It's not fair to either one of you!"

Darr could feel his temper rising. "I grew outta short pants a long time ago, Nick. And I can judge for myself what's fair or not."

"You're absolutely right." Bethany's chin lifted as she faced Nick head-on. "Rushing into something—particularly a marriage—for the wrong reasons isn't good. Neither is tip-toeing your way into one when the reasons are all wrong. And guess what? I've tried both ways."

She slid the ring off her finger and set it beside the water bottle.

Darr jackknifed up again, grunted against the pain that made his head swim and his stomach revolt. "Wait—"

"Wrong reasons," Bethany said, her voice thick. "What if all of it's been for the wrong reason?" Her glistening gaze turned back to Darr.

He reached for her, but she was too far away. "I never loved Celia," he said evenly. "Never. And maybe if I'd have tried harder, I could have kept her from going back again to the guy who beat the life out of her and the baby of his she was carrying. Or maybe not. Because she didn't love me, either.

"I love *you*. That's my only reason. Baby. No baby. Bethany. Barbara. *It doesn't matter to me.* I want a life with you. A future." A cough racked through him. "So the question that leaves is whether or not you love me!"

A tear slid down her cheek. "I do." She bit her lip. Swiped her hand over her cheek. "But what if the reason I feel that way is only because when I'm with *you,* I'm not afraid? I'm sorry." Her voice went hoarse. "Maybe that just makes me like Celia, after all."

She turned on her heel and plunged through the doors.

Darr stared after her, frozen for only a moment before he tore the oxygen tube off and tossed it aside.

Just turning enough to slide his boots off the side of the bed prompted a new symphony of pain to swell inside him. "Move out of my way," he warned Nick, who was still standing there, looking grimly subdued.

Nick hesitated.

Darr glared.

"Here." His brother pulled off his wool coat and handed it to Darr. "You can't go running after her without a shirt."

He could. But he took the long coat, anyway. And alternately cursing and coughing, with Nick's help he managed to slide off the bed onto his own feet, and work his arms into the coat.

Nick took the water bottle and pushed it into Darr's hands. "I'll drive."

"Oh, yeah. *Now* you decide to be helpful." He grabbed his grandmother's ring and pushed through the double doors, nearly mowing down a young nurse who was coming from the opposite direction, a plastic cart of dressings in her hand. "Sorry."

"Lt. Fortune! Where do you think you're going?" She scurried after them. "I don't think Dr. Waite wants you to leave—"

The glass doors slid open and Darr strode through, leaving behind the nurse's alarmed admonitions.

"Over there." Nick gestured toward his Porsche. It was illegally parked in the red zone.

There was no sign of Darr's truck. Which meant that, despite what she'd said, Bethany had chosen to use it.

All the quicker to get away from him.

Nick beeped open the locks and Darr pulled the passenger door open and eyed the low, *low* seat. This was gonna hurt.

There was no grace or finesse involved in the act, but he managed to flop his body down into the car. His teeth were still grinding together over the oaths congested in his throat when Nick drove out of the parking lot.

"Your place?" he asked.

Would Bethany go to the apartment?

He doubted it. Not now.

"Bethany's."

Silently, Nick pulled a U-turn in the middle of the intersection, blithely ignoring the tooting horns he earned, and headed in the other direction. "I suppose karma's going to bite me on the ass for all this."

Darr still had a strong desire to kick his brother in that very spot. "No, but some day…somewhere…there's going to be a woman who knocks you on your ass." He leaned his head back against the seat, breathing very carefully. "And I'm going to sit back and love every—" he searched for a suitable word "—tormented minute she causes you."

"You never could stay mad at anyone for long." The corner of Nick's lip kicked up as he shot him a look before turning through the neighborhood leading to Bethany's street.

Darr could deal with anything that Nick said to him.

What he couldn't tolerate was Bethany getting hurt in the process.

She loved him. He knew she did.

"Drive faster," he told Nick.

The powerful car obligingly leapt forward.

"What are you going to do if she's not there?" Gravel spun beneath Nick's wheels as he turned and flew past John Decker's place and gunned up the hill.

"Find her."

"Where else would she—holy mother." Nick leaned forward, spotting the sight of the helicopter sitting at the top of the hill at the same time Darr did. "You've gotta be kidding me. Bailey-Burdett? She's one of *those* Burdetts?"

Darr eyed the name plastered on the side of the silver bird and swore inside. "So?" He couldn't care less what Burdetts she belonged to. He was a lot more interested in getting to Bethany.

His truck was parked at an angle next to the porch steps. The front door was open.

Beside him, Nick shook his head dolefully. He pulled the car to a stop near the truck and pushed open his door. "Bailey-Burdett is only one of the largest private oil companies left."

He made it around to Darr's side before he could even

manage to heave himself out of the low seat. He grabbed Darr's arms and pulled him up.

Darr wheezed. Hell. "In Texas?"

"In…anywhere. You do *not* look good."

Darr pushed past his brother and made it to the steps. He grabbed the cold, metal railing and grimly planted his heavy boot on the first step.

"—house is an embarrassment, Bethany Ann." A shrill female voice floated out the door. "What were you thinking?"

"I was thinking I was glad to find it because the rent was cheap." Bethany's voice was dull.

Darr pulled himself up the second step.

"Cheap! It's a dump. How could you do this to us? We even had to hear from Charlotte Myers—who is the *biggest* gossip in Dallas—that she saw you on the news tonight. Lyle and your father and I manage to convince all our friends that you're recuperating in the Caribbean, and *you* go and get yourself on the news, looking like some… Orphan Annie!

He made the third step. Impatiently waved off Nick behind him.

"Sorry, Mother, but I just couldn't fit in a trip to the spa when there was fire burning around our ears."

"Do you have any idea of the effort it took to find out where you were living? The favors your father had to call in? Can you imagine his embarrassment when we discovered you weren't even using your own name? And *this* is what we find when we get here? A hovel that's falling down around your ears! Honestly. I just don't know what to say to you. Stuart, *you* talk to your daughter."

"Now, Angela, don't upset yourself."

Darr stepped into the doorway, taking in the tableau.

Bethany, shoulders hunched and hugging her arms around herself, faced off against the other three.

Her father. Her mother—who seemed to find plenty to say as far as Darr was concerned.

And the tall, tight-lipped jerk who was undoubtedly Lyle.

Darr braced his feet in the doorway. "I'd rather you not *upset* my fiancée."

Bethany whirled. Her heart very nearly stopped in her chest at the sight of Darr standing stalwart in her doorway. "What are you doing here?"

"Fiancée!" Bethany's mother lifted her carefully arranged head right up from her gray-haired husband's shoulder at that. Considering all the noisy sobbing she was doing, her makeup had managed to remain impeccable.

"She's all but my wife," Lyle snapped. "I've got a license that only needs signing."

Darr slanted a look toward the man. "Is that a fact?" His voice was even.

Ignoring them all, Bethany took a step toward him, her hands lifting, only to pull back and hug her waist again. "You're supposed to be at the hospital."

"There, we're in agreement," Nick said from behind.

"What kind of circus *is* this?" Angela's voice rose again. "Bethany, I demand to know who these people are!"

Bethany closed her eyes, pressing her fingertips to the pain in her forehead that had been there since she'd arrived at the house only to find her father's helicopter parked in the road, and her worst nightmares standing in the center of her little house as if they were afraid to touch any of the old, simple furniture.

"Angela, be quiet," Stuart ordered, and mercifully, Angela subsided. "Bethany, we're leaving at once. Lyle's been very patient with your nonsense, but enough is enough. Now he's agreed to a quiet ceremony in Judge Dooley's chambers the moment we land in Dall—"

"Recuperating from what?" She interrupted, dropping her hand to eye her mother. "You convinced everyone that I was recuperating. From *what?*"

"Don't take that tone with me." Angela sniffed, looking the picture of wounded motherhood.

"Painkillers," Lyle inserted.

Bethany blinked. "Excuse me?"

"It was a plausible excuse," Angela defended, "to explain away your appalling behavior. Now, as your father was saying, Judge Dooley can perform the ceremony as soon as we arrive back home. We'll make the wedding announcement while you and Lyle go somewhere. Observe at least a brief honeymoon."

"You'd rather everyone think your daughter is hooked on painkillers than that she had the sense to keep from marrying the man you virtually sold her to?" She waved her hand dismissively toward Lyle.

"Sold? Bethany, don't be ridiculous." Lyle reached his hand out toward her.

"Put that hand on her and I'll break it off," Darr said in a low voice.

But Bethany wasn't worried about Lyle. He was beneath contempt and had been all along.

She stepped closer to her father. "Sold," she repeated tightly. "How else would you describe your arrangement with him?"

Stuart's lips thinned. "Nothing more than a business agreement. Don't be naive, Bethany. Bailey-Burdett needs capital and Lyle has it."

"But he was only willing to give it in exchange for me. It didn't matter to you that he had a little problem controlling his *fists*. The only thing *you* cared about was the money!"

"Do you want us to start laying people off, Bethany? Do you want to know that our employees are losing their houses, their cars, all because you won't do your duty for the family?"

"And what about your duty as a parent to me?" She shook her head. Her hand rested on the mound of her child. Her son.

Realization was swelling through her and it was heady. "You know, I was terrified of this moment. Of you finding me. Coming with that almighty confidence that I'd do your bidding. After all, until the wedding, I'd always done just that." She eyed her mother. "I wore my hair the way you wanted. Dressed the way you wanted. Joined the clubs, dated the boys, took the classes. I even agreed to marry a man I knew I didn't love because it was what *you* wanted. I wasn't smart like Bailey or Julia. All I had going for me were my looks. And the connections you made sure I made."

Angela huffed. "And what's wrong with that? Lyle can give you everything you've ever wanted."

"No, Mother." Her lips compressed. "Lyle can give you and Daddy everything *you've* ever wanted." She lifted her chin. "I hope you'll all be very happy together. But for me? We're done."

"What's that supposed to mean?"

Bethany drew herself up to her full height. "Well, Daddy, it means that you're standing in my house and I'm telling all of you to leave."

Her mother looked truly appalled. "But Lyle—"

"But Lyle nothing. He can take his money and buy himself another compliant little bride. And God have mercy on her if she doesn't see through him more quickly than I did."

Lyle's eyes narrowed coldly. "You really are a stupid little bi—"

"You're getting on my nerves," Darr warned.

"And you really are a pathetic excuse of a man, Lyle," Bethany returned evenly.

"Bethany." Stuart took her shoulders. "The last few months have been hard on us all. Try to see reason. The capital we need—"

"How much?" Darr asked suddenly.

"How much what?"

"How much money?" Nick leaned over Darr's shoulder. His smile was as icy as Darr's unsmiling expression.

Stuart glared. "Who *are* you?"

"Darr Fortune."

"I'm his brother. Nick. Fortune, that'd be."

Angela's expression perked. "*The* Fortunes?"

"Get out!" Bethany shouted.

Her mother's jaw dropped inelegantly. "You can't kick us out. We're your parents, for heaven's sake."

"I can. And I am." She pushed her father's hands off her shoulder. "I'll sign over Grandmother's trust to you, Daddy. You can do whatever you want with it. I don't care."

Angela swept her with a wounded look. "Easy to say now that you've got a Fortune on the hook."

Bethany couldn't bring herself to look at Darr. She'd been so afraid of making the wrong decision as far as he was concerned, and that's *exactly* what she'd done by leaving his side for even one moment. *"Out."*

Angela snatched up her fur coat and swung it around her shoulders. "You're an ungrateful, ungrateful child."

"I'm not ungrateful at all, Mother." She patted her abdomen. "You've taught me everything I need to know about what not to do as a parent."

Angela swept past Darr, who'd obligingly shifted out of the doorway.

"This isn't what I wanted, Bethany." Her father stared down at her. She liked to think there was regret in his blue eyes, but knew if there was, it was probably because her grandmother's trust—though substantial—was still merely a fraction of the investment Lyle had agreed to make upon their "I do's."

"It isn't what I wanted, either."

"What will you do?"

"Live my life," she said simply.

His lips pressed together. After a moment, he gave one short nod, and followed after his wife.

"Don't think you're going to get support out of me for that baby." Lyle remained behind. "It's probably not even mine."

"He's not."

He snorted. "Right. You're a cold little fish in bed. If I hadn't wanted to get into Bailey-Burdett so badly, I'd have gotten rid of you after Switzerland. Whose else would it be?"

Bethany looked over at Darr. "His," she said.

Lyle's eyes glinted furiously. "I should have known you were a whore the first—"

"That's it." Darr's fist connected and Lyle's head snapped back.

Bethany gasped and darted forward, even as Lyle straightened, his fists curling. A bead of blood trailed from the corner of his split lip.

She wrapped her hands around Darr's inflexible arm. "He's not worth it, Darr."

Darr didn't blink.

Anger vibrated from Lyle's pores. He faced down Darr for an interminable moment.

"You really want to try?" Darr asked softly.

Lyle's gaze slid from Darr to Nick standing right behind

him. Finally, with a grimace, he turned on his heel and stomped past both of the fierce Fortunes, wiping his bloody lip on his finger.

Bethany realized she was still squeezing Darr's arm. She let go. Folded her arms together. Looked away.

"Think I'll make sure he doesn't get lost on the way to the helicopter," Nick said into the thick silence. He closed the door behind him.

Bethany chewed her lip. Inside, she was shaking. "I'm sorry. They were here when I got to the house. I…I never wanted you to see what they were like. What…I…was like." Her throat tightened with the sudden tears that rose.

"What *you* are is brave. And beautiful."

"I was foolish," she said. Her chest ached. "I had you. And I—I just walked away."

"You still have me."

"You deserve someone so much better than me."

He slid his hands around her face, until she could see nothing but him. His strong face. His steady, steady blue eyes. "I deserve a woman who loves me. Who'll lie with me and laugh with me and fight with me over what—" his voice broke "—what to name our kids."

"People are going to think you're crazy, you know. When they learn I'm not Barbara Burton."

"Barbara Burton is just a name." His smoke-roughened voice slid over her as softly as his thumb stroking over her jaw. "You were never anyone but yourself. And who cares what anyone else thinks? We know what matters."

"But I gave you back your ring." She wanted to wail.

"We can take care of that." He reached into his pocket, wincing at the movement.

"Darr." She wanted to touch him, but was afraid if she did,

she'd cause him more pain. "You need to get back to the hospital. I'll get Nick—"

"I have a cracked rib. Maybe two." He coughed slightly. "Three. But first things…first." He lifted her left hand. Held the ring. "Do you promise to keep it on this time? If you're scared, bothered, whatever. You'll talk to me instead of walking away?"

"I am scared," she admitted. The words felt raw. "I'm scared that you'll realize I'm not what you deserve."

He slid the ring over fingertip. "I'm scared you'll decide I'm not what *you* deserve. I'm a firefighter, Bethany. You've seen what I do."

She pushed her finger the rest of the way through the ring. "I've seen who you are." Tears slid down her face as she leaned toward him. "And I'll never take it off again. I do love you."

"And I love you." His arm slid around her shoulders, pulling her closer, whether the action hurt or not. "Both of you," he promised, sealing his mouth over hers.

When he finally lifted his head, she was the one who was swaying.

"We *are* going to talk about this name business, though," he said. "DJ? I've got a brother who's JR. I used to call him Alphabet Soup."

She slipped her fingers through his hair. It was sooty and singed. If the speed of the last few weeks was any indication, she'd better learn not to blink too much or she might miss something. And she fully intended to savor ever minute of her life with this man. "We'll discuss it," she promised. "On the way to the hospital."

"There's that bossy thing again." He grinned. Wry. Sexy. Wonderful. "Turns me on."

She couldn't help laughing, though her wet cheeks went hot. "*You* are dangerous."

He lifted her hand to his mouth. Kissed her knuckles. "No. I'm just yours."

The truth of it was filling her soul. And it was glorious.

She pulled open the door. "And I am yours." And leaning on each other, they headed out into their future.

Epilogue

"**Y**our face is looking a lot better than the last time I saw you, Darr." Lily Fortune tilted her head around the opened doorway to Darr's hospital room. "Mind if I come in?"

It was two days since the fire at the Double Crown. Two days since Bethany had sent her parents and Lyle packing in that helicopter that ended up being the talk of the town. Two days since Darr had put his grandmother's ring on Bethany's finger.

For a second time.

This time, he knew it was staying there.

"Join the party." He gestured Lily into the room that was crowded with people. Devaney with his arm looped around Lorena's shoulders. Rick and his girlfriend, Elise. Marcus and Joe and their wives.

SusieMae was also there, having brought a huge platter of barbecue ribs and coleslaw, because—as she'd claimed—the hospital food was worse than rat food. Even John Decker, nearly up to his elbows in the ribs, was proof that SusieMae's food was delicious.

Lily's smile widened and she slipped into the room, looking around for some place to set the tall, leafy-green plant she'd brought.

"I can take that." Bethany slid off Darr's bedside and reached for the plant. "There's some room left on the windowsill." It was already crowded with stuff that his visitors seemed compelled to bring. Plastic fire trucks with yellow flowers blooming out the top, balloons, black roses—Devaney's idea of humor, naturally.

"Thank you, dear." Lily leaned down and bussed Bethany's cheek. When she straightened again, her gaze narrowed slightly. "I have to say, you just look lovelier than ever."

Bethany blushed, dashing her hand down the front of her pink blouse. "Thank you."

Lily caught Bethany's hand, holding the ring up for her inspection. "Ah. So *this* is why there's an extra glow." Looking delighted, she scooted past Devaney to lean over Darr and gently hug him, too. "When's the date?"

"Knowing those two, about five minutes from now," Nick deadpanned from his position leaning against one wall. "Afraid if I blink, I'll miss out on best-man duties."

"We haven't set the date yet," Darr said over the laughter Nick earned. His fingers looped through Bethany's after she'd rearranged the windowsill and resumed her spot next to him on the bed.

Her clear blue gaze met his and in them he saw forever. "Don't worry, though," he assured. "We'll keep you posted."

"Well," Lily said. "I do love a wedding. And they always seem to come in batches. Jane and Jorge. The two of you." She smiled again. "I don't want to bother you for long. I just wanted to drop by and thank you again." Her hand waved to encompass the others. "Thank all of you, for everything you did at the Double Crown. If you hadn't been there, I don't know what might have happened."

Darr managed to tear himself out of the depths of his future bride's eyes. "This is two too many fires we've had around here. I should've chased off the idiot who was smoking when I noticed the smell."

"That is not your fault," Lily said emphatically. "There are No Smoking signs posted all over. I just blame myself for not having the alarm system checked before the picnic."

"The alarm might have bought us a few minutes," Devaney said. "But the barn was prime fuel. I don't think anything would've saved it, Miz Fortune."

"At least we got the horses out," Darr said. "Mojito still hasn't turned up yet?"

Lily shook her head. "We're looking."

Bethany's hand stroked his shoulder. "Well." He let out a sigh and focused on something he could do something about. "If you need help cleaning up out there, just call—"

"You?" Lily's eyebrows rose with sudden amusement as she looked over his bandage-bound chest.

"Devaney," Darr finished.

Devaney snorted. "Guy cracks a couple 'a ribs and thinks he can get outta all the hard work. You're going to fit right in with the higher-ups, when you make cap'n."

Her throat felt tight, but Lily managed to keep the smile on her face, as the lively bunch teased Darr. "I've got the ranch taken care of," she assured them. For the first time in a long while, though, her confidence about that fact was starting to crack. "Now, I'll leave you in Bethany's good hands."

It was plainly obvious to her that no matter how recently they'd found each other, those two were meant to be.

It was so easy to remember Ryan looking at her the way Darr looked at Bethany. So easy to remember how she'd felt looking back at him.

She turned to leave, but Nick had pushed away from his loner position against the wall. "I'll walk you to your car."

"Darling, that's not necessary." She shooed him back toward the room. "Stay. Enjoy yourself."

Behind his glasses, Nick's brown gaze was sharp. "Are you sure you're all right?"

She patted his cheek. "Of course."

His brows twitched together. But after a moment, he nodded. "Okay." He leaned down and dropped a kiss on her cheek. "Anytime you want to deal some poker, you let me know." His grin was quick and Fortune-handsome.

She kept her smile in place until she was well away from Darr's private room and the revelry that followed her footsteps down the corridor.

But in her pocket burned the note she'd found after the fire. The note that proved it hadn't been a carelessly discarded cigarette that had caused it.

The note that said, *This one wasn't an accident, either.*

Despite the crowd in his room, Darr eyed Nick when he returned. He could see something unsettled in his brother's eyes. "Everything alright?"

"Just a little poker talk," Nick assured with a smooth smile.

"Poker?" Bethany's soft hair brushed Darr's jaw as her head turned. "I like to play poker."

"No kidding." Nick eyed her, obviously considering.

"Forget it," Darr warned. "If she's anything like she is at Monopoly, she's a shark."

"Hey." Bethany shot him an amused look.

"A beautiful shark," he revised, unable to resist running his fingers through her hair even if there were a half dozen people around to witness it.

Her blue eyes darkened, going from amused to slumberous in less than a blink. "That's a little better, I suppose."

He suddenly wanted his half dozen visitors gone in the worst way. "You know, I...I appreciate everyone coming, but I'm bushed," he said loudly. "I think I need some sleep."

Bethany immediately began to sit up and away from him. "Of course you're tired. This has probably been exhausting for you."

Darr slid his hand up the back of her soft blouse and closed his fingers right over the stretchy waistband of her pants, holding her in place where no one could see. He ignored the startled look she cast him and accepted the knuckle knocks and the careful hugs and kisses he got as the rest of the group began their noisy exodus.

Nick was the last to go. "*Sleepy* my aunt Fanny," he drawled knowingly as he pulled the door closed.

And then there was nothing but blessed silence as Darr looked at Bethany. "See if the door locks."

Her lips rounded. She slowly shook her head. "No. Oh, no. We can't." But her gaze still slid tellingly toward the door. "You're hurt, for heaven's sake!"

"And there's nothing more healing than your touch." His hand drifted from the back of her waistband to the front, spreading across her abdomen.

She exhaled, trying to look disapproving and failing miserably, judging by the faint smile that lurked around her soft lips. "How can you possibly think about...that...when you're all battered and bruised?"

"Lock the door and I'll be happy to explain."

A short, soft laugh escaped her. But she slid off the bed and went to the door. "It does have a lock." She sounded surprised.

For that matter, he was a little surprised, too.

And grateful as all get-out, particularly when, after a quick glance at him, she turned it. Then she leaned back against the door, looking at him from across the room. "We really shouldn't."

"Oh, I think we really should." He lifted his hand, beckoning.

Her head tilted slightly. Her lips twitched. "Are the rest of our lives going to be like this, Darwin Fortune? You crook your finger and I come running?"

"It only seems fair, Bethany soon-to-be-Fortune. You're on this earth and I come running."

Her eyes softened. "What am I going to do with you?"

"Love me," he said seriously.

She slowly pushed away from the door. "Oh, Darr. That I will always do." She carefully lifted her hip onto the bed beside him and leaned over him. "I love you." Her words whispered against his lips. "Now—" her hand trailed lightly down his chest, over the hospital-issue gown he'd been protesting since the nurses had practically strapped it around him "—tomorrow—" she reached the sheet bunched around his waist "—always."

He caught her slender fingers when they crept beneath the sheet. "What about all that *we can't* business?"

She managed to slide beneath the sheet while he was still busy falling headlong into her sweetly sexy, slow smile. "A good fiancée is going to do whatever she can to see that her future husband heals as quickly as possible. After all—" she settled, light as a feather, over him "—we have a wedding date to set."

His throat felt more than a little tight. "Yeah. We can do that."

"Yes." She pressed her lips to his again. "We can."

And they did.

Triple Trouble
by
Lois Faye Dyer

Nicholas Fortune closed the financial data file on his computer and stretched. Yawning, he pushed his chair away from his desk and stood. His office was on the top floor of the building housing the Fortune Foundation, and outside the big corner windows, the Texas night was moonless, the sky a black dome spangled with the faint glitter of stars.

"Hell of a lot different from L.A.," he mused aloud, his gaze tracing the moving lights of an airplane far above. The view from the window in his last office in a downtown Los Angeles high rise too often had been blurred with smog that usually blotted out the stars. No, Red Rock, Texas, was more than just a few thousand miles from California—it was a whole world away.

All in all, he thought as he gazed into the darkness, he was glad he'd moved here a month ago. He'd grown tired of his job as a financial analyst for the Kline Corporation in L.A. and needed new challenges—working for the family foundation allowed him time to contemplate his next career move. And a nice side benefit was that he got to spend more time with his brother, Darr.

With the exception of the hum of a janitor's vacuum in the hallway outside, the building around him was as silent as the street below. Nicholas turned away from the window and returned to his desk to slide his laptop into its leather carrying case. He was just shrugging into his jacket when his cell phone rang.

He glanced at his watch. The fluorescent dials read eleven-fifteen. He didn't recognize the number and ordinarily would have let the call go to voice mail, but for some reason he thumbed the On button. "Hello?"

"Mr. Fortune? Nicholas Fortune?"

He didn't recognize the male voice. "Yes."

"Ah, excellent." Relief echoed in the man's voice. "I'm sorry to call so late, but I've been trying to locate you for three days and my assistant just found this number. My name is Andrew Sanchez. I'm an attorney for the estate of Stan Kennedy."

Nicholas froze, his fingers tightening on the slim black cell phone. "The *estate* of Stan Kennedy? Did something happen to Stan?"

"I'm sorry to be the bearer of unfortunate news." The caller's voice held regret. "Mr. Kennedy and his wife were killed in a car accident three days ago."

Shock kept Nicholas mute.

"Mr. Fortune?"

"Yeah." Nicholas managed to force words past the thick emotion clogging his throat. "Yeah, I'm here."

"It's my understanding you and Mr. Kennedy were quite close?"

"We were college roommates. I haven't seen Stan in a year or so, but we keep in touch—*kept* in touch by phone and e-mail." *Like brothers,* Nicholas thought. "We were close as brothers in college."

"I see. Well, Mr. Fortune, that probably explains why he named you guardian of his children. The little girls are currently safe and in the care of a foster mother, but the caseworker is anxious to transfer custody to you. The sooner they're in a stable environment the better."

"Whoa, wait a minute." Nicholas shook his head to clear it, convinced he hadn't heard the attorney correctly. "Stan left *me* in charge of his kids?"

"Yes, that's correct." The attorney paused. "You didn't know?"

Nicholas tried to remember exactly what Stan had told him about his will. They'd both agreed to take care of business for the other if anything happened to them. He'd been Stan's best man at his wedding to Amy and he definitely remembered Stan asking him to look after his bride should anything happen. Even though their conversation had taken place while emptying a magnum of champagne, Nicholas knew his word was important to Stan and he hadn't given it lightly.

But *babies?* And not just one—*three.*

"The triplets weren't born when we made a pact to look after each other's estate, should anything ever happen," he told the attorney. *And neither of us thought he and Amy wouldn't live to raise their daughters.* "But I promised Stan I'd take care of his family if he couldn't."

"Excellent." The attorney's voice was full of relief. "Can I expect you at my office tomorrow, then?"

"Tomorrow?" Nick repeated, his voice rough with shock.

"I know it's extremely short notice," Sanchez said apologetically. "But as I said, the caseworker is very concerned that the babies be settled in a permanent situation as soon as possible."

"Uh, yeah, I suppose that makes sense," Nick said. He thrust his fingers through his hair and tried to focus on the calendar that lay open on his desktop. "I've got a meeting I can't cancel in the morning, but I'll catch the first flight out after lunch." Nicholas jotted down the address in Amarillo and hung up. It was several moments before he realized he was sitting on the edge of his desk, staring at the silent phone, still open in his hand.

Grief washed over him, erasing the cold, numbing shock that had struck with the news. He couldn't believe Stan and Amy were gone. The couple met life with a zest few of their friends could match. It was impossible to get his head around the fact that all their vibrant energy had been snuffed out.

He scrubbed his hand down his face and his fingers came away damp.

He sucked in a deep breath and stood. He didn't have time to mourn Stan and Amy. Their deaths had left their three little girls vulnerable, without the protection of parents. Though how the hell Stan and Amy had ever decided he was the best choice to act as substitute dad for the triplets, Nicholas couldn't begin to guess.

In all his thirty-seven years, he'd never spent any length of time around a baby. He had four brothers but no wife, no fiancée or sister, and his mom had died two years ago. The only permanent female in his immediate family was Barbara, the woman his brother Darr had fallen in love with a month earlier. Barbara was pregnant. Did that mean she knew about babies?

Nick hadn't a clue. And for a guy who spent his life dealing with the predictability of numbers, in his career as a financial analyst, being clueless didn't sit well.

But he had no choice.

Despite being totally unqualified for the job, he was flying to Amarillo tomorrow.

And bringing home three babies.

He didn't know a damn thing about kids. Especially not little girls.

He was going to have to learn fast….

Charlene London walked quickly along the Red Rock Airport concourse, nearly running as she hurried to the gate. The flight to Amarillo was already boarding and only a few stragglers like herself waited to be checked through.

Fortunately, the uniformed airline attendant was efficient, and a moment later, Charlene joined the short queue of passengers waiting to board.

For the first time in the last hour, she drew a deep breath and relaxed. The last three weeks had been hectic and difficult. Breaking up with her fiancé after three years had been hard, but quitting her job, packing her apartment and putting everything in storage had been draining. She'd purposely pared her luggage down to a few bags, since she'd be living with her mother in a condo in Amarillo while she looked for a job and an apartment.

And a new life, she told herself. She was determined to put her failed relationship with Barry behind her and get on with her career.

She sipped her latte, mentally updating her résumé while the line moved slowly forward. They entered the plane and her eyes widened at the packed cabin and aisle, still thronged with passengers finding seats and stowing bags in the overhead compartments.

Thank goodness I used my frequent flyer miles to upgrade to first class. She glanced at her ticket and scanned the numbers above the seats, pausing as she found hers.

"Excuse me."

The man rose and stepped into the aisle to let her move past him to reach the window seat.

He smelled wonderful. Charlene didn't recognize

the scent, but it was subtle and clean. Probably incredibly expensive. *And thank goodness he isn't wearing the same cologne as Barry,* she thought with a rush of relief.

She was trying to get away from Barry—and didn't need or want any reminder of her ex-boyfriend. Or fiancé. Or whatever the appropriate term was for the man you'd dated for three whole years, thinking he was the man you'd marry, until you'd discovered that he was…not the man you'd thought he was at all.

Very disheartening.

"Can I put that up for you?"

The deep male voice rumbled, yanking Charlene from her reverie.

"What?" She realized he was holding out his hand, the expression on his very handsome face expectant. He lifted a brow, glanced significantly at her carry-on, then at her. "Oh, yes. Thank you."

He swung the bag up with ease while she slipped into the window seat. She focused on latching her seat belt, stowing her purse under the seat and settling in. It wasn't until the plane backed away from the gate to taxi toward the runaway that she really looked at the man beside her.

He was staring at the inflight magazine but Charlene had the distinct impression he wasn't reading. In profile, his face was all angles with high cheekbones, chiseled lips and a strong jawline. His dark brown hair was short, just shy of a buzz cut, and from her side view, his eyelashes were amazingly long and thick. She wondered idly what color his eyes were.

She didn't wonder long. He glanced up, his gaze meeting hers.

Brown. His eyes were brown. *The kind of eyes a woman could lose herself in,* she thought hazily.

His eyes darkened, lashes half lowering as he studied her.

Charlene's breath caught at the male interest he didn't bother to hide. Her skin heated, her nipples peaking beneath the soft lace of her bra.

Stunned at the depth of her reaction, she couldn't pull her gaze from his.

© Harlequin Books S.A. 2009